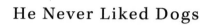

He Never Liked Dogs

Gladdie Deane

He Never Liked Dogs

PALMETTO
PUBLISHING
Charleston, SC
www.PalmettoPublishing.com

PALMETTO
P U B L I S H I N G
Charleston, SC
www.PalmettoPublishing.com

He Never Liked Dogs
Copyright © 2024 by Gladdie Deane

First Edition

Hardcover ISBN: 979-8-8229-2841-1
Paperback ISBN: 979-8-8229-2842-8
eBook ISBN: 979-8-8229-2843-5

Contents

For Grandparents and
English teachers, especially ours, Tom Diffley

Acknowledgments

Thank you to Jodi Bjerke, Mia Bonnie, and Jenny Johnson Zuppan for being our first readers. We're grateful you love dogs and stories. Thank you to the authors and industry experts who generously shared their expertise with us. We would not be where we are today without your help. And a shout out to the Palmetto Publishing team in putting all the pieces of the puzzle together. Finally, to our families, the humans and the dogs, you are the reason we write. Our stories are created from the love you give us.

Prologue

Doc Grady expertly stitched up Barton Moore's forehead, reset Harvey Benson's broken shoulder, dispensed a daily vitamin to Mary Howley, the town hypochondriac, and vaccinated the Wheeler twins, all with the ease of someone making a simple cup of morning coffee. A few minutes before ten, he headed down the hall to his office. Doc Grady sat down at his walnut writing desk, turned on his desk fan, pulled from his back pocket an embroidered linen handkerchief to wipe his brow, and began writing. He heard his nurse's footsteps heading toward his office and breathed a sigh of relief. Nurse Izzy kept his practice running smoothly, the essential cog in the wheel, completing her tasks with the energy of a highly qualified sporting dog.

"Looking for this?" asked Izzy, handing Doc a glass of sweet tea.

"You read my mind, thank you," Doc said graciously, noticing for the first time Izzy's curly auburn hair had a smattering of gray. Could his little Izzy really be old enough to be sporting a bit of gray? Where had the years gone?

"What a morning," said Izzy, shaking her head. "And we still have a line of patients in the waiting room."

"We best get to it then," said Doc, taking a gulp of the sweet tea.

"I declare this weather feels like a three-dog day," reaching for a ponytail holder wrapped around her wrist.

"Feels like it to me," Doc smiled, grabbing his stethoscope. "But what do I know? I'm just a Yankee from the *Noth*."

Izzy laughed at Doc as she gathered her curly, shoulder-length hair, tying it into a ponytail. "There, that feels much better," she said.

Doc and Izzy often spoke fondly of three-dog days, the kind of day where the heat and humidity are so high a person can hardly move without feeling as sticky as a freshly made cinnamon roll. Rather their fond remembrance of a three-dog day came from the day they met, decades ago.

Doc had moved from the Northeast to Fairhope after answering an advertisement in a medical journal looking for an experienced doctor to take over a small-town family practice in a southern coastal town. This was exactly what he needed after losing his wife and young son to tuberculosis, a disease so deadly it killed a quarter of the folks in his small Maine town the previous winter.

The retiring Doctor Rupert interviewed Doc Grady, apparently taking a liking to him right away because he offered him the job that same day. "Might take my patients some time to get comfortable, you being a Yankee and all, but it'll happen."

News of a new doctor from the North spread like the stomach flu. Doc Rupert's formerly bustling practice sat empty, much like the second floor of a library on the first warm spring day of the year.

That is until Izzy came screaming through town like her hair was on fire. Izzy, a scrawny seven-year-old girl, had woken early one summer morning, her freckled skin sticking to the bedsheets like butter to paper. Izzy, Doc Grady would later learn, had quietly sneaked out of the house, heading to the river for a morning swim. It wasn't until her stomach started growling that she returned home to find her three typically rambunctious Labrador puppies lying lifeless on the front porch, still as statues. After a fruitless "Get up! NOW!" Izzy turned toward town and ran as fast as her little bare feet could carry her down Main Street to find a doctor.

Izzy stopped in front of a newly painted door with a wooden sign that read, "Thomas A. Grady, MD." She threw open the door, hollering for help, not caring one iota the new doctor was a Yankee.

Doc Grady rushed out of his office to see what the commotion was about. "Miss, may I help you?"

"It's my pups, please, doctor, sir," Izzy pleaded, her auburn hair curling up like a pig's tail. "They're dying. You gotta save 'em. Patience, Kindness, and Mercy are everything to me."

"Me too," Doc smiled, guessing those were the names of her dogs. The girl was as cute as a puppy herself, with the wild curly wet hair and a smattering of freckles across her nose and cheeks. Doc, seeing that he had no patients, and none likely in the foreseeable future, figured he ought to do what he could.

"Sir, pleeeease, we gots to run, they's close to dying, may even be dead," Izzy sobbed.

He noticed the beads of sweat on the young girl's forehead, her wire-rimmed glasses drooping to the middle of her nose, dusty bare feet peeking out from the hem of her pink-and-white floral print nightgown.

"Shall we take my truck?" Doc Grady suggested.

"Oh no, it's not far, let's run!" Izzy explained to the doctor as if she were addressing a younger child.

Doc Grady grabbed his medical bag and followed the young girl, who took off like a hunted gazelle. Doc Grady, not much of an athlete, did his best to keep up. He could hear a few early morning porch sitters chuckling as he ran behind Izzy with his leather medical bag banging between his right and left knees.

A town as small as Fairhope didn't miss much. Soon the oddly matched pair was followed by the mayor, the grocer and, of course, the town gossip, Miss Martin, who somehow managed to be present at every town emergency.

Izzy dashed up the front steps of a small yellow house with peeling paint to the empty front porch where she'd last seen her puppies. She turned to Doc Grady. "Oh, my golly," Izzy cried, pointing to the porch floor. "They's gone, up to heaven. I didn't even gets to say goodbye."

A small crowd had gathered, watching the child who so obviously loved her dogs.

"Now we *needs* to call the preacher," Izzy sobbed loudly. The nautical blue front door suddenly flew open.

"Izzy, my child. Why you crying so?" asked a pretty woman dressed in a white linen apron over her flowered cotton dress, a mop in one hand, a rag in the other. Her shoulder-length red hair was parted to the side and held back with two hair barrettes. Noticing her porch filled with curious onlookers, she asked, "Sweet reason, Izzy Bartel, what have you done now? Why are all these people on my front porch?"

"Oh Mama, the dogs *is* dead. Patience, Kindness, and Mercy. Gone up to heaven. Just like my Jesus. My heart is so broken!" She threw herself against her mama's chest. Izzy's mama, Liz Bartel, smiled politely at the new doctor and the rest of the folks staring at Izzy.

"Oh, honey, your babies ain't dead," Izzy's mama said softly, stroking her daughter's unruly chestnut-colored hair. "They just got so darn hot. I believe you forgot to fill their water bucket this mornin'. Seems to me you were thinking only of yourself, disappearing down to the river for a morning swim. Not a good thing, Izzy. Ain't safe going to the river all by your lonesome."

Izzy's cheeks, already flushed from the heat, flamed even brighter with shame.

"We'll talk about that later," Izzy's mama said. "I brought the dogs into the kitchen, put water in their bowl. The fan is blowing on 'em. They ain't moving much, but they're breathing. Kinda like the rest of us suffering from this dreadful heat wave the good Lord deemed fit to give us. Now please, everyone, go on about your day. I apologize my Izzy created such a ruckus. The dogs are fine."

"I think it best that the doctor check them over," mumbled Izzy. "'In't that right, Doc?"

"Uhhh," Doc Grady stuttered, "I am a medical doctor." He glanced at the cluster of onlookers staring at him. "But dogs are not really all that different than people. Let's check them over."

The group, led by Izzy, followed Doc Grady inside the Bartel home, where the aroma of coffee and homemade blueberry muffins hit them like an early morning sun. The kitchen was spotless, the floor freshly mopped. In the corner, three gorgeous Labrador puppies, two black and one yellow, had paws intertwined. They lay as contentedly as a growing boy after eating a plate of spaghetti and meatballs.

"Okay, Miss Izzy, let's look these adorable puppies over," Doc Grady said. He knelt down on the wide-plank pinewood floor, examining the pups like they were newborn babes. Doc's gentle touch awakened them, and the two smaller pups began licking Doc Grady's hands. The largest of the three, a black female, stretched and began nipping at the cuff of his gray wool trousers.

"Looks like Kindness has a likin' for your pants," giggled Izzy.

Doc Grady laughed and the others joined in, not a one knowing it was the first time he'd laughed since his wife and son passed.

"Izzy, your mother is right. Your puppies are fine. Days as warm as this one, though, require extra care. Keep a bucket of water filled for the dogs. Let them rest inside or in the shade. You might hose them down now and then. Looks to me these three li'l ones are going to be some of the finest dogs this town has ever seen."

"Did you hear him, Mama?" Izzy said, placing her hands on her heart, looking up to the ceiling. "Like I *says* all along, these dogs are something special. Thank you, sweet Jesus, for blessing me with Patience, Kindness, and Mercy. Amen!"

"Amen!" the group joyfully followed.

As Doc Grady said his goodbye, Miss Martin was right on his heels, determined to get better acquainted, when suddenly the color drained from her face. Her body dropped to the ground like a swatted fly. Heatstroke. That's what Doc Grady proclaimed after he brought Miss Martin back to life with a glass of cold water and a cool washcloth on her forehead. It seemed to the folks standing in the Bartel kitchen that they'd witnessed the new doctor perform a miracle as they watched the color of Miss Martin's face return like the amber glow of a warm campfire.

The story about Doc saving Izzy's dogs and Miss Martin spread far and wide. And like any good story, it grew, eventually gaining wings of its own. Soon the talk on Main Street was Doc Grady had successfully performed mouth-to-mouth resuscitation on three nearly dead dogs and a nearly dead Miss Martin.

By nightfall, Doc Grady's rescue of Izzy's pups led one of the folks in town to christen uncomfortably hot weather a *three-dog day*.

When Doc Grady showed up at his office the next morning there was a line of people waiting to get inside. Izzy was the first in line with a berry pie and three dogs wagging their tails beside her.

Doc Grady's heart skipped a beat, pleased as punch there were finally people waiting to get into his office.

"Morning, Izzy, Mrs. Bartel," Doc nodded politely. "Good to see my patients are doing well."

"Yes, sir. They's doing great," Izzy said. "We's brought you a triple-berry pie. Our way of saying thanks."

"Awfully nice of you. I shall have something to look forward to this evening," Doc Grady said graciously.

Izzy went silent, not quite ready for the task at hand.

"Go on, ask him, Izzy," her mother instructed.

"We's be thinking 'bout you. That you might like one of these pups for yourself," she said as she leaned down to pet the largest of the three. "We's heard you got no family no more. So, I'm giving you this big girl here." Izzy rubbed the pup's belly. "Her name's Kindness, the sweetest dog this side of the Mason-Dixon." Izzy laughed as Kindness licked her face. "She'll sleep right next to you, lick away tears when ya needin' a good cry. She'll cuddle with you, I promise."

The tall, lanky doctor set his medicine bag down, taking Kindness in his arms. He buried his face in the puppy's black fur, hoping to hide the single tear rolling down his rosy cheek.

Kindness became as much an office fixture as the walnut desk in Doc's office. Doc Grady often heard mothers tell their whining child, "Stop your fussing. Kindness will be there."

And Kindness was there, licking tears of crying children fearing a needle, sitting next to people requiring a cast or stitches. Even salty old fishermen needing removal of a badly cast hook appreciated Kindness being by their side. The dog was as much a town hero as the veterans returning from war.

Years later the now greatly beloved Doc Grady credited Izzy for his thriving practice. Izzy disagreed. "It was Kindness, Doc. It was always Kindness."

Chapter 1: The Fall

BOSTON, 2018

Hattie wondered about buckling the seatbelt, usually the first thing she did when she got in a car. At the moment it was impossible. She was handcuffed, sitting in the back of a police car. Her nature was to ask the officer what she should do about the seatbelt. She'd always been a rule follower. She looked at the steel bars between them, realizing how ridiculous her question might seem to the cops who'd just arrested her for murder.

In her thirty-one years, Hattie recalled only once ever seeing police handcuff a woman. Not that she'd seen all that many men arrested. A few times at the Gas & Go, a local scraggy convenience store known as a place to buy illegal drugs near the local high school. She'd watched, alongside other high schoolers who were walking home. By dinnertime, it was a faint memory. She'd felt different seeing a woman arrested, it left an indelible mark, unnerved her still when she thought of it.

It was years ago that she'd watched police outside her childhood home handcuff a middle-aged woman, dressed in a T-shirt, denim cutoffs and flip-flops. The woman looked no different than the moms who drop off their kids at school each day. But on the inside, it was a different story. Mama said the woman was as nasty as a gulp of sour milk. After all, who steals a puppy? Especially Benny? Mama had big plans for Benny.

Benny, a six-month-old golden retriever with a heart the size of Texas and fur so thick it'd keep an Eskimo warm, was as smart a dog as Mama and Hattie seen. Mama been training Benny to be a therapy dog for Henry Dower, a nine-year-old autistic boy in desperate need of unconditional love—something only a dog can supply to a child repulsed by the human touch.

The first time Mama and Hattie met Henry and his family, Henry wouldn't get out of the car, rocking vigorously back and forth. Then he saw Hattie holding Benny. The skinny boy, incapable of opening a car door, wiggled his way out an open car window, crashing to the ground. No tears, though, he picked himself up off the gravel and ran to Benny, all while making screeching sounds like a bat. Hattie gently placed the tiny golden retriever puppy in his arms. The small group watched as Henry buried his head into Benny's fur, Mama promising he could have Benny forever once training was done. There was not a dry eye in sight.

Henry's parents also wanted Benny to protect their son. Autistic kids are prone to run away for no apparent reason, jump in water even though they can't swim, and walk into traffic unaware of an oncoming car. Henry was no exception.

From day one, Benny seemed to understand he had a bigger purpose in life than the average dog. He never joined the other dogs in chasing squirrels or barking at birds. Benny hung close to Mama and Hattie. "By the time Benny is ready to serve as Henry's faithful companion, we'll have put $25,000 worth of man-hours into training him," Mama had told Hattie. Benny was what Mama called a human-dog, a rarity.

Hattie thought of that night years ago when a woman tried to steal Benny. The thief clearly underestimated Mama, who slept at the most four hours a night, often resting on an old military cot in the barn to keep a watchful eye on the dogs she was training. That night the barn was holding summer heat like a Dutch oven, despite the ceiling fans going full blast. Mama and Hattie filled two extra buckets of water for the dogs and let them out late around midnight to do their business. They locked the green barn door and were walking up to the house when they heard car tires rolling up the gravel drive, headlights off.

"Go inside, Hattie. Call 911. I believe we got trouble creepin' around."

"I'm not going in the house without you," said Hattie, deter-minedly meeting Mama's eyes. Hattie already lost her father. She was not losing a mother.

"Fine, we'll make a run for it. Don't turn on any lights in the house. I'll call 911."

Once inside, Hattie stood alongside Mama. The two looked more like sisters than mother and daughter, in work clothes—jeans, barn boots, and long-sleeve shirts. They watched a woman get out of a black SUV and strut confidently toward the barn with steel cutters, ready to pop the padlock on the barn door. She did it quick, easily, as if it was something she did all the time. Quietly the woman slid open the barn door. Dogs began barking, allowing the sheriff to creep up the drive without being heard. Two cops got out of the car with flashlights. When the barn door reopened, and the woman walked out carrying Benny, the flashlights went

3

on, temporarily blinding her as she stumbled toward her car. In seconds the police handcuffed her.

"I recognize that woman," Mama told Hattie. "She came around here a month or so ago, wanting to visit our training center. Told me she had a doodle she might want us to train for her husband, a vet suffering from PTSD. I spent a lot of time with her. Told her what we charge and why. I showed her Benny, what we were doing with him. She asked a lot of questions. I should've known something was up when she asked about the market value of a well-trained dog like Benny."

"She's ruined her life," said Hattie, unable to shake the image of the woman getting handcuffed.

"And she almost ruined Henry's. He's been waiting months for Benny."

"How does someone get bad?"

"Best I can figure is they stop following God's commandments. He made it pretty clear: don't steal, don't lie, don't kill, don't covet. You know 'em, Hattie."

"Yeah. Maybe, it's not so black and white, maybe she had a good reason. Like she has a sick child and she needed money for hospital bills."

"You're young with a tender heart. There's no good reason for stealing someone else's puppies. Plain and simple."

"You're right."

"That's one thing I'll never have to worry about."

"What?"

"You, getting into trouble, being handcuffed by police. You're the best there is, Hattie Brown. My shining star. You're the kind of daughter mamas dream about."

Hattie's thoughts returned to the present. The police car pulled away from her luxury condo building. The handcuffs painfully rubbed on the carpus bone of her small wrists.

"Dear God," Hattie thought, "If Mama were still alive, she'd be so disappointed in me."

Her eyes moved to her beautiful wool navy Brooks Brothers suit, Kate Spade loafers, real pearls, and perfectly combed hair, a lob cut from an expensive Boston salon. Hattie knew she worked harder, smarter, and longer hours than her peers at the investment banking firm where she'd worked since graduating from Harvard. She did everything people asked. And here she was, handcuffed like the bad woman who once tried to steal Benny.

Hattie recalled Mama saying if people follow the ten commandments, they'll stay out of trouble. Hattie followed them, most of them. She attended church, or used to, was high school valedictorian, a graduate of Harvard. She married her first love. She'd done everything right. Everything but marry the wrong guy.

Chapter 2:
A Long Road

FAIRHOPE, ALABAMA, 2008

Hattie Brown was a keen observer of people and dogs, a habit she, for whatever reason, picked up after her daddy died when she was eleven. Daddy taught her to notice things. Things like a dog with its tail tucked under, likely mistreated a time or two. A hunched shoulder man was no candidate for the limelight. Folks wearing T-shirts with slogans, well, they gave off plenty of clues, too.

After daddy passed, she tried her best to remember what he'd taught her. She wondered if he'd recognize her now, five feet eight with long, wavy brown hair. Last time he saw her she was still under five feet, chubby with a short pixie cut. That darn Mema taken the scissors to her.

"The worst cut this side of the Mississippi," Mama shouted, as mad as a hornet when she saw what Mema done to Hattie. Daddy reassured Mama it'd grow back, be even prettier. It had grown back. It now fell loosely to her waist, though most days she wore it in a ponytail. The physical work at Mama's kennel had pretty much gotten rid of the pretween chubbiness. She was lean and tall, and for the most part she'd outgrown her awkwardness. Still at times, at least socially, she felt like a foal finding its legs. Academics was a different story. She was confident. She'd experienced enough success to know she was smart, a quick learner, and it showed. She grinned. She was going to Harvard.

For the past few years Hattie's entire focus was school and dogs, a means to an end. She'd paid her dues. Staring out the finger-smudged Greyhound bus window, Hattie watched a stocky, middle-aged woman with a square face and flat nose bark commands at the elderly Greyhound bus driver. He was attempting to maneuver her suitcase, roughly the size of a small piano, into the bus's baggage compartment. Hattie kept watching, then slapped her head in an *aha* moment. That was it! The woman had an uncanny resemblance to a bulldog.

In her years of working for Mama's dog training business, she and her cousin Beau, who also worked at the kennel, discovered people and their dogs resembled one another. It'd given them plenty of laughs while mopping floors and giving dogs a bath. Hattie worked enough with Mama to know emotionally, people and dogs were different. Dogs forgave easily, loved their people unconditionally. Knew which humans they could trust, and more importantly, which ones to steer away from. Not a single dog Hattie trained—and there'd been plenty—had a mean streak in 'em. Plenty of bark, though.

"Not necessarily a bad thing," her mama, a former southern beauty and professional dog trainer, taught her. "A talker can keep bad folks at bay."

Hattie continued to stare outside, purposely avoiding eye contact with a twenty-something-year-old man who had parked himself directly across the aisle. He gave her the creeps. His pasty-white skin looked like it hadn't seen a ray of sunshine in months. She felt his hooded steely blue eyes on her. When he placed his luggage in the carrier bin across from her, she winced after noticing his inked sleeves with neo-Nazi crap. His body was thin as a starved POW. She guessed he was a druggie. Meth. Maybe heroin. Some of the kids who did drugs at her high school had a similar look: emaciated, dark shadows under the eyes, sallow cheeks. She was glad she'd put a stack of her textbooks on the seat next to her to discourage anyone from sitting there, especially him.

When the haggard-looking driver finally slammed the cargo door shut, Hattie breathed a sigh of relief, willing the bus to stay on schedule. She was desperate to be on time for freshman orientation. Please, God, she silently pleaded, get me there on time.

Harvard was her ticket out of Fairhope. It wasn't that she hated Fairhope. She loved the Gulf Coast, the bay water, her family. A little less heat and humidity and a bigger group of friends would have been nice.

Since graduating high school in May, Hattie worked full time, tirelessly, at her family's dog training center and kennel. Summer's record-setting heat made it brutal, arriving mid-April and sticking around like an unwanted guest.

Unlike Mama, who was at her best when training dogs, Hattie preferred academics. Things like science, reading, and English. She'd taken AP courses and had wanted to take courses at the local community college. But she'd been an essential cog in the wheel of Mama's dog business. They didn't have the luxury of time or extra money. After Daddy passed, she and Mama needed to put food on the table. Hattie, now eighteen, wanted to shake off the adult responsibilities she'd shouldered as a kid. Be a regular college student. Grab a chance at normal.

"Anybody out there need a friend?" the bulldog look-alike screeched, storming onto the bus. She'd definitely grabbed the attention of people on the bus; however, no one offered up a yes to the boisterous passenger.

Trying again, the woman asked, "Any single men out there? I'm available." She waved her stubby naked ring finger to the entire bus, giggling like a schoolgirl.

The man across the aisle, whose eyes had been planted on Hattie since he'd sat down, switched his stare to the new passenger. Hattie took the opportunity to glance at him, noticing the neurotic way his hands, with unusually long fingers and overgrown dirty nails, tightly clung to a black canvas duffel bag. Dear God, she prayed he didn't have a gun in it. His eyes suddenly returned to her. He winked, soaking in her peach-colored tank top, light blue denim cutoffs and tan flip-flops. She regretted dressing for Fairhope's hundred-plus degree heat.

"This bus is headed to Boston, right?" the woman asked loudly like a teacher trying to gain the attention of an unruly class. She didn't need the voice; her outfit alone got her attention as she strutted down the aisle in flowered leggings and a bright-pink, cleavage-friendly tee with silver sparkles spelling out "Vegas."

A dozen or so passengers nodded an obligatory yes, most kept their heads down, consumed with their smartphones.

The woman walked right past Hattie, leaving in her wake a perfumed scent so strong it could be aromatherapy for a pig farm.

Hattie breathed a sigh of relief, digging a yellow highlighter out of her green backpack. Schoolwork had always been her safe haven. And she began to relax, highlighting the main points in her English lit book.

"Ouch!" screeched Hattie when a sharp nail began poking her shoulder.

"You, girl, look like you need a new bestie."

Hattie stared intensely at her book, gathering the courage to explain why the seat next to her was unavailable.

"Excuse me," the woman's voice boomed. "It was a *poe-lite* way of saying, may I sit here?"

"Uh, gosh, uh, I'm so sorry, you may want to find a different seat," Hattie suggested. "I'm starting college tomorrow. I have a huge amount of work to get done before the first day of class," pointing to the stack of textbooks.

Standing up for herself felt good. Hattie sat up straight, pushing back her hunched shoulders.

"Homework? Not on my watch," said the woman, dropping her Hello Kitty luggage right next to Hattie's feet.

"We gonna have some fun on this road trip. O-M-G!" the woman remarked when she took a long look at Hattie's cracked heels and bruised toenails. Hattie had working feet, ones that been crammed into barn boots all day, every day.

"You *gotta* paint those little piggies, pink, maybe blue, *cuz* they *is* something UGLY!"

Hattie blushed.

"Listen up, sweet pea. Not to worry. I've got nail polish in my cosmetic bag to fix all that ugly," pointing to Hattie's toes. "I've got plenty of snacks and diet colas, too. But you're such a skinny thing, you don't need diet anything."

"Uhh," stammered Hattie, glancing to her right. Dang it. There he was again, the hooded, bloodshot eyes staring at her, snickering like a middle school boy.

"I'm guessing a sweet young thing like yourself won't mind if we swap seats, so I can look out the window. Could you move those peanut-size butt cheeks."

"You want to sit right here?" Hattie asked, pointing to her dark blue cushioned bus seat.

"Yes, so kindly scootch toward this here nice fella." The woman stopped talking as she soaked in the young man's appearance.

"Maybe not too close," the woman lowered her voice, nodding her dyed platinum-blond head in the creepy guy's direction.

This was Mama's fault. Hattie wanted to fly to Boston. Mama insisted she take the Greyhound bus. "You'll find a nice grandmotherly type to sit by," she'd said. "And it suits our budget."

"Well, wise Mama," Hattie thought angrily. "What about the creepy guy with his bedroom eyes? Or the loud-mouthed woman ruining my chance to study?"

The woman waited, staring at the coveted seat. Hattie surrendered, picking up her books, she moved over.

"*You's* such a doll," the woman crooned as she climbed over Hattie, her generous bosom plopping into Hattie's face like sand-filled balloons.

"Tight squeeze, too many sugars with my coffees, and between us, those maple-glazed donuts I can't resist," she laughed, pushing her Hello Kitty luggage under the seat in front of her.

"There, all settled," the woman said wiggling her hips like a pig's behind. If *we's* going to be friends, young lady, I'll need a proper introduction."

"I'm Hattie," she said quietly, hoping the man across the aisle couldn't hear.

"Speak up, child!"

"Hattie Brown."

"Nice to know you. I'm Bess Beckman, your new bestie."

Chapter 3:
Getting to Know You

Hattie drummed her fingers on the arm of her seat. The ride was clearly not going as she planned—and she loved a well-executed plan.

She rubbed the sweaty palms of her hands on the back of her neck, trying to release the tension building in her narrow shoulders. Bess's arrival kicked the opportunity to study right out the bus door.

"I listed my hobbies on Match.com as trying out samples of drugstore cosmetics, which is my favorite thing to do, second only to searching for deals at the dollar store," Bess droned on, reapplying her lip gloss. "I'm a good person. Mama used to say I was downright delightful when I wanted to be. Surely there's someone out there who will appreciate me. Right?"

"I believe so," Hattie begrudgingly agreed, the pressure in her chest rising like an outdoor thermometer in the summer. She began scrolling through photos on her phone. It didn't take but ten seconds before Bess was peering over Hattie's shoulder for an uninvited peek.

"Who yo peeps?" Bess asked in a horrible imitation of a rapper, not the least embarrassed she was snooping.

Hattie wanted to say, "None of your beeswax." But she disliked hurting people's feelings. "Family and a close family friend. They came to the bus station to say goodbye."

"Lucky you. I took a taxi, by myself, as usual, to the bus station," Bess sheepishly admitted.

Hattie stared at the photo. It'd been such a sweet goodbye. All the important people in her life came. Mama and Mema giving her last-minute advice and endless hugs. Cousin Beau lovingly teasing her about her smarts. Pastor Luis bestowing her with his well-worn "Pocket Guide to Boston." Bess was right. She was blessed with a good family.

Hattie scrolled to the next photo.

"Would you look at that," Bess smirked as her bright purple nail scratched across Hattie's phone screen. "You got yourself sandwiched like deli meat between two yummy buns. Mmmm, mmmm. One of 'em hotties yours?"

Hattie blushed.

"Uh, no, not at all," stuttered Hattie, pointing to the young man in the photo wearing classic Ray-Ban aviators, sporting a military buzz cut. His broad shoulders and muscular physique filled out the 2XL crimson Harvard T-shirt Hattie had purchased for him, his square chin raised high as if ready for any challenge, "That is my cousin, Beau."

"He's so studly," Bess crowed like a rooster at sunrise. "Bet the young women swoon after him."

"Yeah, he's never had a problem in that category."

"Guys like him never do. What's the scoop with the Mexican guy?"

"He's our pastor, Pastor Luis," said Hattie wondering if Bess was racist. "He's from Texas. And a Harvard graduate. In fact, he's the one who persuaded Mama to let me go to Harvard."

"If that's what Harvard men look like, sign me up," Bess laughed, then coughed, spewing and re-swallowing phlegm. Hattie recognized the smoker's cough, a few of Mema's friends were smokers, or had been in their younger years.

"Oh, no, my cousin's not going to Harvard. I gave him the T-shirt. Beau's more of a hands-on type guy."

"I bet he is," cackled Bess.

Hattie rubbed her forehead, thinking this was going to be a long ride.

"Trade school?"

"No. He had a football scholarship to Alabama, but at the last minute changed his mind. Signed up with the military. He leaves for basic training next week."

Hattie scrolled to the next photo, thinking of Beau, praying he was doing the right thing. Beau and Hattie were only a few months apart in age, and close, far more like brother and sister than distant cousins. Beau's the reason she didn't get bullied by the high school mean girls.

"Woah, back up, girlfriend," instructed Bess.

Hattie scrolled back to a group shot, one that included Hattie's grandmother and mother, taken in front of Mama's 1976 blue Chevy pickup truck.

"Tell me more about your people?"

"Beau's my age. Great football player. Strong as a horse. When we need anything requiring heavy lifting at the kennel, Beau's our guy."

"Your family owns a dog kennel, huh?" asked Bess, applying red rouge on her chubby cheeks.

"A kennel and a dog training center. Mama's got a gift for training dogs, no matter the breed or temperament."

"Is your daddy a dog person too?"

"Daddy was the one who came up with the idea of giving Mama a dog. He passed away when I was eleven, before the business got started."

"That's rough," Bess said, gently patting Hattie's solid hand. "Tell me about the dark-skinned fella?"

Hattie bit her bottom lip, guessing Bess was an unlikely candidate for being politically correct. Still, her heart was in the right place. Hattie could tell.

"Pastor Luis is a good friend of my family's, especially Mema, my grandmother. She's the one standing next to him. They're fishing buddies, gardening buddies. I don't know how Pastor Luis puts up with her at times. He doesn't even like to fish and hardly has the time to help with the church garden. He goes along with it all."

"Sounds like a real nice guy. Not many of those, I guarantee you that."

"Before we left, Mema was worrying about my new luggage going in the truck bed. Told anyone who'd listen it cost a small fortune at Penney's, her graduation gift to me. She definitely didn't want it tossed around as we drove to the station. Being the good person he is, Pastor Luis offered to ride in the truck bed to make sure the luggage didn't fall out. Mema was so pleased. Of course,

Mama had to bring Lily, her favorite dog, along. Mama going somewhere without a dog is like a kid going to school without a phone. Seriously, her lifeline."

"Why she sure is a dog lover, *in't* she?"

"Pastor Luis held one of his arms around my suitcases and his other arm around Lily. His long black hair was blowing around like he was a rock star," giggled Hattie. "We couldn't stop laughing. You'd never guess he was a pastor."

Hattie looked closer at the photo. "He's so different than our former pastor—who underneath his perfectly tailored suits—was as shallow as a worm's grave. Spent as much time on his hair as half the cheerleading team at my high school. Drove a big fancy sedan."

Bess giggled. "You ain't gonna get us hit by lightning, talking like that about a man of the cloth?"

"Not likely. My science teacher explained there's only one chance in 500,000 of lightning striking us. Besides, it's all true. Pastor Griffin was as judgmental as a jury in a small-town court-room. His church doors were open wide for people who liked what he liked. If you were different, why, he slammed the door shut," Hattie said in disgust. "Mema used to say he had such a big ego, he'd have changed the Trinity to Father, Son, and Holy Pastor Griffin, if the bishop allowed it."

"The true character of a person always seeps out. Like this here muffin top of mine when I wear a pair of tight jeans," laughed Bess, pulling on her flabby tummy. "You can only hide the truth so long before it rears its ugly head."

"I suppose," shrugged Hattie. "The good news is Pastor Griffin left, and the bishop assigned Pastor Luis to our church. Honestly, people weren't so sure of him at first. He was a shock to our congregation, showing up wearing sneakers and his black hair tied back in a ponytail. One day he rode his skateboard to church, raised lots of eyebrows that day. Always looks a bit wrinkled. I've never seen him wear new clothes. Says he was born wearing his brothers' hand-me-downs and he'll likely pass wearing hand-me-downs. Such a good guy."

"Maybe the church committee can afford to buy your preacher an iron, now that they ain't paying for luxury *ve-hic-les*," Bess laughed hysterically.

"Honestly, I don't think he'd use it. Wrinkled and well worn doesn't seem to bother him. Mema says people don't even take notice anymore. It's his gentle ways, helpful spirit they love. Pastor Luis is her favorite preacher. And trust me, she's seen a lot of preachers come and go in her eighty years."

"Y'all so young, likely don't know church types are wound as tight as a spool of thread. Preach and preach till the cows come home. Usually I end up falling asleep, then my snoring kicks in. I either get an elbow from folks or the stink eye. I don't go to church anymore. Don't need the stress."

"Well, you are invited to come to my church, sleepy or not," Hattie laughed. "Pastor Luis is like a favorite teacher. His sermons are filled with history, a bit of geography, and lots of wonderful stories. He grew up with seven brothers and a sister, he's got plenty of stories. Stories that make you laugh and cry. You always leave wanting to be a better person."

"I'll think about it. Say, that cousin of yours looks fun, like he enjoys getting in the streets. What about the preacher man? He looks too young and handsome to be sitting at home."

"From what I can tell, he works hard, plays hard. Likes a good time," laughed Hattie. "Beau and Luis were cocaptains of our church softball team this summer. Games drew a good-sized crowd, too. Of course, Beau is Fairhope's pride and joy, being the starting quarterback for Fairhope High. People love watching him play. And folks were curious to see if the new pastor could play a decent game of ball. It was a big surprise when they discovered he plays as well as Beau."

"An athlete, huh? I'm liking it."

"He credits his older brothers for that. Says when he was a little kid, none of 'em wanted him on their team. He practiced day and night so he could hit and catch better than all of them. Beau and Pastor Luis have become good friends."

"You never really think of people hanging out with preachers."

"My entire family hangs out with him. We're like his substitute family—his own family lives in Texas. He loves good food, good music, good stories. Fits right in."

"He'd probably think I'm a bad person since I'm not much of a churchgoer."

"He doesn't criticize Beau for not going to church. Unlike Mema, who has her panties all in a bunch about Beau. Pastor Luis says God can hear Beau's prayers outside of church just as well as inside."

"That's pretty cool."

"He is pretty cool," Hattie said. "He started the first preacher/rabbi/priest cook-off, a fundraiser for Special Olympics. His mac 'n' cheese was awarded second place, only losing to Father Pete, whose fish tacos took first prize."

"Your preacher cooks! Is he single?"

"Yes, ma'am."

"I never dated a preacher. Then again, never wanted to. Until now. Think you could, like, maybe set us up? I'd drive over to Fairhope. Love that charming town."

"Hmmm," stuttered Hattie, caught off guard by Bess's request. "Pastor Luis is a lot younger…"

Bess stopped smiling, furrowed her eyebrows, crossed her arms, resting them on her big bosom.

Hattie backpedaled like a fast-talking attorney. "You're what, in your thirties?"

Bess grinned a smile so wide she'd scare an alligator.

"Fooled you too, huh. It's my expertise with cosmetics," flashing her manicured nails at Hattie.

"Gosh, best I can recall, Mema mentioned that sometime soon Pastor Luis's girlfriend is moving to Fairhope. I think he's taken, Bess."

"Darn, got my hopes up. I was thinking a decent man might be in my future."

Bess kept looking at the photo of Hattie's family. "I can tell that there is your Mama. Same ivory skin as you. Same eyes. And that beautiful red hair. Does she color it?"

"No, it's always been that way. My daddy used to say he could spot her a mile away with hair the color of a copper kettle."

"That's sweet. Surely the woman next to your Mama is your gammy. Looks like a real Southern belle, pearls and all. She's got pretty gray hair, eyes as green as the grass in Ireland."

"Yep, that's my grandmother, Mema. But don't let all that pretty fool you. She can hunt, fish, train bird dogs with the best of 'em. She'd fly to the moon and back if she thought it'd help her family."

"No pearls 'round your Mama's neck."

"Mama's all about the dogs, definitely a jeans-and-boots person."

"Did she ever remarry?"

"No. Never even dated. Who can blame her? Daddy was the kindest, sweetest man. Best plumber in Fairhope. Whole town loved him. Mama says Daddy was her one and only."

"I dream of finding my one and only. Speaking of dreaming, I best get me some shut eye. I was so excited about this trip, the butterflies in my tummy didn't let me rest much last night. Now my eyes are burning like I'm chopping a big ole onion. Mind if I take a catnap?"

"No, yes, absolutely, go ahead, sleep."

The lights dimmed. Gradually, passengers began to nod off. Even the creepy guy. Hattie's seat light was the only one that remained on. She began doing what she did best: open a book and dive in.

✳ ✳ ✳

When the sun began to rise, so did Bess. Hattie watched Bess as she immediately jumped into a morning beauty routine. She pulled out cleansing wipes for her face, put moisturizer on, primer, followed by cover-up, a dash of blush. Then she pulled out a hairbrush. Sprayed a touch of spray on her silver-blond pixie, fluffed her locks, then grabbed her toothbrush and marched to the bathroom.

When Bess returned, she stared right into Hattie's face, while tapping her high-heeled sandals.

"Something wrong?" asked Hattie.

"Honey, don't take this the wrong way, but *you is* a morning mess," Bess said, opening a warm diet cola and taking a loud slurp. "Your hair looks like a bird's nest. I'm not talking hummingbird, I'm talking a big ole blue jay. Then there's those dark circles under your eyes telling me you didn't sleep a wink last night."

"I studied."

"A little makeup will cover up the nasties from all-nighters."

"I'm fine. Really. I'll shower when I get to campus."

"She looks fine, really fine," the creepy guy across the aisle muttered.

Bess and Hattie ignored him.

"Not worth our time," whispered Bess. "Hattie, dear, a piece of advice, choosing to ignore the benefits of makeup is like choosing to be an unfrosted donut. Who wants a plain donut when there's icing and sprinkles? I've worked at Walgreens, cosmetics department, five years plus. Let me give you a hand."

"Great!" said Hattie, faking enthusiasm.

Hattie considered herself average, on a good day, when she wasn't at the kennel covered in sweat and fur. She typically tied her long hair in a ponytail, as humid days made it runaway crazy curly. A shower at the end of the day was as much of a beauty routine as she had.

"Lookie here," said Bess as she opened a green-and-pink cosmetic case. "A little goes a long way. It all starts with a good primer," pulling out a three-inch bottle that read: all-day primer. "Hold still, honeybee, this is how you become Queen Bee."

"Okay," Hattie grimaced, trying to relax. She didn't want to be Queen Bee. Right now, she wanted to be invisible. Then she recalled her grueling high school schedule—up at the crack of dawn, feeding the dogs, letting them out to do their business, hurrying to get to school on time. She barely had time to comb her hair.

The reality was Mama and Hattie kept schedules similar to farmers, rising before sunrise, putting dogs in kennels around sunset. They were lucky if they got to Beau's football games by the end of the first quarter. Even then, Mama wore her work jeans, a Fairhope High T-shirt, and leather boots. Hattie dressed similar, tees, barn boots, and Levi's. Mema was different. She dressed up for Beau's games, wearing her game day royal blue and gold dress, coordinating perfectly with the colors of Fairhope High. Her gray bob fell slightly below her earlobes and was held back with a headband, showing off real pearl earrings.

At the games Hattie sat with Mama and Mema, wishing she was one of the kids who sat with a group of friends. Hattie had quietly admired the popular girls with their carefully applied makeup that glistened under the Friday night lights.

Maybe Bess was right. Maybe Hattie needed to try something new. It certainly was a process: primer, foundation, followed by blush. Bess opened a new mascara, examining the brush as she yanked it from the tube.

"Never use anyone else's mascara. Pink eye, it's the chicken pox of the eyeball," warned Bess. "This tube is brand new, hold still."

Hattie did as she was told, trying her best to stop blinking.

"Now, let's see," Bess said, examining the eyeshadow's color palette like an artist at an easel. "Maybe a touch of brown eyeshadow on the creases. Not too much. You're a natural beauty, baby-soft skin and those freckles. No way are we covering up those ruby jewels."

Hattie finally relaxed. It felt good to have someone doting on her.

"Let's give the brows a tune-up, cuz they's looking like brown caterpillars crawling across your forehead," said Bess.

"That's awful."

"Caterpillars ain't bad. They's just prettier when they turn into butterflies," Bess explained as she took a comb to Hattie's unruly brows.

"Lastly the lips. Pucker up, girl," said Bess as she put lip gloss on Hattie.

The creepy guy leaned over toward Hattie. "You got sexy lips."

"Keep that thought to yourself, please," Bess snarled, giving the creepy guy the stink eye. "She's not interested."

"Next stop, Logan Airport," the bus driver announced.

"Lucky us, just in time." Bess pulled from her purse a pink pocket mirror with painted yellow daisies on it. "Look at you, belle of the ball!"

Hattie looked in the mirror, expecting to see a clown face looking back at her. What she saw was a prettier version of herself. Nothing was overdone. It was as if Bess's fine-tuning brought out the best in her features.

"I love it!" Hattie hugged Bess, feeling pretty for the first time.

"Me too!" the creepy guy winked at Hattie.

Bess leaned over Hattie to stare him down. "Leave my friend here alone. Don't make me say it again," threatened Bess, holding Hattie's hands in hers.

"Listen up," said Bess to Hattie, "you's smart and beautiful and most important, kind. Someday you'll be flying first class, not taking the bus with folks like me, and, unfortunately, him," nodding toward the creepy guy.

"Bess, thank you so much."

"You's welcome. We're friends now, right?"

"For sure," said Hattie, grabbing her backpack.

As she moved to the aisle, the creepy guy stood. Clutching his black duffel bag like it was a baby, he moved in close behind her.

"I was going to get off in Braintree, but I think hanging out at Harvard Square might get me some action tonight," he whispered into Hattie's ear as she waited her turn to exit the bus.

Hattie, unsure what to do, glanced back at Bess, who was already pushing her way toward the creepy guy. Why, she's strong as a bulldog, thought Hattie, watching as Bess yanked his earplug and he reeled in pain.

"Best sit yourself back down," Bess instructed the creepy guy, pushing down his shoulder.

"You're not the boss of me," he snapped.

"If you get off this bus and stalk my friend, I swear on my mama's grave, I'll have an entire Boston precinct tailing you quicker than a hummingbird flaps its wings. My cousin Ray is a cop here in Southie. He's so good, he's bad. That makes him someone you *really* don't want to cross. You get what I'm saying?"

Hattie never turned around. She walked straight ahead, praying the creepy guy wasn't following her. Not until she got her luggage and found the airport entrance, did she dare to look back.

The bus was taking off, black exhaust fumes consuming its back wheels. Through the smoke, Hattie could see Bess giving her the thumbs-up sign. The coast was clear.

Chapter 4:
Curbside Pickup

HATTIE, 2008

Car doors slamming. Horns honking. Important-looking people in suits, women in stiletto heels rushing in and out of the
terminal. Hattie paused, soaking in the chaos of a large city airport.

Once inside the airport terminal, she went straight to the
women's restroom, managing to squeeze into the stall with her
suitcase. She unzipped it just enough to pull out a nicely folded
light blue polo shirt and crisply starched chinos, thanks to Mema,
who had ironed all of Hattie's clothes.

Hattie wiggled out of the cutoffs and yanked off the tight tank
she'd worn for the past twenty-four hours, dropping her clothes
on top of her suitcase. She was never wearing that outfit again,
shuddering at the thought of creepy guy's warm breath invading
the back of her neck.

She raised her arms, pulling on the polo shirt. She felt better
already. She slid one long leg into her pressed pants, then the other. Fresh clothes felt as wonderful as sweet tea in the summer. She

barely managed to squeeze the shorts into her suitcase, which was bursting at the seams.

As she washed her hands, she looked in the mirror. Better, much better. This outfit looked familiar, comfortable. She took a second look and her hopeful smile disappeared when realized she looked like a walking advertisement for school uniforms at the private high school in Fairhope. Her chest deflated with a sigh. Was this what college students wear? The look wasn't awful, less cowgirl, more preppy.

As Hattie exited the terminal, she recited Mama's travel tips. "Stand with your shoulders back. Look confident. Pay attention to your surroundings. Don't focus on your phone, it makes you an easy target."

Mama's instructions seemed over the top, bordering on paranoia. Hattie didn't want to live in Mama's world of fear. She didn't blame her, not after Daddy's death had left them shattered like broken crystal. Mama suffered severe panic attacks, and she was constantly texting Hattie to confirm her safety, her whereabouts. Frankly, it was stifling. In an effort to help Mama, she'd taped on the fridge one of Pastor Luis's favorite Bible verses: "Don't worry about anything, but in prayer and supplication, with thanksgiving, make your requests known to God, and the peace that passes all understanding will fill your heart and mind through Christ."

You couldn't miss it. And despite Mama getting half-and-half out of the refrigerator every morning for her cup of coffee, the verse had yet to give off a light bulb moment.

Hattie got in the line for a taxi, taking a minute to send a text to Mama: *Made it to Boston. At the airport. Waiting for a taxi.*

"Next!" aggressively shouted an airport employee in his neon orange safety vest. Hattie quickly strode toward him, and he gestured for her to walk to a green-and-white taxi. The cab driver jumped out of the car and grabbed her luggage, placing it in the trunk.

"Where you go?" he asked in broken English.

"Harvard University."

"Fine, thank you. Twenty-minute drive."

Hattie climbed in the back, attempting to suppress her grin. She, Hattie Brown, a nobody from Fairhope, Alabama, was heading to Harvard.

The taxi driver stepped on the gas, the sedan surging full throttle into an endless stream of traffic. The blare of car horns intensified. Long gone were the genteel ways of Fairhope, where a toot of the horn meant a friendly hello, or a cautionary "Be careful."

Hattie's phone pinged. Mama texted back, asking for a description of the driver and name of the cab company. Hattie ignored the request. If she sent a description of the driver—a man in his midtwenties with a thick foreign accent, sporting a way-long beard—Mama would have a panic attack. And surely as the cows come home, Mama be on the next flight to Boston to bring her home.

Hattie finally stopped staring at the driver as if he was a criminal and began noticing her surroundings. The back sides of brownstones with tiny balconies. Wrought iron fences encasing charming café tables and chairs. Richly potted plants and flowers in window boxes. She wondered how people could enjoy outdoor balconies with the frenzy of traffic down below. She glanced to her right, and it took her breath away, a handful of Sunfish sailboats bobbing

28

back and forth on the Charles River. Red, white, and blue sails glistened on the water. An endless stream of runners, walkers, and bikers on a path that paralleled the river.

As the taxi crossed the bridge from Boston to Cambridge, the weight of attending Harvard descended on her shoulders like concrete slabs. The excitement turned into sheer terror. What if she wasn't Harvard material? Her mind started racing with the traffic.

The sudden screeching of brakes put an end to Hattie's anxious thoughts. The driver sucked in air as if it were his last breath when his taxi stopped inches from the rear of a green Subaru Forester with a BU sticker on the back window.

"Accident," remarked the driver.

The air inside the cab was stuffy, overly warm. She needed fresh air, and rolled down the window. There were lots of people walking dogs. From the looks of it, Boston was proving to be a dog-friendly town. Hattie unexpectedly longed for one of Mama's dogs. They'd calm her nerves. Lily, Mama's first and favorite dog, always lay close to Hattie, especially when Hattie was sad or anxious. Stroking a dog's fur was calming. Hattie hadn't been without a dog since she was eleven years old, the year Daddy died. She ached for the familiarity of the kennel, a pack of dogs simultaneously barking. Their long noses clamoring for her attention. She grinned thinking of Lily's wagging tail when she'd walk in the door after school.

Hattie, so eager to escape small-town life and cleaning kennels, never guessed she'd miss it all. Jeez, maybe she was more like Mama than she realized, more like Mama than she wanted to be.

Memories of Lily flooded her. Lily was a miracle from heaven. After Daddy passed, Hattie's mother, Beth, could barely get out of bed in the morning, leaving eleven-year-old Hattie responsible for running the household. Each morning Hattie made breakfast before heading off to school. All Mama could stomach was a couple bites of toast and a few sips of coffee. Hattie needed more sustenance in her, or her stomach growled like a lion. The kids sitting close to her at school would giggle at the gurgling. Hattie wasn't keen on cooking eggs like Mama once done, ensuring her family left each morning with full tummies. These days Hattie filled her own bowl of cereal, Rice Krispies, milk, topped off with blueberries and a heaping tablespoon of white sugar. Lately she'd gone without the blueberries. Mama had stopped going to the grocery store, asking Hattie to handle the shopping. Kroger was too far for a young girl to walk, so Hattie shopped at the Gas & Go convenience store near their house, not exactly a mecca for healthy, fresh food.

Thank God for school. It gave Hattie a sense of normalcy. She earned excellent grades, loved learning. It was after school that the sadness wrapped around her like a mummy. The new normal was Mama resting in bed, most the day, most the night. Mama no longer did mom things. No cooking, cleaning, or seeing friends. She barely spoke. Each day, Mama looked a little skinnier, a little bonier, a little crazier. Eleven-year-old Hattie had no idea what to do. Mema did. Mema, with a personality so strong a hurricane would turn the other direction, took charge.

"I brought supper," Mema said to Hattie as she plugged in a Crock-Pot filled with beef stew. "Where's your Mama?"

"She's sleeping."

"At four in the afternoon?"

"Yes," whispered Hattie to her grandmother. "Mama is having a real hard time since Daddy passed. I think we best let her rest."

Mema looked around the house. Stacks of unopened mail on the kitchen counter, used paper plates in the sink, the kitchen garbage overflowing.

"Dust 'round here is as thick as molasses," Mema announced. "Drapes drawn as if it's World War II. The floors need a good mopping."

Mema opened the refrigerator and gagged. "Sweet reason, there's still salads and casseroles in here from the luncheon after your daddy's funeral."

Nine weeks to be exact. Hattie been counting.

"Half-and-half expired two weeks ago," exclaimed Mema, shaking her short gray bob.

"I'm trying my best," said Hattie in a wrinkled school dress and unmatched socks.

"Looks to me like things around here have gone to hell and a handbasket," Mema screeched, storming into Beth's bedroom.

"Your daughter needs tending, and from the looks of it, so does your home," Mema sternly scolded Beth. "If you don't start caring for Hattie, I'm taking her home with me. She's hurting too. You ain't the only one with a broken heart."

Beth stared blankly at her mother.

"Seems to me, Beth, you's at crossroads. Monroe's not coming back, so you best start asking the good Lord to give you the strength to go on without him," lectured Mema as she pulled off the sheets and duvet covering her daughter.

"I don't want to go on," sobbed Beth, "not without Monroe."

"Fine. I'll be back tomorrow to pick up Hattie. That is, unless I see some improvement around here. I'm talking a fully stocked kitchen, a good dusting, mopped floors, and folded laundry for

starters. You have twenty-four hours to get your house in order—
for the sake of your daughter. Oh, and the fridge smells like a dead
raccoon rotting in the summer sun. Please toss Martha's potato
salad, if Hattie gets ahold of that, she's going to suffer food poi-
soning."

Hattie pressed her ear up against the bedroom door to listen.
She loved Mema. Living with her was another matter. Mema could
be as entertaining as a New Orleans jazz band. She was also bossy
and talked nonstop and held a busy social calendar. Surely as the
stars shine on a clear night, Mema be dragging Hattie along to
garden club meetings, bridge club, fishing with friends at the pier.
Least her mama let her be a bookworm.

And poor Mama, she looked like a rabid, starved animal, hardly strong enough to pick up the newspaper at the end of the drive,
let alone get groceries and clean the house before tomorrow. Hattie wondered whether to postpone an already-late book report, or
jump in to help Mama. Getting to the grocery store was a problem,
Kroger was a half mile away. And she couldn't walk it, not while
carrying groceries. Groceries would have to wait. But if she started
now, cleaning up like Mema asked, she could make everything
look better.

Dinner first. Hattie fixed boxed macaroni and cheese, substi-
tuting the quarter cup of milk with water. And who needed butter?
She certainly didn't. Mama wouldn't notice. She never touched
her food anyway. Hattie took a bite of the watered-down mac 'n'
cheese and lost her appetite. She opened the fridge, breathing in
a putrid smell. She began tossing almost everything, filling a large
garbage bag. After dragging the bag outside, she began the dusting. The yellow feather duster made her feel like Mary Poppins.

Nothing hard about dusting. Then the vacuuming, why, that was easy enough. Last thing on the list was to mop floors. As Hattie was filling the bucket of mop water, she knocked over the entire bottle of Pine-Sol cleaner.

Dang it. The floors look dirtier than when she started. Frustrated, she gave up and began working on her book report. Half past midnight, she finished her report. It'd be turned in a day late but it was done.

Exhausted but unable to sleep, Hattie opened her bedroom window, looking to the heavens above. The full moon and brilliant stars gave her a celestial feeling, like heaven was reaching out to help her. She needed help. Practical help.

"Dear Lord," Hattie whispered. "You've got to help Mama and me. I'm plum tired. My teachers keep asking why I can't stay awake in class. Mama's fallen apart, taken to her bed all day and all night. I'm doing the cooking, cleaning, the laundry. I'm buying groceries from the Gas & Go Station because Mama's not up to driving to a grocery store. To be honest, for a while, I was buying lots of candy, cookies, and colas. But my stomach started to hurt something fierce, guessing it was all the sugar. I never used to get away with skipping vegetables and fruits. Mama doesn't notice, not anymore, doesn't much care." Hattie teared up, crying.

"God, there used to be folks dropping off food for us, checking on us. No one comes anymore cuz Mama keeps telling 'em we're fine. Just need our privacy. We're about as fine as a thirsty horse in the desert."

More tears slipped from the corners of Hattie's eyes.

"Mema's getting herself all wound tight about Mama grieving. It's a mess. We sure could use some help down here. Oh, and if my daddy can hear me, Daddy, if you're listening right now, it's so awful with you gone. I'm not trying to make you feel bad. I'm just sharing. I hope you can hear me up there, I sure miss you down here, just wish I knew that you're still watching over us, somehow."

Hattie's shoulders heaved with sobs, and she cried herself to sleep.

Next morning Hattie quietly made a peanut-butter-and-sugar sandwich for school. Beth took a few sips of coffee, hugged Hattie, and returned to her bedroom. Neither spoke. Both sporting swollen eyes from crying all night. Hattie hollered goodbye, wondering if Mema be waiting for her when she got home.

Chapter 5:
Mama's Turnaround

1996

Hattie came home after school expecting to find Mama in bed or, worse, Mema there, packing Hattie's suitcase. Hattie wandered into Mama's bedroom to check on her. The bed was unmade, Mama not there. Hattie panicked. Where was Mama? She needed her mother, even if it meant taking care of the caregiver. She loved her quiet Mama. She prayed Beth was okay.

"Mama!" Hattie screamed out in a panic. "Where are you?"

"We're in the backyard, honey," hollered Mama. "Come out back."

Who was this we? Mama never had friends visit anymore, not since the funeral. Hattie pushed open the gate, stepping through overgrown grass. Must be important for Mama to get out of bed and go outside. Hattie silently prayed it wasn't Mema in the backyard with Mama.

"Hattie, come meet the cutest puppy on God's green earth," said Mama. "Isn't she pretty? The color of butter. Careful though, her teeth are as sharp as a tiger's."

Hattie slowly walked toward Mama, who was holding a beautiful yellow Labrador retriever with perfectly round brown eyes and a wagging tail thumping excitedly against Mama's chest. Mama and puppy looked like they were meant for each other.

"Why, she's adorable. Who does this cutie belong to?" asked Hattie, looking around to see who was visiting.

"Us!" Mama exclaimed.

"What?"

"It was quite a morning."

"I'll say."

"I was in bed, after you left. And someone started knocking on the front door. I wasn't up for company, so I tried to ignore it. The person kept knocking, so I tossed on Daddy's old bathrobe and opened the door, just a crack to see who it was."

"Who was it, Mama?"

"Doc Grady. Standing there with this pudgy yellow Labrador." Mama hugged the puppy.

"Apparently, your daddy asked Doc for a favor before he passed, quite a huge favor."

"Really?"

"He, uh, wanted us to have one of Arlo's puppies. You remember Doc's retriever, his office dog."

"Sure I do. Sits by me when I have to get my finger pricked."

"Doc breeds a litter every once in a great while for special people. I guess we're one of 'em, per Daddy's request."

"What? This cutie is ours!"

"It's a surprise to me too. Doc says it's Daddy's way of looking out for us. Your father always called us the perfect sandwich family, he and I the bread, you the sweet strawberry jam in between. It's his way of putting the sandwich back together."

Beth wiped her eyes.

"Doc says the only time he ever heard Daddy brag was when it was about you, Hattie."

Hattie smiled, with a teardrop dripping down her left chin. The puppy's long tongue started licking Hattie's cheek, and she couldn't stop giggling.

"So Daddy wanted us to have her, huh?"

"Yes. Doc warned me puppies are much like having a newborn baby around. People have to really want to care for one."

"Are you up for it, Mama?"

"I didn't think I was. I haven't been taking good care of you lately. I'm sorry for that."

"It's okay. I understand."

"It's not okay. I just know when Doc Grady handed the puppy to me, along with a puppy information packet and a twenty-pound bag of dog food, that it stirred some life back into me. Her name is Duchess. But I think I'll call her Lily."

The puppy began pulling on Hattie's white knee-high socks.

"Seems more like a menace than a gift," Hattie giggled as Lily attempted to pull Hattie across the lawn.

That night Hattie heard the screen door open and close, Mama taking the puppy outside to do its business. How did Mama know puppies need to pee every few hours?

"You two are up early," Hattie said in a sleepy voice as she passed them in the hallway on the way to the bathroom.

"Lily has to go pee every few hours, hope we didn't keep you up."

"I'm good. You're the one who's got to be exhausted," Hattie said, leaning over to pet Lily. "Guess all that cuteness s'pose to make up for no sleep, huh, pretty girl?"

Hattie observed Mama fall into the rhythm of a new routine, round the clock care for a needy pup. One morning, as Hattie walked out the front door to head to school, Mama was standing outside in the pouring rain, an umbrella in one hand, a dog leash in the other.

"Bye, Mama," said Hattie, noticing Mama's white Keds tennis shoes were soaked.

"Your daddy," whispered Beth, looking up at the ominous gray skies shooting down heavy raindrops, "should have included a pair of rain boots with the puppy."

Chapter 6:
Same Town, New Rhythm

"Grab the food, will you, please?" Mama asked Hattie as Lily and Mama came inside the house.

Mama was wearing Daddy's red Alabama sweatshirt and jogging shorts; the outfit hung on Mama's thin body, making her look like a teenage boy.

"Quick," pleaded Mama. "Lily had an accident in the car, I have to clean it up."

Better you than me, thought Hattie, walking away with the food. She inhaled the aroma of freshly baked chocolate chip cookies from one of the bags. Was there anything more delicious? She doubted it. She peeked in the nicely packaged food boxes from Fresh Provisions, a café on Main. One box contained the jumbo-sized chocolate chip cookies. The other box cradled two turkey, cranberry, and apple sandwiches on multigrain bread. Nestled in next to the sandwiches were two mini yogurt parfaits topped with fresh fruit. After weeks of boxed cereal for supper, this was going to be like a dinner from a fancy restaurant.

Hattie carefully placed the sandwiches and parfaits into the fridge as if they were precious jewels going into a safe. As she folded the paper sack, a big yellow paw reached for the box of cookies.

"You touch my supper, you'll be sorry as a fox caught in the chicken coop." It'd been a long time since they'd had a good meal like this.

This week alone, Lily chewed apart Hattie's coveted three-ring science notebook and ripped the tongue of her Converse tennis shoe. Not to mention the countless times the dog jumped up on her and scratched her bare legs. Lily was a walking disaster. The only good thing was the dog kept Mama from sliding back into a deep black hole of grief. Once when Mama temporarily drifted back into a sad, dark place, ignoring Lily's needs, she discovered a chewed table leg and a torn-up needlepoint pillow. Lily forced Mama to be present. Hattie thanked God. The dog seemed to be the catalyst of Mama's return from the living dead. Mama began doing mom things, things like picking up light bulbs from Ace Hardware on Main Street, colas from Sam's Club, and bread from the local bakery. Mama also brought Lily with her, wherever she went.

The house was a different kind of messy than what had sent Mema into a tirade a few months backs. Rather than dirty dishes and unopened mail, it was tennis balls and dog toys. Occasionally a chewed sock. Once in a while a puppy accident. Mama said it was to be expected, and she seemed totally okay about getting on her hands and knees and scrubbing Lily's messes with a mix of water and vinegar.

One afternoon Hattie came home from school and found stacks of books on the kitchen table. She gravitated to the table to take a look. She was thumbing through one of the piles when Mama and Lily burst through the front door after a walk.

"It looks like you robbed the library," Hattie commented.

Mama laughed. "Who knew the library have so many dog-training books?"

"You're obsessed."

"I feel something special. A nudge. To learn as much as I can about dog training." Mama looked at Hattie and pointed to the heavens above. Hattie shrugged, not quite knowing what to say.

"Sounds a little crazy, I know."

"One can never have too many books," laughed Hattie.

"The librarian thought I was a lunatic," admitted Beth. "I caught her eye roll when I asked for an exemption on the number of books a person is allowed. Wouldn't be surprised if there's a rumor going around Fairhope that I've turned into the crazy dog lady."

"Better than a crazy cat lady," teased Hattie. "Besides, Mrs. Rowell owns that title. Kids at school says she's got at least twelve."

"That's a lot of litter boxes."

"How'd you swing all this?" asked Hattie, pointing at the stack of books.

"I was honest. Told her I'm just getting back on my feet since Monroe passed and our new puppy is ruining our home. I said I need help. Books might just be the thing."

"And that worked?"

"Not at first. I was certain the librarian, the one who wears the thick red glasses, was going to say no, I really did, until Maggie Peters intervened."

"Who is Maggie Peters?"

"The director of the chamber. Daddy used to refer to her as Fairhope's middle-aged cheerleader. You can't miss her, wears the power suits around town, loud and proud like she's a presidential candidate."

"Can't say I know her."

"Well, Maggie started talking to me, about how busy she is and has no time to train the family's new dog, a rescue with a horrific habit."

"Let me guess…jumps on people like Lily? Sharp nails, hurts. Totally annoying. I get it."

"No, not even close," laughed Mama. "Apparently, the dog really likes chewing her boys' dirty socks and boxers. Maggie thinks it's the smell, says the boys are going through puberty and have all sorts of unique smells. She's so loud the whole first floor of the library could hear her. I could hear people laughing."

The important thing was Mama was laughing. Hattie couldn't help but join in.

"The librarian was desperate to get Maggie to be quiet, she started checking out my entire pile of books."

"Holy moly!"

"Maggie also gave me her business card. Asked me to call her. She'd like to set up a time for me to train her dog. She'll pay me! Can you believe it?"

"Yes! You're a natural, Mama. You really are."

"Thank you, sweetheart. I really hope I get good at this. Maybe people will hire me. And I could eventually start my own dog business."

"Best start with Lily," giggled Hattie. "I'm so tired of her biting my pant leg like she's fighting off a big ole alligator. When I told my science teacher, 'Lily ate my homework,' she accused me of fibbing. I'm the only kid in the entire school who actually likes her class."

"Hattie, I'm going to do my best to master this whole dog-training thing. Like you do school. I feel something good is going to come from this."

"You better start soon," Hattie said, pointing to the steps. "Looks like Lily's gnawing her way to China."

Mama sighed, seeing the teeth marks in the knotty pinewood planks. "I just finished a chapter on the importance of keeping a pup in a crate when no one can watch it. I best start tonight."

The first night in the crate, Lily whined, barked, then howled, sounding like a brokenhearted teenager.

"Mama, I've got a test tomorrow, you've got to get Lily to be quiet," begged Hattie. "I can't sleep."

"Sorry, Hattie. It takes time for dogs to adjust. Patience, please."

"Try telling my math teacher that," Hattie snapped, "after I fail the test tomorrow because I didn't get any sleep."

"You're a female Einstein. You'll do fine, sleep or no sleep."

Lily eventually fell into a deep sleep, as did Hattie. But it definitely was a short night.

Mama was as dedicated to learning about dog training as a law student studying to pass the bar. And she loved sharing what she was learning, even if Hattie wasn't all that interested.

"Hattie, there's no crash course to a well-behaved dog. Training requires consistency, time, and repetition. Reward and praise are key."

She and Hattie purchased treats and toys to put into the crate, creating a sanctuary for Lily. It was working. There were still puppy challenges. Lily proved to be an escape artist, the likes of Houdini. There was no stopping her when the front door opened. She relished a mad dash outside much like a racehorse out of the gate. Hattie and Mama scolded Lily as if she were a kid at school who pulled the fire alarm. Still, Lily didn't learn.

One night when Hattie was working on math, she heard Mama laughing. Mama rarely laughed anymore. Hattie, curious as to what was so funny, got up and went into Mama's room.

"Mama, what are y'all laughing about?"

"Listen to this, this is so us," said Mama as she began reading from one of the library books.

"'It is counterproductive for dog owners to scream at their dog like the house is on fire when it doesn't respond to the 'come' command.'"

Mama giggled.

"Hattie, that's exactly what we do." Mama continued reading aloud, "'Adding in a scolding when the dog returns makes obedience even more difficult. It is not surprising many people have problems getting their dogs to follow commands. A more productive method is for the dog owner to use a happy, enthusiastic voice when calling the dog, resulting in the dog wanting to return to its owner.'"

Mama sat silently.

"We've been doing it all wrong, Hattie."

"Guess so."

From then on Hattie could hear Mama's new happy voice. Mama also kept a few dog treats in her pocket, in case of emergencies when the happy voice wasn't enough. Hattie still wasn't sold on the whole happy-voice thing.

"Mama, Lily's misbehaving," Hattie ranted, pushing Lily off her bed.

"A firm *no* only, please, Hattie," lectured Mama. "Catch her doing something good, praise her for something wonderful she does."

Hattie raised her eyes brows. Finding the good in Lily? Who was Mama kidding? Did she mean like when Lily pulled on her pant leg or running away? Hattie found it easier giving Lily a good spanking on the behind than to sound happy when Lily did wrong.

"The training books say you have to catch her doing good," Mama again suggested.

"How?" Hattie demanded. "She's bad, Mama, bad, bad, bad."

"No, she's a puppy."

"She's a nightmare," Hattie muttered as she stomped upstairs. "I'm so sick of her. I'm sick of you. And I'm sick of not having daddy here!"

Hattie expected to get a lecture, but Mama held her tongue, grabbed the leash, and silently exited the front door to take Lily for a walk.

Eventually Hattie began to notice Lily listening to Mama. Sit, come, stay, at least for a couple of seconds. When Mama wasn't training Lily, she was studying books about training.

"You and that dog are like peas in a pod."

"Oh, Hattie. I s'pose it seems like I spend all my time with Lily. I needed a purpose. Training Lily gives me that. You're growing up so fast, you hardly need me."

"That's not true, Mama."

"Oh, honey, it's okay. It's the cycle of life, you growing up and all. Lily needs me. And at the end of the day, when I miss your daddy the most, I need her. She snuggles up close to me, softens the arrows piercing my heart. I'm guessing school is the balm that does that for you."

Mama was right. School did take her mind off missing Daddy. And the prayers she was saying every night seemed to be helping. Look at Mama now. She always had one particular book out on the kitchen counter, *No Bad Dogs*. Doc Grady gave Mama the book when he gave her Lily. One night, when Mama, Hattie, and Lily gathered on the big bed to watch TV, Mama grabbed the book from the nightstand. A folded piece of notebook paper fell out.

"What's that?" Hattie asked.

"It's a note of some kind," said Mama, unfolding the lined paper. "Oh, Hattie, it's a letter from Daddy." Mama began tracing over each letter with her fingertip, tears dripping down her pale cheeks.

"Mama, read it to me please."

Mama paused, silently taking in the words before sharing.

"Mama!"

"Okay, okay," continued Beth.

Dear Beth & Hattie, by now Doc Grady has presented you with my gift, a puppy. Beth, you likely were mad at first. You never liked surprises. Hattie, I imagine you giggled like only you can do. Did Doc tell you the puppy comes from the legendary line of his first dog, Kindness? Kindness was Doc's first office dog. Doc was having his own hard time after his wife and son died. Only way he could get through those days was with Kindness. Along the way, he discovered how much comfort a dog provides to his patients. Ever since he's had an office dog. Hattie, remember when you had stitches and Doc's dog Romeo was right by your side? You felt better, braver. I'm hoping our puppy does the same for you two, protects you when I'm gone.

Bethie, you're patient and kind. Hardworking. Doc says you have all the skills to be an excellent dog trainer. I'd bet the farm you become one of the best trainers Fairhope has ever seen! Hattie, I know school's more your thing, but this pup is going to be a good friend to you. Help your Mama with him or her.

I love you two. To heaven and back. Family was the best thing that ever happened to me. Someday we will all be together again. Until then keep the faith. Love, Daddy.

That night Mama told Hattie she was putting the note inside of her Bible. "It's time I do better," said Mama. "I gave up reading the Bible—too angry with God for taking Daddy from us. His letter renewed my faith."

She carefully placed the letter in the Bible next to her favorite verse, Jeremiah 29:11. *For I know the plans I have for you, plans to prosper you and not to harm you, plans to give you hope and a future.*

Hattie pulled Lily between them. All three snuggling in close. Daddy was right, a dog by your side did make you feel better. On lonely days, when Hattie was missing Daddy so much she could hardly breathe, she'd open Mama's Bible and reread Daddy's note. She'd seen Mama do the same thing. One thing Hattie knew: more dogs were coming their way. Daddy was helping Mama find her calling.

Chapter 7:
A New Normal

FAIRHOPE, 1997

Hattie's father had worked every Saturday morning. "Prime time for a small-town plumber," he'd told Hattie. So, Mama and Hattie had their own Saturday morning ritual. Daddy called it "girls' morning out."

Rain or shine, Hattie and Mama went to town on Saturday mornings. First stop was for Mama to get a hazelnut coffee from the Wake-Up Call. Then, it was Dahlia's Delights to buy a glazed blueberry donut. They'd run into friends, visit the farmers market, walk to the pier. Some Saturdays they'd window shop. Mama always made sure they headed home just in time to meet Daddy as he walked in the back door.

After Daddy died, everything changed. Mama wouldn't go to town. Told Hattie it was too painful. Hattie felt it too, no fun-loving Daddy to come home to. Plus, Hattie noticed how people avoided her and Mama now, as if they had something contagious.

It'd been over a year since Daddy passed. Saturdays were spent helping Mama with household chores. Then one Friday night, Mama marched into Hattie's room.

"Hattie, let's go into town tomorrow morning, like we used to. We'll take Lily. Get coffee and donuts."

"Seriously?"

"Yes, it'll be good for Lily, good for us."

"Uh, okay, sure."

"It'll include a training session for Lily, you okay with that?"

"For blueberry donuts, I'm okay with just about anything."

The "girls' morning out" returned. Hattie noticed people who once avoided them now made it a point to stop and say hello to Lily. After all, who could resist Lily, with her soulful brown eyes and those darn paws the size of tea saucers? Lily was the icebreaker people needed. The mother-daughter duo was approachable again, like when Daddy was alive. Hattie asked Mama if she noticed it too.

"The way I see it," said Mama, "is folks simply feel better knowing we have one of Doc Grady's pups by our side."

One of Beth's friends, Olivia Lupin, a beautiful blonde wearing a navy tennis skort and a pink quarter-zip popover, stopped Beth and Hattie as they exited the Wake-Up Call. Olivia was attempting to walk her dog Posey. By the looks of it, it wasn't clear who was walking whom.

"Beth, Hattie," exclaimed Olivia, breathing heavily as she gripped the leash. "You two are just the people I'm looking for."

Hattie noticed Mrs. Lupin was struggling to control the dog, a handsome black doodle who was as playful as a set of twin toddlers. She also noticed how pretty Mrs. Lupin looked with her hair tied in a messy bun and lightly applied makeup. Hattie cringed looking at Mama wearing old cutoffs and one of Daddy's Alabama T-shirts, three sizes too big.

Hattie had to admit, though, when it came to dogs, Mama was the one who shined. Lily followed Mama's commands, never pulling or jumping on people. She didn't growl or bark at the other dogs they met on their walks.

"Maggie says she ran into you at the library," Olivia said. "Says you're training dogs now. Is it true?"

"A slight exaggeration. I've been working a great deal with Lily," said Beth. "And spending my free time reading up on the whole dog-training thing. It's a good hobby for me. Like tennis is for you."

"Well, then, it sounds like you're just the person I need. Taking Posey on a walk is about as pleasant as being dragged behind a school bus by a towrope. I'm going to need replacement surgery for my shoulder if things don't change."

Lily sat quietly at Mama's feet while Olivia spoke.

"Your Labrador is so darn sweet and good, a real peach," said Olivia, working to keep an excited Posey from jumping on Hattie. "I want that," Olivia said, pointing to Lily lying on the ground like a perfect angel.

"I'd be happy to *try* training Posey, she's adorable. But I can't guarantee anything, I'm a newbie at this."

"Come on, look at Lily. She didn't train herself, Beth. Listen, I'll pay you good money, give you my firstborn, if that's what it takes," laughed Olivia. "Then again, that's not much incentive, who wants a teenager? Oh, except if the teenager is you, Hattie, you're one of a kind, amazing, really. Mine, is such a…"

51

"…jerk," Hattie thought to herself. She went to school with Olivia's teenage daughter, Tisha. Popular Tisha. Outgoing Tisha. Super pretty Tisha. But a total jerk, even to her mother. Mostly Tisha was a jerk to the unpopular kids at school, including Hattie. She knew the only thing that stood in the way of Tisha and her friends bullying her was Hattie's cousin Beau.

"Seriously, Beth, say yes, please," Olivia pleaded.

"Do it, Mama, you're so good at it."

They needed the money, and what did Mama have to lose?

"Okay, let's try it."

Beth put the training theories into action. Even Hattie picked up Mama's mantra: repetition, reward, repeat. Practice every day.

In two weeks, Posey no longer jumped on her family's legs. In four weeks, Posey no longer pulled on the leash. By the end of training, Posey came when called. Olivia was over the moon, paying Mama for her time.

Word of Mama's dog training skills spread.

The client list grew. Hattie overheard Mama tell Mema, "The money I earn from training dogs is paying the mortgage and puts food on the table. I'll never get rich, but I love the work."

Eventually Mama saved enough money to turn the old red barn, where Daddy stored a 1973 black Camaro he used to tinker with, into a dog-training center and kennel.

Training classes were held every day of the week, including Saturdays. Hattie knew Mama's routine. Before a new training session started, Mama spent time getting to know each dog, watching their movements, level of eye contact, their playfulness, their level of aggressiveness. "It's as if you read their souls," Hattie told Mama as she watched her adapt her training techniques to fit the dogs' personalities.

Mama worked night and day. Living in jeans, T-shirts, and work boots. Her red hair always pulled back in a long braid. She wore a baseball cap to keep the sun off her fair, lightly freckled skin. It was the same routine every day, except on Sundays. Sundays were the Sabbath, a day of worship and rest for the Brown family. When Daddy was alive, Mama attended church in feminine floral dresses, ankle strap sandals with three-inch heels, her red hair flowing down her back. She held hands with Daddy, who wore a suit. Mama on one side of Monroe, Hattie on the other side.

These days Mama's pretty auburn hair no longer flowed down her back. She'd cut it to her shoulders. It was either in a ponytail or tucked behind a headband. Getting "dressed up" for church these days meant Mama wore khakis and a white button-down oxford blouse. As for makeup, "No time," she claimed. It was obvious to Hattie: Mama's pretty days died with Daddy.

Chapter 8:
All Business

2 0 0 7

"I'm going to need you to start helping me more with the dogs, mostly cleaning kennels," Mama told Hattie one night as they sat down for supper. Swanson's chicken pot pie. Mama considered it a home-cooked meal—at least as much of one as Hattie was going to get from Mama.

"I was planning on—" said Hattie, interrupted by the home phone ringing. Likely another person wanting to hire Mama as their personal dog trainer. Mama stood tall, strong—all the walking, cleaning, and grooming dogs had changed her thin, frail stature.

"I can't get Tank in until October, does that work? Okay fine. We'll see you then." Mama hung up the phone, returning to the kitchen table.

"You have lots of customers, Mama. Phone never stops ringing," noted Hattie when Beth sat back down.

"Business is good, great, even. But I'm only one person. I can't keep up. As I started to say, I'm gonna need your help. Part time only, of course, during the school year, full time in the summer."

Hattie looked at the dirt under Mama's nails, the grime on her jeans, the sweat stains under her armpits. She didn't want that.

"The dogs are more your thing, Mama. You best hire someone else," Hattie suggested. "I'm applying at McDonald's this summer, some kids I know work there, and I hope to take some class—" Mama interrupted.

"I can't afford to pay anyone else besides you; they'll expect a living wage. I'm counting on you, Hattie."

Hattie swallowed the words that had been hanging on the tip of her tongue, waiting to be shared at the opportune moment. She planned on asking Mama if she could take an AP college-level class at the community college this summer. Her high school counselor suggested it'd be a great way of beefing up her transcript for college applications. Now it was out of the question.

Hattie begrudgingly agreed to help Mama, before school feeding dogs, after school cleaning out the kennels, and both tasks on weekends. Eventually, Hattie did the cleaning, feeding, and walking dogs; Mama focused on the training. It was physical work. School was like a coffee break.

One morning before school, Mr. Barnard, the high school math teacher, wearing a wool cardigan with brown patches on the elbows similar to the ones Fred Rogers was known for, pulled Hattie aside.

"Your SAT scores are back."

Hattie couldn't breathe.

"I've discussed the results with the school counselor. Based on your scores, we've got a list of colleges we think are a good match."

He smiled, handing Hattie a sheet of paper with a list of schools. University of Alabama, Vanderbilt, Tulane, Stanford, Harvard, and University of Washington.

"Your scores are outstanding, as are your grades. The only area of weakness is a lack of extracurricular activities, and that is explainable. You work in a family business. We encourage you to apply to all of these schools. Some are reach schools. We'll help you in any way we can."

Hattie took a long look at the list. Harvard was on the list, her dream school. She twirled around like a ballerina, bursting with happiness.

* * *

Hattie heard his Jeep around 7:45 a.m. Beau helped out at the kennel on Sundays. He'd recently added a performance muffler to make it extra loud, just for kicks. It drove Hattie crazy. Beau was a total gearhead. She owed him though. He always had her back.

"You best get that muffler fixed," teased Hattie, as she watched her six-foot-three cousin jump out of the Jeep in jeans and a Fairhope Pirates football T-shirt. He wore beat-up work boots and a baseball cap pulled low, covering a good portion of his thick blondish-brown hair and the top half of his green eyes. Beau's good looks, easygoing way, and celebrity-like status as Fairhope's record-setting quarterback had girls fawning all over him.

"Beau definitely got the looks in that family," a Fairhope cheerleader once commented to her cheer team, not realizing Hattie was sitting in the row directly behind her. Hattie's eyes had burned with tears. She blinked them back, telling herself she'd rather have brains than beauty any day.

"It's so frickin' loud, you freak out the dogs," Hattie scolded. "Doesn't help you floor the gas."

She noticed the stubble on his chin and bloodshot eyes. He looked tired, dark circles under his eyes.

"Late night?"

"Something like that."

"Too many cheerleaders wanting to party with the quarter-back?"

"I wish. Nothing like that. Got a lot on my mind."

"Heavy-duty stuff, like which girl to ask to the prom?"

"No, serious stuff."

"Like what?" asked Hattie, skeptical he'd ever had a serious thought in his life.

"Like do I accept the scholarship to play football at Alabama, or do I serve my country?"

"Gosh, that is huge," said Hattie, feeling bad she'd poked fun at him.

"Damn straight. But you got your own tough decisions to make."

"Hey, let's take a break from it all this morning. I've already fed the dogs, come to church with us, it'll do you some good."

"Can't."

"Why?"

"More like *could*, but won't."

"Why?"

"Hattie, it's like this. From where I stand, Pastor Griffin and his entire family are the most judgmental people I've had the misfortune of meeting 'round here. The only thing I've learned from going to church is Griffin's a bigger hypocrite than a Washington politician. And that's not easy. I'm better off listening to Herb, the manager of the local Gas & Go, talk to me about tires."

"Well, then, you'll be pleased to know Pastor Griffin is no longer at First Methodist."

"Someone finally get pissed off and run him out of town?"

"Not exactly. But there were big changes last week. Turns out Pastor Griffin wasn't good at taking the bishop's advice to put out the welcome mat to all folks, not just the ones Griffin liked. Griffin parted ways with First Methodist, new preacher starts today. Come meet the new guy."

"No thanks, I'm good. Let me know if the new preacher looks like he can play a decent game of ball; Ronnie broke his ankle and we're short a ball player for the summer rec league. In the meantime, I'll be listening to good ole Herb."

She pinched his arm good.

"Okay, then, we'll be heading out. Stick around for lunch."

"Only if Mema's doing the cooking. Yours or Aunt Bethie's I can do without."

Hattie laughed and stuck out her tongue.

Chapter 9:
Old Church, New Song

Mema, Mama and Hattie arrived early, just as the bishop was asking the church secretary to make sure the church bells rang in a celebratory rythm. "We're welcoming this new chapter in the church's history. Make the bells ring!"

Bishop Wendell had a formidable presence. Hattie heard he was a former professional football player for the Minnesota Vikings, and looked it, at six feet two with broad shoulders. Today he wore the traditional clerical robe and purple stole, indicating his bishop status. Standing next to him was the new pastor, a younger man with jet-black hair and deep brown eyes. He had the build of a soccer player, lean and agile.

Hattie figured the new pastor was in his early thirties and by far the cutest guy she'd ever seen. He might increase church membership based on his looks, she thought. The only imperfection she could see was a cowlick at the back of his head. She watched as he subconsciously brushed his hand over it, though it bounced back up, refusing to lie flat. When the new pastor turned his head, she noticed his dark black hair was in a ponytail. Wow, that's a change. He wore a slightly wrinkled pair of brown pants and a navy blue blazer over a white button-down dress shirt with his cleric's collar. Unlike the leather loafers the bishop wore, the new pastor sported a weathered pair of black Nikes.

When the church bells stopped chiming, the bishop stepped to the pulpit, nodding hellos to the sparse congregation.

"Welcome all of you. I commend each of you for being here today. You are part of a church with a history of being a leader among the Methodist churches in the South," began the bishop. "I credit the Lord for its success, and all who have dedicated your lives to service here. Thank you. And of course, I'd be remiss if I failed to also credit God's geography. We stand here, blessed, our church high on the bluff, overlooking the water, with a tiered steeple that can be seen from land and sea, as if announcing this is a safe place for all.

"I'm told fishermen and fisherwomen have nicknamed First Methodist their spiritual lighthouse. Thanks to the church custodian, who leaves a few lights on when she leaves, a sign we are open any time. Some stop in to pray before they head out to net their catch, others come here after a rough trip at sea. Let me make it clear: anyone who seeks a quiet place for prayer and meditation is welcome here.

"I asked Pastor Griffin to open the church doors wider, to welcome all different kinds of people after hearing some folks weren't feeling welcomed. He resisted the change. I did a lot of praying for Pastor Griffin, suggesting that he should follow Jesus's own example of caring for the tired, broken, ridiculed, divorced, the sinners.

Society's outcasts. Jesus invited them to his table. Some of those very outcasts becoming his disciples. In practice, Pastor Griffin was uncomfortable with this.

"Since 1862 we've served as a safe haven during storms, literally and figuratively. Storms don't pick and choose where they go, or who is affected. When it comes to helping those in need, we cannot pick and choose either. These church doors will be open for all who knock. Our job is to let them know they are never alone in their storm.

"Pastor Griffin and I ultimately agreed to disagree; he handed in his resignation and I accepted it. This issue has left this church divided. We need a healer, a positive force to bring us together again. I am pleased to introduce Pastor Luis Gonzales."

Bishop Wendell began reciting Pastor Luis's credentials: undergraduate degree in philosophy from Trinity College in San Antonio, graduating summa cum laude. Captain of the soccer team. Student body president. A master's degree in theology from Harvard's divinity school. Numerous mission trips to Honduras, Guatemala, and El Salvador; associate pastor at Central Station Methodist, Boston, Massachusetts, where he turned a fledgling congregation into a dynamic, growing church. "A feat considering this is a part of the country where church membership has dramatically declined," noted the bishop.

The bishop covered boards and committees Pastor Luis served on. Hattie noticed the new pastor was sweating profusely, his leg nervously bouncing up and down. She watched him observing the same five people nodding off, one of whom was snoring loudly. Hattie continued to watch Pastor Luis look around at the handful of other adults who were wiggling like third graders waiting for recess. Hattie felt sorry for him. She'd seen in the bulletin he was to talk this morning about the newly approved strategic plans. How boring was that? That likely put even more people to sleep.

When the bishop finally passed the baton over to Pastor Luis, Hattie saw the new pastor rise, rub his palms on his pants. He had no notes and she hoped that meant he'd be brief.

"Thank you, Bishop Wendell, for your introduction." Pastor Luis nodded respectfully at his pastoral leader. "I promised the bishop I'd speak on the strategic plans approved at the Southern Conference of Methodists, and I will soon—not today, though."

Hattie saw the bishop raise an eyebrow and brush his hand over his thinning hair. He didn't look happy. Still, the new pastor continued. "Bishop Wendell did an excellent job of sharing with you what I refer to as 'resume stuff.' For a moment, I wasn't even sure he was talking about me. What do I know? I'm the new guy, right?" A handful of people laughed, nervously.

"I believe to get off on the right foot, I'll share with you the more personal side. Everyone's got a history, and a story that's part of them," continued Pastor Luis. "And sometimes if you know their story—or at least some of it—it's easier to understand them. So, this is mine."

Hattie noticed a few seemed to have perked up.

"You might wonder how a Texas kid ends up in Boston and now, Alabama. It's a love story, of sorts. My mother is Irish Catholic. She grew up in Boston. My father's family are field pickers in the great state of Texas. They found each other at a bar on Padre Island. It was her one, and I might add only, spring break in college. Nine months later my oldest brother came along."

The congregation was so quiet you could hear a sneaker stick to the glossy hardwood floor.

"I'm part Latino, part Irish. Which may leave you wondering if your new pastor is a bad-tempered man who enjoys siestas."

Mema hooted with laughter, along with several others, enjoying the new pastor's self-deprecating sense of humor.

"I'm the middle child of eight kids. My hometown is San Antonio, Texas. I was raised Catholic. Like all good Catholic mothers, mine encouraged me to become a priest. I had such great interest in theology that she thought I was a shoo-in. Trouble was I wanted what my parents had, a loving family. I'm a romantic kind of guy. I hope to marry and have a family someday. I believe marriage, love, and preaching can go hand in hand. I figured my chances of changing the Pope's mind were close to zero. Over time, in my graduate studies, I found myself solidly aligned with the beliefs of the Methodist Church," he said, nodding in deference to the bishop.

"I'm a hand-me-down kind of guy." He looked down at his feet, pointing to his tattered Nike tennis shoes. "And these are my younger brother's shoes. I borrowed them last Thanksgiving and darn it, I've yet to give them back." He shook his head. "Even pastors make mistakes."

More people laughed. Hattie knew people were warming up to him.

"I was blessed with a scholarship, giving me the opportunity to attend Harvard Divinity School. I lived rent free. My mother's side of the family boasts a Flannery cousin on every street corner in Southie, where I could sleep on their couches. I'm deeply grateful, and fairly certain I will someday find myself with back problems."

Hattie was glued to Pastor Luis's every word. He'd gone to Harvard! She couldn't wait to meet him. Harvard was her top choice for college, a reach school. She had a million questions she wanted to ask him.

"Until we find an organist and a pianist, it's me on the guitar. Anyone musically inclined, please help me out. The five campfire songs I've mastered on the guitar are going to get old pretty quick." He took a few deep breaths and wiped the sweat off his brow.

"I love dogs, any kind. I cry at the drop of a hat. My dad's the same way; go figure that my mother is tough as nails. My favorite movie is *Father of the Bride*. I dream of someday having a little girl who I get to walk down the aisle when she grows up. I'm an uncle to nine nieces and nephews who think I'm a pretty fun guy, mostly because I make really good chocolate chip pancakes, heavy on the chocolate.

"I'm not the tidiest person. I'm always behind on my cleaning and yard work. I seldom iron my clothes, which disappoints my mother. Trust me, when she visits here soon, these pants will be pressed."

He smiled, a real smile. His teeth slightly crooked, far from a mouth perfected by an expensive orthodontist. "I knew I liked this town when I drove down Main Street for the first time and I saw two craft breweries on the same street. I'm a fan of craft beer, so don't be shocked when you hear your pastor is drinking at the local brewery. I'm a double-IPA kinda guy. Every once in a great while I step outside my comfort zone and try a sour. I stick to one beer, savoring the rich taste. And frankly, one beer is all my budget can afford." A few more people laughed. The bishop was smiling.

"While enjoying a beer, I usually find one or two people who need help from a church like ours, a denomination called to serve. I find people are more relaxed with me when we're sitting at a pub, sharing a story or two. If you see me sitting at a table by myself, please join me." He looked out at the congregation and paused, then smiled. "For those of you who don't like beer, I won't hold it against you," he teased.

This time it was Beth who laughed loudly. She loved a good beer and so had Hattie's daddy.

"I'll gladly order you a cola or a sweet tea. I'm here to serve." He raised his hand toward the sky. "Seriously, call me any time… except when the Dallas Cowboys are playing." Pastor Luis grinned. "My apologies to the bishop. I know it's not his team."

This time the bishop broke out into a belly laugh.

"In all seriousness, First Methodist is a place for renewal of your spirit so you can go out in the world and be the person God intended. We all need help facing life's challenges. That's what church is all about. No one should face storms alone. I'll try to keep my sermons brief but meaningful, the music inspirational, and the doors open for all. That includes the broken, addicts, divorced people, same-sex couples, people with special needs. You can dress up for our services, you can dress casual. Come naked for all I care."

Hattie got the giggles, shaking silently, attempting to stifle her laughter.

"Let's all do our best to leave judgment of others at the door. Life can be difficult outside these godly walls, let's not make it harder. My hope is that when you leave the service, you take away something that helps you, and in turn, you're able to help someone else. If I achieve that, I shall make God, and my parents, proud. Thanks to our Father, for it is he who has brought me here. I look forward to our journey together."

The bishop and Pastor Luis stood at the front doors to greet people as they left. Mema, Mama, and Hattie were the last to leave.

"Pastor Luis, this here is my granddaughter, Hattie. She's been accepted at Harvard. Smart as Einstein."

"Mema, stop!" declared Hattie, blushing.

"And this here is my daughter, Beth, best dog trainer in the entire state of Alabama. Runs a fine kennel as well, with my grandchildren's help."

"Hattie, a pleasure, and congratulations on your acceptance to Harvard," Pastor Luis said, reaching out to shake Hattie's hand. "I am happy to answer any questions you have about Harvard. I loved my time there. And Beth, you will be the first person I call when I am blessed with a dog of my own. And you, ma'am, I did not catch your name, but I'm certain we shall be good friends. I can tell."

"Call me Mema, that's what my friends and family call me. I'm in charge of the church's garden club and keeping track of my family."

"Looks like a job well done, on both counts. Mema, it is a pleasure."

When the three women got in the car, mama spoke up first, "I like him. What y'all think?"

"You like him because he likes dogs and beer," Hattie pointed out.

"You got that right," laughed Mama.

"I like him, too," Mema commented. "I think he's got a good head on his shoulders. Maybe he can get Beau to start coming to church."

"It's a sign, maybe my dream will come true. He, Pastor Luis… the one for me," Hattie said dreamily.

"What?" Mama and Mema simultaneously screeched so loudly they stopped Hattie in her tracks.

"Hattie Brown, that is inappropriate," mama said. "He's at least ten years your senior."

Hattie laughed and shook her head. "Before you interrupted me, I was going to say, he, Pastor Luis, went to Harvard and loved it. I think it's a sign, a God wink. I think Harvard's the school for me!"

"Oh, good gravy, we thought you were crushing on the new preacher," Mema scoffed.

Hattie rolled her eyes. "No, that's more like you two. I'm thrilled I met someone who went to Harvard. He offered to tell me about his experience there, answer my questions!"

"I'll invite him to supper," said Mema. "The sooner the better."

A week later, Pastor Luis was joining the Brown family for Mema's famous brisket, deep-fried okra, and garlic roasted potatoes. Mema gussied herself up in a colorful floral dress with her pearls. She spritzed herself with perfume and dotted her lips with rose-red lipstick. Hattie showered after working in the kennel and threw on a pair of clean jeans and a clean tee. Mama, busy with the dogs all afternoon, washed her hands in the kitchen sink and left it at that.

"Beth, dear, you'll be changing clothes, yes?"

"Why? It's Wednesday-night supper, not a holiday."

"Company is coming, the new preacher. Surely, you realize you've been working with dogs all day."

"I believe the preacher said to leave judgment at the door. So, quit judging me. My workday isn't over. The kennel is full and I've got dogs to train later," Beth snapped.

Hattie cringed. She hated when Mama and Mema argued.

Pastor Luis arrived five minutes early, wearing jeans, a short-sleeved plain white button-down shirt, and Chuck Taylor sneakers that looked more worn than the Nikes he preached in. Jeez, thought Hattie, if the worn Nikes are his Sunday best, then he must have even less money than we do.

"Pastor, can I offer you iced tea?" asked Mema.

"Or, how about a beer? I've got IPA's in the cooler," Beth offered.

Luis looked from one Brown woman to the other. "I'll start with a beer and have sweet tea with supper."

"Perfect, please come sit down."

The Brown women watched as Pastor Luis made himself comfortable. He updated them on all the people he'd met the past week while devouring Mema's brisket like a stray dog finally getting a meal.

Hattie finally got up the nerve to ask him about Harvard.

Pastor Luis was honest, telling Hattie the good things and the not so good. Nothing he said scared her enough to change her mind.

"And if you end up going to Harvard, there's a great burger joint at Harvard Square, Bartley's. I order the Tom Brady."

"What's the Tom Brady?" asked Hattie.

"A hefty, half-pound beef patty, cooked medium rare, topped with guac and a slice of cheddar. The tough choice is whether to have fries or onion rings."

"My kind of place," said Mema. "Perhaps you can take me there, Pastor, if Hattie goes to Harvard."

"Surely as the sun rises," promised Pastor Luis.

"What would you order for me?" asked Mema.

"For you, let me think," paused Luis. "Are you a cheddar and bacon kind of gal?"

"You bet I am."

"Grilled onions?"

"Of course."

"Aww, then I'd suggest you order the Joe Bartley. Can't go wrong. How about you, Beth? What do you like?"

"No need to share what I like. I have no plans of going anywhere outside of 'bama."

"Oh, Mama," complained Hattie.

"Don't you 'oh, Mama' me."

Hattie flushed in embarrassment.

"Pastor Luis, tell me, what exactly does Harvard have that University of Alabama doesn't, besides uppity people?"

"Hmmm, let me think," Pastor Luis said. "Snow and cold for one thing. Hattie will definitely need a warm coat, boots, and a hat and mittens to survive New England winters."

Beth smiled. "Well, at least you're smart enough not to try to BS me."

"And frankly, there's no place in Boston that sells brisket as good as this, not anywhere. This is off the charts. I can't remember a meal this good."

"You should join us for dinner more often," invited Mema.

"Sign me up. Ladies, on that note, I should be heading home and answering my deluge of nightly emails and text messages. Listen, Beth, I promise you, if I didn't think Harvard was a good fit for Hattie, I'd tell her. But it's a more diverse community these days. Students like Hattie, brilliant, motivated to learn, are there on scholarships. Yes, some students, as you say, 'wealthy and all fancy,' go there. But there's students who are from backgrounds like me. I encourage you to pray on it. All of you, it's a big decision."

"Were you intimidated going to Harvard?" Hattie asked.

"A little, at first. Until I realized having six brothers all bigger than me is far tougher than getting a master's degree from Harvard."

All three women laughed.

That night Hattie prayed for Mama to let her attend Harvard. In the middle of the prayer, she stopped. She remembered Luis's sermon on Sunday. "God's will be done, not my will." She then instead asked for God's guidance on schools. Still, she couldn't help hoping it was Harvard, telling the good Lord why it was a good fit. She knew she'd be good either way. Truth was, she couldn't say goodbye to high school fast enough.

A week later Mama gave Hattie her blessing: yes to Harvard. Hattie spontaneously hugged Mama tight, something they rarely did. Hattie was determined to make her family proud and of course, her new pastor, who already in his brief time in Fairhope had changed Hattie's life.

Chapter 10:
The Alpha and Omega

HARVARD, 2008

"Sir, excuse me," Hattie said more boldly than she felt. "Can you drop me off at Apley Court, a residence hall on campus?"

"What is the address?" he said, staring at her in the rearview mirror.

Hattie scrolled through her phone. "16 Holyoke, Cambridge."

The driver nodded, typing it into his phone.

Her head hurt. A dull ache from a lack of sleep left her feeling like she had the flu. Her phone pinged, a text from Mama. *Let me know when you get to campus.*

A left turn, then a right, and the driver swiftly pulled to the side of the street. He pointed to campus. "This is as close as I can get you."

"Yes, of course, thank you."

She paid him in cash, tipping generously, something she learned from her dad. "Wait, miss. I help you with your luggage."

"Thanks, but I can get it."

"I insist, please. Someday if my child goes away to school, I hope someone helps her."

Hattie smiled. The driver looked way too young to have children.

Apley Hall was located in the historic part of campus, one of several stately old brick buildings with ivy ambitiously climbing red brick walls. She was relieved to see other students getting out of taxis. She guessed they were international students. They looked worldly, sophisticated, and well dressed. She felt like a hick.

Her phone pinged, another text. This time from Beau. *Eat some lobstah!*

Yep, they were all hicks from Alabama.

Two upperclassmen carrying clipboards, wearing crimson-colored polo shirts with an embroidered Harvard logo, checked Hattie in, giving her instructions and a key. "Your room is on the second floor. No elevator. Kicking it old school."

"Can we help carry your luggage to your room?" offered the young man with red hair and a smattering of freckles matching Hattie's own.

"I can manage, thanks. Y'all just point me in the right direction."

"You must be from the South," the other young man, tall with an unruly brown beard, said.

"As you can see, we're a bright group, here, at Harvard," the ginger teased. "What part of the South are you from?"

"Fairhope, Alabama."

"My dad and I golfed at the Grand Resort in Fairhope, a few years back. Loved it. Great place to stay."

"It is," smiled Hattie, knowing it was a small white lie since she'd actually never been there.

"Are you positive you don't need any help?" the young man asked again.

"I'm fine. Really."

Hattie climbed two flights of stairs to room 206. The hallway was filled with a flurry of activity. Students moving in, parents helping. Mothers teary eyed. Fathers carrying boxes. Hattie greeted each one warmly, desperately trying to not sound so Southern. She was sweating something fierce, noticing it was as hot and humid here as back home. Surely, this building has air-conditioning. It didn't feel like it, though.

Once inside her dorm room, she tossed her belongings on one of two empty dormitory twin-sized beds. The room was all hers, no roommate yet. Hattie breathed a sigh of relief and flopped on the bed. It felt so good to stretch. The room was stuffy and warm, and smelled like mothballs, reminding her of Mema's attic. She had no energy to get up and open the window. She stretched, closed her eyes, promising it'd be for just two minutes. She couldn't recall ever being so exhausted, even after the long days at the kennel.

As she began nodding off, the door flew open. "My room-mate!" Hattie thought, bolting straight up.

A small group of people were staring at her, holding a set of matching luggage, including a duffel bag the size of a human body, a large trunk, a suitcase, and a rolled-up rug. The upperclassmen who greeted Hattie outside were now standing, arms full, with her roommate's family, staring at her.

"Greetings," the man who must be her roommate's father said, stumbling through the door with the rug flung over his shoulders. "You must be Hattie Brown."

He had soft gray hair, nicely trimmed, and spoke with a British accent. He was breathing heavily after climbing two flights of stairs. He reached out to shake Hattie's hand.

"I'm Charles Reade; this is my wife, Claire, and our granddaughter, Eleanor, the one you'll be rooming with. We're her token butlers," Charles teased, wiping his sweaty brow with an embroidered handkerchief he pulled from his pant pocket.

"It's a pleasure," Hattie said, noticing how relaxed and at ease they seemed at one of the top schools in the country. The grandfather wore pressed chinos, a plaid button-down shirt, and loafers without socks. The grandmother was dressed in a white golf shirt and a madras skirt that looked like a hand-patched quilt. She was elegant, carried herself like royalty with her shoulders back and graceful manners. Her outfit was a beautiful contrast to her light golden tan. Hattie's new roommate was wearing a pink-and-green sleeveless dress with coordinating green flip-flops. Hattie suddenly felt self-conscious in cargo pants and the "Go Navy" T-shirt she changed into. It was Hattie's third change of clothes in a day, way out of character, but she kept trying to fit in with the students she saw on campus. Now observing her roommate, maybe another change of wardrobe was required. But Hattie didn't own anything close to a dress like that. Hattie wondered why her roommate's grandparents were moving their granddaughter in. Secretly, she was glad she wasn't the only freshman whose parents weren't there to help.

"Ladies, the first orientation meeting begins at four this afternoon," Claire said, frantically tapping at her Apple watch, the orange band matching her orange suede loafers with gold buckles. "It's already three. Ellie, dear, put this mattress pad on over the stained mattress. Lord knows what bacterial fungus is growing on it."

"Pathetic, isn't it, Gammy? Good thing we bought the bigger mattress topper, too."

"Are your parents here?" Charles inquired.

"No sir, I took the Greyhound bus from Alabama."

"A great way to see the country, I hear," Charles remarked.

"More, like, way inconvenient," Ellie quipped. "Don't you have airports where you're from?"

"Of course we do," Hattie laughed nervously, clearing her throat, "Uh…my mother is terrified of letting me fly. I'm her only child. She panics when I leave home. Frankly, she worries when I do anything—ever since Daddy passed."

Hattie knew she was rambling, but her roommate's condescending comment hurt her feelings.

"My Mama had a really difficult time after Daddy passed. She's gotten a lot better thanks to Lily, our dog."

The room grew uncomfortably quiet, all eyes resting on Hattie.

"I best finish unpacking," Hattie said as she pulled her favorite jeans out of her suitcase and put them on a shelf in the closet with several T-shirts. It was all so awkward. She hung up two button-down blouses, one blue, one white. Bless Mema and all the clothes she'd ironed and folded. Hattie was almost to the bottom of her suitcase when she discovered a surprise. Tucked beneath towels was an expensive-looking pair of gray wool trousers, a beautiful gray cardigan, and an elegant white silk blouse. *"Every young woman needs a classy outfit. You'll be the classiest young lady at Harvard."*

It was so sweet Hattie wanted to cry. She missed her family. Going away to college sure changes things.

Hattie continued unpacking, placing her Muck boots—the ones she'd worn for the past three years cleaning kennels—in the back of the closet. The boots were indestructible. She was certain they'd get her through a New England winter.

She organized the small dorm closet, following Mema's rule of "everything has a place and a place for everything." Unlike most college students, Hattie had plenty of storage room left over.

She organized her desk, finding places for her laptop, books, folders, and notebooks. She loved the small wicker basket from the Fairhope farmers market. It was perfect for her pencils, paper clips, and tissues. Everything was neat as a pin. She sat down at her newly organized desk and opened her laptop, double-checking details for freshman orientation. Out of the corner of her eye, she watched the take-charge grandmother and granddaughter disagree on where to put the mountain of clothes, towels, and toiletries, noticing her new roommate had enough skin and hair products to fill an entire closet.

"Y'all, uh, excuse me," said Hattie. "I've got extra storage in my closet, please feel free to make use of it."

"No, thank you. I don't share my things," Ellie piped up.

"Eleanor, you're being rude," scolded Claire. "Hattie was kindly offering you additional storage space."

"Fine," scoffed Hattie's new roommate.

"Hattie, please don't mind Ellie, she's mad at me, so she's sharp with her tongue."

"Yes, ma'am," Hattie said softly. She'd heard New Englanders were more abrupt. Guess it was true.

"I really won't use any of your things. I have more than what I need."

"Thank you," Ellie said, turning her back on Hattie.

"Gammy, we need to figure out where I can put the microwave and my small refrigerator. I can't imagine living without a real kitchen to cook in. This is all so lame."

Charles sat quietly at his granddaughter's small dorm desk. Hattie could tell he was watching her as she unpacked photos.

"Is that a photo of your family?" Charles asked Hattie.

"I guess you could say that," Hattie laughed softly, a long strand of brown hair flopping forward, landing on her freckled cheek. She pulled it back, wrapping it around her tiny ear with a pearl earring.

"Mind if I take a look?"

"No, yes, please," she said, handing him the picture frame. "Mama's pride and joy."

Hattie figured Charles expected to see a photo of Hattie's family, mostly people. The photo Charles was looking at was of Mama surrounded by a litter of Labrador pups, three black, four yellow, falling all over her, one biting at her hair, which was pulled loosely in a side braid. Hattie loved how the photographer had captured a look of sheer joy on Mama's face.

"Your mother, I assume?"

"Yes, sir."

"Your family must be fond of Labradors?" Charles inquired.

"Reckon you called that right," Hattie said. "Dogs are pretty much the reason for Mama's existence. The bane of mine, at least sometimes. The photograph is of our finest, Whistling Dixie's litter. Dixie came from one of Lily's smallest, and likely the best litters we've had. All gentle souls, easily trainable, every one of 'em. Mama says she would have won the Westminster Dog Show with any of the pups from that litter."

"May I ask what it is your mother does?" Charles inquired.

"She owns a kennel and trains dogs—never met a dog she couldn't love or train," Hattie explained. "She's a natural. Beau and I help her, of course, but Mama's the star."

"Beau is a brother, yes?"

"Might as well be. Beau's my cousin. We're the same age."

"It's nice to be from a close-knit family," Charles told her. He kept staring at the photo. "Your mother's dogs have particularly strong jawlines and big paws. Some of the best-looking retrievers I've ever seen in the States. Is your mother from a long line of breeders and handlers?" Charles asked.

"Oh no. Mama's the first. Mema, my grandmother, heads up the garden committee at church, which she believes is perhaps the most important job at First Methodist, right up there with the pastor's."

Charles laughed.

"The dogs, they're all Mama's, well, maybe a little mine, a gift from my daddy. Mema likes to say it was the 'angels come a knocking'…all part of God's plan. Mama says it was Daddy's backup plan."

"Backup plan?"

"After Daddy discovered he was sick and wasn't getting any better, he gave us a puppy to watch over us after he passed away.

Lily is from the finest lineage on God's green earth, all starting with Kindness, according to Doc Grady," Hattie explained with pride.

"Kindness?" Charles asked. "A most interesting name."

"Kindness was Dr. Grady's first retriever. Name was perfect. Story is that's what she gave to Doc's patients. Kindness became a Fairhope hero. Doc still has an office dog to be by the side of his patients needing, well, some kindness." Hattie laughed. "He breeds a litter once in a blue moon. It's a lot of work if you're doing it right. Doc keeps a list of special folks, ones having a tough time in life like Mama and me, or some for service dogs, some for family pets. Daddy's dying wish was Doc give us one of his dogs. Mama named her Lily. Lily helped Mama discover her gift to train dogs."

"I'm sorry about your father," said Charles, lowering his voice. "Ellie experienced something similar when she was very young." Charles paused, looking around to see if Claire and Ellie were within earshot, his voice a mere whisper. "She'll tell you in her own time, but until then, may I ask for your discretion?"

"Yes, sir, of course."

"Ellie lost her parents in an accident. She was only seven years old. We've been her guardians since the accident."

"I'm sorry."

"Me too. Here's my business card. Call us if you need anything. And please, watch over Ellie. She acts tough, but her heart is tender. Be patient. Ellie won't let you in right away, it'll take time with her."

Hattie's phone pinged. A text from Pastor Luis. *Praying for you. First few days of college may feel overwhelming. You might even get homesick. Perfectly normal. Trust in Him. All will be well. Look up Philippians 4:13 tonight.*

"Charles, shall we get these two to their first official Harvard freshmen event?" suggested Claire.

"Yes, indeed."

Claire put her long, tanned arms around Ellie's and Hattie's shoulders.

"We'll say so long here, ladies. Call us if you need anything, anytime, that includes you, Hattie. We're minutes away and will be extremely cross if you don't call or visit, particularly if you need help. Don't be strangers, you two."

"I know, I know," Ellie said as she hugged her grandparents. Charles and Claire also hugged Hattie goodbye. Maybe, thought Hattie, Pastor Luis was right, all will be well.

Chapter 11:
Harvard, a Fast
Learning Curve

2008

Hattie had a comfortable routine. After dinner, she'd head to the library. Second floor. Her usual spot, by the history books. For some reason, being surrounded by history books made her believe anything was possible. She was hunched over studying, in an oversized gold "Go Navy" sweatshirt Beau sent her. She was lonely. She'd watched her roommate Ellie get ready to meet friends at a pub. Hattie wasn't sure if or when Ellie studies. But in the style department, Hattie admired Ellie. Earlier tonight she watched as Ellie changed into jeans with a white blouse and a retro black leather jacket. She looked cool with a confidence Hattie wished she had.

Hattie rested her head on the walnut desk. Her eyes were tired, bloodshot from the endless reading professors assigned. At this point, it was useless to study more. She was exhausted. She slid her homework into her backpack, and when she exited the library, she turned her phone on. She always looked forward to getting messages. Beau's texts made her laugh or crazy mad. Mama, of course, sent photos of dogs. Pastor Luis sent thoughtful messages. Mema never texted, but called once a week. Hattie was painfully aware her social life at the moment was even more pathetic than in high school. Her phone pinged, a message from Beau.

I don't think you have to be all to smart to serve in the military. Some of these peeps are idiots.

Hattie texted back: *It's not 'to' it's 'too.'*

Beau: *Always showing me up.*

Hattie: *Once a grammar queen, always a grammar queen.*

Beau: *Basic training is tough.*

Hattie: *Harvard's not exactly a piece of cake.*

Beau: *Miss u, cuz, lights out.*

Hattie*: Miss you too. Notice the correct spelling?*

When she unlocked her dorm room, it was pitch black. Ellie still wasn't home, out with her seemingly infinite number of friends. Hattie hadn't made a real friend yet. She tried, helping fellow students with their homework; greeting people on the campus sidewalks, even those who made no eye contact. And did they respond in kind? No, welcome to the East Coast.

Admittedly, while her social life was nonexistent, her classes made up for it. Her education at Harvard was exceptional. She loved every minute, well, almost. At the beginning of the semester, a few of the students snickered when they heard her Southern drawl. She guessed they thought she was a hick, and she became hesitant to answer questions in class. She knew it would cost her—participation was part of her grade.

God, help me, she prayed. I'm so, so self-conscious. Her phone pinged. A text from Pastor Luis.

She is clothed in strength and dignity, and she laughs without fear of the future. When she speaks her words are wise and she gives instructions with kindness. Proverbs 31:25–26. Chin up, kiddo. Be bold. Be Brave. Blessings, Luis.

Sometimes, it was as if Pastor Luis read her mind.

From then on, Hattie challenged herself to speak up in class and answer even the most challenging of professors' questions. Her voice shook in nervousness. She discovered generally her answers were spot on. Her confidence grew. The questions she raised during lectures created insightful class discussion. She no longer heard the snickering when she spoke. Academically, she was more than holding her own. Still, she ate in the dining hall alone, walked to class by herself, and had yet to have a real conversation with her roommate. It was already the first of November. They hadn't moved beyond the "how's it going" small talk.

Maybe, it was because they were complete opposites. Hattie hopped out of bed the minute her alarm rang, getting ready for her 8:00 a.m. class. Ellie, on the other hand, set her alarm for 10:00 a.m. Then it was a good couple times of slamming the snooze button before she crawled out of bed for an 11:00 a.m. class. Somehow, though, Ellie managed to get up immediately when her alarm went off at 6:30 a.m. for her twice-a-week yoga class.

Hattie wore T-shirts, jeans, and hoodies. Ellie always looked like a model, especially when she went out at night. She must have a million guys after her, thought Hattie, with her long blond hair, daring sense of style, and those long legs usually paired with stiletto heels. Ellie was definitely the queen of an informal Harvard social club. Hattie noticed she always came back to their dorm room at night, leaving a trail of going-out clothes and heels scattered on the dorm room floor. At least one of them was having a grand time at college.

In early November, when Hattie returned to her dorm room, she got on the computer to check the airfare to Fairhope over Thanksgiving. Mema offered to pay for her flight. Hattie scanned the internet. Airfares were ridiculously high. It made more sense to spend Thanksgiving break at school. She'd use the time wisely, get schoolwork done, start studying for finals. Mema could fly her home for Christmas. If they booked now, the cost wouldn't be terrible. It'd make a wonderful Christmas gift. And since Mama wasn't paying for the trip, she wouldn't have a say in the mode of transportation Hattie chose.

Exhausted, Hattie shut her laptop and climbed into bed. She'd email Mema the news in the morning. Her eyes ached. She thanked the good Lord she could sleep late the next day. Despite how tired she was, sleep avoided her like an ex-boyfriend. She kept worrying about, of all things, her roommate. Strange, they weren't close, heck, it was an exaggeration to even call them casual friends. Why did she feel so unsettled?

At 5:30 a.m. Hattie got up to go the bathroom. She still hadn't really slept, at least not the good kind. Ellie's bed was empty. Should she call Ellie's grandparents? Stop, she thought. Maybe her roommate met the man of her dreams last night. Maybe Ellie had partied too much and stayed with friends, or maybe she'd actually gone to stay at her grandparents.

Hattie climbed back into bed and finally fell into a deep sleep, only waking when she heard Ellie unlocking the door.

Hattie opened one eye, and she looked at the clock. Ten in the morning. She glanced at Ellie, who looked like the loser of an

MMA fight. A deep purple bruise on her neck. Mascara was running down her cheeks, her hair matted. The chambray blouse Ellie had worn the previous night was torn on the side, as if someone tried to rip it off her. What the heck had happened?

Hattie lay still, her mind wrestling. She should ask Ellie if she was okay. But Ellie was an "it's none of your business" type person. Hattie remained silent. She secretly glanced at Ellie, who was staring blankly in the mirror, frantically twisting the strands of her long, silky blond hair. Then Ellie's legs buckled, crashing to the floor, looking like an overserved bar patron.

"Ellie, are you okay?" Hattie whipped off her blankets, jumping out of bed to help.

"I'm fine. A wicked migraine, I think."

"Let me get you a glass of water."

"Water'd be great, thank you," whispered Ellie, remaining on the floor.

Hattie raced to the compact refrigerator on the other side of the room, grabbing a bottle of Fiji water from Ellie's unending supply.

"Here you go," said Hattie, handing the cold water to Ellie, who was now curled up on the patterned rug covering the tiled floor. "Is there anyone I should call? Your grandparents, maybe?"

"No, absolutely not," Ellie snapped back to life. "I'm fine. The water helps. I've got to get up to shower."

Hattie extended her hand. Ellie was shaking like a leaf in the wind.

"I know this is absolutely none of my business," Hattie acknowledged. "But did something bad happen to you last night? If so, we should report it. We can go to the police, together."

"I just came from there and the hospital. And you're right. It's none of your business," Ellie snapped as she grabbed her towel and headed to the shower.

Hattie paced nervously, no idea what to do, how to help. Pastor Luis's words came to her. *God is always there. Ask him for guidance.* She did a quick, desperate plea to God for wisdom.

When Ellie returned to the dorm room, she was quiet. She blow-dried her hair, put moisturizer on her face, wiped away the remains of yesterday's mascara. She threw on a Harvard sweatshirt with jeans and white tennis shoes.

Hattie sat at her desk, trying to study. She couldn't concentrate. It was obvious Ellie didn't want her help. Hattie decided to head to the library. The room felt stifling. She tried to get up, but her feet felt stuck like they were in cement.

As Ellie was putting clothes in a laundry bag, her cell phone rang. She answered. "Hi Poppy. Yes, I'm fine. Busy. Classes and stuff. Sorry I haven't called. I don't know. I, well, we don't really hang out together, different friends. I suppose I can ask."

Ellie was looking over at her.

"No, I hadn't planned to," continued Ellie. "Fine. I'll think about it. I'll let you know."

Ellie hung up, and instantly her phone pinged. Hattie glanced over at Ellie, who was staring at her phone, her cheeks turning from a sickly white to a deep red. Dropping her phone, Ellie reached for the garbage can and vomited.

Hattie grabbed a bath towel, handing it to Ellie. She raced to the shared bathroom to dampen hand towels. When she returned, Ellie was sitting in her desk chair, head between her knees.

Hattie handed Ellie one of the dampened towels. "Here, put this on your forehead, it will cool you off."

Ellie tilted her head back, placing the dampened towel over her face. Hattie couldn't ignore the muffled sobs underneath the towel. She desperately wanted to call Ellie's grandparents. Instead, she grabbed another dampened towel and a hairbrush. "Let me help get this stuff out of your hair," referring to the vomit on the strands of Ellie's hair.

Ellie did not refuse.

Hattie slowly cleaned and brushed Ellie's long blond hair, eventually tying it gently into a loose ponytail away from her face, in case Ellie got sick again.

After years of cleaning up after dogs, Hattie was immune to smells and things that bothered most people. She reached into her storage bin of towels and supplies and grabbed a small bottle of white vinegar and a shower bucket. It was second nature to Hattie, mixing vinegar with water for a cleaning solution. She'd done it every day at the kennel. She poured the mix on the vomit that had splattered on the rug, scrubbing until it was spotless.

"Sorry for all this. It's disgusting, I know. I'm just so wretched sick. And I was rude, it's not okay."

"It's fine," Hattie said. "I understand."

"I had a really bad night," Ellie continued hoarsely, as if someone had his hands around her throat to prevent her from freely speaking. "I'm pretty sure some asshole slipped a roofie in my drink."

"What happened?"

"I only had one drink, and I can't remember a thing. When I woke up this morning, I wasn't here. Obviously. I was somewhere else, a place I would never go, with someone I would never go home with. Something happened to me. He denies it of course. I know better. He's scum," Ellie said, writhing in disgust. "The police confirmed it looks like someone gave me a date-rape drug in my drink. It's a mess. I'm underage. I used a fake ID."

"How can I help?" Hattie asked calmly, praying she was saying and doing the right thing.

"You can help me kill the son of bitch," snapped Ellie, venom raging in her voice. "I was raped, and I know who did it."

"Ellie, I'm so, so sorry."

"Me too. Let's keep this between you and me. My grandparents don't need to know, okay? They worry enough about me."

"Fine, sure."

"Oh, by the way, Charles and Claire invited us to come to dinner tonight at their home in Back Bay. Can you join us?"

"Uh, I think so."

Actually, it was the last thing Hattie wanted to do. Ellie was intimidating enough on a regular day. Now this. Hattie's phone pinged. She looked down, a message from Pastor Luis.

One of my professors at Harvard Divinity routinely quoted the great John Wesley. "Do all you can, where you can, when you can." Even at college, even when you hardly feel like it, you can be of service to God.

"Ellie, I'd love to come."

"Great, meet me here at five."

Chapter 12:
Being There

ELLIE, 2008

Hattie was at the library all day, attempting to study but mostly working at taming thoughts about Ellie. Poor Ellie, what a nightmare. As Hattie walked from the library to the residence hall, she hoped Ellie would tell her grandparents. They'd know how to help her far better than she did.

Hattie had yet to go across the river and visit Back Bay. She read in Luis's much-used *Guide to Boston* that Back Bay was an affluent area with pricey brownstones. Award-winning restaurants and boutique shopping all close by. She'd wear the outfit Mema got her, the one from the boutique in Birmingham. The gray pants and cardigan sweater would be perfect for November.

When Hattie arrived back to their room, Ellie was getting ready, swirling a scarf around her neck. Hattie guessed to cover up the bruise on her neck. Ellie slipped a navy blazer over a pink flowered blouse with jeans and clogs.

Hattie felt tongue tied. What do you talk about with someone who less than twenty-four hours ago was drugged and raped? What do you say to her family? Instead, she tried to act as if nothing happened. "Hi Ellie, I'll shower quick and change."

After she showered, she put on her new gray wool trousers and cashmere sweater. It was the nicest outfit she'd ever had, and tonight was the perfect time to wear it.

"Wow, nice outfit," Ellie complimented Hattie.

"Really?"

"Of course, I wouldn't say it if I didn't think it."

"Well, thanks. Mema, I mean my grandmother, gave it to me."

"She has good taste."

When they got in Ellie's car, neither brought up the previous evening's events. Instead, Boston's cityscape became their icebreaker.

Charles and Claire's home was a three-level brownstone on the cross streets of Beacon and Dartmouth. Their home had lovely window boxes outside filled with fall-colored pansies, kale, and tiny white pumpkins. Hattie instantly fell in love with their home.

Rainy weather had settled in, and the girls were grateful to get inside, where a fire was burning in the fireplace of the home's library. Rich oriental rugs covered dark hardwood floors. The front rooms were decorated with cozy furniture upholstered in colorful floral prints and gingham. The study was filled with old books. Antique wood pieces were perfectly scattered throughout the home. Hattie knew if she ever had a home, this is what she'd want it to look like.

"Sit down, girls, please," invited Claire. "Hattie, make yourself at home."

Hattie noticed how comfortable and plush the sofa felt as she sat down, sinking in, cushions around her. It was like being wrapped in a down comforter on a cold winter night. If she wasn't careful, she'd nod off to sleep. It felt wonderful to be in a home, and ever since Hattie first arrived in Boston, she hoped to someday see inside a brownstone.

"Your home is lovely," Hattie complimented Claire.

"Thank you. It works well for us. Three levels. Ellie's room is on the third floor. She'll have to show you around. Plenty of room for you to stay overnight, if you tire of the residence hall and need a reprieve."

"Thank you, that's very kind."

Claire, dressed in a navy cashmere turtleneck and black trousers, handed the girls a hot apple cider, followed by a plate of warm bruschetta. Hattie took one slice, she hadn't eaten all day. Fresh tomatoes and basil, a touch of garlic. She desperately wanted a second, but was afraid she'd break some sort of etiquette rule about appetizers.

"Ellie, dear, how is school going? Are you keeping up?" asked Claire.

"Gammy, it's the weekend, let me relax, please."

"Hattie, I assume Ellie has told you how much she enjoys cooking?" asked Claire, changing the subject.

"No, actually she hasn't mentioned it."

"It's Ellie's passion," said Charles, greeting them with a warm smile. He was dressed in a checkered blue-and-gray sports coat, coordinating with navy slacks. "I'm so pleased the two of you are here to join us this evening," smiled Charles. Hattie returned his smile. She could tell Charles meant it.

"I'm also pleased Ellie is cooking for us. Since she left for college, we survive on takeout."

"What my grandparents haven't shared is that I'm the only one in this family who can cook. These two are absolutely terrible cooks."

"Not terrible, dear Ellie," laughed Claire. "We just don't meet your standards."

"Seriously, Hattie, my grandparents are the worst. The Brits aren't exactly known for their delicious food. That said, I'll be in the kitchen. If my grandparents start interrogating you, come find me. They can be nosy."

Hattie laughed nervously. "I'll be fine," she said, watching in amazement as Ellie left for the kitchen, looking remarkably together. It was as if last night had never happened. How was Ellie doing it?

Hattie shifted uncomfortably, then attempted to make conversation. "So, what made you move to the States?"

"I'm the responsible party," Charles began. "I wanted to see the world. My parents suggested I could start by expanding the family brewery business to the US."

"Exciting!"

"Yes, and no. It was far from the travel adventure I envisioned. But there was a far bigger problem."

"What was that?"

"I was in love with a beautiful, feisty English woman I met at Trinity. Smart as a whip. Eyes the color of sapphires."

Hattie smiled, knowing it was Claire.

"Claire was the only child of a prominent London businessman. Her father raised her to understand business. I couldn't leave England without her."

"Of course not," interjected Claire. "You needed me. Charles and I had a lovely wedding in the English countryside, packed our bags, and honeymooned on the *Queen Mary*. We arrived in Boston and never looked back," Claire said lovingly. "Though, I do recall starting out was a bit rough."

"A bit rough?" exclaimed Charles. "It was like paddling a canoe across the Atlantic Ocean."

"Charles, you're exaggerating."

"I hardly think so. Hattie, I was appointed head of sales for the US market, and we didn't have any. The only office space we could afford was the second floor of a brownstone that suffered smoke damage. Stunk like a burnt roast."

"We learned Americans preferred cheap beer in large quantities, or at least they did back then," remarked Claire. "We knew we had a mountain to climb. Charles's family produced small-batch beer, more expensive, but far richer taste."

"We wrongly assumed business would flourish here," commented Charles. "Claire poured over the financials, working the numbers to cut expenses until I garnered up sales. I kept peering over her shoulder. She finally told me to get out of 'her' office and drum up some business, fast."

"How did you do that?" asked Hattie.

"I called on all the prospects I could find in the city. So, I flipped a coin. Heads, I'd head north to Maine. Tails, I'd head south to Cape Cod. I was told both had a bustling summer tourist trade, which I hoped might be our niche, tourists might be more willing to spend more for a quality delicious beer while on holiday. It was tails, so I got in my twenty-year-old Range Rover, which had its own set of problems, headed south, leaving the city behind.

Once I got over the Bourne Bridge, I relaxed, soaking in the beauty of seagrass, water, white sand. I parked the car, stepped outside to enjoy the fresh air, and watched the fishermen. Cleared my head."

"The good Lord threw him a lifeline," Claire said.

"What was it?" asked Hattie.

"A dog," laughed Charles. "A monstrosity of a dog, hair as thick as thieves, black, the size of a bear. A beautiful Newfoundland with no one around to claim it. The Newfie was howling, crying really. But wouldn't come to me, either."

"Poor thing. Mama says Newfies miss their families as much as babies miss their Mamas," sympathized Hattie.

"Evidently," nodded Charles. "I'd never heard such a painful sound from an animal. I found a dog tag on the collar, gave me the information I needed.

"The tag read: *Stuart's my name. Property of the Cod & Core General Store.* I pushed and pulled Stuart into my car, mind you, it was like lifting an elephant into a circus tent. No cell phones back then, so we drove to the nearest gas station to get directions. Turned out the Cod and Core was only a short distance away. A good thing, too, because the amount of drool on my front seat could have watered a garden."

"They can be big droolers," giggled Hattie. "Mama has trained a few."

"Stuart's tail began wagging the minute we arrived at the general store. We walked in together, and we both felt as if we'd come home. Familiar brands of British coffees and teas lined the shelves. Fresh quality produce in bins, quality dried goods from the UK and Ireland. Stuart immediately flopped down on the floor. I began looking for someone to help me. A short, stocky red-haired man, on the phone behind the counter, nods at me, covers the receiver, and says, 'Be with you in a minute, I've lost me dog, making an inquiry.'

"I mouthed back, gesturing wide with my hands, 'Black? The size of a bear?' And pointed to the wood floor, where 150 pounds of fur was now contentedly sleeping under the counter.

"The shopkeeper's name was Jack O'Keegan, smiled big at me with tobacco-stained teeth, and says to the person on the other end, 'Happy out, found Stu.' He slams the phone down and says to me, 'That's 'im. Righto. Thank you, Jesus, Mary, and Joseph! You too, good sir.' And like a leprechaun, plops down next to Stuart, puts his arm around him, looks the dog in the eye, and says, 'Bloody hell, Stu, you gave me a scare. Damn glad you're back.'

"The owner gets up off the floor, shakes my hand, and introduces himself. And there was my opportunity. I mention to him I have something in my car that he needs. Went and got our best ale from the cooler. A couple of Reade beers later, a few stories, and some laughs, Jack tells me to come back with a contract the next day. He'd love to sell my beer."

"That is amazing," said Hattie. "Mama would love that story."

"I needed a lawyer pronto, to draw up an American contract. By the time I got back to Boston, it was five thirty at night. I couldn't exactly start calling attorneys out of the yellow pages. But there was a young lawyer who rented the first floor of our office. He was my best bet, though, I was skeptical of him."

"Why?" asked Hattie.

"I'd never seen a client walk in or out of the law office. Turns out, the lawyer, Jim Dubois, was one of the first Native Americans to graduate from Harvard Law, top of his class. Wrote the legal contract up for me in no time flat."

"A Harvard grad, huh? I wonder if I'll hear about him."

"If you study law, you will. Jim is the grandson of the chief of the Wampanoag Indian tribe. Today, he's one of the top lawyers in Boston. Back then, he was like us, struggling for business. Jim offered to go with me to get the contract signed. Later he confessed he didn't have anything else to do."

"Times certainly have changed, Jim has more clients than he can handle," said Claire.

"He works way too hard, does way more work than one person should be doing. Different back then, though, we were all having a rough go at it. Jim and I began referring business to one another. Our relationship grew from business acquaintances to best friends. If you ever find yourself in trouble, Jim Dubois is the man to call. There's a lesson in this story. Hattie, if you can keep rowing through rough waters, keep the faith, it'll lead to something better."

"Dinner is served," Ellie said, walking in with a bowl of steaming hot pasta. "Please, everyone, take a seat at the table."

The table, with a breathtaking view of the river, was set with blue-and-white china and a fresh bouquet of hydrangea flowers.

Ellie served a Caesar salad tossed with homemade dressing topped with garlic croutons, Bolognese pasta, and baguette bread.

"Ellie this is wonderful, you are an outstanding cook," Hattie said. "This is the best meal I've had."

"Since you left home?" teased Charles.

"No, the best meal I've ever had, in my whole life."

They all laughed.

"I swear," claimed Hattie.

"I appreciate that, really, I appreciate everything you've done for me." Their eyes locked. Hattie knew Ellie meant every single word.

The evening wrapped up with Charles sharing a story about his courtship of Claire, and the number of times he proposed before she finally said yes.

"Four times to be exact," Charles said, shaking his head. "Worth every humbling no she gave me."

Hattie was surprised how much she enjoyed herself, Ellie's rape temporarily forgotten. The evening reminded her of the nights Pastor Luis joined her family for supper. Good food and storytelling. Southerners and Northerners weren't all that different.

On the way home, Hattie sat silently, unsure if Ellie was going to crack after an evening of pretending everything was normal.

"My grandparents really enjoyed your company this evening," Ellie said as she drove them back to campus.

"They are wonderful. Thank you for bringing me. And, wow, I hadn't realized I was living with the next Julia Child."

"Cooking is my passion. College is the hoop I need to jump through before I get there. I promised my grandparents."

They crossed over the bridge from Boston to Cambridge.

"I sure wish Gammy and Poppy would lighten up about my classes," Ellie admitted. "They'd freak if they knew I'm pretty much failing everything, except art history. And that's only because Gammy dragged me to every art museum in the world. Jeez, I probably know more than the professor."

"I could help you with your classes, if you like."

"I don't know."

"Sometimes it just takes the right trainer."

"Trainer?"

"I meant tutor. I've spent way too much time around Mama and helping her train dogs." Hattie shook her head.

"Whatever you want to call it, I need it. I'm circling the drain."

"I'm happy to help out with school and, well, whatever you need. Ellie, with the other, um, last night? Are you okay?"

Ellie shrugged. "I'm mad at myself."

"You know, it's not your fault."

"I keep telling myself that. I just wish I believed it."

"I will help you through this, and your classes."

"Hattie Brown, after this morning, the one thing I know is that you would do anything to help me."

Chapter 13:
Night Terrors

ELLIE, 2008

"Stop it!" screamed Ellie. "Leave me alone. I don't want to. You son of a..."

The screaming woke Hattie, who bolted out of bed, rushing to Ellie's side.

"No, no, please stop," Ellie said, sobbing, kicking, and flailing her legs and arms while Hattie attempted to wake her.

More sobbing. "Stop!" Ellie's angry voice fell to a desperate plea. "Please, stop."

"Ellie, it's me," Hattie said, still shaking Ellie. "Wake up. It's a bad dream, only a dream."

Ellie's eyes finally opened. She was gasping for air.

"Oh God, it was him, again. He wouldn't stop," Ellie sobbed.

"You're okay, honest. Just a bad dream. I promise," said Hattie, patting Ellie's shaking legs to calm her. "You're here with me. No one else is here."

Ellie grabbed a tissue, wiping her tears. "Did I hurt you?"

"No, not at all," Hattie said convincingly, though she was sure she'd have a bruise or two on her arms.

"I don't think I can fall back asleep," Ellie mumbled, getting out of bed. She began pacing. "This sucks so bad. These nightmares seem so real."

Whenever Hattie couldn't sleep, Mema worked her magic, rubbing Hattie's feet until she relaxed and nodded off. "Ellie, you know, sometimes, when I can't fall asleep, back home, Mema gives me a foot massage. In less than five minutes, I'm out like a light. Guaranteed. I can try it, it might work."

"I haven't had a good night's sleep since that night," Ellie admitted. "Just who is this *Mema*, anyway?" she said, plopping down on Hattie's bed, placing her two beautifully pedicured feet on Hattie's lap.

"My grandmother, she's some *kinda* wonderful," said Hattie as she gently rubbed Ellie's feet.

"Sounds like it."

And just like Mema done for Hattie over the years, Hattie massaged Ellie's foot, gently squeezing the arch and Ellie's perfectly manicured toes. She rubbed the sole of her foot. Each foot, twice. It took less than five minutes and Ellie was asleep. Hattie imagined Mema saying, "Works like a charm, remember, it's been a kind thing to do since biblical times." Her grandmother knew all the secrets to good living.

"My apologies for keeping you awake last night," said Ellie the next morning. "Night terrors. I can't shake this. I need to see my psychiatrist."

"You have a psychiatrist?" asked Hattie, immediately regretting her words. She sounded like a backwoods judgmental hick.

"Pretty much on speed dial."

"You seem so together."

"Hardly. I've seen a therapist since I was little. After my parents' accident. Kids suffer from PTSD, too. Night terrors, panic attacks, sleeplessness. Lack of an ability to focus. I used to have them all the time, after the accident. It got better during high school. I was good, really, the best I'd ever been. After the rape, it's all coming back. At night I can't sleep, during the day I'm agitated. I feel like I'm crawling out of my skin." Ellie anxiously rubbed her arms. "I'm going to see if I can get into my doctor this morning and get on new meds, maybe EMDR. Might have to step it up on yoga, too. Do it more than twice a week."

Hattie had no idea what EMDR meant, but had done yoga in her PE class and knew it was a healthy thing for the body and the mind. She'd read about vets having PTSD, but hadn't realized ordinary people suffer from it too.

"If you have time, maybe later today, you can help me with my statistics homework. "

"Definitely."

"I'll text you when I'm back on campus. We can have dinner at the dining hall, then head to the library."

"See you then."

Hattie googled PTSD and EMDR. One website described posttraumatic stress syndrome as a mental health condition triggered by a terrifying event. Symptoms include anxiety, nightmares, depression, reliving the trauma, difficulty concentrating. Sounded like Ellie. Hattie then looked up EMDR. It was a type of specialized therapy, using the eyes, for people suffering from trauma. Hattie felt for Ellie. The after effects of trauma were intense, complicated.

Life altering. No one treatment worked for everyone. Poor Ellie. Two horribly traumatic events before she was twenty years old.

Ellie texted Hattie that she was back on campus.

Let's meet for dinner at six in the dining hall.

Hattie's social anxiety skyrocketed when she saw Ellie seated with a bunch of other girls at a long rectangular table. Hattie prayed she didn't say something stupid and lose the opportunity to make friends.

"Hattie, we're over here," Ellie hollered. "We saved you a seat."

Hattie smiled. Never once in high school did anyone, besides Beau, save her a seat in the cafeteria.

"Thanks."

Ellie made socializing easy, introducing her. A couple of the girls were from Boston, one from San Francisco, and two from the Midwest. The conversation focused on the pathetic food served at school and how much homework they had to get done. By the end of dinner, Hattie felt almost comfortable.

"Well, girls, we gotta run." Ellie stood, grabbing her backpack. "Hattie and I are heading to the library. She is a total *brainiac* and is going to help me pass statistics."

"It was nice to meet you, Hattie, hope to see you around," several of them chimed in as Hattie gathered her backpack.

"Same here," smiled Hattie, thinking that this is how college should be. Who knew something as simple as sitting with friends in the dining hall could be so wonderful.

The two roommates walked to the library.

"Why aren't you in statistics?" asked Ellie. "I thought every freshman had to take it?"

"Uh, well, I didn't have to."

"Why not?"

Hattie paused. "Uh, one less class I had to pay for, so I tested out of it."

Ellie laughed. "I must have done something right to get you for a roommate."

Hattie was good at tutoring. Honestly it was similar to training dogs. Patience. Clear communication. A mutual understanding. Praise.

"How am I ever going to repay you?" Ellie asked as they walked from the library to their dorm room. "I finally understand how to do the problems."

"Let me think…maybe put your high heels away at night, so I don't trip and break my ankle," she teased.

"Maybe I can do one better, and talk my grandparent's house-keeper in to coming to our dorm room to make our beds, hang up clothes, put my shoes away."

"Seriously?"

"No," laughed Ellie. "Claire would wring my neck. It's a nice thought though, isn't it?"

The girls laughed, together, like friends. One dressed in jeans, an old sweatshirt, and Converse shoes; the other dressed in design-er slacks, a tan cashmere crew neck sweater, and expensive leather riding boots. Hattie intuitively knew that even as different as they were, they were better together.

Chapter 14:
A Cottage Holiday

2008

The fall semester flew by, and students at Harvard were eagerly packing for the Thanksgiving break, while Hattie was making a list of groceries she'd need to stock up on for the long weekend. Harvard's dining hall was closed on Thanksgiving. And it looked like she'd be eating deli turkey this year. Beau was required to stay on base. The Brown family's Thanksgiving was definitely going to be different.

Hattie tried to put a good spin on things. She'd work on homework, start preparing for finals. Christmas break was only a month away. She could do this, she'd be fine. Lonely, but fine.

"Ellie, do you mind if I put food in your refrigerator over break? The dining hall is closed on Thanksgiving. I'll be eating in our room until it reopens."

"Absolutely not," Ellie said in disgust.

The words were a slap in the face to Hattie. She'd been tutoring Ellie for weeks now, and Ellie was passing all her classes.

"Uh, okay, no worries," uttered Hattie, stunned by her roommate's response.

"Not okay," Ellie said. "You are not staying here over break. That sounds horrible. I can see it now, a Cliff bar for breakfast and a take-out turkey sandwich for Thanksgiving dinner. Not on my watch. You are spending Thanksgiving with my family."

"I don't want to impose."

"Impose? Charles and Claire would love it. We celebrate on the Cape, at Poppy and Gammy's cottage. It's all very relaxed. We'll eat good food—compliments of yours truly. As you may recall, my grandmother is a terrible cook. We'll go out to dinner too, play cards, watch movies. Not exactly exciting, like going to New York to watch the Macy's Thanksgiving parade like we did when I was a kid. I've outgrown that, anyway. You will love Cloudberry Cottage."

"Sounds really nice. Maybe you should ask, just to make sure it's okay?"

"Fine, I'll ask, only to ease your concerns. I know what their answer will be. Start packing your bags, girlfriend! Sweaters and sweatshirts, it's November on the Cape."

Charles and Claire picked the girls up from the residence hall the Wednesday morning before Thanksgiving. Hattie felt like a child going on a family vacation. Once they crossed the Bourne Bridge, Hattie felt a sense of calm. The traffic eased, as did the frenzy of Boston. The ocean was a breathtaking deep blue from a low November sun. It was cold enough to snow. Hattie kept her fingers crossed, hoping to see snowflakes fall over the holiday weekend. She saw a sign for Hyannis and the ferry. Twenty miles later, they got off route 6A and took a narrow two-lane road into the town of Chatham.

Charles took on the role of tour guide. "Three sides of the town are surrounded by ocean. Chatham, historically, was a small fishing village, and the fishing community is still strong, but summer tourism has skyrocketed in the last twenty years."

"As have home prices," remarked Claire. "We bought our cottage for a song, back in the day. The value has quadrupled, we could make a fortune if we sold it—not that it's ever leaving this family, nor getting torn down for some big monstrosity of a mansion. I simply won't have it."

"Of course not, dear." Charles patted her hand lovingly. "The town is quiet right now. I love it off season. Come summer, tourists start pouring in."

"I'll bring you back here in the summer," Ellie interrupted. "It's so much fun. The beaches, the Cape Cod baseball league, the seafood. We can grab dinner at the Red Nun, a great burger-and-fries place, before a ball game. Best college players in the country, nice to look at, too. We can party with 'em."

"Eleanor!" exclaimed Claire.

Ellie and Hattie giggled like sisters.

As they drove down Shore Road, Charles pointed out the majestic Chatham Bars Inn overlooking the Atlantic. "It originally was a hunting lodge, back in the early 1900s."

"Our cottage is just outside of town," Charles said, driving down a gravel road past several cottages. At the end of the gravel lane was a single gray-shingled cottage with a charming pink door and matching shutters. A sign that said *Cloudberry Cottage* hung above the door. The back door opened up to a dirt path that led to a tall dune, hiding the beach.

"Here we are," said Claire. "We better turn the heat on, get settled. Ellie, we should head to town soon, get our groceries before everything closes up."

They unloaded the car and went inside. Despite the chill in the air, the cottage felt warm and inviting. They entered a cozy family room with a stone fireplace as its focal point. The kitchen had light gray painted cabinets. It was tiny but well equipped, a Sub-Zero refrigerator and a Wolf range and stove.

"You can put your luggage in the mermaid room," said Ellie. "Follow me."

"The mermaid room?" Hattie asked curiously.

"You'll see."

As Hattie opened the door, the first thing she noticed was a beautiful wood mermaid hanging above the queen-size bed as if in charge of watching over the guests who slept there. A white wicker chair with a blue cushion was tucked into the corner. A lovely hand-hooked rug with a montage of nautical images covered the wide-plank pinewood floors.

"I love it!" exclaimed Hattie, flopping on the bed.

"You'll sleep like a baby in here," said Ellie. "Claire swears it's the mermaid who provides serenity. In reality, it's the great mattress."

Hattie laughed.

"The other bedrooms are on the opposite end of the cottage. One is the Cotswold room, Charles and Claire's room. It's decorated in English country, of course. I'll be sleeping in the map room. It's a showcase of vintage maps from all over the world, hand selected by my grandfather. I'm certain he will show you every excruciating detail on his legendary maps. Trust me, it will be painfully dull."

"Remember who you're talking to," teased Hattie. "Dull is my middle name. I'll enjoy it."

"No wonder why my grandparents adore you, you're an old soul in a young body."

Claire and Ellie worked on the grocery list. While Charles gave Hattie a condensed version of the history of his map collection, talking of things like topography and roads and how it affects how people live. Hattie listened attentively. Ellie rolled her eyes, mouthing a "thank you" to Hattie. As expected, Hattie hardly minded. She was thrilled when Charles offered to take her to the Maps of Antiquity shop in Chatham on Saturday.

Hattie slept like a baby that night. When she finally rose at nine the next morning, coffee and pastries were waiting on the kitchen table. The aroma of a roasting turkey consumed the entire cottage.

"Good morning, Hattie," greeted Claire. "Charles and Ellie ran into town to get some last-minute things. Please help yourself to coffee and pastries."

"Thank you. This is all so wonderful, a much-needed break."

"Ellie says you've helped her a great deal with academics. We appreciate that."

"School and tutoring are sort of my thing, like cooking is Ellie's. I'm happy to help."

The door blew open with a gust of chilly wind, and Charles and Ellie entered with a package of freshly made dinner rolls from the local bakery.

"Lucky us, we grabbed the last batch of fresh dinner rolls, right before the bakery closed," Ellie said, proclaiming victory. "It simply wouldn't be Thanksgiving without these. Even I can't bake rolls as delicious as this."

"Can I help in the kitchen?" Hattie asked.

"Thank you. But no. You relax, or better yet, go study. If I know you, you'll feel guilty if you don't. I have plans for us, including a spa day at the Chatham Bars Inn this weekend. Now's your time to get your work done."

"Well, then, I think, I'll get at it."

"Good because we'll be playing card games tonight, maybe a game of Clue. Prepare yourself, the Reade family takes games seriously."

"I'm all in," Hattie exclaimed.

Despite feeling perfectly at home with the Reade family, Hattie missed her own family. The coziness of the cottage reminded her of Mema's home, the smells of Thanksgiving dinner, and evening card games—it was like her own holidays in Fairhope. It was anyone's guess who would be at Thanksgiving dinner. Mema invited friends, and a few strangers with no place to go. Sometimes there was an unusual pairing of guests, be it the mayor and his wife, or the divorced garbage collector and his children. This year Pastor Luis was in the mix. Hattie's chest felt heavy thinking of them together, laughing and storytelling without her.

She'd call home later, for now she'd dive into her studies.

At three, Ellie announced dinner was ready. Claire gave Hattie candles to put on the table, and the cottage glowed with a holiday warmth. The table displayed a mouthwatering feast of roasted turkey baked golden brown, cranberry sauce, mashed potatoes with a touch of fresh garlic, roasted vegetables, sweet potatoes, and dinner rolls.

"Charles, would you please say grace?" Claire asked.

"Yes, of course."

Hattie folded her hands, bowed her head.

"Dear Lord, let us be grateful to the farmers who worked the land to provide us food and of course, Ellie, who so wonderfully prepared it all. Thank you for my dear wife and granddaughter. A special thank-you to Hattie's family for sharing her with us this holiday. Amen."

"Amen," the foursome said in unison.

Claire insisted they each say what they were thankful for this year. When it came to Ellie, "I am most grateful for my newest and dearest friend, Hattie."

"And I you," said Hattie sincerely. It dawned on her that she and Ellie had become really close after Ellie's rape, best friends through tragic circumstances. Hattie wondered if this is what Pastor Luis meant when he said God will make something good out of bad things.

After a second helping, Hattie felt as if the top button on her jeans was about to pop like a champagne cork. After the dishes were done, the foursome put coats and hats on and headed out to walk on the beach. Clouds and fog moved in. The winds whipped cold air from the north, temperatures hovering in the low forties. Still, it felt good to be outside in the fresh air. There were a couple of other families walking the beach and two young boys playing Frisbee with their goldendoodle. Seeing the dog instantly made Hattie miss Lily. Lily would love running on the beach.

The wind off the ocean had picked up, sending a chill into their bones. They returned to the cottage and Charles built a fire in the stone fireplace. Claire served freshly brewed coffee and pumpkin pie with whipped cream.

Later that evening Hattie called home to wish her family a happy Thanksgiving. She first spoke with Mama, who then passed the phone to Mema, who passed the phone to Pastor Luis, who eventually passed the phone to Doc Grady and, per Mema's insistence, a few people Hattie hadn't met. The phone finally returned to Pastor Luis.

"Well, that's a cast of characters at Mema's," said Hattie, laughing. "I don't even want to know where Mema found Henrietta, who by the way says she has twelve cats and is hoping for lucky number thirteen."

"You don't know the half of it," laughed Pastor Luis. "It's been a priceless experience. I've heard stories to last me a lifetime."

"Awww, Thanksgiving at Mema's. A gathering of the lost, odd, and quirky. Funny thing is, I miss it."

"Can't say there's anything quite like it. Are you enjoying the Cape?"

"Ellie's grandparents' cottage is charming, cozy, and warm. It's been so relaxing. I didn't know how much I needed this. We walked Harding Beach this afternoon. It was so cold but so beautiful. We're going to an antique map store tomorrow. They want to show me Lighthouse Beach. Ellie has a spa day planned for us at Chatham Bars Inn."

"A favorite of mine, too."

"Spa days?" Hattie asked.

"No," laughed Luis. "Never done the spa thing. My brothers get wind of that, and I'd never live it down. Sorry, I meant to say Lighthouse Beach. One of my favorites. Years back, one of my divinity school classmates invited me to his parent's place in Chatham."

"It's breathtaking, isn't it?"

"It is. And from what I recall, we spent a good share of our evenings at the Chatham Squire. I'm sure Ellie will take you. Excuse me, Hattie, Mema's waving me back to the table. Her pumpkin pie is being served. So, we'll see you at Christmas, right?"

"Wouldn't miss it."

Chapter 15:
Life Changes

2012

After they returned from Cape Cod, Ellie and Hattie became inseparable. Freshmen year flew by like migrating geese. Hattie made the dean's list. Expanded her circle of friends. Renewed her hard-earned scholarship. At the end of the spring semester, she returned to Fairhope for the summer, training dogs and cleaning kennels.

As promised, Ellie invited her to Cape Cod over the Fourth of July. They sailed and watched fireworks and partied with a couple of Cape Cod League ballplayers they met at the Squire. Six weeks later they were back on campus, and this time it was Hattie and Ellie, now sophomores, holding the important-looking clipboards, helping new students move in.

Sophomore year was far calmer. Hattie and Ellie were in sync, comfortable with each other, like sisters. Charles paid Hattie a stipend for tutoring Ellie, which helped pay for books and food. Ellie fell far short of Hattie's academic excellence, but she was holding her own, passing all her classes. Hattie was proud of Ellie, who continued to see her psychiatrist regularly. She still experienced night terrors, but they were far less frequent than the previous year.

Then, in a snap, sophomore year was over. Hattie's favorite professor from the English department encouraged her to major in a field she was passionate about. She was embarrassed to share how much in student loans she'd have to pay back. She heard enough to know Harvard business majors had job offers in hand before graduating. She couldn't count on that with a degree in English or history, both majors likely requiring graduate schooling. In the end, she took the less risky path, declaring finance and economics her majors. She'd still be able to sneak in an English or history class each semester. Ellie also declared her major: art history. Of course, Ellie had the luxury of well-to-do grandparents. Hattie did not.

Mema informed Hattie, confidentially, Mama was having body tremors. Her muscles frequently ached. Mama's legs didn't move like they should. "It's like her brain is telling her one thing but her body isn't listening," Mema told Hattie.

After several months of doctor appointments, Beth was officially diagnosed with Parkinson's. Doctors prescribed drugs that helped Beth maintain a fairly normal work life.

By spring semester of junior year, things had changed, Parkinson's was like a thief, stealing Beth's ability to train dogs and run the kennel. Beth had good days and bad days. She hired two dog handlers to help her with the business. As her condition worsened, Mema became Beth's caregiver.

The summer before senior year, Hattie accepted an internship at Citibank in Boston. Her only chance to return home was a long weekend before the start of senior year. When she returned to Fairhope, she was shocked to see Mama could no longer stand without help. Parkinson's was grinding away at Mama's good life and Hattie hated it.

"Do Fairhope doctors even know what they're doing?" demanded Hattie.

"I've seen doctors, lots of 'em. Even gone to specialists in Atlanta. I'm doing all I can." Beth grimaced in pain.

"I can't believe this," Hattie cried as she slammed the back door. "I need some fresh air."

Hattie put on her running shoes and left for a run. She needed to think, to breathe. If Mama couldn't work with dogs, she had no life. My God, why her mama? Her father already been taken from her. Hattie didn't know what to do, where to go. She kept running until she couldn't breathe, ending up outside of her church, First Methodist.

She found Pastor Luis in the church gardens, in jeans and a green and blue windbreaker, on his knees weeding, of all things. If Hattie weren't so upset, she may have found it funny, knowing Mema likely put him up to this.

"Pastor Luis, I need help," she said, sobbing.

"Please, sit with me, on the bench," he said wiping the dirt from his hands on a towel he pulled from his back pocket.

"Why can't God give my family a break?"

Hattie, sweaty from running, with flushed red cheeks, sat down, her arms crossed, anger causing creases between her eyebrows.

"The Bible says in this world, we will have trouble; and believe me, I have searched, but cannot find any chapter that tells us if we believe in God and are good Christians, we will have smooth sailing. Smooth sailing comes in heaven, where there are no more tears, no more sorrow."

"Why should we even pray?"

"Because God helps us through our troubles. He may not, for reasons only he understands, remove us from difficult situations, but he always helps us through it. He is with you today. He is with your mother. He loves her more than we can comprehend."

"Yes, well, *he* has a funny way of showing it."

Hattie got up, thinking of her once strong mother, who'd trained hundreds of dogs and who now required a walker to get around. Hattie's anger inside burned like an out-of-control forest fire.

"I'm sorry, I know you're trying to help." Hattie stood. "I've got to go. I need to finish my run."

She ran to the water, near the pier, where the cool Gulf breeze blew on her, drying her tears. She searched the water, trying to find her faith, trying to find hope.

She was standing at the end of the pier, in running shorts and a Harvard T-shirt, when Luis found her. The wind whipping her brown ponytail.

"Hattie, believe me, I know how hard this is. I know your heart physically aches. I know it. Because mine does too. Your mother is in a terrible situation right now. I wish I could fix it. I promise, though, there is a better place for her, a place where there will be no more pain, no more tears. A place where your father and Lily await her arrival. It's heaven. Your mother believes it, in fact, she's counting on it. Her only worry now is you. She desperately wants you to be okay. To be happy. To graduate from Harvard. Go home to her. Let her tell you."

Hattie turned and looked at him. For the first time, she noticed that he'd cut his long hair, no longer ponytail length. It fell just above his shoulders, long enough that he still looked more like a member of a rock band than a pastor. The cut was bad, uneven. It dawned on her. Mema cut his hair. Who else would have given him such an awful cut? She was always trying to help people save money, trying things she had no idea how to do, Hattie thought, recalling her own bad pixie cut thanks to Mema. His darn cowlick was still there, popping up like a weed. His windbreaker made him look younger than his years.

"Go home, Hattie. She needs to know you'll be okay."

"I'm not sure I will be," Hattie cried.

"That's why I'm here. To make sure. Mema too. And Beau. I promised your mother. I promised God. You are not alone in this. Come on, I'll walk you home." He put his arm around her shoulder and they left together. He was right, she was not alone. Still, she was heartbroken.

The remaining time in Fairhope, Beth, Mema, and Hattie spent most of their time on the front porch, playing with puppies from Mama's litter, looking through old photo albums, playing cards, drinking sweet tea. Telling family stories. Sunday evening, Hattie desperately wanted to stay and help, but Mama refused the offer.

"Now's your time to learn, grow, follow your dreams. Learn as much as you can, maybe someday carry on the family business. You're a natural at dog training,"

"Not like you, Mama."

"Yes, you are, child, but you're young. Go for your dreams. See the world. Teach, write, get a PhD. It makes me happy you're doing what you love. It's the only thing that helps me get through this," pointing to her walker. "Hurry now, go get packed before you miss your flight."

Hattie hadn't mentioned to Mama she changed her major to business, something that would be more financially secure, a safer bet. She leaned down to give Mama a kiss goodbye.

"I'm still mad you made me take the bus to school when I was a freshman," teased Hattie, attempting to lighten a somber goodbye.

"You're a better person for it. I love you, kiddo, make me proud. And for heaven's sake, take one of the Labrador pups along with you to the airport. They need to get comfortable with going in the car. Luis won't mind. He's stopping by later anyway."

Pastor Luis, Hattie, and a ten-week-old Labrador named Fiona, got in his silver Tacoma truck.

"This is a step up from your 1999 Corolla," teased Hattie.

Fiona, the biggest puppy of the litter, pawed at her long brown hair. Hattie buried her head in its golden fur. Was there anything as wonderful as puppy smell?

"Looks like someone's fallen in love," teased Pastor Luis.

"She's melting my heart. I can't believe I'm saying this, but I've gotta get one of my own someday."

"Me too," laughed Pastor Luis. "Haven't quite convinced Lauren." Lauren was his girlfriend, who followed him from Boston. His phone rang.

"I need to answer this, it's Lauren. She misses Boston, city life."

"By all means," Hattie said, scrolling through her phone, trying not to listen.

"I will be home right after I drop Hattie off at the airport," he promised Lauren, who hadn't yet realized she was on speaker.

"Why can't her own family bring her?" whined Lauren.

"I am family," he quietly responded.

And then there was dead silence on the other end. Hattie was 100 percent certain his girlfriend had just hung up on him.

An awkward silence hung in the air until Fiona went to sit on Luis's lap, small enough to wiggle under the steering wheel.

Neither spoke until they arrived at the airport.

"Do you think you can sneak Fiona on the airplane?" teased Pastor Luis while helping Hattie with her suitcase.

"I wish."

"I'll watch over Beth and Mema. And the pups," Luis said, while scratching behind Fiona's ears. "Doc Grady and Izzy are helping out, too."

"I know, it's the only reason I can leave. One more favor, please."

"Anything," he smiled gently.

"Would you help Mama place these pups in extra special homes? They're Mama's last..." She couldn't finish. Instead she gave Luis a hug goodbye, clinging to him like a young child fearing kindergarten. She abruptly grabbed her luggage and ran into the terminal, afraid to look back, knowing if she did, she'd never get on the airplane.

* * *

Despite conflicted feelings about returning to campus, Hattie was surprised how good it felt, the familiarity of an academic routine stabilizing to her like an anxiety medication.

By mid-October Hattie's sense of security caved like a car crashing into a concrete median.

Hattie entered her dorm room, finding Ellie writhing in pain, unable to walk. Hattie called 911. EMTs were there in four minutes.

"All the signs of appendicitis," the head EMT told her. "We're taking her to Mass General."

Hattie called Charles and Claire, arranging to meet them at the hospital. She ordered an Uber. She hung up and instantly her phone buzzed again.

"Mema, I can't talk right now, Ellie's sick, they think it's appendicitis. I'm on my way to the hospital."

"I'm sorry, dear. I know this is a bad time, horrible. I want you to be the first to know, your Mama, my Bethie, passed away this morning."

Hattie couldn't speak, dropping to the floor as if someone had tripped her. She curled into the fetal position. "No, not my Mama," sobbed Hattie.

By the grace of God, Hattie gathered her strength and her backpack to meet her Uber driver outside the residence hall.

Hattie stumbled and the woman driver got out to help Hattie into the car. When the phone rang, Hattie unknowingly pressed the speaker button.

"Mema, it's me."

"Don't hang up. Listen to me, the doctors tried, Hattie, there was nothing more they could do. God's truth. They did everything they could to save your Mama. Hattie, I'm so sorry. Bethie's gone to heaven. Come home to Fairhope. We'll get through this together."

The driver, a petite Indian woman with olive skin and soft brown eyes, drove silently. Hattie knew she'd heard every word. When the driver pulled into Mass General, she parked, got out of the Prius. Taking Hattie's elbow in her hand, together, they made their way inside to the surgical waiting area. Charles and Claire were there. Hattie, in shock, sat down. She watched the driver speak softly to Charles and Claire. Claire immediately went to Hattie, reaching for her, rocking her like a small child. Charles made phone calls.

"Hattie, I've arranged a private aircraft to fly you home as soon as possible," said Charles. Hattie hugged him. He was the father she didn't have.

The Uber driver drove Hattie to a general aviation airport twenty-five minutes from the city. From there, the pilot of the jet met the car at the fixed base operation. Taking over, he gently grasped Hattie's hand, helping her board the corporate jet. Hattie knew it was God and the kindness of friends and strangers helping her get back home.

* * *

Mama requested the memorial service be outside, rain or shine, by the red barn where she'd spent her days training dogs. She requested only family, close friends, and the dogs she'd trained and their humans be invited.

Beau, now training to be a Navy SEAL, received a special leave to attend Mama's funeral. Beau was giving the eulogy. Hattie noticed how he'd matured, distinguished in his dress blues, looking dignified. He had a mourning badge on his uniform, and it made Hattie's heart ache so deep she slumped in pain. He'd grown up. She knew public speaking never was Beau's thing, something he avoided like a three-hundred-pound lineman going after him. Still, Beau rose to the occasion. He began slowly.

"Beth Brown was a second mother to me. My own Mama left for greener pastures when I was in high school, looking for a different life in Alaska. I wasn't interested in joining that adventure. So Aunt Beth took me under her wing. I became one of her own. Even after a full day of dog training, tired to the bones, she came to every one of my games with her barn boots still on. You'd never hear her cheer, she was a quiet woman, suppose the opposite of me, a guy whose voice is loud enough to make a Remi gun sound quiet. Beth changed me, taught me quieter ways work wonders.

"On my first day at the kennel, I was rounding up the dogs. One darn Aussie refused to come in. I was tired and mad and yelled at the top of my lungs, words not worth repeating. The dog was playing cat and mouse with me. I was pissed.

"Aunt Bethie came outside, holding a piece of a hotdog. 'Treat,' she said to the dog in a happy voice. That darn happy voice. Sure enough the dang dog trotted right up to her.

"Aunt Beth later pulled me aside. 'Beau, ever wonder why there's a thing called a dog whisperer?'

"'Never much thought about it,' I told her.

"'I didn't think so. Come sit down here on the bench.'

"I knew I was in for a lecture. It went something like this:

"'Screaming at a dog like you was doing is like a coach yelling at his players when he ain't yet taught them the plays. Takes a lot of energy, doesn't make anyone feel good, and the team only gets worse. You yellin' is confusing to a dog. Hears nothing but loud. Can't make heads or tails of what you want 'im to do. Starts running for safety, which is away from you. Good dog communicators don't yell. They stay in control. Speak kindly. That's why their dogs come to them. You got it?'

"'Yes ma'am,' I told her.

"'Okay, then, the only time I ever want to hear y'all holler 'round here is if the barn is on fire. Give dogs love and praise, and they'll jump over the moon for you.'"

Beau looked out at the crowd. Blinking back man-size tears, he continued, "I learned dogs are better than us humans. Except for Bethie, she was one of 'em. And I mean that in the best way. Everyone needs a hero. Aunt Bethie was mine. Godspeed, my trainer, my soul mother. You were best in show."

Pastor Luis played "Amazing Grace" on the guitar. Pastor Luis's girlfriend, Lauren, sang the Lord's Prayer so beautifully there wasn't a dry eye. She was pitch perfect and was lovely in a chiffon black dress. Hattie had heard Lauren had the voice of a Broadway star. Now that she'd heard it, she knew it was true.

After the service, a group from the church served lunch to all the guests: Mema's brisket sliders, potato salad, and fruit. After the lunch, Mema spoke.

"Thank you everyone for coming today to celebrate the life of Beth. This here barn and the land meant a lot to Beth. We think it's a pretty special place. Beth made it even more special when she began training dogs here, her God-given gift. There was no trainer like my daughter. Hattie and Beau were good with the dogs, better than most. But Bethie, well, she was the star of the family."

Mema took a hankie from her pocket, dabbed her eyes. She cleared her throat.

"My daughter would want me to share that no one, absolutely no one, feel sorry for her. If she couldn't be here, there's no other place she'd rather be than in heaven with her husband, Monroe, and a dog or two by her side. I'm betting she's got a heaven-made leash in her hand as I speak."

Mema was right. Mama was where she should be.

After the luncheon, dogs and their people walked solemnly to their trucks and cars. Not a dog barked or growled, as if respecting everything Beth Brown taught them. Far off in the distance, as the sun was setting beyond the barn, Hattie and Beau stood together by a newly dug memorial stone that read, *Beth Brown, Beloved daughter, wife, mother, & aunt, and forever dog trainer.*

Chapter 16:
The Real World

2012

By May of Hattie's senior year at Harvard, she had received her first job offer from an investment firm on State Street in Boston. She accepted the position immediately, not weighing the pros and cons. She needed to support herself. She wasn't like her classmates looking forward to a summer traveling Europe before new jobs or grad school in the fall. There was no city Hattie would rather live in than Boston, and Ellie invited Hattie to live with her family. Ellie was going to work for her family's business, Reade Brewing Company.

Beau, now stationed somewhere he was not privy to share, was less and less communicative. His last message was unsettling. *I have to go silent. In case of an emergency, message this number, 612.633.4954. Someone will contact me. No worrying. God's got this.*

She sure hoped so.

Hattie invited Mema to her graduation ceremony along with Pastor Luis and his girlfriend, Lauren. Perhaps Lauren would begin feeling part of her family like Pastor Luis did.

At the last minute, Lauren changed her plans, deciding instead to join old friends on Cape Cod, skipping the ceremony in Boston and canceling plans to meet Luis's relatives in South Boston.

Mema and Pastor Luis sat next to Charles and Claire at the ceremony. Harvard graduation was filled with all the pomp and circumstance Hattie hoped for.

The Reade family hosted a celebratory dinner after the ceremony, inviting Hattie's family to join them at the Ritz Carlton. At the end of the dinner, Charles gave a toast to two talented graduates. He concluded with an open invite. "This is a spur-of-the-moment thing…I hear some of you have had weekend plans canceled. So join us at our cottage on Cape Cod, all of you. Please. It's a great way to let Ellie and Hattie relax before they begin working. The weather will be perfect."

"I'll be in charge of the Memorial Day cookout," Ellie announced. "And pretty much all the cooking, all weekend."

"Never been to Cape Cod, I'd love to go," remarked Mema. "And if you by chance have an extra fishing pole I can use while I'm there, I'll be as happy as a seagull with a French fry."

"That's my Mema," laughed Hattie.

"Can we count you in, Pastor Luis?" asked Claire.

"I was planning on seeing family while here. They were excited to meet Lauren," he admitted, looking like a disappointed little boy who didn't get what he wanted on his birthday.

"Need I remind you," chided Claire. "Your girlfriend is staying at a luxury, five-star resort on the Cape. We've plenty of room for everyone at Cloudberry. I promise it's far better than staying in the city on Memorial weekend."

"Please say yes, Pastor Luis. I'll feel better if you come—in case my old heart stops beating," teased Mema.

"Well, in that case, how can I say no?"

There was plenty room for all at Cloudberry. Ellie cooked delicious meals. Hattie read and slept on the beach while Mema and Luis fished. Saturday night after dinner, they sang campfire songs around the Reades' fire pit. Pastor Luis borrowed Charles's guitar, and when he sang "Sitting by the Dock of the Bay" by Otis Redding, Hattie and Ellie joined their arms, singing at the top of their lungs. Mema howled in laughter at the girls. Charles and Claire, wrapped in a Thunder Bay wool blanket, softly sang along.

"This is what cottages are for," remarked Charles. "Family and friends."

"I wholeheartedly agree," said Claire. "Thank you everyone for coming."

On their final night at the cottage, Mema, Hattie, and Pastor Luis gathered on the beach to say a prayer in honor of Mama. Pastor Luis took their hands in his. It'd gotten chilly, a strong wind from the north. Luis's hands were warm and comforting. Hattie noticed how handsome he looked in his Nantucket red shorts and the gray Black Dog T-shirt Mema purchased for him from a local shop on Main Street. Luis was barefoot and as relaxed as Hattie had ever seen him. It was as if the sand, ocean, and sun brought out the best in him. His olive skin was dark brown after three days of sun, his windblown hair messy. Luis took out his pocket Bible. "I have two verses I'd like to share that remind me of Beth. The first is from the book of Psalms: *For all the animals of the forest are mine...I know every bird on the mountains, and all the animals of the field.*"

Hattie loved the Bible verse. Surely, God must know how much Mama loved her dogs, how much Mama did for dogs.

"The second verse is from Proverbs. *Those who do what is right take good care of their animals..."*

"That was my Bethie," Mema said tearfully.

"And that was my Mama," Hattie said proudly.

The stars flickered like candles, as if Beth and Monroe were personally greeting them from heaven. "Mama and Daddy are watching us from heaven," said Hattie, looking out at the ocean. "I feel it."

Pastor Luis put his arms around two of his favorite people, walking them slowly back to the cottage.

The next day the heartfelt goodbyes began, graduation weekend coming to a close. The college journey coming to an end. Hattie and Ellie clung close to each other. It was hard to think of moving forward. They had talked frankly, learning neither was thrilled with their future jobs.

After packing and cleaning Cloudberry Cottage, they got on the road, stopping to drop off Pastor Luis at the five-star resort where Lauren was staying. He and Lauren would ride separately, take her rental car to Boston. They'd all meet up at Logan Airport, where Pastor Luis and Lauren would accompany Mema back to Fairhope.

Lauren's brunette bob was perfectly coifed with a pink-and-orange headband. She wore a white tennis outfit, an Arnold Palmer drink in one hand, a tennis racket in the other. She politely greeted the group in the lobby of the resort's main building.

"It can't be that time already," Lauren pouted, her bright pink lips quivering. "I don't want to go back to Fairhope, Luis."

Pastor Luis put his arm around Lauren, pulling her toward him.

"The last day of vacation is always difficult."

He kissed her on the lips and Lauren's mood instantly changed. She possessively squeezed his behind. Hattie turned away. PDA was not her thing. When Lauren finally let her possessive grasp of Luis go, she soaked in the two Harvard graduates like a lioness sizing up its prey. Hattie noticed Lauren's eyes glaring at Ellie. She'd seen it before; other women glared at Ellie simply for being beautiful, having no idea the childhood tragedy she carried inside her.

"I can't believe everybody stayed together in one teeny cottage. Where did everyone sleep?" asked Lauren.

"Cloudberry's really not so 'teeny.' Granted a couple of us had to share rooms, but somehow we managed," shrugged Ellie. "We're like one big happy family."

"How nice," Lauren commented, turning to Luis. "I'm more of a resort person. Luis, we must come back here and stay. The spa is to die for."

Ellie looked over at Hattie and mouthed, "High maintenance."

Hattie smiled. She loved Ellie like a sister.

"We better get everybody on the road before traffic lines up at the bridge," suggested Charles. "If we leave now, we'll have you at Logan in ninety minutes."

At the airport Mema hugged Hattie tight, as if it was the last time they'd see each other, neither wanting to let go.

"Remember, you are strong. And wise. And most important," Mema raised her eyebrows, "a great woman of faith. Don't let anyone change the wonderful person you've become."

"I won't, I promise," said Hattie, holding back tears. "When I get some vacation days, I'll come home for a visit."

"Good. We'll sit in the rockers, enjoy sweet tea on the front porch."

"Thank you for coming to my graduation. I love you!"

"Love you back! I best get on my plane. I miss havin' grits. I can't imagine life without grits."

Hattie saw Lauren roll her eyes. Seriously? Who makes fun of a wonderful elderly woman who misses Southern food? Apparently Lauren, who now reminded Hattie of the mean girls in high school.

* * *

"Put your big-girl clothes on like a real working woman," directed Ellie. "We'll go practice walking in heels. Maybe around Copley Place, Star Market."

"To learn to walk in heels, seriously?"

"Do I ever kid about anything related to fashion or your well-being? First, we'll practice on the sidewalks. Then the cobblestones, then slippery waxed floors."

"I don't want to do this," Hattie whined, staring at the navy stilettos. "I want to wear my Converse."

"Converse won't do a thing for your career. You'll be an outcast. Employees will talk behind your back and say you're weird."

"I am weird," laughed Hattie.

"I know that, but they don't. Take your heels off and give them to me for a minute. Trust me. You don't want to land on your tushy the first day of work."

"Being a grown-up is hard."

"You're telling me. Like I want to work full time for my grandparents. I don't know how Charles and Claire do it every day, and oddly, they enjoy it. Their office is so, so not me. No one has any fashion sense. Women in turtlenecks and corduroys, men in khakis."

"You're going to be a dynamo in sales and marketing."

"We'll see," Ellie said doubtfully. "Let's go, girlfriend. We've got heel practice."

They walked to the Prudential Center and Copley Place then back.

"I felt awkward," admitted Hattie as they entered Charles and Claire's brownstone.

"Awkward doesn't come close to describing it. You're a gorilla on rollerblades. You must have banged into every little old lady at the market."

"It's not funny."

"I know," Ellie howled with laughter. "You could have seriously hurt somebody."

"Stop laughing!" giggled Hattie.

Monday came all too soon. Hattie arrived at the investment banking firm in a dark navy pantsuit with coordinating heels, looking very grown up. She felt like she was playing dress-up. The elevator took her to the fourteenth floor, where she met her person in charge, Richard McCabe. He looked like he was in his late forties, dressed in a typical conservative business suit. Hattie interviewed with him a few months back, recalling he was all business, no small talk.

"Welcome, Hattie, the new employees are meeting in our conference room," Richard said politely, pointing to where a small group was gathering. Ten other new hires were seated at an oblong conference room table, all wearing similar dark suits. Hattie noticed one of the young men had accidentally left the price tag on the sleeve of his new suit. She was secretly glad, knowing he was an imperfect newbie too.

Hattie assumed corporate training would be similar to college classes. A wrong assumption. The corporate trainers were investment bankers, not professors. Hattie missed writing college papers, doing research. Participating in lengthy class discussions. Corporate classes at the firm were all about rules and numbers. Still, Hattie was determined to succeed, and threw herself into learning spreadsheets, securities and exchange rules, and company policies. She learned the business of selling stocks and bonds. It wasn't awful, but didn't spark the same enthusiasm she had for her college courses. She worked like her life depended on it. And in a way, it did. She had to support herself.

One afternoon during the last week of training, Hattie's phone kept vibrating. Trainees were only allowed to check their phones during breaks. Still, everybody did it during class, and she secretly glanced to see who was calling. Pastor Luis. He usually texted. Something must be wrong.

"I've got to take this call," whispered Hattie to a coworker sitting next to her. "It may be an emergency." She stood and left the training room.

"Pastor Luis, hello," Hattie said hesitantly.

"Hi Hattie, is this a good time to talk?"

"Uh, sure, yes, it's fine," not letting on that it was so not fine with corporate management.

"Dear friend, bad news, Mema had a stroke, she's in the hospital. She's asking for you."

"Oh, no. When? How is she?" Hattie began gnawing at her already short nails.

"This morning, she was gardening at church. Collapsed. She's in ICU. How soon can you get here?"

"I'm in the middle...I'm not sure they'll let me come home. Can you tell Mema I'll call her doctor on my break?"

"Hattie, I can't tell you what to do. But I believe it's important for you to come see her," Pastor Luis advised.

"Okay, let me see what I can do." Her mind raced. This was her first job in the real world; she couldn't afford to blow it. What should she do? She texted Ellie.

"Screw work," messaged Ellie. "I'll have Claire book you a flight to Fairhope."

Hattie's boss proved much less accommodating. "You'll need to make up the training you miss, and it will be on your own time."

"Of course. Richard, I apologize, but my pastor says its serious. And my mother recently passed away, my cousin is in the military, I'm the only one who can help."

"No need for personal details."

"Okay, then," she said quietly. "I promise to be back as soon as I'm able."

Hattie arrived in Fairhope at midnight. She headed straight to the hospital. The night nurse let Hattie in, even though visiting hours were long over. Mema was sleeping, her complexion gray. She looked unusually frail. When her eyes finally opened, she smiled weakly at Hattie.

"I knew you would come. I needed to see you."

"I needed to see you too," said Hattie gently combing through Mema's hair with her fingers, "to know you'll be okay."

Mema paused, soaking in the sight of her granddaughter. "Sweet pea, I loved you the moment your mama told me she was pregnant. I loved lying the palm of my hand on Bethie's round tummy as you grew inside of her. You were always kicking and moving all around, showing off to us. You weren't even born yet and I knew you was something special. Every day since then, every darn day, my love has grown for you. I'm bursting with love for you, like the flowers blossoming in the church garden. You are my sunshine."

"And you're mine," Hattie said.

"Watch out for yourself in the corporate world. Some of 'em folks have no ethics. It's money, money, money. They'll work you to death and not think a lick of it."

"Mema, you know I can take care of myself. I made it through Harvard."

"Yes, well, we all need help from time to time. Even me, and I'm as tough as old shoe leather."

"I promise I'll ask for help."

"Go to church. It keeps us from losing our way. Even if the sermon is boring, take in the music. Music is good for the soul. Oh, and one final thing. Marry a husband who is funny. Humor will get you through the tough times. And he should be a hard worker. Who needs lazy? He should be patient and kind. And please, let him be a great man of faith."

"I will, someday."

"Remember, love is kindness. And don't you take the first guy who comes along. Wait until I give you a sign."

"A sign?

"When you meet the right one. I'll let you know."

"Of course you will. You've never been anything but frank with me. Why change now?"

"Trust God, Hattie. And I believe Pastor Luis...he's..." Mema whispered, closed her eyes. She'd spoken her last words.

Chapter 17:
When It Crumbles

2013

First Methodist Church was overflowing, folding chairs added in the narthex to accommodate the Fairhope crowd who showed up to honor Mema. Despite the ceiling fans blowing full force, people were fanning themselves with the church bulletins. The air conditioner hummed and then hiccupped, clearly underperforming for this large of a crowd. Never before had Hattie seen the church so crowded. It moved her.

After the hymn "How Deep Our Father's Love," per Mema's request, Father Luis stood to deliver her eulogy. He was dressed in a dark suit with a purple tie, Mema's favorite color. Pastor Luis shuffled awkwardly, slowly to speak. He accidentally tripped as he reached the wood pulpit; the crowd gasped. Thankfully he was able to catch himself before falling. He looked up to the roof of the church, held his stare for a few seconds, as if personally communicating to the heavens above. Maybe he was.

"Today we honor the life of Elizabeth Alice Brown. Mema to many of us. Our Lord Jesus has welcomed her home to a house of many rooms, where she will be welcomed with open arms.

"Mema was a great woman of faith. Our glorious church gardens reflect Mema's love for this church and her desire to display all of God's glory. Blossoms await all who come here. She believed the welcome begins outside, displaying God's gift in colorful flowers.

"Our Mema was unafraid of hard work. She was a taskmaster and an overseer. She certainly kept me on my toes. I was the only one who arrived each day at church as early as she did. So, she put me in charge of making her coffee. Our routine went something like this. We started our day with a morning prayer. 'Keep it short,' she'd say. 'Coffee's waiting. We got work to get done.' Coffee in hand, we'd make our to-do lists. Mema then headed to the gardens, me to my office.

"One day, after a particularly wet spring, she expressed her concern about a lack of garden committee volunteers. She'd asked several people. None wanted to work in the monsoon-like weather we'd been experiencing. Her calendar said it was planting time. She asked me to pray for a special volunteer. I did that very evening.

"The next day I arrived promptly at six thirty. I made the coffee. Didn't see Mema. I went to my office, where I found a pair of Carhartt overalls on my chair with a note. *'Your prayers were answered. Meet me in the garden. Best put the overalls on, you's about to get real dirty.'*"

The crowd in the church chuckled.

"Then there was the time she insisted I needed to relax on my day off, enjoy myself. I mentioned that I preferred to spend my day of rest quietly, sometimes at a bookshop or the library. Darn if

137

she didn't show up at my house the next day at the crack of dawn with fishing gear. I've fished pretty much every Friday morning with her since."

He paused.

"Then there was the time, I was on the phone with the bishop. She marched in my office. I covered the receiver and told her I was speaking with the bishop. I expected she'd understand, returning when I was available.

"'Tell the bishop I have an emergency,' she whispered to me. 'Something needs your attention, immediately.'

"I reluctantly got off the phone, and asked what was so urgent.

"'You wear sneakers at church, even on Sundays.'

"'These, yes,' I said, pointing to my shoes.

"She handed me a pair of Frank's dress shoes. 'Try these on.'

"'This is your emergency?' I asked.

"'Yes, as a matter of fact it is. I bought these leather shoes for Frank before he passed. Someone needs to be using them. They've hardly been worn.'

"'These are a size fifteen, I'm barely a ten.'

"'Thick socks will help. Try 'em on.'

"I did. But only to show how ridiculous it would be for me to wear them.

"'Perfect,' she said.

"'No, not perfect,' I told her. 'I am not wearing Frank's dress shoes. It's dangerous to walk in these, they're five sizes too big.'

"'Tennis shoes don't belong in church,' she huffed.

"'The good Lord does not care about the shoes I wear in church. You, however, seem to.'

"She stewed a minute or two.

"'I just want someone dear to me to wear Frank's shoes,' she said, teary eyed. 'So I don't forget him.'

"God bless that woman," said Father Luis as he wiped his brow, tears the size of diamonds dripping down his cheek.

"Last night as I looked through my closet to make sure I had clean clothes ready for today, I felt a nudge. I tried to ignore it. The nudge wouldn't go away. I couldn't sleep. I knew what I had to do. I got up and called Hattie at two in the morning. I asked if she would be so kind as to find those shoes. She did. Today, I stand in Frank's shoes, not because sneakers don't belong in church, but to honor Mema."

Laughter echoed from the pews.

"Mema fixed me chicken noodle soup when I was ill, always followed by a shot of bourbon. Which I didn't want, but as many of you know, it is very difficult to say no to Mema. She was my first friend here, my best friend." Pastor Luis started to weep. Hattie wondered if he could finish the eulogy.

She felt a nudge. Help him. She stood, made her way to the pulpit. She wore a simple navy dress, pearls, and high heels. She felt far different than the girl who'd once cleaned kennels and trained dogs.

Pastor Luis gave Hattie a grateful smile, and handed the mic over to her. He looked like a small boy instead of a grown man. It was his tears and the oversize shoes. And his cowlick.

"Mema once told me," said Hattie, looking at the diverse group of people sitting in the pews, old and young, black and white, "if I ever came home with anything less than a 3.0 GPA in school, she'd have to spend less time fishing and more time tutoring. The very thought of my grandmother tutoring me was as painful as stepping on a nail. I worked my tail off to earn straight As. Fear, at times, is a good motivator. She used that tactic a few times with me, and more than a few times with my cousin Beau."

The crowd in the church laughed.

"Mostly, though, she gave us unconditional love, every single day. Inside that burly personality of hers was a heart of gold. She'd help anybody, even strangers. And I promise you, they didn't stay strangers long.

"After my grandfather passed away, she spent most of her time gardening and fishing. Inviting people to sit in a rocker on her porch, relax, especially Pastor Luis. She saw a lot of Frank in Pastor Luis," smiled Hattie. "Maybe that's how the whole silly shoe thing started." Several in the church laughed.

"Mema was toughest on those she loved most. If she tried to whip you into shape, like she did me, Beau, and Pastor Luis, rest assured, it was out of love."

Pastor Luis finally had control of his tears, and laughed along with everyone else.

Hattie continued: "Mema would expect each of us to become great people of faith, try our best to follow the Ten Commandments. Be Christlike. This church is filled with her soul. Today, when we leave here, this sacred place she so loved, do something kind for someone. Because up in heaven, Mema is watching us. I imagine she's pushed and shoved her way right next to the good Lord himself.

"And, Mema, while you expect us to march on, our hearts are aching today. We're not sure how to do it without you. You left this world a far better place, me a far better person. I love you."

Hattie walked back to the pew, noticing Lauren and Pastor Luis holding hands tightly. He with his beautiful olive brown skin and Lauren's light cream-colored skin looked like a match made in heaven. They were beautiful together.

A week later Hattie returned to work. She walked up to the building; her chest felt tight. Mema's warning rang in her head like a foghorn. As she entered the office, she promised herself she'd do this job for only one more year. And then follow her heart, apply to grad school. Until then, she must survive. So, she did the thing she'd seen Mama do to survive grief, work night and day. The only difference: Mama loved her work.

* * *

Eventually, Hattie moved out of the Reades' home, renting a small apartment close to work. It looked more like a generic hotel room than a home. She spent so little time there, it didn't matter. The only people she socialized regularly with were Charles, Claire, and Ellie, and even that was becoming less frequent.

Richard, her boss, took notice of Hattie's zealous commitment to work. She outperformed everybody, becoming his prodigy. Richard promoted her to his investment banking division, handling IPOs, privately owned businesses deciding to go public. It required a detailed, astute individual with ethics; nothing could be leaked before a public stock offering. Hattie was perfect for the job.

Three years later, Mema's warning had been put on the back burner so long it was forgotten. Hattie's client list was growing faster than anyone else's at the firm. She was earning a top salary, saving most of it, a nest egg for grad school, someday in the near future. In addition to her regular duties, she was asked to serve as a member of the corporate training team. Her sixty-five-hour work weeks became longer. Sundays turned into workdays. She ignored Pastor Luis's suggestions of finding a church and volunteer. In theory she agreed with him, but he had no idea the pressure she was under.

One Monday morning, after working all weekend, Hattie headed to the conference room to prep for the arrival of a new group of trainees. Richard met her there and asked she do a dry run of her presentation for him. "Flawless," he complimented her after she finished. She glowed.

"I'll welcome the trainees," Richard instructed. "Then turn it over to you."

The new trainees began filtering in, all dressed in similar dark banker-looking suits. At eight o'clock sharp, Richard was ready to begin. The group exchanged professional courtesies. All were present except one trainee, a man named Asher Sinclaire. Richard proceeded without him, asking Hattie to step forward to speak.

"The firm is divided into three divisions," explained Hattie. "I work in the IPO division, and started out like each of you, in the corporate training program."

The door to the conference room flew open, and there stood a sandy-blond-haired man in his late twenties, wearing a sharp-looking herringbone suit, a duffel with the logo GRIT in one hand, a brown leather backpack in the other. He was six feet two with shoulders the width of a refrigerator. His steely blue eyes looked around the table, as if assessing each individual.

"Hello all, I apologize for my tardiness, ran into parking trouble after an early morning hockey game," he said casually.

Richard stood up. "Asher Sinclaire?"

"Righto," Asher said as he took a towel out of the duffel to wipe a bleeding cut on his nose.

"Do you realize you're bleeding?" asked Richard.

"You should see the other guy," Asher laughed.

A few laughs erupted from two trainees in the back.

"Other guy?" asked Richard.

"Some nutcase in a Prius stole my parking spot, it went downhill from there. For him," wiping his scratched cheek with a white handkerchief.

Asher's easygoing confidence reminded Hattie of Beau, and she couldn't help but smile as she watched him.

"I jacked him around, just enough to teach him a lesson. He shouldn't mess with a guy who plays hockey," the new trainee bragged. "Then the idiot goes and scratches me like a girl." He suddenly noticed Hattie. "No offense."

"No offense taken," smiled Hattie.

"Mr. Sinclaire, you've had quite a morning," chided Richard. "This is a conservative investment banking company. We don't have time for that kind of thing here."

Richard was furious, his face was beet red.

All jocks are the same, thought Hattie. Beau would have done the same thing.

"Won't happen again, sir."

"I hope not."

"Okay, then, let's get Mr. Sinclaire caught up with the group," said Hattie, attempting to make him feel welcome. "I was sharing with everyone the structure of the firm. There is a handout on the table, please take one. As I said to the others, stop me any time to ask questions."

Someone asked about the division she worked in. Then Asher raised his hand. "When do we get assigned to our divisions?"

Richard stepped in. "Trainees need to successfully complete eighteen months of training, pass the industry test, and then you'll be assigned to a mentor. The mentor helps determine your career path here."

"Who was your mentor?" Asher asked Hattie.

"Richard," Hattie said, nodding her head respectfully toward her boss.

"Awww, so you were the star of your training class?"

"I wouldn't say that," Hattie said humbly.

"I would," Richard affirmed. "Hattie is a Harvard grad, a workhorse, passed her tests with flying colors. Watch and listen to her; she's going places most of you can't even imagine. Now, let's break for lunch. Catering will be here shortly."

"What do you think?" Richard asked Hattie as they walked down the hallway to their respective offices.

"They seem bright, eager."

"What about the hockey player?"

Hattie blushed, her freckles feeling like they were candles on a birthday cake. "Ahh, I have no idea. What do you think?"

"Big ego, argumentative. Seems like he could be testy."

"Anyone can get testy trying to find a parking space in this city."

"Maybe. He rubs me the wrong way. I wouldn't have hired him."

She silently said to herself, "Because he's not a corporate robot like the rest of us."

After two months into the training program, one of the trainees Hattie really liked from the Midwest dropped out of the program, deciding instead to go to graduate school, an MFA program in Iowa. Hattie was envious; she'd procrastinated exploring grad schools. The firm consumed her life and with the added training responsibilities, she didn't have time to research grad school and complete applications.

She comforted herself with the fact that the group of trainees was doing well, with one exception: Asher Sinclaire. Asher was struggling, his test scores barely passing. His strengths were his social skills, being the life of the party among the trainees, providing the group a needed reprieve in an otherwise intense training program. On Fridays he organized a happy hour for the trainees after work. With the exception of Richard, Asher charmed everyone. Hattie looked forward to seeing him, even just for a minute or two, every morning.

"Hey, super star," Asher said to Hattie one Friday afternoon. "Want to join us lowly trainees tonight for happy hour?"

Hattie had nothing planned for the evening; however, as a trainer, she didn't know whether it was appropriate to socialize with the people she was training.

"Thank you. I have plans. Maybe next time."

"Promise?" Asher asked.

"Actually, no, I can't promise," admitted Hattie. "I need to check our corporate policy. As a trainer, I'm not sure whether fraternizing with the trainees is permitted."

"We're having a drink or two, not breaking SEC rules."

"No, I know. I, uh, uh, just don't know if its proper."

"Well, I hope not. Didn't proper go out of style with Jane Austen?"

Hattie laughed. At least he knew Jane Austen.

"Hey, we let off some steam, a couple of drinks after a tough week. Don't make it complicated." Asher tossed his suit coat over his shoulder and left the building, never looking back.

Hattie watched him. She felt lonely and socially awkward. Her only weekend plans were work and brunch Sunday with Ellie. Even that was a rarity these days. Ellie traveled extensively, marketing the company's specialty beers in the Australian and Asian markets. Customers adored her, and the Reade market share was increasing. Still, Ellie recently admitted to Hattie she was itching to take her cooking more seriously.

The two young women met at Piattini on Newbury Street. Ellie wore a gray cashmere cape over jeans, and Hattie wore a crew neck sweater, jeans, and loafers. After they ordered mimosas, Ellie crooned, "I have big news."

"Do tell!" Hattie said, thinking Ellie may have met someone special.

"I'm finally going to pursue my dream!" Ellie squealed in excitement. "I've decided to quit my job and go to culinary school."

"Congratulations! You'll make an incredible chef, it's your calling. Seriously, you're so talented."

"Thank you, I really think I can do this."

"I didn't know Boston had a culinary school?"

"It doesn't."

"Oh, no. New York?"

"Paris, France."

Hattie teared up. "What will I do without you?"

"You'll be fine, you've got your work. And maybe it's time you look into pursuing your own dreams. Heck, you'll likely meet the man of your dreams while I'm away."

"Not likely. I haven't dated since Harvard."

"You haven't wanted to. You're unapproachable. You give off an aura that you don't want anyone to get close to you."

"I do not."

"Yes, you do. Seriously, the next guy who asks you out, say yes."

"Okay, and what if he's Ted Bundy's twin brother?"

"Charles will rescue you. Heck, I'll come save you. Paris is only an airplane ride away."

* * *

Charles, Claire, and Hattie gathered at Logan International to say goodbye to Ellie. As the three returned to the parking terminal, Charles gave Hattie an extra hug. "Don't be a stranger," Charles told Hattie.

"I won't, I promise. I'll call you soon, Sunday brunch."

"Please do," Claire said tearfully. "We can't lose you both, you're a part of this family."

Hattie worked even more hours. Her bonus that year was close to $200,000. She put the entire amount into savings. Her big expenditure was going to be a vacation to Paris to visit Ellie and she promised grad school, in another year or two. But there was always another deal to work on, another deadline.

One Friday night, while still in the office, she was feeling unusually lonely. She sent a text to Beau, knowing the likelihood of a response was close to zero. *How is Fairhope's fav QB? Still a legend in your own mind? Ha!*

She followed with a text to Ellie. *Seeing Charles and Claire Sunday. Will let you know how they are doing.*

Hattie waited, mentally calculating the time difference. Six in the morning in Paris. Nothing. Why did her two besties have to be on the other side of the world?

She sent a third text to Pastor Luis. Lately, she had been horrible about responding to his texts.

Finishing up a busy week. How is Fairhope?

Her phone pinged immediately.

I miss fishing with Mema. She was right, you know, being outdoors is good for the soul. I convinced Lauren to go fishing tomorrow with me. Her first time. I'll let you know how we do. Blessings, Luis.

Pastor Luis's mention of Lauren and the "we" thing made her feel even lonelier.

"Still here, huh? You are a suck-up," said a familiar voice.

Hattie looked up. Asher was standing there, his tie off, striped shirt collar loosened up, briefcase in one hand, hockey gear in the other.

"Just finishing up."

"Hot date tonight?"

"No," she laughed. "I imagine you can't say the same."

Asher leaned uncomfortably close to Hattie and asked, "Did you ever check on that policy, the one about trainers fraternizing with trainees?"

"I did not. No time. Sorry." He made her feel jittery.

"So, you don't *really* know whether it's permitted or not?"

"I guess you could say that."

"So, if I ask you to join me for a drink tonight, you can't use the excuse it's against corporate policy because you have no idea."

"Asher, I don't think it's a good…"

He interrupted. "Join me for one drink. Honestly, you look like you could use a break from the office."

Hattie looked into his blue eyes, his handsome, confident smile. "I suppose I could join the group...for one drink."

"I'm asking you to join me, you and me."

Hattie blushed, a deep rose on her cheeks.

"If you're uncomfortable being alone with me, I can call my mom and she'll give a reference."

Hattie laughed. Asher was funny and good looking. Why not? "Sure."

"Let's go to Sonsie," he suggested. "We can take my car."

Asher and Hattie left the office together.

"This is it," Asher said, pointing to a shiny black Audi.

"Wow," Hattie said incredulously.

"Wow, yourself," Asher mocked.

"The pay grade for a trainee at the firm must have doubled since I started. Look at this car."

"I may be just a trainee at work. Outside of work, I'm a Sinclaire and we Sinclaires like our nice cars, we're upper class," holding Hattie's door open for her.

Sonsie was a hip, upscale Boston restaurant. It was crowded with a sophisticated-looking Friday night crowd. She took a deep breath, insecure at how stiff and businesslike she looked. Hattie casually pulled out her ponytail holder and let her hair loose. She ran her fingers through it. Asher gently grabbed her elbow, escorting her through a sea of people waiting for tables. The hostess, a young twenty-something African American woman with the most beautiful brown eyes Hattie had ever seen, greeted them. "Mr. Sinclaire, good to see you. How many for dinner this evening?"

"Good to see you, Charise, two of us."

Reaching into the hostess stand, she grabbed a couple of menus. "Follow me, please."

The elegant hostess seated them at a small table overlooking Newbury Street. Hattie slipped off her navy blazer, hoping she looked less formal, unbuttoned the top button of her blouse. She wished she had pearls on like Mema.

"How do you rate getting us a table?" asked Hattie.

"Connections," admitted Asher.

"Nice," said Hattie. "I guess it pays to know people."

"Tell me about it. Is that how you got your job? Was it a 'who you know' type thing?"

"Maybe."

Hattie shared that her best reference was from Charles Reade of the Reade Brewing Company. Ellie, his granddaughter, had been her college roommate.

Hattie could have sworn Asher flinched when she mentioned Ellie's name. She was about to ask if he knew the Reades, but someone with a drink walked by, tripped, and spilled their drink all over her blouse.

"You owe my date an apology," Asher demanded as he stood up to face the drunk.

"Sorry, didn't mean to," the man slurred. "I'll pay for the dry cleaning."

"Darn right you will," exploded Asher. "Look at her blouse."

"It's fine, Asher, really. I'll get the stain out later."

"No, it's not fine," said Asher as he shoved the man.

"Here," the drunk said, tossing Hattie a couple of twenties. "I'll pay for the dry cleaning. Tell your boyfriend to lighten up."

"He's not my boyfriend...and he's just trying to help."

"He's looking for a fight," muttered the drunk, who sauntered away.

"That was kind of nice."

"Nice?" questioned Hattie, rubbing a wet napkin across the stain.

"That he thought I was your boyfriend. A huge compliment to me. You're a beautiful woman. Smart. The firm's golden child."

Hattie blushed. Asher spontaneously leaned over and kissed Hattie in a way she'd never been kissed.

"I hope that was okay," Asher laughed.

"I'm not sure," she said.

"You are definitely a challenge," Asher said. "I'm not leaving you alone for someone else to snap up. We'd be good together."

Hattie had to pinch herself.

In the weeks that followed, Asher romanced Hattie. Candle-light dinners. Drives to the North Shore. Drinks on his rooftop apartment building. And parties, lots of parties.

They kept their relationship under wraps. The secrecy seemed to heighten their attraction to one another. His tailor-made, slim-fitting suits showed off his athleticism. And it wasn't just his good looks she was drawn to; it also was the confident way he carried himself. She'd been friends with plenty of men at Harvard, casually dated two of them, one sophomore year, one junior year. Both men were intellectuals. They were what Ellie called "coffee shop guys," the kind who linger over a cup of coffee and discuss things like the latest political fiasco, or the important issues facing the United Nations. None was the confident, athletic type like Asher.

Asher and Hattie began spending more time together than apart on weekends. Friday evenings they were always with a group of Asher's many friends partying. Weekend days she helped Asher study for the SEC exams. After nine weeks of dating, Asher's practice test scores climbed from 62 percent to 83 percent.

When the training program was nearing the end of its curriculum, the trainees took the official exam. Asher scored 87 percent, higher than anyone expected.

"How did the hockey player pull those kind of scores? I've never seen him work a minute past six since he started," Richard asked Hattie.

"I heard from other trainees he put in extra study time on weekends," said Hattie.

"If that's true, good for him. He still seems slippery to me."

"Slippery?"

"Yeah, I can't put my finger on it," said Richard. "I don't trust him."

"I think you may be wrong. The trainees seem to really like Asher."

"You're young, unjaded," scoffed Richard. "Watch and see. Eventually, someone's true character surfaces."

She wished Richard appreciated Asher's qualities, or at least stopped trashing him. Asher was good for her. For the first time in her life, she was not the academic kid, the quiet girl everyone in school ignored. She was Asher's girlfriend and was desperately trying to be outgoing, flirtatious, and fun. His friends enjoyed her company. She finally was part of the in crowd, and she liked it.

The firm assigned Asher to the firm's real estate division. He'd mentioned his uncle worked in real estate for years. She thought it was a good fit for Asher and the firm.

One Thursday afternoon at work, Hattie received a text from Asher.

Family wants to meet for dinner tonight. Can you join us?

She was working one of the biggest deals in the firm's history. She was feeling overwhelmed with all the work needing to be completed.

Richard asked me to stay late.

She prayed there'd be another chance to meet his family. Her phone pinged. *This is important. Family.*

Chapter 18:
A New and Different
Hattie

Hattie rarely told a lie. When she did, it was only a white lie, something said to prevent hurt feelings. Like when Mema asked, "Is the dress perfect for the fall festival?" And Hattie would say yes, even though it looked like it sat in the attic for decades.

Hattie desperately wanted to meet Asher's family. One white lie. Once. Not a big deal. She wouldn't do it again.

"I have a small family emergency I need to tend to this afternoon, is it okay if I leave early?" asked Hattie as she stopped into Richard's corner office. He was facing his computer and swung his chair around to look at her. His reading glasses dropping midnose, his eyebrows furrowed. He actually looked concerned.

"Of course, is it your cousin, the one in the military?" Hattie had recently shared Beau was in the SEALs, which Richard greatly admired.

"Oh, no, nothing like that. Some things I need to take care of for my grandmother's estate."

"Do what you need to do. We'll see you early tomorrow."

"Thank you, I'll be in early, five thirty."

Hattie sent a text to Asher. *What time is dinner and where?*
Capitol Grille. 6:00.
I'll be there.

Then she prayed she wouldn't run into anyone from the firm, particularly her boss.

At four Hattie logged off her computer, grabbed her briefcase and walked to her apartment. She searched her closet for the right outfit to meet Asher's family. She had a closet filled with business suits, but few dresses, and those were far more professional than social. She had a black sleeveless dress that could work. She usually wore a blazer over it. But she'd wear it as a separate. It would have to do. As she brushed her long hair, she thought about Ellie living in Paris. Mema was gone. Mama was gone. Hattie missed being part of a family.

She looked forward to meeting Asher's parents, a family. Maybe even some day…She stopped herself.

Asher instructed her to valet her car. She rarely used valet, seemed like a luxury. She wanted to arrive on time and did as Asher suggested.

"How may I help you?" the host, an elderly man in his seventies, asked when she arrived at the restaurant.

"I'm meeting the Sinclaire family," Hattie said. "Have they arrived yet?"

"Yes, they are in the bar area," said the host. "I believe they decided to eat in there."

"Oh," said Hattie, somewhat surprised.

It was dimly lit in the bar. The Boston Bruins hockey game was playing on the flat screen above the bartender.

"Hattie, we're over here," hollered Asher, waving her over. He was sitting on a barstool, next to him a man, larger than Asher, but definitely a family resemblance with sandy brown hair and the same piercing blue eyes. She guessed it was Asher's father.

Asher stood, giving her a sweet peck on the cheek. Her knees weakened.

"Hello, you," he smiled. "Ditched the rigid business attire tonight, huh? Good call. You look amazing," running his fingers down her sleeveless arm.

"Thank you," flushed Hattie, hating that she acted like a schoolgirl every time he complimented her.

"Hey, Asher, you *gonna* introduce me to this beauty?" said the middle-aged man with gel-slicked hair tucked behind his ears. He was good looking like Asher, except that he carried a notable paunch, which protruded over his extremely tight gray pants. He wore gold chain bracelets on his right hand and a diamond ring on his left pinky finger.

"Hattie, this is my Uncle Monte, my father's younger brother. Monte moved to Boston from Chicago. He's in commercial real estate."

"A pleasure to meet you," Hattie said warmly, extending her hand to shake Monte's.

"Yeah, babe, you too."

"We thought we'd eat in the bar, less formal," said Asher.

"Will your parents mind?"

"My parents?"

"You said your family was coming, right?"

"Yeah, right, my uncle. Monte is interested in what you do, specifically the IPOs. Maybe we can figure out how the firm can help fund his real estate business. You, two, go ahead and talk business. I've got to hit the men's room."

"Bartender," hollered Monte. "A drink for the young lady!"

"What can I get you?" the bartender asked, placing a cocktail napkin in front of Hattie.

"A glass of rosé."

"And you, sir?"

"Scotch on the rocks."

Once the bartender stepped away, Monte bent his head in close to Hattie. She could smell his cologne, musky. It was overwhelming.

"Asher tells me you got a lot of pull at the firm. You're, uh, like the corporate superstar."

"I try my best."

"You are such an innocent babe," teased Monte, putting his arm around her shoulder. "A virgin, huh? A virgin investment banker. I bet Asher is eating you up like a caramel apple."

Monte was crude. If she worked for someone like him, she'd ask him to remove his arm or report him to her boss. But this was Asher's uncle.

She breathed a sigh of relief when she saw Asher returning to the table.

"Did you give Monte useful info?" asked Asher.

"We were just getting to know each other," Monte laughed. "She's a sweetheart."

"That she is. Hattie, tell Monte about what you're in charge of."

She wanted to please Asher and was explaining her job when a few of Asher's hockey buddies showed up for a postgame celebration.

"Sinclaire, what the hell are you doing here?"

"Same thing you are," Asher hollered back. "Having a couple drinks, dinner."

"Is this her?" One of the players dressed in a Bruins hockey jersey asked. "Are you really this loser's boss?"

"No," Hattie laughed. "Coworker."

"You're all Asher talks about these days," the player teased. "He never plays hockey with us anymore. Says he has other priorities."

"I see why," another player, dressed in a wool men's dress coat, commented in a Canadian accent. "Sinclaire's right, you are beautiful. Says you're smart too."

Hattie smiled.

"You are the best," Asher whispered to Hattie as he leaned over and kissed her, this time on the lips. His hockey pals cheered.

"Hey guys," Monte interrupted. "Don't mean to bust up the party, but we're having a business dinner. So maybe find yourselves another place to...act stupid."

A handsome dark-haired, dark-skinned man wearing a navy quarter zip, who Hattie later learned was team captain, took Hattie's hand in his. "If ever the Sinclaire men mistreat you, call me."

"Or call me!" another of the players chimed in. Another hollered on his way to a different table, "She's way too classy for you, Sinclaire."

"Ditch him while you can! He's trouble," said another player.

Hattie laughed. Asher, however, was as red as a beet.

"Man, I need to relax, the guys teasing you got me all jacked up," said Asher, rolling his neck around. "I'll get us another round."

Hattie had to be sharp tomorrow, up early. She set her drinks aside, sticking to water. Meanwhile Monte and Asher had downed three drinks each before dinner.

"You ever give out the family and friends stock tips before the IPOs?" asked Monte.

"No," Hattie said firmly, shaking her head. "Strict rules about insider trading."

"People do it all the time," commented Monte. "How else do you think the rich get richer?"

"Not where I work. If you'll excuse me, I have to use the ladies room."

She was exhausted and starving. Monte's conversation felt more like an FBI interrogation. She looked in the bathroom mirror. Her mascara was slightly smudged and her dress wrinkled. She wanted to go home, wished she'd never made up a story to leave work early. This whole night had snowballed. Why did she feel like it was turning into a dangerous avalanche?

When Hattie returned to the table, dinner was waiting. Finally. After dinner Monte ordered another round. Hattie cringed, hoping the evening would end soon. When the drinks were served, Hattie moved hers to the side.

"Asher, I should head home soon. I've got an early morning tomorrow."

"Okay, but first a toast, to us, and new opportunities," slurred Monte.

"Finish your drink, Monte ordered for you, and we'll head out," encouraged Asher.

She forced it down.

The next morning Hattie woke with a jarring headache. She couldn't recall leaving the restaurant, or how she got home. Her thoughts were fuzzy. Her body ached like she had the flu. Despite feeling awful, a train wreck couldn't stop her from being at the office today. Richard was counting on her.

She climbed out of bed to go the bathroom and grabbed her phone to see how much longer until her alarm went off.

Her phone read 8:30 a.m. She took a second look.

"This can't be happening, not today," Hattie said. She jolted out of bed, panicking. She heard her apartment door open. Someone was entering her apartment. She grabbed her phone, ready to dial 911.

"I have coffee and scones, sleepyhead," said Asher, whistling.

"How did you get in here?" a startled Hattie asked.

"You gave me your key, remember?"

She looked at him blankly.

"Last night you insisted I take it. I drove your Jeep home for you, you were a little unsteady," winking at her.

"I don't remember, sorry. I think I've got the flu, but I've got to get to work," said Hattie in a panicked voice. "I promised I'd be there at five thirty this morning. I need to call Richard. And let him know I'm running late. Jeez. How did this happen?"

"Relax. I emailed Richard and said you weren't feeling well, a stomach bug."

"What?"

"I sent it from your email, used your laptop, pretending to be you. Richard has no idea it was from me."

"Asher, why?"

"Hey, I did you a favor. You got really crazy last night. Work certainly wasn't on your mind. And then you passed out."

Hattie didn't recall drinking much at all. The only drink she actually finished was the last round ordered when she was in the restroom. She recalled setting all the others aside. Or at least she thought she did.

"Listen, forget about work for once, Richard will survive. If you ask me, they don't appreciate you enough. I want to take care of you today. You were so sweet to Monte last night."

"Uh, sure, yes, of course."

"Good. I want to make you feel better. I'm serving you breakfast in bed."

After breakfast, Hattie watched as Asher pulled off his shirt and jeans. He was the kind of guy who dated women who looked like models. Still, he reached for her, and as always, it surprised her.

Chapter 19:
Life in the Fast Lane

It was past ten when Asher and Hattie finally climbed out of bed. While Asher showered, Hattie grabbed her robe, made coffee, and sat down at her desk to check emails. Several emails from Richard, the first was hoping she was feeling better. She was grateful he seemed sincere. The remaining emails pertained to the IPO deal. She began hammering away on the keyboard, determined to make up for today's transgression.

"Hattie, I'm heading to the gym." Asher leaned over to kiss her. "I don't know what's up for the weekend, I'm thinking I might join the guys at Stowe, play some hockey, maybe snowboard."

"I was hoping," she hesitated, "we might spend time together today, since I'm home."

"You know me, I can't sit still," Asher laughed. "Get some rest. I'm going to work out, then later this afternoon catching a ride to Stowe. I'll see you Monday."

Her heart sank as he slammed the door. She missed him already.

Her phone pinged. She smiled, betting he missed her too.

Instead, it was a text from Pastor Luis.

Good people leave memories that bless us. Proverbs 10:7. Your family is good people, leaving me with wonderful memories. I miss Beth and Mema. I miss you.

While reading Luis's text, Hattie smelled a whiff of lavender, Mema's favorite. If Mema were still alive, would Asher have come with her to Fairhope, meet her family? What would he have thought of her grandmother with a heart the size of Texas who fished from the town pier and loved digging in dirt? What would Asher think of her hometown?

Hattie sniffed again, wishing she could have introduced Asher to Mema. The lavender scent, however, was gone.

* * *

Hattie finally caught up on emails. She showered and was hanging up the clothes she'd worn last night. She felt something in the pocket of her dress. Reaching in, she found a credit card receipt from last night's dinner at Capitol Grill. A whopping $685. She examined the receipt. It was charged to her card, her signature, albeit shakier than usual. She broke out in sweat.

"Asher wouldn't stick me with the check from last night," she thought. "He invited me." She studied the receipt, numerous drinks, two filets, and a salmon salad. Monte and Asher feasted like kings, drank like fish, and she'd paid the tab. She rubbed her forehead, recalling Asher mentioning he sometimes maxed out his credit card waiting on a commission check. That must be it. She thought of texting Asher to ask. But it felt awkward. Surely Asher would pay her back.

It was a solitary weekend for Hattie, spending most of it working. She arrived at the office around 5:30 a.m. on Monday. Like clockwork, Richard arrived at six.

"Glad to see you're back, feeling okay?"

"Yes, thank you. It must have been a twenty-four-hour stomach bug."

"You did great work Friday afternoon, all while keeping your germs at home. Good call. Which reminds me, corporate security contacted me. Someone attempted to log in on your computer at 1:00 a.m. Friday, unsuccessful hack. Attempted opening a couple of the confidential IPO folders. I assume it wasn't you, you were down and out, right? The IT department needs me to verify that it wasn't you?"

"No, yes, you're right. It wasn't me." Hattie was shrouded with guilt about lying and calling in sick.

"That's what I thought. Don't worry about it. It happens. I'll have the tech folks check into it."

All morning Hattie kept glancing out her office, wanting to get a glimpse of Asher. Most employees arrived by seven thirty. Asher finally made his grand entrance a little before nine. He looked relaxed, happy, and devilishly handsome in what looked like another new suit. He saw her watching him and winked. Then turned left, heading to his cubicle. Seeing Asher made her heart flutter. She did her best to suppress her grin.

Asher and Hattie's relationship flourished like daisies in the summer. They kept it under wraps, neither ready to make it public, Hattie dreading the attention of an office romance.

They typically saw each other one or two nights during the week and on the weekends, often meeting Asher's friends for happy hours. She worked hard to fit in, laughing a bit too loud at jokes and smiling until her face hurt.

One morning when Hattie was grabbing a cup of coffee in the employee break room, she overheard a couple of the administrative assistants from the real estate division talking. She couldn't help listening. Asher worked in their department.

"He's always going somewhere really cool, like this past weekend. He was skiing at Stowe. He told me he's going to Atlantic City with his uncle," one of them shared. "He's a total jet-setter."

"And a hottie," said the other young woman.

Hattie took her time adding cream to her coffee, listening. Asher was in Stowe last weekend, but he hadn't said a thing about Atlantic City.

"I heard his manager is getting really miffed because he hasn't made his quarterly sales numbers," said the other executive assistant.

Hattie quietly exited the break room.

She returned to her desk and texted Asher. *Need to talk. Tonight?*

He texted back. *No can do. Headed to Atlantic City tonight.*

Business? Hattie texted.

Guess you could call it that.

Hattie frantically texted back. *Management frowns on taking vacation days when you haven't made your numbers.*

She waited, staring at her phone.

He didn't text back.

Hattie couldn't sleep that night, worrying she'd upset Asher. She kept checking her phone every few minutes.

Sunday night her phone pinged.

Back in town. Missed u. —A.

Hattie said a grateful thank-you to God. Asher was back. He missed her.

Monday morning, Hattie set her alarm fifteen minutes earlier, taking time to put on makeup, something she seldom did. She tried to remember the makeup techniques the woman on the Greyhound bus taught her. What was that lady's name? The middle-aged woman who was so funny and kind. The one who said something like makeup was like Miracle-Gro to a flower. Bess. Bess had taken care of her on that trip, keeping the creepy guy away from her. Mema was right, God works through people. Hattie smelled lavender, and mentally drifted back to Fairhope, thinking of her quiet Mama and her feisty, loving Mema. Where was the scent coming from? Her memory?

When Hattie got to the office, Richard asked her to step into his office, closing the door behind her. He seemed nervous, pacing like a caged lion.

"Today is going to be unpleasant around here," conceded Richard. "There's going to be a layoff. Ten percent of our personnel."

Hattie's heart sank. She'd worked her tail off since day one. What would she do now? Where would she go? Back to Fairhope? Nothing was there for her. She loved Boston. What about she and Asher? Hattie was shaking her leg nervously and began chewing her already short nails.

"Hattie, calm down, it's nothing you need to worry about. The layoff mostly affects the firm's real estate division. It's a brutal business, dependent on the economy. We've taken some big hits this year. We're getting rid of the low performers."

She thought about Asher, who hadn't made his quarterly numbers.

"The rumor mill will begin around nine, after several employees are called to Human Resources. Then, the laid-off employees will be escorted out of the office around ten thirty. It's important not to let this layoff distract us. You're doing a great job. Keep it up."

It happened just like Richard said it would. As she was returning to her office, she heard voices in the hallway. She stretched her neck to see. A small group of employees were carrying boxes, walking to the exit. Asher had his arms around two young women brokers, one who had been in his training class. Both women were crying, one leaning her head on Asher's shoulder. The other wiped her tears while Asher squeezed her shoulder. Hattie wondered where Asher was going with those women.

No one seemed to do any work after the layoff. Even Hattie was having a difficult time. She was feeling survivor's guilt. She had sent Asher two text messages checking on him. He never responded. She wrapped up her work around seven. Hungry and tired, she headed to her apartment.

After Hattie changed into a T-shirt and jeans, she sent Asher another text. *How r u?*

Her phone pinged. *Partying with friends. Want to meet us?*

Honestly, she didn't. What she really wanted was to talk to him one on one. Let him know she was there for him.

She texted back. *Where?*

She waited. No message back. Fifteen minutes went by, then thirty. An hour. She fell asleep on the couch, hoping for a message that never came.

* * *

Hattie's alarm went off at five in the morning. Once again, she grabbed her phone. Still no message from Asher. Maybe he needed some space from her. After all she was gainfully employed, still the darling of the firm as Asher liked to point out. By six she was at the office. She logged onto her computer to begin financial analysis of her latest client when her phone pinged. She grabbed for her phone as if saving the life of someone clinging to the side of a building.

Pulled an all-nighter. Working on Sunday's sermon. It's titled: What We Can Learn from Dogs. The things your mom taught me. I sure miss seeing the Brown family seated in the front pew. Sending prayerful thoughts your way. In Him, Luis.

Hattie wished it'd been Asher rather than Luis. Her phone pinged a second time. What wisdom did Luis have for her now? she disappointedly thought.

Way hungover, babe. I gotta sleep it off. Dinner Saturday?

Hattie breathed a sigh of relief. He still cared. Saturday worked perfectly with her schedule. She had Friday dinner plans with Charles and Claire and absolutely couldn't cancel again.

Of course. U ok?

Wounded but not dead. C U soon.

She and Asher would get through this, together. They'd figure out his next opportunity. He was too entrepreneurial for a conservative banking firm. He'd find something better, something that suited his vibrant personality. She stood taller. This actually might be a good thing for their relationship.

Chapter 20:
An Unexpected Visitor

*W*here *r u? Asher texted.*

Hattie was at Charles and Claire's home getting the latest news on Ellie's culinary adventure in Paris. It felt good to be with them. The Reades were like family. The dinner was delicious, roasted chicken. Hattie hated that she'd let them become a low priority in her life. She excused herself from the table to respond to Asher's text.

Back Bay. Having dinner with a friend's parents. All okay?

No. I'm at your apartment. I need you. NOW!

I'll be there shortly.

Hattie returned to the table, explaining a friend needed help, car problems. Another white lie. She raced to her apartment. Asher was waiting in his black Audi, the music cranked. She knocked on his car window. He smiled, rolling down the window. His car smelled like bourbon.

"I want to talk about our plans," slurred Asher.

"Our plans?" Hattie was confused.

"Yes."

"You want to come up?" she offered.

Asher parked his car. Hattie waited in the lobby for him.

As they rode the elevator, Asher reached for her hand, holding it tight. "I want you to meet my family tomorrow night, dinner at my parents' house."

"Of course, I'd love to."

Hattie could hardly stop herself from grinning. Finally.

"What should I wear?"

"Nice casual. I'll pick you up at a little before six."

They got off on her floor.

"Hey," Asher said, running the inside of his thumb down Hattie's cheek.

"Hey yourself," she said, trying to be flirtatious.

"Are you sure you weren't out with some other guy tonight? Like Richard? You're his 'go-to girl' who can do no wrong. I bet he has the hots for you."

She rolled her eyes.

"Seriously, Asher. Richard is happily married."

Asher looked into Hattie's eyes. Her long wavy hair which she always kept in a ponytail at work, flowed freely down her back. She was dressed in a classic white button-down blouse and jeans. Leather loafers. "You're a classy babe," he said, nuzzling the side of her neck. "I love when you wear something other than uptight business suits."

Asher left at the crack of dawn the next morning to play a pick-up hockey game with his former teammates. When Hattie woke, she felt rested and excited. She, Hattie Brown, was going to meet her boyfriend's family. This was a big deal. She sorted through her closet, trying to figure out what to wear. Nothing in her wardrobe was quite right. She threw on jeans, her Converse, a gray tee, a yellow cardigan, and left for Newbury Street to shop. She wanted to look perfect. The people she met tonight could be her future family. She was so excited, she hugged herself.

By noon, she'd picked out a dusty pink hibiscus flowered dress with bell sleeves from Anthropologie. Flirty and fun, nothing serious like what she typically picked out.

"The dress looks beautiful on you, you're a real Southern belle," the saleswoman exclaimed. "And your accent is equally lovely."

"Thank you, that is so kind."

Hattie hurried down Commonwealth Avenue back to her apartment. She passed an elderly couple walking arm in arm, and thought of Mema and her grandfather, Frank. The scent of lavender surrounded her. Lately, whenever Hattie thought of love or family, she smelled lavender. It likely was coincidental. But it reminded her of when Mema told her, "I'll give you a sign when you meet the right one." Was this it? Asher?

An hour before Asher was to pick her up, she received a text message from Beau. A rarity these days. He'd been assigned to a special forces unit.

You'd be proud of me, working super hard. Guess I'm more like you than I thought. It's you and me now. And we got Luis. We are family. Don't forget it. Miss u.

Her doorbell buzzed, and instantly she had butterflies.

"Ready to meet the family?" Asher was dressed in a blue sports coat, a plaid button-down shirt, faded designer jeans, and a new pair of Italian loafers.

"I don't know," she said nervously. "Is anyone ever ready to meet their significant other's family?"

"They'll love you," Asher said confidently. "Just don't say y'all and they won't make fun of you."

"Seriously?"

"Yeah, the whole Southern accent thing makes you sound like you're from a Podunk town in the South. It slips out every now and then."

That stung. The salesclerk who helped her select a dress for tonight said she adored Hattie's Southern drawl.

There was a moment of awkward silence.

"So, uh, let's head out to the 'burbs. I'll brief you on my family. What to say, what not to say."

"Okay," Hattie said hesitantly, suddenly feeling the excitement drain from her and nervous exhaustion taking over.

Asher floored the gas out of the parking ramp like he was in the Indy 500.

"Fun, huh? The purr of the engine. Love it. Okay, listen up. My dad, John, is Monte's older brother. Dad started out in the brokerage business, he now sells software for cybersecurity. Makes a good living. He wanted to sell the cyber software to the firm, no chance now. He's gonna be ticked when he finds out I'm no longer working there."

Hattie remained quiet, not certain how to respond.

"My mom, Francine," continued Asher, "is a former beauty pageant queen, Miss Illinois."

"You're kidding, right?"

"No, my friends used to tease me about how hot she was. Dad's really into having a good-looking wife. Four kids later, and she looks like a model. No fat. No wrinkles. We call her the Botox Mama."

"That's awful."

"Not really. She looks good. That's what matters. I love my mom, but she can be a snob. It's all about who you know, what you have, where you live. You'll see. She grew up with no money. My dad says that's why she's a big social climber. If you get to know her, Mom's a lot of fun, loves to party. And Dad teases her that she loves to spend his money." Asher laughed.

"What about your dad, what's he like?"

"You're about to find out," said Asher, pulling into a circular driveway. Parked in the circle drive was a blue Jeep Cherokee, a black Porsche, and a white Lexus SUV.

"Home sweet home."

Hattie's eyes widened. Asher's family's home was a six-bedroom modern house so different than the small farmhouse she'd grown up in.

"It's huge!" exclaimed Hattie, thinking of Mama's simple farmhouse and Mema's quaint cottage on the Gulf.

"Cool, right? A pool in back, too. In the summer, it's the ultimate party house."

Asher's mother answered the door, looking as if she'd walked off the cover of a women's magazine. Hattie noticed her perfect makeup, worn like a news anchor for the camera. Shoulder-length jet black hair. Francine wore black slacks and a gorgeous silk blouse. Her simple, elegant outfit was offset with an abundance of jewels, rings on every finger.

"Come in, you two, we're so curious to meet you, Hattie," admitted Francine. "It's not every day Asher invites a young lady to a family dinner."

"Yeah, it's more like a dozen girls invited over when you and Dad are out of town. Pool parties with his BC babes," said one of Asher's brothers, who walked by with lacrosse gear.

Hattie blushed.

"Shut up, Harrison," said Asher.

"Why? It's true."

"Boys, please. We have a guest. Let's head into the living room," Francine suggested. "Hattie, would you care for a cocktail?"

"A glass of wine would be perfect. Thank you."

"Red or white?"

"White, thank you," said Hattie, noticing the variety of artwork in the home. Modern pieces, a Picasso-type look. It was a colorful, energetic room.

"Your home is lovely."

"Thank you. My favorite is the art in this room, it cost us a fortune. Worth every penny."

"Only you, sweetheart, think it's worth the money you spent on art," Asher's dad announced as he walked in with a swagger even Asher couldn't match. He dressed remarkably similar to Asher, sans the jeans, instead wearing sage green chinos.

"I could paint that crap," pointing to the piece above the fireplace, "with a dozen martinis under my belt. Speaking of martinis, Fran, where is mine?"

"John is teasing about the artwork, not about the martini," said Fran, immediately walking over to the fully stocked bar. "If he doesn't have one by six, he growls like a guard dog."

"Heavy on the vermouth tonight, sweetheart," he directed his wife.

"Forgive me, Hattie, an unusual name by the way, I'm John Sinclaire," extending his hand out toward Hattie. "Asher tells me you're a fireball in the IPO business."

John had the grip of an athlete. Hattie's grip was clammy. Nerves did that to her.

"Thank you," said Hattie. "I've heard great things about you as well."

John and Hattie exchanged pleasantries. While the others found a seat, John stood by the marble fireplace mantel, drilling Hattie with questions about the firm.

"Enough business talk," Francine interrupted. "Asher, please call your sister and brothers down to join us, dinner will be ready soon."

"Dinner. Now!" hollered Asher.

"Asher, really?" his mother scolded him. Hattie, though, could tell how much she adored her eldest son. His father, John, on the other hand, seemed standoffish toward his eldest.

Asher's brothers raced each other down the stairs.

"Where do you want us to sit?" asked Harrison, the taller of the two younger brothers.

"Hey, he brought a girl," Sean, Asher's youngest brother, said, as if Hattie weren't standing right there.

"This is Sean, and you already met Harrison," Asher said. "Dumb and dumber. Guys, this is Hattie."

"Nice to meet you both."

"Same," said Sean.

"Asher, please sit to the left of your father. Harrison, Sean, you two may sit over here. I'll sit close to the kitchen," instructed Francine. "Hattie, please sit across from Asher. Where is that daughter of mine?"

"Right here, mother," snapped Asher's sister, Addy, as she strutted in the room wearing a black lacy, low-cut blouse with a skin-tight purple skirt and ankle boots. Addy was gorgeous, a younger version of Asher's mother but with longer hair. Same beautiful brown eyes, red lips, perfect posture.

"Addy, dear, please introduce yourself to Asher's friend, Hattie," Francine suggested as she dished up lasagna and salad.

"Hi," said Addy, plopping in the remaining dining room chair.

"Hello Addy," Hattie cheerfully said. "It's good to finally meet you in person. Asher has told me how much fun y'all have together."

"Y'all? *Whaaat?*" Addy remarked rudely. "Are you from the South or something?"

"Hattie graduated from Harvard," Asher interrupted.

"Doesn't sound like it," Addy said snidely.

"I love Southern accents," Francine interjected. "It's refreshing."

"Southerners sound stupid," Addy said, glaring at Asher.

"Don't take Addy personally," John interjected. "Ever since Addy became a teenager, she's been busting my chops, too."

"She's the only one that gets away with it," teased Asher.

Hattie sunk lower in her chair, embarrassed. No one seemed to notice her. Hattie listened while the Sinclaire family discussed the party Addy was going to this evening—a group of girls from school who played hockey. Hockey was a foreign sport to Hattie. She listened closely, looking for an opportunity to say something, be part of the group. Her phone pinged. She discreetly glanced down to see if it was someone from work. No, it was Pastor Luis. A photo of the sunset over the water in Fairhope: *Our Creator's gift.*

Asher's brother Sean asked Hattie about Harvard. Finally, her opportunity to talk. "One of the best experiences of my…" began Hattie.

"May I be excused," interrupted Addy. "I promised my friends I'd drive to the party, and this is boring."

"Yes, dear, thank you for joining us," said Francine.

"Be home at a decent time," commanded John.

"Yeah right," Addy laughed.

Harrison and Sean followed their sister's lead, excusing themselves.

Hattie was secretly relieved. She'd barely said a word at dinner, finding it difficult to join a family conversation of sparring inside jokes and sports talk. Maybe now, in a small group, it'd be easier to converse, get to know Asher's parents and them her.

"Anyone want another drink?" John asked.

Asher grabbed a beer. Francine made a gin and tonic. Hattie passed on a second glass of wine. She didn't want a repeat of what happened the night they were with Monte.

"Hattie, you're in the IPO division, maybe you can help my younger brother, Monte. He needs venture capital to grow his commercial real estate business. He's thought about taking his company public. Great guy, you'll love him, I'll introduce you."

"Actually, I've met Monte."

"Great, then you know what a good guy he is. I look forward to the firm helping him. Monte's making a real impact in Boston, moved here from Chicago. He's big into gentrifying neighbor-

177

hoods, and goes to a bunch of charity events, good for business connections, you know what I'm saying."

"Married and divorced three times," Francine interjected. "Monte can't keep his you-know-what in his—"

"Fran, you love to insult my family. Like yours is anything to brag about."

Husband and wife went back and forth, cutting down each other's family.

This definitely was different than her family dinners with Pastor Luis, or for that matter, dinner with Ellie's family. When John's sparring with Francine ran its course, it seemed he was ready for a new opponent.

"Asher, by the way, if you think I'm going to let you screw your old man out the rent money you owe me, you're dead wrong," chided Asher's father. "Get me paid ASAP. Or I'll boot you out of there. I gotta list a mile long of people who want to rent in that building."

"Yeah, about that, Dad, you may have to give me a break. There was a layoff at the firm."

"Jeez, and I bet you're gonna tell me you were one of 'em. What the hell you gonna do now?"

"Easy, Dad. I'm going into commercial real estate, like Uncle Monte. Maybe even partner with him on a few deals. Monte and I and, actually, Hattie talked a few weeks back."

"Monte's got cash flow problems up the wazoo, he can't pay you much. And it's not easy, commercial real estate, you need money, experience."

"I'll be fine, I've got this figured out."

"What do you think, Hattie?" asked John.

"I think," Hattie said thoughtfully. "Asher will do really well, at whatever he wants to do."

"I agree," said Francine. "He's a remarkable young man."

John ignored them both. "Let's get one thing clear, Asher, I'll have three kids in college next year, if your sister is lucky enough to get accepted. Get the rent paid, even if it means working at Dunkin'."

Asher downed his beer. His cheeks burned. Hattie could tell he was embarrassed.

"I got this, Dad. Actually, we got this, Hattie and me. You know, she makes close to what you do, and she's half your age."

She recognized pride in Asher's voice.

"Half a million bucks?" scoffed John. "Yeah, right. A mere thirty-something-year-old."

"Yep, Dad, half a mil last year, my girlfriend."

That was, in fact, exactly what she'd made. It'd been a record-breaking year for the IPO division and their bonuses reflected it. She was Richard's right-hand person; he paid her well. He knew headhunters contacted her regularly with job opportunities. She wondered how Asher knew what she earned last year. They never discussed her salary.

"So, don't worry about me paying you the rent, we're, uh, well, we're"—pointing to Hattie—"better than fine, we're great. Really great. I was going to do this later, but I think I'll do it right here, right now with the people who got my back. Right, Dad?"

Asher was mouthy after a few drinks, more aggressive than usual. She silently prayed they could leave soon. She was mentally exhausted and tried to catch Asher's eye to let him know they should leave. But Asher got up from his chair, wiped his palms on his jeans.

"Dad, why don't you get us a couple of your best Cuban cigars?" Asher smirked. "I think a celebration may be in order."

"A celebration? Son, you've got no job, you're behind on rent. Your future plan is working with my brother. Hardly cause for celebration."

"John, please," begged Francine.

Hattie sat quietly, taking in the dining room's decor. Purple-and-gold paisley wallpaper with a dramatic, almost gaudy gold chandelier. Velveteen fabric in zebra stripes covered the chairs. Earlier in the evening, she thought it breathtakingly glamorous; now it seemed suffocating, she could hardly breathe. She saw the reflection of Asher in the wall of mirrors. He was walking around the dining table toward her. She gasped when he knelt down next to her. What in the world was he doing?

Asher cleared his throat, then looked directly into Hattie's eyes. She could see their reflection in the mirror. They made a handsome couple.

"Hattie Brown, will you marry me?"

"Me?" questioned Hattie, wondering if Asher was drunk.

"Yes, you, funny girl."

Chapter 21:
Yes or No?

All eyes were on her. They were looking at her, waiting for an answer.

"Yes, of course I will marry you!" said Hattie squeezing Asher's hands.

"Welcome to the family," Francine said warmly as she got up from her chair to embrace Hattie. "Asher, dear, I hope you asked Hattie's father first."

"Oh, I didn't need to. Hattie's parents passed away," Asher said kissing Hattie. "We're her family now."

"Well then, I'm sure your parents are looking down from heaven, and are happy for you," Francine said sweetly.

Hattie looked around at the luxurious home. Daddy would be uncomfortable in this home, with these people. He was a down-to-earth guy. The vocal boxing match she witnessed this evening was as foreign to the Brown family as the fancy house. Daddy loved being a plumber, Mama a dog trainer. They wouldn't have fit in here. Hattie suddenly ached with intense loss. She needed her parents right now. Their advice. Their approval. She'd dreamed about this moment, but she didn't feel happy. Why didn't she feel happy? Then, as quick as a falling star drops from the sky, she mentally scolded herself. She was getting what she longed for: a handsome husband with a successful East Coast family.

"Congratulations!" said John. "A good marriage is like a good business deal, both sides win. Well done, son."

On the drive home, Asher, typically talkative, was unusually quiet.

Hattie took the first step.

"Asher, wow, this is all a big surprise, a shock, really."

"Yeah, I know. It's a good thing, I mean a great thing. Right?"

"Of course, I'm just caught off guard. You never indicated we were headed this direction. So soon…"

"We make a great team, a future power couple. And it's a bonus my dad can't hassle me about finding a job or past-due rent. Not when my future wife makes more than he does."

"Yeah, about that, until you find a job, maybe I can help you with rent."

"Or, maybe we could just move in together?" He smiled.

She smiled back, not letting her reservations show about how fast this was all happening.

When he parked the car, Asher swept Hattie in to his arms. "I love you," he whispered into her ear. "We're good together."

* * *

Asher went golfing, giving Hattie the much-needed alone time she craved to wrap her head around the marriage proposal. She felt like she was on an emotional rollercoaster, one moment flying high, the next panicking. She grabbed her phone and FaceTimed Ellie, desperate to talk to someone.

"How's my favorite chef?" Hattie asked, noticing Ellie was dressed in her chef's uniform on a Sunday evening. Her long blond hair was tied back in a ponytail and she wore no makeup. Still, Ellie was stunning.

"I didn't know you had culinary school on Sundays?"

"I normally don't. I went in today to hone my skills. These French instructors are like sharks, circling the weak, ready to devour the less talented souls. I don't want to get eaten up by them."

"They can stop circling. You're way too talented."

"You're sweet. Thank you."

"How is Paris?"

"I can't say I've seen much of it, too busy cooking."

"You look great, as always."

"Awwww, thanks, not compared to the French women. What they say is true, they're all beautifully dressed and thin as toothpicks. I'm like a big ugly catfish swimming among trout," Ellie remarked.

"Never in a million years. You look happy, Els."

"I am," she admitted. "I was born for this."

"Any social life?"

"Sort of," Ellie grinned. "There is this one deliciously handsome culinary instructor who seems to have taken an interest in me."

"And?

"Typical Parisian man, well dressed, well mannered. Cooks like a dream. He's taught me so much. I really like him. I've been alone for so long, it's good, it's time. Do you know what I mean?"

"I know exactly what you mean. And I have some good news of my own. And it's not job related!"

"Whaaat?" exclaimed Ellie. "Do tell."

"I know this might be hard to fathom, but guess who has a boyfriend?"

"No way! Who is it? I know. Ethan? I thought you two might get together at Harvard, but he spent that year abroad and hooked up with Katie. I heard they're no longer together. You two would be perfect!"

"No, it's not Ethan. It's someone I work with, or used to work with. I met him when I taught in the corporate training program, one of the trainees."

"A younger man?"

"Same age as us. Late starter. Played minor league hockey out of college."

"An athlete, that's so unlike you."

"I know, right? He's soooo good looking. Honestly, he seems more like the type of guy who goes after women who, I don't know, I guess women who look more like you than me. I'm just a flat-chested plain girl from Fairhope, Alabama."

"Stop! You always sell yourself short. Women pay up the wazoo to stylists for hair like yours. Plus, you're smart, and wise and wonderfully kind to people. Even God thinks he outdid himself when he made you. Listen, you deserve the best. Where's he from?"

"Boston. Graduated from Boston College."

"BC, huh? Some of the kids from my high school went to BC. What's his name?"

"Does the name Asher Sinclaire ring a bell?"

"Are you dating Asher Sinclaire?"

"Dating Asher, no…" she nervously giggled.

"Thank God. You should stay away from…"

Hattie interrupted Ellie. She couldn't wait one minute longer. "I'm not dating Asher Sinclaire. I'm marrying him!"

"Excuse me, what did you say?"

"I said, we're getting married!"

"The connection is really bad, I can hardly hear you," sputtered Ellie. "Listen, I'll call later."

"No worries. You sound exhausted. Get some rest. Love you!"

∗ ∗ ∗

Hattie thought about it all the time, becoming Mrs. Asher Sinclaire. The actual planning was a whole different matter. She and Asher had no designated church at which to get married in Boston. Asher's parents were nonpracticing Catholics. She never joined a church in Boston, despite Pastor Luis's encouragement to do so.

A hometown church wedding was an option. Pastor Luis would love to officiate. The catering committee at First Methodist would prepare a delicious Southern supper with all the bells and whistles for a traditional church reception. Hattie guessed they'd encourage her to have the wedding in the church's garden, honoring Mema. It'd be lovely, glorious, in fact. If it rained the reception could be held in the church basement. They'd miss the garden views outdoors, of course. Still, the delicious food would make up for it. It'd be the perfect venue if Mema, Daddy and Mama were alive, and if she was marrying someone besides Asher.

She heard him say time and time again his family was upper class. Her family friends back home were salt-of-the-earth-type people, not the country-club crowd like the Sinclaires. She stopped thinking about Fairhope as an option.

* * *

Despite Hattie specifically asking for a simple gold wedding band with the date of their nuptials engraved on the inside of the ring, just like Daddy done for Mama, Asher went overboard.

"You need at least a carat ring. What you wear is a reflection of me, my success," Asher lectured. "Speaking of success, your future husband has good news."

"Do tell," said Hattie snuggling up to Asher.

"I've decided to partner with Uncle Monte. We're forming an LLC to buy up rundown properties and rebuild. I'll help Monte secure funding for the real estate projects. Maybe, you can help us."

"I'd love to."

"Believe me, this is a much better fit than my job at the firm. Monte even offered me stock in his company."

"Sounds perfect for you."

"Which reminds me. It'll cost us two hundred fifty thousand to purchase stock. You okay with that, using your savings to purchase stock?"

"Of course."

Hattie wrote Asher a check for stock. He in turn surprised her with an engagement ring that would make her the envy of the office.

Chapter 22:
The Hidden Truth

"I'm so glad you called, perfect timing," answered Hattie. "We've decided on a destination wedding, next month."

"You're kidding?" Ellie said.

"No, why would I joke about that?"

"Hattie, slow down, weddings take months to plan. Couples are typically engaged for a year."

"We have no reason to wait. It's going to be a small wedding. You'll be my maid of honor, won't you? Asher's brother Harrison is the best man."

"Hattie, seriously, I need to tell you something important."

"Okay."

"Asher and I have a history. Remember at college our freshmen year? Asher, well, he was the…"

"Oh, you don't have to explain," interrupted Hattie. "I know all about it. Asher told me everything. You went to school together, partied together, and what was it he said? Oh, he says you're like a sister to him. He can't wait to see you. So mark your calendar. The wedding is Saturday, March 25, in Turks and Caicos. Promise me you'll be there?"

"Charles and Claire are in Africa then. A safari, for their fiftieth wedding anniversary. They love you dearly and would want to be there for you."

"Oh, about that. Asher and I decided on a more personal wedding. You, of course, and Asher's family. Asher may invite a few of his hockey friends, who are like brothers. But he's not inviting people he doesn't personally know. It's important to him that it's small, no outsiders."

Hattie waited what felt like several minutes for Ellie to respond.

"What about Pastor Luis? Surely you want him officiating at your wedding?"

"I haven't had a chance to touch base with him. I've been so busy with work and the engagement. By the way, my ring is gorgeous! It seems like I haven't talked to Luis in, like, forever. Anyway, the resort has a justice of the peace who can marry us. They do it all the time."

One month later, Hattie was walking down the aisle wearing a sleeveless white satin dress, sleek and short, slightly above her knee. Francine told her it was perfect for a tropical island wedding. Not really Hattie's style, but she was desperate to please her future mother in law and Asher.

Ellie had arranged a crown of white tropical island flowers she clipped to Hattie's hair.

"You look beautiful. Any man in the world would be lucky to marry you," Ellie told her, reaching for Hattie's hands. "Are you sure you want to do this? You two haven't been dating all that long."

"I am," glowed Hattie.

Asher wore a white tux with a floral bow tie. His family cheered when they saw him in flip-flops as he walked down the red aisle runner to meet Hattie at the ocean's edge. Hattie had never seen Asher more handsome. He looked like a movie star as he high-fived guests with his left hand, carrying a margarita in his right.

Every folding chair placed beachside was filled with Asher's family: siblings, aunts, uncles, and cousins. Some friends. Hattie's family and friends were nonexistent, except for Ellie, Beau unable to get leave on such short notice.

After the "I do's," Hattie began partying alongside her new in-laws. She drank a shot handed to her from Asher's Uncle Monte, then another shot, and a third shot. The DJ began blaring rock music, and Asher's sister, Addy, talked a couple hockey players into getting on the tables to dance with her. She pulled Hattie up too. Asher jumped up to join them. At the end of the evening, Hattie looked around for Ellie, but her best friend was nowhere to be found. A note was left at the front desk. Ellie wished her the best and was heading back to Paris a day early to be with Jean Paul.

Chapter 23:
A Honeymoon
Hangover

Mimosas in the morning. Margaritas in the afternoon. Cocktails in the evening. "This is our honeymoon and we're living it up," Asher told her. He seemed elated when she finally threw caution to the wind and joined in the hedonistic island lifestyle, leaving behind the worry of the wedding that almost never happened.

Right before they decided to have the wedding in Turks and Caicos, Asher asked Hattie for another $250,000 for additional stock in Monte's company. She insisted on having an attorney draw up legal documents.

"It's not how the Sinclaires do business," he'd told her. "We avoid lawyers and their big legal fees."

"I have a friend in the firm's legal department who will draw up an agreement for no cost."

"You don't trust me?" Asher argued.

"It's not that. It's important to protect our assets."

She wanted to tell him she didn't trust Monte, but kept that quiet, not wanting to further rock the boat. In an effort to appease

Asher, she'd agreed to a destination wedding, a big party, and to pay for it all.

After the honeymoon on the flight home, the flight attendant announced they could use their laptops. Hattie, for the first time in ten days, pulled out her computer and began checking work emails.

"Can I get you two a drink?" asked a pretty flight attendant with beautiful brown eyes and long black hair.

"A gin and tonic for me," said Asher.

"And you?" the flight attendant smiled at Hattie.

"A water, thanks."

"Oh jeez," groaned Asher. "You're back to the same old Hattie. Honeymoon is over."

"I've got to work on Monday. I've been gone almost two weeks. Drinking alcohol in the morning isn't going to help me."

"It helps me," he said curtly. "Makes me less uptight."

Hattie was aware, once again, she'd disappointed him. But seriously, how could she maintain her work schedule and keep up with her husband's party lifestyle?

The flight attendant returned with Asher's cocktail and Hattie's water. Asher was tan and handsome in a linen white shirt, jeans, and his flip-flops. Hattie witnessed her new husband wink at the stunning flight attendant, who smiled back flirtatiously.

"Is there anything else I can get you?" she asked.

"Yes, I changed my mind," said Hattie. "May I please have a mimosa?"

"Of course."

As the flight attendant walked away, Asher turned to Hattie. "That's my girl," lovingly kissing the side of her neck.

* * *

She dressed in a dark conservative suit, lightly kissing a sleeping husband goodbye so not to wake him. She walked to work like usual, except she had a two-carat diamond on her left hand. As soon as she sat down at her desk, her phone rang.

"Welcome back," said Richard.

"Thanks," she said, catching a glimpse of the huge stack of paperwork Kayla, her assistant, had neatly placed on her desk. Had she really only been gone ten days? It looked like a month's worth of work.

"Let's get together this afternoon, I'll bring you up to speed on what you missed. My office, around one."

"See you then."

"It's good to have you back."

Hattie's diamond ring sparkled like a star on a cloudless night against her sun-kissed skin. She loved peeking at it and was staring at it when Kayla walked in.

"How was island life? You look like you had some sun," Kayla commented.

"Island life was bliss. Not sure I'm ready to return to the real world."

"Yeah, it kinda sucks. I'd love to be able to travel."

"You will. It took me time too. I didn't go anywhere until after college. Richard's on pins and needs for this contract. Would you make five copies?"

"Woah! Wait one minute. Who did you get engaged to on your vacation? The king of England? Look at the size of that diamond!"

Hattie blushed, then the floodgates opened. She shared the details of her island wedding. By lunchtime, word of Hattie's nuptials spread through the office. Hattie couldn't turn a corner without someone congratulating her.

A couple of young women from administration hugged Hattie when they heard. "You're so lucky. Asher is so handsome. We miss him working here. He was so much fun," giggled one of them.

Hattie walked to Richard's office. She figured by now he'd heard. She knew this conversation might be uncomfortable, Richard never had warmed up to Asher.

"I hear congratulations are in order," Richard said, peering over his readers as Hattie walked into his office. "You had me fooled. I'd never guessed you and Asher were even dating. Congratulations. He got a good catch."

"Thank you."

"I hope he doesn't mind you working late."

* * *

Hattie knew business was slow in commercial real estate, and kept attempting to build Asher's confidence. When Asher and Monte finally won a bid of a commercial property turned into condos, they celebrated.

"It'll be so glam, so fantastic," Asher enthusiastically told Hattie over dinner at the posh 76 Club where Asher was a regular. "Boston's old-school ways are changing, lots of new money in this town, and we're going to change the skyline, starting with a luxury condo building."

Hattie loved the old, the Beacon Hill rowhomes, cobblestone streets, historic buildings on its college campuses. She knew, however, Asher was a modern visionary. His architectural plan called for condominiums, ultramodern, with floor-to-ceiling windows. A concierge and doorman 24-7 on call to fill tenants' every need.

Asher celebrated the closing with Hattie, handing her a hot-off-the-printer purchase agreement for the top floor condo in the building.

"It'll be perfect. Imagine our condo a showplace, we can host elegant parties for potential buyers. Our first real home!"

They called Asher's parents to share the good news. Asher's mother, Fran, immediately called her decorator, Mimi Fitz, to help Hattie. Mimi was a few years older than Hattie and dressed as if she'd walked off the pages of *Vogue* magazine. She was blond and ultrathin, except for her lips—they were big, lusciously lined with lipstick. Mimi loved long working lunches at the Ritz with clients. Hattie joined Mimi and Asher for the first couple of two-hour lunches. After that Hattie politely declined. Asher had a far more flexible schedule and met Mimi regularly, selecting colors and furnishings. Hattie observed her husband and Mimi shared a fondness for modern design with its monochromatic colors and woven fabrics.

When Hattie got a look at the final fabric selections with an invoice nicely tucked inside, she realized her husband and decorator had spent a whole lot of time together picking out a whole lot of white, which long term was impractical, when they had kids or a puppy, but they would be down the road.

Chapter 24:
The Simple Movement

Mema's will dictated that the porch rocker be given to Hattie. As worn as it was, Hattie loved it. The sentimental value was priceless. Mema had loved the calming effect the rocker had on people who sat in it.

At first glance, the rocker looked to be an ordinary, much loved rocking chair. To a skilled craftsman, this piece was a feat, the finest of art. The grain of the mahogany wood resembled waves in the ocean, the finer grains looked like sea grass.

And as much as Hattie loved the rocker, she knew with all the modern white-on-white formal decor, it stuck out like a sore thumb. As she unpacked boxes, she tried the rocker in the dining room. Earlier that day, the decorator's truck had delivered a glass-top dining table that sat twelve people comfortably. The rocker definitely didn't fit; it was like a sunflower tossed in among red roses.

Hattie moved the chair to the family room under a newly purchased, wildly expensive piece of black-and-white artwork by a hip Brooklyn artist with a cultlike following that included Mimi and Asher. She knew Asher would hate the rocker placed near his modern art.

She finally moved the rocker to the kitchen corner, close to the all-metal barstools. Surprisingly, Mema's rocker logistically fit in the kitchen, and it was far more comfortable than the new sleek metal barstools. She plopped down in the rocker. This is how furniture should feel. She stared at the expensive metal barstools. Ugh. She and Asher sure had different tastes.

Asher arrived home to find Hattie eating lo mein noodles, sitting in the rocker. She was wearing sweatpants and a navy sweatshirt, working on her laptop.

"What are you sitting in?" he snapped.

"This?" said Hattie, rubbing the rocking chair's smooth wood. "Don't you remember, Mema gave me this rocker in her will. I know it doesn't match the barstools perfectly, but it's so comfortable. I love rocking in it."

"Come on, Hattie. First of all, calling your grandmother 'Mema' makes you sound like an uneducated redneck. Call her what she is, your grandmother. And secondly, donate it. It's old."

"Everyone in Fairhope called my grandmother Mema."

"We're not everyone, are we? I don't get why your grandmother gives you a frickin' rocking chair and your cousin inherits a cottage on the Gulf. Waterfront property is worth real money. It's so unfair," said Asher. "Maybe we should contest the will."

"Beau serves in the military. He'll need a place to live when he returns to the States. He doesn't make nearly the salary I do. Honestly, if you saw the cottage, it needs a lot of work. Trust me, we got the better deal," Hattie said sweetly.

"Fine," Asher said. "Monte and I have a cash flow problem. You know the real estate biz."

She was far too kind to throw in his face that she'd already given him half a million for his business.

"I've got a bonus coming soon. We'll be fine."

"I hope so. I'll stall Monte as long as I can. In the meantime, better up those commissions you earn. Are you working as hard as you can?"

"Of course I am."

"Maybe they should pay you more. Look, I'm tired, long day, I'm gonna watch something on Netflix," he said, grabbing a beer out of the refrigerator. "Oh, by the way, we're hosting a party here a week from tomorrow, an open house to show off our digs. Look your best, something glam you'd wear out clubbing, no boring banker-looking stuff."

Asher took great care in hiring the best caterer in Boston and reupped his wardrobe for the party. He was a showman. Hattie preferred the back seat, but did find a little red dress to wear with gold hoop earrings to avoid looking like a banker.

Hattie had little to do with the execution of the party; the caterer handled everything. Asher entertained the crowd. All she was responsible for was the bill.

"It was a great party," Hattie complimented Asher. "Everyone says our place looks like it belongs in a magazine."

"I know, right? A friend of mine in PR says she'll pitch a story about my real estate business to the editorial guys at *Architectural Digest* and *Boston Magazine*. Something like, 'Up-and-Coming Real Estate Developer Changing Boston's Skyline One Condo at a Time.' Not bad, huh?"

"You've got great business acumen, amazing real estate vision. I'm proud of you," said Hattie while massaging the back of his muscular neck.

"Yeah, but if no one knows about it, it won't do us any good," Asher pointed out. "My friend says it might even be worth it to hire her agency to get us some good press."

"They will adore my handsome and successful husband."

A month later, Hattie came home to an enraged husband who had a six pack of beer in front of him, four of which were empty.

"So, tell me, when did you decide to steal my PR idea? Land yourself on the cover of the *Globe*'s business section. Look at this," he said, tossing Hattie the paper.

The headline read, "Former Dog Trainer Turned Investment Banker."

"You just can't stand it that I might be better than you at something," screamed Asher.

"This isn't what you think," stuttered Hattie. "There was no PR agency. It just happened."

"Yeah, right," said Asher, flushed with alcohol, seething with anger.

"I swear I did not steal your idea. One night you were out with friends. I went for a walk. There was a woman who was having trouble with her puppy, an adorable goldendoodle. The puppy was literally dragging her down the sidewalk." Hattie laughed nervously, noticing Asher was not amused.

"I stopped and helped her. I showed her how to hold the leash and what to do if the dog pulled. She asked me how I knew so much about dogs. I mentioned to her that my mother, when alive, had been a dog trainer. She asked if she could hire me. I explained

I was an investment banker. That I didn't train dogs anymore. I had no idea she was a reporter and would want to write a story."

"You don't get ink like that without an agency."

"Asher, wait a minute. Yes, you can," said Hattie throwing up her hands.

"I don't think so," chugging his fifth beer. "I'm going out."

"Please, stay. I did not hire a public relations person, I swear. I always put you first."

"Right. Just like when I asked you to get rid of that stupid chair."

"Hey, I'm sorry, it's one of the few things I have from my childhood."

"Which I wasn't part of. But that doesn't seem to matter to you," snapped Asher as he grabbed his green Barbour raincoat, slamming the door.

And once again, she was alone.

Fortunately, Asher sold two more condos. It seemed to make him upbeat, forgive her for being in the news. Then sales stalled.

The frequency of cocktail parties increased as Asher got more and more desperate to get condos sold. Hattie did as Asher asked, hiding the rocker in their bedroom. Inevitably, when Asher went to bed inebriated, he'd trip over the rocker, banging a body part in the process.

"Do we really need that piece of old crap in here?" he snarled like a mean cat.

The more Asher complained, the more important the family heirloom became to Hattie.

"This is my grandmother's favorite piece."

"I've heard your song and dance before."

"Please listen and try to understand. Mema wanted me, us, to have it when I married. She said it's magical, calms people. Someday we'll use it to rock our fussy babies to sleep with a dog or two by our side."

"Babies! Don't even go there. You start talking like a suburban housewife you'll bore me and my friends to death. And a dog? On our designer furniture? I don't think so."

Hattie was crushed. Her posture caved as she tried to protect her heart. The smell of lavender circled around her. Was the rocker worth arguing about? Their marriage was too new to talk about babies. She should have known better. Her phone pinged. Pastor Luis.

I was feeling overwhelmed today, trying desperately to please everybody. And failing miserably. I found this Bible verse, and taped it to my desk. You're a lot like me, so thought I'd share. "For I the LORD thy God will hold thy right hand, saying unto thee, Fear not; I will help thee."

Luis. Sending her a gentle reminder God wanted to help. She'd let her faith take a back seat in her life. She needed to fix it.

Sitting in Mema's rocker, Hattie devoured a mouthful of caramels. She had her laptop and was checking incoming emails while wondering if the lonely feeling in the pit of her stomach was typical of a newly married woman. Do newly married husbands spend more time with their friends than their spouses? Daddy always rushed home after his plumbing jobs so they could eat dinner as a family. Maybe it was different for a business owner like Asher, maybe going out at night was part of the whole networking thing. She let it go.

One night she heard him quietly creep in. He didn't turn the light on. He didn't see the rocker. He tripped. Losing his balance. Asher hit his forehead on the dresser.

"Damn it, Hattie! I told you to get that worthless antique out of here. I'm so sick of the 'it means so much to me' crap. If I hear one more story about your Mema, I'm going to slap you!"

The room filled with the scent of lavender. A strong scent, so strong it was pungent.

"I'm sorry, really, I am so sorry." Hattie jumped out of bed, reaching to help him.

"Don't touch me," Asher said, pushing Hattie's hand away.

"I'll get a washcloth and some aspirin," she said softly.

"Forget it," Asher said, grabbing the white duvet. "I'll sleep in the guest room. I need my space."

Space? Who was he kidding? She let Asher do what he wanted, buy what he wanted, see who he wanted. They rarely spent time together anymore. Hattie couldn't sleep. She got up, showered, wrote a note of apology to Asher, and left for work. She wasn't going to ruin her marriage over a rocking chair. This whole thing was ridiculous.

She left the firm at exactly at five o'clock, deciding to permanently move the rocker to storage in the basement of the condo building. She had to get it done before Asher got home.

She changed out of work clothes into sweats and a T-shirt, began moving the rocker out of the bedroom. With the exception of running into one of the white walls and leaving a few black marks, transporting the chair into the carpeted hallway was relatively simple. She didn't run into trouble until she tried to push the mahogany rocker into the elevator. It felt as heavy as a sofa. She put

201

the chair down, took a couple of breaths. Attempted to push it into the elevator. No luck. Didn't fit. She tried again, from a different angle. Same thing. This was proving as difficult as getting a dog to sit still for a nail trim. Hattie was tempted to call the building custodian to help her, but it was well after six. She'd have to wait until the morning. She reluctantly moved the rocker back into the condo, doing her best to tuck it into the corner of the bedroom.

She worked on her laptop until close to midnight. Her three text messages to Asher remained unanswered. Finally, after taking melatonin, she fell asleep.

She woke at four in morning. Asher's side of the bed untouched. She grabbed her phone, ready to dial 911, he must be hurt. She quickly disconnected when she saw a text message. *Drank too much, staying with Hawk, a buddy. Let's meet after work today. PURO ceviche bar.*

Chapter 25:
Office Politics

"**G**ood morning, Kayla," Hattie said as she walked by her assistant's desk. "We've got a lot on our plate today. Can you bring me the Federal IPO file?"

A few minutes later Kayla appeared in her office. "I can't find the file. Would someone have taken it?" Kayla asked.

"I don't think so. Federal's my client. I'll check with Richard, maybe he needed to look at it."

Kayla blushed a deep red.

"You okay, Kayla?"

"Yes, just warm. I'm not feeling all that great. A virus is going around at home, probably got it from one of my brothers or sisters. Something's going around."

"I'm sorry. I've been working you way too hard. Do you need to take a sick day?"

"Nah," Kayla said. "A cup of hot tea will bring me back to life."

"Funny, that's what Asher always says when he's not well. You two think alike. By the way, will you schedule me out for about an hour today at noon? I need to get a new outfit for tonight."

"Something special going on?" Kayla inquired.

"Kind of," Hattie shyly admitted. "Dinner with my husband. We've both been so busy, going opposite directions lately. We haven't spent much time together. Asher asked me out for dinner. And honestly, I don't splurge often. But today I am buying a new outfit, something stunning. I want to impress that handsome husband of mine."

And maybe, Hattie prayed, he won't stay out all night with his friends.

"Any suggestions, Kayla? With all those young brokers asking you out, you must have an idea of what men find pretty."

Kayla always had a full social calendar. Hattie recently heard through the office grapevine Kayla was dating one of the new brokers. Office romances were frowned upon, but Hattie knew all too well they happened. And why not? That's how she found her husband. Maybe Kayla would? She was gorgeous, long red hair, pearl-colored skin, curvaceous figure, and a flirty, fun personality. The men in the office enjoyed being around her. She certainly brought a positive energy to what could be a dull office environment.

"I can't help you. Sorry, I'm just not myself today."

Kayla always had an opinion. Something must be getting her down. She had dark circles under eyes, and her cheeks were flaming like a baby sparking a high fever.

Hattie left the office at 11:45 a.m., heading to a Newbury boutique.

"I need something for a special dinner with my husband. Can you help?"

"Possibly," said the sales clerk, drumming her perfectly manicured nails on the counter. She was dressed in a flowing black skirt with a black silk blouse. She looked Hattie over, frowning. Hattie noticed.

"I work in banking," explained Hattie. "I have to dress conservative at work. But after work, I can be more flexible."

"Flexible?"

"I mean, prettier, dresses. That sort of thing."

"Let me see what I can do."

The clerk selected three outrageously priced dresses. The first was a black scallop V-neck, sleeveless dress. Definitely a classic. But it seemed too traditional to catch Asher's eye. The second was a royal blue long-sleeve sheath dress. Almost perfect. A contender. It was a dress she was comfortable in, she looked nice. But she was looking for something stunning, something to let Asher know she was still the woman he married in Turks and Caicos. The third dress, a deep burgundy, off the shoulder with a maxi hemline, was promising. The low cleavage showed off her pale, creamy skin. She slipped on the store's sample black heels.

"Let me see you in it," the clerk said, tapping on the dressing room door.

Hattie walked out, standing in front of the three-way mirror.

"That's the one. Makes you electrify the room. You are not the same woman who walked in here. You look exotic. I love what I've done for you."

Hattie wanted to roll her eyes. But the saleswoman was right. It was beautiful. "I think my husband will love it."

Hattie returned to work later than planned. She refused to feel badly, she owed herself this. She owed it to her marriage.

When Hattie sat down at her desk, the Federal IPO file was on top. "Phew," she thought, "Kayla found it." The rest of the afternoon, Hattie studied the file, making sure everything was in order. This was her biggest deal ever and the execution must be flawless. The entire firm was counting on her.

Asher texted Hattie to meet him at Puro around 7:00 p.m., which would work out well, giving her time to head home and change.

She was going all out. She changed into her new dress. Then took time to apply an extra coat of mascara and carefully select a lipstick to match her dress. She studied herself in the mirror. She'd never, not even on her wedding day, looked this stunning. Hattie smiled. Asher was going to remember why he married her. She was going to make sure of that.

Chapter 26:
The Bouquet of a
Lifetime

She'd done her best. Makeup. New dress. Stiletto heels. Her brown hair shined so beautifully even the staid maître d' dressed in a black tuxedo took note, complimenting her. "I seat beautiful women like you at our best table."

"Thank you."

"I am going to bring a glass of prosecco, on the house. It looks as if this evening is special for you."

Hattie sipped slowly on her wine, scrolling through her phone. Twenty minutes later, Asher blew in like a hurricane, nervously running his hands through his rain-dampened hair. He hadn't shaved, wore a slightly wrinkled button-down shirt with a navy blazer. His sloppiness gave him a carefree look, making him even more handsome. Hattie felt like the luckiest woman in the world. He was so good looking.

"You are a very lucky man," the maître d' said as he handed Asher a menu.

"Yeah? Why's that?" asked Asher, looking up from the menu.

The maître d' nodded toward Hattie. "Your wife is a most beautiful woman."

"Wow, look at you. What's the deal? Something big going on at work?"

This was hardly the response Hattie was hoping for, but at least he noticed.

"No," Hattie said shyly. "I wanted to look nice tonight, for you."

"Oh yeah, you do, trust me, here you go," he said handing her a dozen yellow roses.

Her spirits soared. "Thank you. That is so sweet. I love them. Let's stop and get a vase for them before we go home tonight."

"Yeah, about that…"

"Sir, can I get you something to drink?" a waiter dressed in black-and-white formal attire asked.

"Scotch on the rocks. Thanks."

"When did you start drinking scotch?" Hattie asked, knowing scotch was not Asher's usual drink, but was Monte's.

"Don't start acting like you're my mother, wanting to know everything I do. You are so uptight."

"I apologize. I meant nothing by it, just making conversation."

"I, unlike you, like to mix things up because life gets boring."

"I'm sorry if it seems like that."

"Look, this is the thing." Asher paused. "I need space. Marriage makes me feel totally claustrophobic," Asher said, loosening his tie. "A guy like me needs a night out now and then. You know what I'm saying?"

"I think I've been really pretty good about that."

"I guess," he shrugged, staring blankly at the crystal salt and pepper shakers on their table.

"Asher, I'm trying to give you what you need to be happy. I really am," Hattie said desperately.

"Dear God," she prayed silently, "help me be a better wife. Help me make my husband happy."

Asher interrupted her thoughts. "I guess what I'm trying to say, is maybe, I need more space and, like, a judgment-free zone."

"I'm sorry, I don't understand."

The waiter appeared with Asher's glass of scotch. "Are you ready to order?"

"Uh, we're just having a couple of drinks. No dinner tonight. Thanks."

"Fine, then," the perturbed waiter collected the menus, visibly annoyed at the turn of events.

"We're not staying for dinner?" Hattie asked. "I wish you'd told me ahead of time. I don't have anything for us to eat at home."

"Hattie, the thing is…I'm not coming home."

"What?"

"This whole marriage thing, I think we rushed into it. It's not working for me."

Too shocked to speak, she mentally went into autopilot, grabbing her Michael Kors purse, the one Asher's mother had given to her for Christmas. Unable to catch her breath, she ran for the exit. Once outside, she stumbled, regained her balance, and leaned against the building to steady her wobbly legs. It was pouring rain. She dug through her purse to find her phone. She'd Uber home. Where was her phone? She cursed the rain. An old-time yellow taxi pulled up next to her. A driver got out, opened an umbrella. He called out, "Miss, you look like you could use a ride." The elderly man was wearing a classic wool flat cap.

"Uh, yes, thanks, I do," said Hattie, wiping away her tears. The man smelled like lavender.

"How did you know I needed a ride?"

"A woman standing alone outside in the pouring rain always needs a ride," the driver said politely. "Where to?"

Hattie gave the elderly male driver her address. It reminded her of the first taxi she hailed years ago when she arrived in Boston, fresh off the bus from Fairhope. She'd been so young and naive. Good Lord, Hattie thought, ten years of living in the city and a degree from Harvard, and she was still so naive. How could a man like Asher ever want to stay married to someone like her? She was a fool.

Cooper, the always helpful doorman at her building, helped Hattie out of the taxi, kindly protecting her with a huge umbrella from the downpour.

"Good evening, Mrs. Sinclaire." Hattie rubbed her red eyes. "Are you okay?" asked Cooper.

"Just tired, thanks."

Hattie got in the elevator. Her heart hurt so bad, she felt like she'd been stabbed. Once inside the condo, she collapsed into bed, suddenly remembering she'd left the bouquet of yellow flowers in the back seat of the taxi.

When her alarm went off the next morning, Hattie longed to put the covers over her head, hide in bed. Survival instinct told her she needed this job. The money she made was the one thing that

Asher loved about her. It might bring him back, especially with the hefty bonus she'd earn from the Federal deal.

Hattie arrived at the office around six that morning.

"Hattie, you don't look well?" Richard asked, noticing the dark circles under her puffy eyes.

"I'm fine. I've been burning the candle at both ends the last couple of weeks for the Federal IPO."

"Listen up, after the Federal deal closes, take some time off, recuperate. I can't have my star employee getting run down."

Hattie nodded and smiled as if everything were perfectly normal.

Kayla, her assistant, arrived around eight, bringing with her a pile of paperwork for Hattie.

"So, how did dinner go with Asher? What did he say about your new dress?"

Hattie looked at Kayla. The young woman had the most beautiful red hair, emerald green eyes, and a Marilyn Monroe–like curvy figure. Kayla wore a body-hugging shamrock green dress. It was stunning. Hattie realized Kayla was everything Hattie was not. Spontaneous, fun, sexy. She worked hard, played hard. Hattie wished she was like that. She was proud of Kayla. A young twentysomething who juggled work, night school, and— from what Hattie observed—an active social ife. She enjoyed mentoring Kayla, trusted her like a sister.

"Kayla, I need to talk to you. Can you shut my door, please?"

"Uh, sure."

Hattie's phone pinged. She grabbed it, thinking, hoping, praying, it was from Asher. The text, however, was from Pastor Luis.

Beau's back in town. Might be a good time for you to come visit. He's not well. Doesn't want you to know. Pray for him.

Hattie threw her head back, rubbed her forehead. What next? She looked up from her phone. Kayla's cheeks were flushed.

"Are you feeling okay?" asked Hattie.

"I'm fine," said Kayla, looking down at her feet. "It's, well, you never ask me to shut your office door. Kinda makes me nervous."

"Please don't think it's something you've done, not at all. You're doing a great job. This isn't about work. I just need to talk to someone."

Hattie began sobbing silently, her shoulders shaking so hard it was a miracle a rib didn't break.

"Hattie, what's wrong?"

"It's my cousin, Beau. He's not well. He's back in the States from a tour in Afghanistan. I received a message this morning."

"A kid from my high school returned from a tour there. Came back and is a mess. That's a bummer."

"And then, last night, Asher left me. He doesn't know if he wants to be married. I'm so sad. I can't imagine life without him. I don't know what I'm going to do."

"Did Asher say why he was leaving you?"

"He says he needs some space. Apparently marriage is cramping his style," Hattie sobbed.

"Let me get you something to eat and drink. We've got to keep your immune system strong. You've got the deal of a lifetime happening this week. For now, focus on work. After the deal closes, then you can cry your heart out. Until then, it's my job to help you keep it together."

"Thanks, Kayla."

"First thing is a cup of coffee. Trust me. I know this place, not far from here, that serves such a strong cup of coffee it practically brings back the dead. I'll be back shortly."

Hattie gave her a half-hearted smile. What would she do without Kayla? She began to think about those she was close to. She'd lost touch with them. Beau was home, but didn't want her to know. She hadn't made any attempt to stay in touch with Ellie since the wedding. And she'd completely lost touch with friends like Charles and Claire. Pastor Luis took time to regularly check on her. She'd barely responded back. What had happened?

"Here's your coffee, black, right?" said Kayla, returning from the coffee shop. "I'll grab lunch for you later," Kayla offered. "I'm here to make sure Federal's IPO goes smoothly. Give me a checklist. I'll get it done."

"You're the best. Thank you."

"Not a problem," Kayla said confidently.

Hattie noticed Kayla had never looked happier, more beautiful. She bet Kayla never had a man tell her she was boring.

At times during the workday, Hattie could hardly breathe. When she felt like crying, she'd crush up balls of tissue, hold them against her swollen eyelids to damn the flood of tears she blinked back. Kayla kept her going with food, drinks, and moral support.

Hattie finally finished her work at two in the morning, falling into bed. She reached for her pillow, hoping it would lessen the pain in her heart. Exhausted, she fell asleep. An hour later, she woke to the creaking of the rocking chair.

"Asher?"

The rocking stopped.

"Asher, is that you?"

Hattie narrowed her eyes, trying to focus. She saw the outline of a petite woman sitting in the chair. An elderly woman in an old-fashioned dress, the kind Mema used to drag down from a trunk in the attic. The woman's hair was braided in a long ponytail, shoulders slightly hunched over, a string of pearls around her neck. Sweet Jesus, it looked like her Mema. Hattie felt the blood rushing to her head. Was exhaustion and a broken heart making her crazy? She flopped back down, closing her eyes.

"Hattie, sweet pea, go home, find Henry," said a voice. "It's time to go home, child."

What in the world? Hattie reached to turn on the light. It was so bright it hurt to look. She blinked her eyes a couple of times. The rocker was empty.

Hattie tossed and turned until her alarm went off at 4:45 a.m. In the shower, she told herself that stress causes the brain to think strange thoughts, dream strange dreams. She'd learned about it in a neuroscience class she'd taken at Harvard. She'd have to slow down, manage her anxiety better after the IPO. But not today. Today was the biggest deal of her career, taking Federal public to provide the company funding for development of a drug that helps kids with autism. She thought of Pastor Luis and surprised herself by taking a minute to text him.

Received your text about Beau. Closing on a huge deal today that may change the world for the better. Pray for me. I'll keep you posted.

Her phone pinged. *I pray for you every day. —Luis*

The execution of the IPO was flawless. Hattie's boss, Richard, was so excited he was like a teenager who was given his first car.

"Take Asher to dinner tonight to celebrate," said Richard. "Expense it. My treat."

Hattie faked a smile. "That's kind of you."

She walked home, praying Asher had had a change of heart. She imagined him at home waiting for her. That they'd order take-out from their favorite Chinese restaurant, talk about how to help Beau, make love, sleep late. She prayed again for her marriage.

Hattie's doorman opened the door. Cooper always had a cheerful smile for her. He was a sweet young man, a law student at Northeastern, working part time as the building concierge.

"Welcome home, Hattie."

"Thanks, Coop, good to be home."

"Someone was thinking of you," he said, handing her a small bouquet of blue delphiniums, purple anemones, and eucalyptus.

"These are lovely," said Hattie, breathing in the scent.

Her heart soared. An apology bouquet from Asher. He'd changed his mind. He wanted her back. Flowers were his thing. Once inside her condo, she ripped open the card.

Praying for you on this important day. Blessings, Your Fairhope friends, Lauren & Luis.

Hattie instantly dropped the bouquet as if it were a hot pan. She couldn't breathe. Her chest felt like a heavy door had fallen on top of her. Too tired to remove her cream silk blouse and brown wool trousers, she collapsed into bed. Sleep came instantly. Similar to the previous night, Hattie woke to a familiar voice.

"Go home, child. Find Henry. Henry will save you."

Good Lord, what was going on? Mema's voice. She flipped on the ceiling light. The room was so bright it hurt her eyes. By the time her eyes adjusted, there was no sign of Mema. Relieved, she turned off the light and climbed into bed. Still unsettled, Hattie flipped on the small lamp on her nightstand. She pulled up the covers, closed her eyes. Her rapid breathing returned to normal. It was then she heard the empty rocker moving back and forth.

Chapter 27:
The Changing Season

Something was calling her home. A ghost. The Holy Spirit. She didn't know. Her whole body shook in anxiety. She knew she had to go.

"Dear God, help me safely get to Fairhope," prayed Hattie. "Beau needs me. And I beg you, help me make my marriage work."

She logged out of her computer and grabbed her navy backpack from under her desk. Hattie stopped in to say goodbye to Richard.

"I'll check in throughout the week. Call if you need anything."

"No worries, it'll be a quiet week. Enjoy a week off."

"Kayla, can I see you in my office?" Hattie asked as she walked by her assistant's desk.

Kayla looked up from her computer.

"Of course."

"Thank you for all your help this week, professionally and personally. I couldn't have done it without you."

Hattie was dressed in a brown pantsuit with her hair pulled back in a chignon bun. No makeup. She noticed Kayla dressed like she was going out on a fun, twentysomething night on the town, a tight faux-leather skirt, a satin low-cut red blouse, and black, shiny stilettos. She'd have to talk to Kayla about dressing more appropriately at work, if she wanted to move into a professional job after she got her degree. But today she had to save her own sinking ship.

"I'm taking next week off, heading home to Alabama," Hattie told her. "You may need to get on my computer and help with client calls. It should be relatively quiet now that the Federal deal is done. You've got my password, right?"

"Yep."

One of the firm's receptionists knocked on Hattie's door. "Excuse me," she said softly.

"Yes?" Hattie asked.

"There's a visitor, someone special here to see you."

Hattie's heart soared.

"Please, tell him to come in."

"She, actually," the receptionist said.

Hattie felt like a boxer receiving an unexpected blow.

"Uh, okay," Hattie stammered. "I'll come to the lobby. I can't imagine who…"

"Yes, you can, if you think really hard," Ellie said, barging into Hattie's office, looking like she owned the place. Ellie wore a tan cashmere-wool topcoat with a cream blouse underneath, black trousers, and tasseled leather heel loafers. Confident. Classic.

"Because only your best friend would fly nine hours from Paris and immediately come to see you. Best friends keep in touch with each other. Best friends respond to text messages." Ellie walked over to hug Hattie. "Shame on you."

"I'm so, so sorry. It's been insane around here."

"Jeez, girl, you're as thin as a toothpick. And what are you wearing?" Ellie said, noticing Hattie's dull brown pantsuit, the same shade as her loafers.

"You look remarkably similar to the headmistress I had at prep school."

"I work for an investment banking firm, remember? We're bankers."

"Apparently the Vegas pole dancer over there didn't get the memo," Ellie commented, nodding her head toward Hattie's assistant.

"Kayla, please ignore my best friend. She's teasing, of course."

"Not really," snapped Ellie. "And what about the circles under your eyes? Hattie, what's going on?"

Kayla excused herself.

"Don't go too far," Ellie said rudely. "I may have to corner you to find out exactly what is going on around here."

"What!" Kayla exclaimed.

"Just teasing, but do count yourself in for a few questions, if your boss doesn't fess up and tell me why she looks like crap."

Kayla's cheeks flamed as she exited the office.

"Easy, tiger lady," Hattie warned. "I'd hate to lose my assistant. I cannot believe you are here! You, by the way, look terrific. Paris has been good to you."

"Too good. I'm ten pounds heavier than when I left the States."

"You're the most beautiful, well-dressed friend I'll ever have."

"Thank you," beamed Ellie. "Speaking of beautiful, that's a hot little number you've got working for you. She must make the men here pant like a dog in heat."

"She does attract her fair share of attention. Great young woman. I'm mentoring her. First generation to go to college; she attends Framingham Community College. Says she wants my job someday. I like that she is ambitious."

"I bet," Ellie said, looking around Hattie's large corner office. "You're obviously doing well in your career. No doubt. Is it the job that's putting dark circles under your eyes?"

"I can always count on you to tell me like it is. I just pulled off the deal of a lifetime. I'm exhausted. I'm taking next week off to recover."

"Nice. Heading to a tropical island?"

"No, I'm going to Fairhope."

"Wow! How'd you talk Asher into visiting hillbilly haven?"

"I'm going by myself."

"Hattie, do you really think Fairhope is the right place to go relax? I mean, so soon after the death of your mother and Mema."

"Beau's back from Afghanistan. It's been way too long since he and I have spent time together."

"I don't know, Hattie."

"It's fine, really. I have a feeling Mema wants me to go home."

Ellie raised her eyebrows. "Excuse me?"

"I'm so tired I'm talking nonsense," said Hattie, realizing her slipup. "Pastor Luis suggested it."

"Can I bring you to the airport?"

"I'm driving the Jeep."

"To the airport?"

"To Fairhope."

"The twenty-year-old Jeep, the one with over 150,000 miles, that belongs to your cousin?"

"That's the one."

"Absolutely not."

"Beau will need a car. He's back in the States. Listen, I've got a cell phone. AAA membership. The quiet time in the car will do me good." Hattie purposely left out that Asher had maxed out their credit cards, spent all her money. Driving was her only option.

"You're exhausted. You've lost so much weight your pants could slide right off you. Frankly, I'm slightly jealous of that, but you're in no shape to drive alone across the country. If you're driving, I'm going along."

"Ellie, I appreciate the offer. I really do. You need to spend time with Charles and Claire. They'll be thrilled you are home."

"I'm surprising them for their fiftieth!"

"Fifty years, that's incredible."

"Let's both surprise them!" suggested Ellie. "Come with me."

"I can't." Tears welled up in Hattie's eyes, and she blinked several times to hold them back. "Everything is such a mess."

"Let's get out of here," Ellie said, reaching out to gently squeeze Hattie's hand. "You're not alone anymore, I'm here. We'll figure this out."

Hattie nodded.

"I need to let my assistant know I'm leaving."

"I'll let her know. Get your stuff together, go out the back entrance. No one will see that you're upset."

"Okay. Meet me on the fifth floor of the parking ramp."

Hattie left with tissues in one hand, her brown leather briefcase in the other.

Chapter 28:
Together Again

"This Jeep has definitely seen better days," commented Ellie as she opened the door, wiping off the seat before sitting down. "I bet if I slam the door, the whole thing falls apart."

"One man's trash, another man's treasure," teased Hattie, in an attempt to lighten the mood. "This Jeep is Beau's pride and joy. I promised I'd watch over it while he was overseas. Honestly, I don't drive it much. Asher occasionally uses it when his car is in the shop. Today I had a meeting out of the office."

"Ten bucks it dies on Boylston Street."

"Ten bucks it doesn't," said Hattie, gently pressing on the accelerator.

The engine roared like a souped-up hot rod.

"Holy moly!"

"Beau's a total car nut. He did something to make the engine hum like a helicopter."

"You must terrify every pedestrian on the street. If you don't get a new car soon, I'm buying you one."

"Stop!" Hattie scoffed, realizing how much she'd missed her best friend.

"Lookie here," Ellie laughed when she opened the glove box. She twirled a red lacy thong around her pointer finger. "Did one of your cousin's groupies leave this behind?"

"Who knows?" Hattie said, shaking her head.

"I guess you Southern belles don't like leaving much to the imagination."

"I grew up wearing Hanes. We never had money for fine lingerie."

"I'm not sure this," pointing to the red thong, "classifies as fine lingerie."

"Asher and I are separated," Hattie randomly blurted out. "Probably because I don't wear things like that."

"No. Absolutely not. Asher is a total jerk. You don't know the half…" She abruptly stopped talking, as if someone coiled duct tape over her mouth.

"What?"

"I was going to say people don't get separated because of underwear. If Asher wanted you to wear things like this, he could have bought it for you."

"Beau once told me I'm an old soul in a young body. He's right. I might as well be walking around in Mema's undergarments."

"You are perfect, Hattie. What happened?"

"If I start talking about it, I'll fall apart. I just need a break from here. Get my thoughts together. And Pastor Luis says Beau's not well. His last tour was tough on him."

"You cannot go by yourself in this Jeep."

"I can. The oil is changed, the engine checked out fine. Honestly, I don't mind driving. I'll download a book, make some work calls, chew on sunflower seeds when I get sleepy. I'll be fine."

"If you're going, I'm going with you. I have a two-week break from culinary school. I'll spend a week with you, a week with Charles and Claire. Go get packed. Beau needs you."

"Seriously, you don't need to do this."

"Trust me. I want to."

Hattie pulled the Jeep Wrangler into the circle drive of her condominium building. Cooper, looking the always professional doorman in his concierge uniform, opened Ellie's door, then crossed in front of the Jeep to open Hattie's door.

"Good afternoon, ladies."

"Hello Cooper," Hattie said. "Is it okay if I leave the Jeep in the circle for five minutes? I'm going to run upstairs and pack."

"Sure thing, going anywhere fun?"

"Home...to Alabama. My best friend Ellie here is coming with me. We were roommates at Harvard."

Cooper gave Ellie the thumbs-up sign.

"Ellie, I'll head upstairs and throw some things in a suitcase. I'll be right back," said Hattie.

"No hurry. I'll wait here."

Hattie returned with a small suitcase, backpack, and briefcase. "I'm ready. Let's get on the road."

"How long do you plan to be gone?" Cooper inquired.

"We'll be back in a week."

"Safe travels."

Chapter 29:
A Hitchhiker

The Jeep roared onto Interstate 95 south.

"What's the plan?" Ellie asked.

"We'll blow through New York, DC, Virginia, the Carolinas, Georgia, and then sweet home Alabama. It's a twenty-one-hour drive."

"We're going to need sustenance," Ellie said. "I'm craving Chick-fil-A."

"O-M-G, you, a culinary student at the finest cooking school in the world, and you want a fried chicken sandwich? Are you kidding me?"

"I never joke about food. It's too important to my happiness."

"It's good to know Paris hasn't made you thumb your nose at American food."

Ellie fell asleep after a fried chicken sandwich and waffle fries, looking like a content baby after nursing. Hattie attempted to listen to a book on Audible, but it was impossible to focus. She was crawling out of her skin, trying to figure out how to save her marriage.

"Dear God," she prayed. "I don't know what I'm doing wrong, help me fix it."

Hattie's phone pinged. Please, let it be Asher. As she anxiously reached for her phone, it slid between her seat and the console. She squished her hand down the narrow slot, but was unable to reach it. She had to know who texted her, praying it was Asher. She took the next exit, pulling off to the side of the road. She threw the car door open, stood, and bent over. Stretching her arm out, she successfully reached her phone.

Beau received an honorable discharge. Last mission rough. He's moved into Mema's cottage, working at the brewery. Explain more when you get here. Pray for him. Safe travels.

Her heart sunk like a marble in a glass of water. She wanted to throw her phone she was so disappointed it wasn't a message from Asher wanting her back.

How could two people be so in love, and then suddenly one of them change his mind? She didn't understand. She needed Beau to be fine. She didn't have the energy to fix his life when her own was unraveling like a ball of loose twine.

She reluctantly got back on the interstate heading south, the opposite direction of where she longed to be, back in Boston working things out with her handsome husband.

After a long nap, Ellie woke to find they were on the DC beltway.

"That nap was satisfying," yawned Ellie. "Like a whoopee pie filled with white buttercream frosting."

"You needed sleep."

"Factoid. Did you know the brain has a hard time determining whether you're tired or hungry? Usually people need more sleep, less food. I, however, am wired just the opposite. I need more food, less sleep."

"Speaking of food, still game for a dinner at Founding Farmers?"

"Love to, my treat."

Hattie breathed a sigh of relief, wondering how long her money was going to last. Asher had plundered every account except a childhood savings account she still had at a Fairhope bank.

"I'm going to attempt to parallel park this beast." In no time flat, she'd parked between a Lincoln Navigator and a Honda.

"Perfectly done. Face it, Hattie, you're as close to perfect as people come."

"Hardly."

"No, seriously. You're pretty perfect. It's about time you realize that. Don't let this bump in the road fool you. It's an Asher thing, not a you thing."

Founding Farmers Restaurant was crowded, a twenty-minute wait for a table. Hattie and Ellie found a seat at the bar. A handsome African American bartender sporting a blue nautical bow tie with a coordinating blue gingham shirt smiled at them. Ellie returned his smile.

"May I talk you ladies into one of our signature cocktails made with our own proprietary spirits?"

The word spirit sent shivers down Hattie's spine. What was it the past few nights waking her? She wondered if she was headed to some sort of mental breakdown.

"What do you recommend?" Hattie asked the handsome bartender.

"If you like a sweet citrus flavor, I suggest the Farmer Jon."

"A Farmer Jon it is."

"And for you?"

"I'll pass on a Farmer Jon, more of a city girl myself. I'd like a glass of rosé, preferably, a French wine."

"I recommend the Côtes du Ventoux rosé," the bartender suggested.

"That sounds perfect."

Hattie and Ellie had barely touched their drinks when a hostess announced their table was ready.

"Did we die and go to heaven," exclaimed Hattie as she read the menu. "All my Southern favorites—fried green tomatoes, corn bread, chicken and waffles."

"The butternut squash ravioli sounds divine. I'm going with that."

The two friends ate slowly, savoring every bite. Ellie dominated the conversation with stories of Paris, occasionally scrolling through her phone to show photos of delicious French cuisine and Jean Paul, Ellie's new love interest. Hattie guessed he was ten years older than Ellie. Handsome dark eyes, curly hair; he wore dark shirts, with slim-cut jeans and expensive-looking loafers. Definitely European. Definitely gorgeous.

"Jean Paul looks like a movie star, are you sure he's a chef or just playing one in a movie?"

"I'm sure. He's incredibly talented. He wants me to come work for him."

"I dare say you and Jean Paul are smitten," teased Hattie in her best fake French accent.

"It's ironic, isn't it? I've battled my weight my whole life, and I'm dating a Parisian chef who loves to cook for me. And if all that's not enough, I'm a stress eater. I had to lay on my bed to get these jeans on."

"You haven't gained an ounce."

"I have. A good ten."

"You are glowing with happiness. Cooking is your passion, you were born to do this."

"You really think so?"

"I know so, you're at your best in the kitchen," Hattie said. "And if it becomes too stressful, you can always get a dog. It's medically proven pets reduce stress."

"A dog, maybe someday when the time is right. Hattie, I'm sorry about what you're going through, what can I do?"

"Being right here, right now, with me, is the best thing for me, really. When I'm alone, I get so incredibly sad."

"Can you tell me what happened?"

"I honestly don't know," said Hattie tears welling in her eyes. "It's as if one day Asher woke up and didn't love me."

"Can I interest either of you in dessert and coffee?" the waiter interrupted.

"Coffee, please," Hattie said, dotting her teary eyes with her napkin.

"Me too. And we'll share a slice of your signature apple pie." Ellie insisted on paying the bill.

"Hand me the keys," said Ellie. "It's my turn to drive."

"As a matter of fact, I could use some sleep."

* * *

Hattie slept for three hours, waking when Ellie pulled off the freeway.

"My bladder is about to burst. I've got to pull into this rest stop," explained Ellie.

Hattie was drowsy, her turn to drive. She got out of the car, hoping the cool night air would shock her into being awake enough to drive.

A black Ford pickup truck pulled in to the rest stop at the same time, parking right next to the Jeep. A heavyset man in his sixties wearing an Atlanta Braves ball cap unrolled his window, blowing out smoke, letting cigarette ashes fall to the ground. Hattie smelled the smoke and turned. A brown-and-black-colored dog speckled with white spots jumped from the passenger side of the car onto the burly guy's lap.

"Get the hell off me," the bearded man shouted with a cigarette hanging from his mouth. Hattie and Ellie turned to look inside the truck just in time to see the man violently shove the dog off him. They watched in horror as he hit the dog. They heard the dog yip, then a pained, high-pitched bark.

"That's it!" Hattie said as she stomped over to the truck, slamming her hands on his windshield. "Stop hitting your dog, creep!"

The man glanced up, lowered his ball cap so his eyes were covered, and started his engine. He began backing up. Then the truck door opened and the man pushed the dog out onto the sidewalk. They watched in horror as the dog landed on its back and the man tossed his lit cigarette onto the dog's underbelly.

"I'm calling the cops!" hollered Ellie.

"None of your damn business," spewed the man, an unlit cigarette hanging from his mouth. He revved the gas and took off, leaving the whimpering dog lying on the ground.

Hattie and Ellie ran to the speckled dog. Hattie slowly ran her hand over the dog's stomach to check for any sign of a burn. It had an unusually long body and short, squatty legs. It flipped over onto its legs. The dog seemed okay. Best Hattie could figure, the dog had a body of a corgi with the head of a retriever. No collar or tag.

Ellie came over to pet it.

"Careful, Ellie, we don't know if the dog has its vaccinations; if its abused, it could be scared, try to bite, to protect itself."

The dog chased its tail, then sat down, right next to Ellie's feet as if they'd known each other for years.

"People can be so cruel. The idiot dumped his dog at a frickin' rest area. Now what? We can't just leave it."

"Let's google animal shelters in Atlanta, make some calls. We'll explain the situation. Surely one of the shelters will have room and we can drop the dog off."

Hattie grabbed a bottle of water, pouring it into an empty coffee cup.

"Here, pup, help yourself."

The dog got up, lapped the cup dry, and returned to sit next to Ellie.

As they got back into the Jeep, the dog began whining.

"I bet the dog has to go the bathroom," said Hattie.

"I'll take her," Ellie volunteered, pointing to the grass. "The pet area is over there. I saw it when I pulled in."

"Okay, remember, after the dog does her business, give her lots of praise. Tell her good dog."

"Okay, mom."

"Seriously. Praise is everything when it comes to dog training."

"I forget you once trained dogs."

Hattie watched as the quirky-looking dog followed Ellie over to the pet area. Sure enough, the dog did its business and began wagging its tail. Happy. The dog, clearly, was comfortable around Ellie.

When Ellie and the dog returned to the Jeep, she asked, "Do you think we could we find a Krispy Kreme donut shop? I'd love one of their originals, fresh off the line with a cup of coffee."

"You crack me up, what would your French boyfriend say?"

"He'll never know," Ellie said, laughing.

They sat outside Krispy Kreme, eating a glazed donut, sipping coffee while making phone calls.

"That's the fifth shelter I've called," groaned Hattie. "No luck."

"I've called four. They all said the same thing," said Ellie as she licked the sticky donut glaze off her fingers. "No room."

"I suggest we take the dog with us," said Hattie. "I'll see if Fairhope's shelter has space. I know the vet in Fairhope. I'll have her check the dog over."

"Did you hear that, li'l doggy? You just bought yourself a road trip."

Chapter 30:
Hidden Scars

"I've got a second wind. I'm happy to drive," said Ellie, wired with two cups of strong coffee.

"Great, I'll get caught up on work stuff, make some calls and check emails. Shouldn't take too long, then we can switch."

"The perfect corporate executive," Ellie teased.

Hattie winced. Asher ribbed her constantly about being a corporate robot, it gnawed at her.

"Lost in space?" Ellie teased.

"Sorry. Just thinking."

"About?"

"Stuff. Work."

"And…"

"And Asher."

"Aww, yes. Men."

Hattie took a few deep breaths as if she were preparing to dive off a steep cliff.

"Do you still love him?" Ellie asked.

"I've never felt anything like what I feel for Asher. But it's so hard to please him. Everything I do right now annoys him. He says

I spend too much time working, the first to arrive at work and the last to leave. The kind who tries to please her boss."

"Is that a bad thing?"

"It bothers him. Along with…I have no spontaneity. I am too serious. I don't know how to have fun. I'm too quiet. I need to be sexier. He's right. Look at me, I'm as about as sexy as the goofy dog sitting next to you."

"That's ridiculous, you are so pretty," snapped Ellie. "He's partying like a frat boy in college. Asher needs to grow up. What does he do for work now that he's left the firm?"

"Commercial real estate development. He works with his uncle who is a big-time commercial real estate developer from Chicago. Asher admires his uncle's hedonistic lifestyle."

"Of course he does. It's the Sinclaire family way."

"It's so hard to make him happy."

"Making your husband happy is not your job," Ellie said, her voice consumed with anger.

Hattie rolled down her window, hoping to keep her tears at bay.

"Maybe he's just a messed-up guy," Ellie said, rolling down her window too, letting the wind blow through her long blond hair.

It was a beautiful spring day in the South. The countryside was green, pastures were filled with majestic-looking horses and grazing cows and calves. The small towns resembled one another: a gas station or two, feed store, grocery, and two or three churches. Then scenic green pastures with livestock. Huge Chevy and Ford pickup trucks with oversize wheels and "Go Bama" stickers on the rear windows passed them with a friendly honk and a wave. They were getting close to Fairhope. Ellie stopped at a Chevron station just outside of Fairhope to fill up with gas and get a bottle of water.

"I'm going to use the bathroom. Be right back."

Hattie wasn't going in; the last thing she wanted was to run into Rex. She saw him through the window at the cash register, an older man wearing a stained gray T-shirt and greasy mechanics overalls, sporting a long, white, Santa-looking beard. He'd watched as Ellie filled the tank. Hattie slouched down so as not to be seen.

"Rex says hello," remarked Ellie when she returned to the Jeep. "Speaks highly of you and your quarterback cousin. Says your mother was a Southern beauty. I think he may have had a crush on her. He, however, was incredibly intimidated by your grandmother. Overall, says you come from a fine family."

"Welcome to small-town America."

"Yes, well, apparently, you trained his beagle. He's very appreciative, by the way. Look there's a 'Welcome to Fairhope' sign."

"Ellie…"

"Yes?"

"Thanks."

"For what?"

"For this, driving with me."

Chapter 31:
Soul Sisters

"The Spanish moss hanging from the trees is beautiful, reminds me of Savannah," commented Ellie, brushing her long blond locks behind her ears.

"This is the historic section of town," pointed out Hattie.

"I feel like I stepped back in time, waiting for my own Rhett Butler to scoop me up and kiss me. Is he here? Hattie, is he?" Ellie teased, faking a southern drawl.

"Sorry, dear Scarlett, your best life is waiting for you in Paris, France."

"Well, I can tell I'm going to like it here this week," Ellie said, soaking in the flowers. "Being a member of the garden club must be a full-time job here."

"I'd forgotten just how beautiful it is."

Hattie breathed in the warm, humid air, smelling a touch of wisteria. The warmth relaxed her, easing some of the tension in her neck and rounded shoulders.

"I assumed when you said you were from a small town there was maybe a post office, a couple of churches, an American Legion club. You never said a thing about gardens, craft breweries, restaurants, and shops. And, look at that, the beautiful white church over there, on the bluff, how it overlooks the water. It's a perfect place for a wedding."

Hattie flinched, instantly regretting her destination wedding in the Caribbean. She should have been married here, in this town. Mema's dream was for Hattie to walk down the aisle at First United Methodist—where three generations of Browns were baptized, confirmed, married, and eulogized.

"That is the church my family attends, or used to," said Hattie. "Mema practically owned the front pew. We arrived fifteen minutes early every Sunday to claim our spot."

Hattie noticed the dog nudged closer to Ellie's shoulder.

"Your pup is growing fonder of you by the minute."

"Stop! She's not mine."

"She's looking at you as if you're her forever human," teased Hattie.

"Not my time."

The dog gave Ellie sloppy licks on her cheek.

"Better not tell her that," said Hattie,

"You need to call the local shelter, pronto," Ellie demanded. "I'm returning to France in ten days. And I can't leave this quirky, but oh-so-sweet, puppy homeless," Ellie said, reaching over to scratch the dog behind the ears. "You on the other hand, you're here in the States, it might be time you have a little pal to hang with."

"Asher would hate a dog," admitted Hattie, suddenly realizing she still thought of them as married.

"Who cares what he thinks?"

"Yeah, well, I work too many hours to even think of having a dog. I'll call the shelter when we get to Mema's cottage. Let's make a quick stop at the Buzz Coffee Shop, I need caffeine."

"Can we leave the dog in the Jeep?"

"The Buzz is dog friendly. They'll let us bring her on the patio."

"Maybe we should give 'her' a name?"

"Let's see. My guess is she's part retriever, part corgi, maybe part terrier."

Ellie turned her head side to side, looking at the dog. "Let's name her Queenie."

"Queenie it is!"

Hattie, unaccustomed to the heat, took off the Harvard sweatshirt, displaying a Go Navy T-shirt. A gift from Beau. Asher criticized her wardrobe, suggesting Hattie dress more like his eighteen-year-old sister. Ridiculous. Hattie earned a living as a banker. If there was anyone Hattie aspired to dress like it'd be Ellie, she thought, noticing how great her best friend looked.

"How do you do that?" Hattie asked.

"Do what?"

"Look that good after traveling across the Atlantic, and then another twenty-one hours in a Jeep. I look like I just got off work after a twelve-hour shift at the kennel, you look like you're ready for a meeting with the prime minister of England."

"A little secret. I cleaned up at Rex's gas station," admitted Ellie. "The women's restroom was spotless by the way. I took the opportunity to brush my teeth, moisturizer, a dash of blush and a splash of Coco Chanel. It's the little things."

They entered the coffee shop, immediately greeted by Hattie's former neighbors, then her former dentist and his wife, all extending their sympathies about Mema's passing. Thank goodness no one asked about Asher. Her chest already felt as if it was sliced open.

Hattie and Ellie ordered the house brew and found a café table outside on the patio.

"You, girl, have been hiding this gem of a town from me. It's like a Southern version of Martha's Vineyard."

A man in his thirties wearing Ray-Ban aviators, Nantucket red cargo Bermuda shorts, and a gray T-shirt walked quickly past them. Hattie saw the cowlick.

"I think Luis just stepped into the coffee shop," Hattie said.

"You better go say hello. I'll take Queenie for a short walk. She's panting like crazy."

"Okay, there's a town park across the street, you'll have to clean up after Queenie. I know that's not really your thing, but there's complimentary doggie bags and trash bins everywhere. Oh, and praise her if she does her business."

Ellie rolled her eyes. "It's like having a child."

"You got that right."

"I don't believe I'm cut out for it."

Hattie gently tapped Luis on the shoulder. "Have time to join an old friend on the patio for coffee?"

Pastor Luis turned, his square jaw dropping in surprise, his eyes sparkling with delight at the sight of her.

"I always have time for you. And if I didn't have time, I'd make time."

"We have a table outside, come join me."

She noticed a deep sadness in his brown eyes. She wondered if Beau's situation was weighing heavily on him.

"I can't think of a better way to start my day than enjoying a cup of coffee with one of my favorite people."

"I bet you say that to all your parishioners," she teased.

"No, just the Brown family," he said, taking a seat.

"Well, thank you."

"You're welcome. Shall we begin with a morning prayer?" Pastor Luis suggested before sipping his latte. "I get my daily strength knowing I've got the Lord by my side."

Hattie nodded, wondering why she never took the time to pray in the morning.

"*Dear Lord,*" he began. "*Let my dear friend Hattie know what a blessing she is to us. Her kind ways reach far and wide. Help her to recognize the gifts you have generously bestowed upon her. And may she use those gifts for your purposes. Let her know I am always there for her and Beau. Amen.*"

"Amen."

"Did you travel solo?"

"Ellie came with me. We picked up an extra passenger along the way, a furry one, a stray dog at a rest stop needing a home, which reminds me, I need to call the Fairhope animal shelter and see if there's room."

"Not sure you'll have much luck. I went to a fundraiser for the shelter a few months back, they're maxed out most the time. An expansion is in the works. Certainly can't hurt to check."

"Darn, Ellie's going to freak if they can't take the dog. Enough about that, it's not your concern. How are things at First Methodist?"

"Hattie, your concerns are mine. I'll pray for the right owner, send a few feelers out to people at First Methodist. Plenty of new members, maybe I'll find a taker. It's a growing, busy congregation. Sometimes even chaotic."

"If anyone can handle it, you can. Mema said you were her favorite."

"Mema's support for me was unwavering from day one. You know, she was my number-one supporter, putting parishioners in their place when they'd exhausted my sometimes overly sensitive soul. It's not the same around here, not with Beth and Mema gone. I miss them terribly. Sometimes I head to the church gardens where I feel Mema's presence. Do you know what I mean?"

"I think so," Hattie said softly.

"Thank God for loved ones to help us through life's difficulties. Speaking of which, how is Asher?"

Hattie flushed, momentarily unable to speak, blinking back watery drips. "He's fine," she said softly. "It's hard, marriage."

"You're not the first to say that. It's not uncommon to struggle in the first year of marriage," Pastor Luis shared. "My mother likened it to living through a kitchen remodel, uncomfortable and messy, but in time, it comes together, and the result is something even better."

Hattie wondered if that was it, normal growing pains. Or if it was a bad remodel, poorly designed from the start.

Pastor Luis hands were relaxed around his coffee mug. He wore a Harvard class ring. Asher never wore the simple platinum band she had specially engraved with their wedding date. He claimed rings felt uncomfortable. As far as she knew, he'd never taken it out of the box.

"It's been a while since I've been home," said Hattie, changing the subject. "It's as if I'm seeing Fairhope for the first time. The gardens. The pier. Downtown. I'm wondering why I was so dead set on leaving this place."

"You gain a new perspective when you've been away."

"It feels good here." The warm winds off the bay blowing on her were calming. "Is the key to Mema's cottage still in the same place?"

"Under the same gray stone. You'll be pleased how nice the cottage looks."

"Really? I figured the cottage would be in dire need of some TLC."

"Beau's been working hard fixing it up. It's looking good."

"I'm sorry he's having a hard time adapting to civilian life."

"Me too. Beau calls it collateral damage."

"What do you mean?"

"War affects even those who come home physically intact. Many are traumatized. Beau's body is fine. His mind is not. He attends church now, says the music is comforting, helps slow his mind down," Pastor Luis shared. "He can't always sit through the whole service, but he takes in as much as he can."

"Beau goes to church?"

"He sits in the same pew your family used to."

This was role reversal. She hadn't been to church in ages.

"The VA diagnosed Beau with PTSD. Prescribed him pills, but he doesn't think the meds work all that well."

"Gosh, I've been so consumed with my own life, I hadn't realized…"

"Don't be hard on yourself. The good news is God calls us when and where we are needed. You're here now. That's all that matters."

"Beau's always been so darn stable. I'm somewhat surprised."

"Living in terror, fighting day in and day out, it takes a toll, even on the best of them. Beau's just one of several veterans around here needing help."

"How can I help?"

"Start with prayer, ask for God's wisdom. PTSD is a complicated mental illness. Be mindful around Beau. No loud voices, no surprises, no entering a room without giving him a heads-up. If Beau senses you're upset, it can lead to him becoming emotionally dysregulated."

"Wow, yeah, I'm still not sure I get what I'm supposed to do when I'm around him."

"It's like being a duck, calm on the surface while you're paddling like crazy underneath. It's acting calm, even if you're not. You happen to be naturally even tempered. It's not you I'm concerned about. It's other people's actions that can be a trigger for him. It causes a fight-or-flight reaction."

"Meaning?"

"He either runs from the perceived danger or feels the need to fight."

The conversation came to a screeching halt when Ellie rushed up to them.

"Queenie got loose. I can't find her!"

"Gotta run!" Hattie jumped up, turning to Luis. "I'll call you."

Chapter 32:
Guests Welcome,
Maybe?

"The dog took off after an adorable terrier, with little pink bows in its ears," Ellie said breathlessly. "I lost my grip on the leash. She's lost in a town she doesn't know."

"Don't panic. We'll find her. She likes us. Likes the food we give her."

Queenie was in the park, happy as a clam, chasing a squirrel that appeared to be running for its life.

"BAD, BAD DOG, GET OVER HERE!" Ellie screeched at the top of her lungs. "NOW!"

"Woah, girlfriend," warned Hattie. "Talk to Queenie like that and she's running for greener pastures."

"How's she ever going to learn right from wrong if we don't yell at her?"

"Watch and listen."

"Come!" Hattie said in a happy voice, like it was a reunion with her long-lost bestie. Hattie also dropped her hand near her thigh, wiggling her fingers.

"Come!" she said excitedly.

Queenie stared at Hattie, interested, but not ready to give up freedom.

"Come! Here, girl!" Hattie tried one more time.

This time Queenie sprinted to Hattie.

"Good girl!" Hattie said running her hands through Queenie's fur. "Attagirl."

"You're good," said Ellie.

"I learned a thing or two after working for Mama. I was never fond of dog training back then."

"Why? You're so good at it."

"I don't know, probably because I didn't choose it. Mama did. Anyway, she used to say to use a happy voice with a dog. It's kind of like the saying, you catch more flies with honey than vinegar."

"When I get a dog, I'm hiring you."

"You have a dog," teased Hattie. "And I'm helping you."

"Very funny," Ellie said, holding Queenie tight.

"Let's head to Mema's cottage. I'm feeling road grunge. I need a shower."

"I can't wait to see it."

"It may be a mess on the inside, Beau lives there now. Who knows what we'll find."

"Likely string bikinis and empty beer cans," teased Ellie. "Say, how is the good-looking preacher friend of yours? I noticed you two were in a deep conversation before I interrupted you."

"Luis is fine. He was telling me about First Methodist. He credits Beau for the increase in attendance."

"Your cousin?"

"Since Beau began attending church, female membership has skyrocketed."

"Women will do almost anything for a man."

"Yep," acknowledged Hattie, realizing the lengths she'd gone to keep Asher happy, doing things she normally wouldn't. "Pastor Luis says Fairhope isn't the same without Mama and Mema. They were all such good friends. He still senses Mema's presence."

"Excuse me?"

"He feels her spirit."

"Okay, that's a little strange, don't you think?"

"I'd normally agree. But this past week I've felt something similar." Hattie paused, wondering whether to continue. "Ellie, promise you won't get all wigged out?"

"I'll keep an open mind."

Hattie shared her recent encounters.

"I thought I was having weird dreams because of so much stress. Now that Luis shared that he experienced something similar, I no longer think I was dreaming."

"Why then hasn't Mema's ghostly spirit been watching over you?"

"What do you mean?"

"Why didn't she intervene, stop Asher from acting like a drunk frat boy?"

"Maybe she was," shrugged Hattie.

"How?" inquired Ellie, raising her perfectly lined brows.

"After Mema passed, I inherited her rocking chair. It was a fixture on her front porch for as long as I can remember. She wanted me to have it, handmade. Luis shipped it to me in Boston."

"Nice."

"I thought so too. I moved the rocker into our condo. Whenever Asher came home late, after partying or whatever, no matter where the rocking chair was, he'd trip over it. Sometimes fall, bruise himself."

"Like it was jumping out at him?" exclaimed Ellie, looking pleased.

"Kind of like the rocking chair was in the right place at the right time type thing. In Asher's case, the wrong place at the wrong time. The thing is, I'm not normally attached to material things, but this chair, I don't know, I protected it like a mama bear protects its cubs. Asher would get so mad, so I'd move the rocker to another spot, and sure enough he'd somehow run into it again."

Ellie giggled. "Justice from the spiritual realm."

"That's not even half of it. A couple nights ago, I woke and heard the chair rocking back and forth."

"Okay, now I'm weirded out. But go on."

"I woke in the middle of the night. An elderly woman was sitting in the chair, telling me to head home to Fairhope to find Henry. Says Henry will save me. The woman had a white glow around her, so bright I couldn't really see her, but it was Mema's voice."

"Who exactly is Henry?"

"That's the other strange thing. I have no idea."

They drove silently past the inlet of turquoise water glimmering under the noon day sun.

"I love your town," Ellie said, breaking the silence.

"It feels good to be here."

"My grandmother Claire says the ocean is a great healer."

"Look, there's Mema's cottage, the white clapboard house between the brick house and the bungalow on the corner."

Mema's Cape-style cottage was freshly painted, white with ocean blue shutters and a matching blue door. The front porch sported a newly installed porch swing. Window boxes were filled with red and white geraniums, toppling over with green ivy and purple tidal wave petunias.

"Oh my gosh, Hattie. All this time I felt sorry for you having to grow up in the South. I was a fool. Your town is wonderful, this cottage is absolutely charming."

Hattie parked the Jeep on a short gravel drive.

"Grab your luggage, we'll go around the back, find the key."

Ellie and Queenie followed Hattie down a flagstone walkway to the back of the cottage. Hattie bent over two large gray stones by the back door, lifting the second of the two while Queenie sniffed the garden beds.

"Aha! The extra key is exactly where it should be, lucky us, some things never change."

Hattie unlocked the back door, which led directly into a mudroom. It looked the same, with a coat rack hanging on the wall and an old pine sitting bench with a pair of men's brown work boots and gray running shoes tossed underneath. A giant-sized yellow raincoat hung on one of the coat hooks, along with a gray hoodie splattered with paint stains. The remaining hooks held a steady stream of baseball caps.

"Your cousin must love baseball," Ellie pointed to the collection of baseball hats.

"Beau's a sports junkie. He was a superstar in every sport he played in high school. Honestly, we are about as opposite as two cousins can be."

As they entered the kitchen, Ellie marveled at the copper pots and pans hanging from a black pot rack. The stove looked vintage, the farmhouse sink, the real deal.

"I feel like I've come home," Ellie said, rubbing her hands across the sink. "I could be perfectly happy cooking in this kitchen for the rest of my life."

The nautical blue painted cabinets matched the outside view of the bay waters. There was a whitewashed round kitchen table with four Windsor chairs. The flowered yellow wallpaper was peeling at the seams, but the matching pleated curtains still held their charm. The wide-plank pinewood floors were swept and mopped, almost spotless—with the exception of tiny pebbles of sand burrowed in the cracks after years of Hattie and Beau's sandy feet.

Hattie took a deep breath. "The cottage smells like Mema. Clean, fresh, with a touch of lavender, her favorite. She used to say lavender relaxed the nerves. She'd put a little lavender in a cup of tea to cure a headache."

The rest of the cottage proved equally as charming. The family room featured a floor-to-ceiling stone fireplace surrounded by two dark brown leather chairs and a dark green love seat covered in coordinating plaid and chintz pillows.

"Come see Mema's favorite room," said Hattie as Ellie and Queenie followed her into a formal dining room with green-and-white toile wallpaper and a mahogany dining room table.

"Mema loved to serve supper in here."

"Was she a good cook?"

"Yes, tremendous! Unfortunately, only Beau inherited that particular skill."

The hallway leading to the main bedroom was lined with framed family photographs, including photos of Beth's Labrador retrievers and Mema with family and friends, and a row of school pictures of Hattie and Beau. "I love these," commented Ellie.

The main bedroom, decorated in periwinkle and off-white, contained a full-size bed with a small nightstand and a spindle chair in the corner. The flowered wallpaper added an old-time charm.

"Claire would love this cottage."

"Perhaps Claire and Charles will come visit sometime. This was Mema's room. Why don't you sleep here? You'll have your own bathroom. It looks like Beau is staying upstairs."

"Perfect."

"Let me check and see if there's clean towels, Beau doesn't seem like he'd think of that type of stuff."

Hattie found freshly laundered towels in the linen closet, Red-ken shampoo and conditioner, Dove bodywash. She pulled out a drawer in the vanity, new toothbrushes and toothpaste. There was a hair dryer. It was as if he was expecting guests. It dawned on her. Beau likely had a lady friend who spends the night.

"Looks like Beau's got everything you need. I'll be upstairs unpacking, go ahead and shower."

Hattie lugged her belongings upstairs. Beau had his things in what Mema referred to as the "blue room," the same room he stayed in as a kid. The twin bed was made military-style, corners precise, sheets tight. Hattie laughed, thinking of her six-foot-three cousin sleeping on a small twin. Then again, after sleeping nights outside in Afghanistan, a twin bed with clean sheets likely felt pretty darn good.

A pile of laundry was haphazardly tossed on the floor. Gym shorts and boxers shoved in the corner. On top of the beechnut bureau was a folded pile of Beau's T-shirts, a pair of Jordan basketball shoes, and some framed photos, including a five by seven of Beau in his football uniform, a larger eight-by-ten frame of Beau in his blue naval uniform. And much to Hattie's surprise, a framed photo of her giving the valedictorian speech. God love him, she thought.

She put her duffel and backpack in the "yellow room." The furniture was the same as when she was a little girl, including a bird's-eye maple writing desk and a matching bureau. The room was painted a soft buttercream yellow. At the foot of the bed was a handsewn blue-and-yellow plaid quilt she'd made in 4-H years ago. It was as if Mema was personally welcoming her home.

Hattie's phone pinged. She dashed across the bedroom, reaching into her backpack for her phone. Asher?

No. Pastor Luis sent a text.

Can you meet this afternoon, my office?

She responded immediately, jumping in the shower and changing into clean clothes. As Hattie was brushing through her long thick hair, Queenie wandered upstairs with a pair of Beau's boxers hanging from her mouth.

"Leave it," Hattie commanded, leaning over to gently pry the underwear from Queenie's jaw.

Queenie refused to let go, wagging her tail back and forth.

"Leave it," Hattie said again, this time successfully removing the boxers.

"Good leave it," praised Hattie. "Good girl."

"Can I come up?" Ellie hollered from the bottom of the painted steps.

"Of course," Hattie said, holding her cousin's boxers in her right hand.

"What's that?

"Queenie was enjoying Beau's dirty laundry."

"Dogs are disgusting. Which reminds me, did you get ahold of the animal shelter?"

"I did. Queenie is on a wait list. She's hanging with us for the time being. Listen, I've got to stop by the church to pick up a folder from Pastor Luis, do you want to come?"

"Actually, I need to go to town and pick up a few new things to wear. I only packed for March in New England, not the Gulf Coast."

"You go shop. Fairhope has great boutiques. We can meet up around four at the Fairhope Brewery. We'll grab a drink and let Beau know we're in town."

"Is Beau going to be okay with this, us, me, here?"

"I think so, but..."

"But?"

"Sadly, my once happy-go-lucky cousin is having a rough re-entry into the civilian world. Pastor Luis is going to bring me up to speed, give me some information."

"Maybe I should check into a hotel?"

"No, Beau would hate that. So would Mema."

"Okay, then. I'll see you at four, Fairhope Brewery."

Chapter 33:
Don't Let 'Em Fool You

Pastor Luis's assistant was nowhere in sight, so Hattie breezed past the receptionist area, knocking on Luis's door. Luis warmly welcomed her with a much-needed hug, making her feel like everything was going to be okay. His long hair, slightly wrinkled plaid button-down shirt, and cargo pants made him look more like a graduate student than a pastor. She wished they'd been at Harvard at the same time. They'd surely have been good friends.

"Can I get you an iced tea, a water?" asked Luis.

"Water, thank you. I'm not used to Fairhope's heat, I look like I sprinted here," pulling her T-shirt away from a sweaty body.

"I'll grab a couple bottles of water. Be right back."

He returned, handing her a water and a manila folder filled with articles.

"This is the information I wanted to share with you. It should help you get through this week with Beau."

"Get through this week?" she asked with trepidation.

"It's a huge adjustment being around someone with PTSD. Experts equate it to walking through a minefield; one misstep and a bomb can go off."

Hattie shrank into herself, rubbing her forehead. She didn't know how much more she could take.

"It's like this, Hattie. People who suffer from PTSD have certain things that trigger them. Beau's triggers are things that make him feel as if he's returned to Kabul, fighting to save his SEAL team. Loud noises remind him of explosives; gunshots remind him of snipers. Angry people remind him of the enemy. Triggers are things that cause his brain to think he's in danger, real or unreal. The fight-or-flight emotion kicks in."

"What determines if it's fight or flight?"

"Difficult to predict."

"I feel so bad for Beau. How do I help?"

"Our job is to help him calm down, find his way back to the present where he is safe. Give him a diversion. Something that redirects his focus. It's easier said than done."

"Aren't there therapists who can help him?"

"Some of the best trauma experts in the country are in Boston, and it may be wise, someday soon, to encourage Beau to seek help there. Especially since Beau's not seen any improvement on his meds. In fact, things have actually gotten worse."

"Worse?"

"Look at these," Pastor Luis said, handing Hattie a small pile of local newspapers.

She began sorting through the pile, reading the headlines. *Hometown Hero Beau Brown Returns; Fairhope Brewery Names Beau Brown New Manager; Beau Brown Involved in Taproom Brawl; Local Police Arrest Former Navy SEAL.*

"This is unbelievable," Hattie said.

"You're welcome to a couple of books I have on PTSD and trauma. I've learned a great deal."

"I'll take you up on that, thanks."

A quiet knock interrupted their conversation.

"Yes?" Pastor Luis asked.

"Your three o'clock is here," said LeeAnne, the church secretary, a friendly woman in her fifties who was a lifeline for Luis and pretty much everyone in Fairhope. "Good to see you, Hattie Brown!"

"You too, LeeAnne," said Hattie, noticing people in Fairhope still used her maiden name.

"We've missed you, terribly."

"And I you!"

"I miss your whole family, feel like I lost a part of me after Mema passed. And darn, we miss your mama as well. Dogs 'round here just ain't the same. It brings me peace, knowing they're all together with your daddy now. If you have time, I'd love to buy you a cup of coffee."

"I'd love that."

Hattie began gathering the materials Pastor Luis shared.

"Hattie, the absolute biggest thing you can do for Beau is to love him unconditionally. He doesn't need another someone judging him, correcting him, giving him consequences for his behavior. Meet him where he is. Love him as he is, with all his mental wounds. They're as real as if someone stabbed him with a knife. And please, call me if you need anything. If I don't answer, LeeAnne can always track me down."

"Thank you, for everything," she said, wondering how long it was before he and Lauren announced their engagement. He was such a great guy, one in a million.

She exited the church, her mind swirling with thoughts of how she could help her cousin. She prayed for Beau as she walked through the church garden, and then it dawned on her. For the first time in almost a year, she was focused on helping someone other than Asher.

Chapter 34:
Trauma's Toll

Hattie glanced at her Garmin watch: A Christmas gift she bought herself after Asher said husband and wives don't need to buy each other Christmas presents.

She had some time before she needed to meet Ellie, and headed straight to the library, finding a reading desk back in the corner on the second floor. Hattie poured over Pastor Luis's information. What a deal. Nightmares, flashbacks, anxiety, depression. The list went on: agitation, irritability, hostility, hypervigilance, self-destructive behavior, social isolation. Most disturbing was how difficult it can be to function in everyday life. PTSD was a nightmare for those suffering from it and the people living with them.

She googled treatments. Some doctors prescribed cognitive therapy and medications. Others recommended daily yoga, music, and meditation. Newer treatments included an eye movement desensitization process known as EMDR, neurofeedback, and the assistance of service dogs. Mama would have loved the service-dog idea for Beau.

She tapped her pencil on the library desk. Recovery is iffy. No easy answers. Pastor Luis was right, the leading trauma centers in the country were in the Northeast. Could she get Beau there? She looked at her phone, it was close to four. She sent a quick text to Ellie: *Heading to the cottage to let Queenie out. See you at the brewery in a few.*

Queenie was thrilled to see a familiar face, jumping up on her hind legs, almost knocking Hattie to the floor. The trainer in Hattie took over.

"No, off," Hattie commanded in a stern voice, gently leading Queenie's front paws off her thighs and gently down to the floor.

Hattie anxiously brushed her hands through her long hair. She needed to help Beau. His life was mess, hers a mess. Add a new dog in the mix, and it was sheer insanity. She prayed God give her strength.

She let Queenie out, then fed her. After seeing Queenie had chewed a pillow, she brought in one of Mama's old dog crates stored in the garage. Before she left, Hattie put a defiant Queenie in it. When Hattie left the cottage, Queenie was still whining, bringing back memories of when Mama first began crating Lily. Oddly, it conjured up a good feeling.

Chapter 35:
Finding Common
Ground

"**H**ey!" Beau shouted across the taproom, "We don't serve just any valedictorian who walks in off the street here. We've got standards."

Everyone turned to look at Hattie who broke into a smile the size of a melon. She rushed the bar, giving Beau a hug, the type a child gives to her daddy after he comes home from a long day at work. Beau picked her up off the ground and twirled her around.

"Thank you, God, for bringing him home," Hattie whispered.

"I spent ten years in the military. I know a broken heart when I see one. We're going to be okay, Hattie. I promise."

Hattie nodded hesitantly, then turned her attention to Ellie. "Did you get a chance to meet my friend, Ellie?"

"Boy, did I ever," Beau laughed. "She's been interrogating me about our beer. You know, she's incredibly picky."

"She should be! Ellie's the granddaughter of Charles Reade, Reade Brewing Company."

"Well, I'll be darned. I was thinking she thought Southerners are only good at making moonshine."

"Nope, Ellie knows her beer."

"Stop talking as if I'm not here," Ellie scolded them both. "And yes, I do enjoy high-quality IPAs."

"...and high-quality food, designer clothes, and expensive cars," Hattie teased.

"I believe that. Hey, I'd have picked you two up at the airport. Why didn't you call?"

"Didn't need to. We drove here."

"Really? Let me guess, one of you has a brand-new white Range Rover that called for a joyride."

"No. As a matter of fact, we drove your Jeep," Ellie pointed out.

"Did y'all think I'd need it?"

Hattie shrugged, wondering what he'd think if Beau knew she could no longer afford the price of an airline ticket. The Jeep was her only choice.

"I bought me a big honkin' Chevy pickup truck after my last tour."

Hattie made eye contact with Ellie, who swiftly swooped in and covered for her.

"We took the Jeep, because, uh, we brought a dog with us, we actually found a dog. I mean, it's now temporarily our dog," Ellie rambled. "I guess we're fostering it. We didn't want our cars to get dirty with dog hair, so we decided to drive yours."

"Awfully, good of you to think of yourselves," Beau scoffed. "But I always did love that car, had me some good times in the Jeepster."

"I'll say!" Hattie teased. "We found empty beer cans stuffed under the seat. Ellie also found one of your girlfriend's scanty panties in the glove compartment. You are bad, Beau Brown."

"I never leave the evidence behind."

"Well, maybe one of your groupies did, maybe you were so focused on her G-string, you didn't notice what she was drinking," teased Hattie.

"I tossed the scanty panty out the car window," Ellie said, rubbing her hands like she was removing bugs.

"Fine by me. Those don't belong to any lady friends of mine," Beau said smoothly.

Chills went down Hattie's spine. Had it been Asher?

"Beau, I'll take a glass of your finest. Tell me how this whole brewery thing got started."

"Y'all really want to hear it?"

"Yes!" Hattie and Ellie said in unison.

"Okay, then. We started by hiring the best brewmasters in these parts, Travis and Lionel. Our guys are old school. Got themselves a lifetime of stories, some will make you laugh, some bring you to your knees. The recipes are all theirs. They do the quality testing. We serve only their best batches. Less profitable, but the right thing to do. Travis carries a shotgun in the back of his truck and is missing a few teeth. But I never met a finer man. Ole Lionel learned how to brew from his grandfather, who learned it from his grandfather, who was a slave, forced to learn the brewing trade to please a nasty old slave master."

"I love a good story behind a good beer," Ellie admitted, clapping her hands in delight. "Where did the brewmasters get their equipment?"

"Right here in the good old US of A."

"American is good. The equipment out of Liverpool is even better."

"Our guys do the best they can with what we can afford. Our customers are happy."

"That's the point," agreed Ellie. "How about the ingredients, what makes yours special?"

"Ma'am, are you trying to steal trade secrets?" teased Beau.

"No, absolutely not. I'm a foodie, an aspiring chef. I love hearing about ingredients."

"Well," grinned Beau. "Our *special* ingredients are classified. If I told you, I'd have to kill you. All I can say is I've yet to have a dissatisfied customer."

"Okay then, I'll have your IPA."

"I'll do the same," said Hattie.

"Ladies, going for the gusto, huh?"

"Yes, and I haven't eaten all day, so I'd like to know what food pairings you have with your beer. Maybe something simple, like goat cheese and fresh fruit, or a pâté," Ellie asked.

"Beer, we do. Don't know much about pat-ay."

Hattie shook her head and laughed.

"Seriously, you two," pouted Ellie. "Food pairings are important."

"Well, then, lookie here, we have pretzel snack mix from Costco. Two flavors, original and jalapeño. A buck a bag," Beau smiled, pleased with his answer.

"That's pathetic. Good beer, or any good drink for that matter, should be paired with good food. It's a culinary standard at the school I attend in Paris."

"Paris, huh? I ain't hearing much *parlez-vous français* in your voice. You sound more like a Yankees fan, maybe Red Sox."

"Red Sox. Definitely. Boston's my hometown."

Ellie jumped in about culinary school. Hattie could tell Beau loved hearing about the food. Then Hattie began talking hedge funds and IPOs in the investment world. Beau and Ellie's eyes were glazed over.

"Neither of you have any idea what I'm talking about," said Hattie.

"No idea," Ellie and Beau said in unison, laughing.

"Story of my life," admitted Hattie.

"You're nothing like how Hattie described," said Ellie, staring at the man bun. "Not exactly," pointing to Beau's hair, "the high-and-tight military cut."

"Recon."

"Pardon me?"

"SEALs call crew cuts 'recon.' High and tight is cadet talk. Anyway, I left the navy, honorable discharge. I can wear my hair any way I want these days."

"I like long hair on men," Ellie complimented him.

"You wear it well," Hattie agreed.   .

"Hate to say it, but sharp scissors or searing clippers anywhere near me makes me shake. It's a war thing."

"Gotcha," said Hattie.

"Where y'all staying?"

"At Mema's cottage."

Beau's jaw dropped.

"Yikes, you look completely uncomfortable with that. We'll find a hotel."

"Wait, it depends."

"On what?"

263

"If Hattie brought her husband," Beau said. "What the heck is his name, Edgar, Ebbit?"

"Asher, his name is Asher," Ellie said with disdain.

"Excuse me," Beau interrupted Ellie, placing his hand on top of hers as if applying the brakes.

A boisterous, sunburnt group of tourists stumbled into the brewery. Hattie noticed Beau tense, veins in his neck popping.

The noise and chaos must bother him, she thought.

The women were dressed in tees and cover-ups haphazardly thrown over bikinis, and the men in sleeveless tanks with sunburnt shoulders.

"I bet their day began with Bloody Marys," commented Beau.

"First round is on me," a heavyset man with slicked-back hair hollered to his buddies, who had taken over the taproom like weeds in a garden.

After Beau had served the new group, he poured Ellie and Hattie a second glass of the brewery's award-winning beer.

"Ladies, pleased to say we've been voted the best of the South."

Beau left to fill more drink orders.

"Your cousin isn't the country hillbilly I thought he'd be."

"He's a great guy. I can tell Beau likes you," Hattie said nonchalantly.

"Stop!" Ellie blushed.

"Not in that way, silly. He's a smart guy, he knows you're way out of his league. What I'm trying to say is, I can tell he respects you, your knowledge of craft beer."

Hattie and Ellie watched as Beau adeptly managed a now-chaotic taproom, serving beer, chatting it up with customers. It was obvious the women in the brewery enjoyed his attention. He flirted a tiny bit, enough to be polite, the makings of a good bartender. They watched as he carried himself with a confidence few have. Hattie referred to it as SEAL swagger.

One of the women from the tourist group wiggled out of the friends' circle, attempting to get right up next to Beau. She was a thin, pretty, dark-haired brunette, with a pale peach bikini top and flowered sarong.

"Good evening, ladies," said Beau. "Looks like y'all enjoyed some sun on the water today. What can I do for you?"

"Nothing that I can say in public," the tipsy brunette laughed. "Especially with my boyfriend over there," pointing to the man with slicked-back hair.

Beau ignored the comment. "Do you have any questions about our beers?"

"I got a question," the boyfriend of the brunette hollered. "Why the crap does a glass of beer cost so damn much here?"

"Ernie, shut up," the brunette scolded her boyfriend. "This is a classy beer joint. Look around."

"Who cares?" Ernie shouted back.

"Well, if the beer isn't worth it, looking at the hot bartender is," Ernie's girlfriend told her friends, who giggled.

"You gotta thing for that girly man bartender?" Ernie demanded.

"You have no business talkin' to me like that after the way you chased Missy all day on the boat."

"Hey, I'll be happy to give each of you a sample of our beers," offered Beau, working his bartender magic. "If it's not to your liking, no hard feelings. You're not out a thing."

Hattie and Ellie watched as the brunette made a second attempt to rub up against Beau as he took orders. Somehow, he managed to keep a healthy distance, successfully avoiding a confrontation with the woman's boyfriend.

Once the taproom customers were served, Beau returned to his conversation with Hattie and Ellie.

"How'd we rate, Miss Fancy Pants?" Beau asked Ellie.

"It's not bad, seriously. Definitely one of the better beers I've tasted in the States."

"I'm liking what I hear," said Beau.

More people filed into the brewery, which was quickly becoming standing room only. Hattie was exhausted but hesitated leaving. Pastor Luis told her uncontrolled crowds could be a trigger for Beau. She noticed beads of sweat above Beau's furrowed brows. He looked agitated. She breathed a sigh of relief when an additional server arrived to help Beau.

Hattie overheard the brunette's boyfriend tell his friends, "I'm going slap her up if my lady keeps staring at the girly man bartender."

"No one slaps me around," she hollered back. Ernie grabbed her wrist, yanking it hard, her glass of beer crashing to the floor.

Hattie watched as the glass hit the cement floor, shattering into a million small pieces. The newly arrived server, a woman in her midthirties, blond hair in a ponytail, wearing a white brewery T-shirt, swooped in like a seagull to clean up the glass, accidentally cutting her hand. Blood began dripping on the front of her tee. The crowd. The noise, the blood. Triggers.

Chapter 36:
A Kabul Memory, A
Fairhope Nightmare

Beau was throwing punches at an invisible enemy who seemed as real to him as his cousin Hattie.

Hattie attempted to worm through the crowd to get to him.

"I've got to stop him," she told Ellie.

"I'm right behind you," followed Ellie.

Hattie knew not to get too close to Beau or she'd become an unintended target. She remained at arm's length.

"Hey, Beau," Hattie said softly. "It's me. It was just a glass that broke. We're all fine. No worries."

He had a glazed look in his eye. She recalled Pastor Luis's advice: no abrupt movements. She kept still. Just breathe, she thought. He can't calm down until I am calm. She breathed slowly, deeply.

"Beau, can I close out our tab, Ellie and mine? We're ready to head home to Mema's."

No response.

Hattie tried again. "I think I'll have Ellie sleep on the main floor of the cottage, in Mema's old room. You and I will be upstairs.

Remember, we have a dog with us, her name is Queenie, You'll like her. She's your kind of pup."

No connection. His eyes were still glazed over.

"You've done a great job fixing up Mema's cottage. Mema couldn't keep it up, not with Mama so sick. Uunfortunately, I didn't get back here to help you. I'm so glad you're home now, *here in Fairhope*. And I'm so grateful to be *here, in Fairhope*, with you, where we are safe."

Beau stopped thrashing.

"Sorry, Hattie, I'm sorry," said Beau, vigorously rubbing his temples. "I get these crazy spells. You, okay? Is your friend, okay?"

"All's good."

"No one got hurt?" he asked hesitantly.

"No. The obnoxiously drunk group left a few minutes ago."

"I get flashbacks."

"I'm sorry. We'll wait here until things, uh, calm down before we go."

Beau grabbed a bar towel, wiped his face, and tossed it over his shoulder. He was back taking orders from a few customers who fortunately missed the entire unnerving episode. Hattie saw the main door to the brewery open, anxiously wondering who was coming in. She sighed a breath of relief when she saw him, Pastor Luis. He wore jeans, a flannel plaid shirt and a Dallas Cowboys ball cap. She watched as Luis sat down at the end of the counter. Beau walked up to him, shook his hand, and served him a glass of beer.

Chapter 37:
Southern Ways

"What was that all about?" Ellie asked Hattie, who returned to their table.

"I'll tell you later. Let's pay our tab and head to Mema's cottage. Will you let Beau know we're leaving? I see Luis at the bar and want to mention this to him."

Hattie sat down next to Pastor Luis.

"You just missed Beau having some sort of crazy outburst. I'm afraid to leave him alone."

"I got a text about it. Hurried down here. I'll nurse a beer until the brewery closes, make sure Beau gets home okay. Friend, go get some rest."

"Thank you, for everything."

It felt good to walk outside, breathe fresh air.

"I couldn't love your town more," said Ellie kindly. "I met an artist this afternoon who moved here from the Berkshires. Loves it, says the town is a magnet for creative types."

"It is, though I didn't have much exposure to that when I was a kid. New techniques on dog training was about as creative as my family got. Hey, we're home. Thank goodness, I'm beat."

The cottage looked inviting, warm, and welcoming. Mema's pet peeve was coming home to an unlit house. She always left a light on in her front window. And Beau had apparently inherited the same habit.

Flood lights flashed on them as they followed the stepping stone path around back.

"Those are new."

"Bright enough to keep a burglar out."

"Bright enough to blind a person."

A swing hung from a huge oak tree in the backyard. There was no breeze, yet still it was rocking back and forth. Hattie and Ellie both noticed. Hattie unlocked the door, and they heard Queenie whining.

"I bet Queenie needs to go the bathroom."

"I'll take her out," Ellie offered.

"I'll come with you."

Queenie happily followed her new human friends outside, busy sniffing new smells and listening to the outdoor noises, mostly other dogs in the neighborhood barking. Queenie ran up to the swing, sniffed, and then began to chase her tail.

"Take a break," Ellie commanded. "Quick, please, we're exhausted."

"You'd make my Mama proud. Bet you had no idea what you signed up for when you came on this trip," Hattie said, breathing in the salty humid air. "You are a saint."

"Never a saint, just a good friend who loves you. Speaking of which, we need to eat, how about breakfast for dinner. Scrambled eggs, bacon, and toast?"

"Sounds good. I'm starved."

After they ate, Hattie shut off the lights and went upstairs. She lay in bed, thinking about Beau. She'd intended to come to Fairhope mostly to figure out *her* life. A trip to get *her* head together. Beau's problems were an afterthought. And now his problems had landed in her lap like a glass of spilled milk. She thought of the dream, Mema insisting she find Henry. Whoever Henry is, maybe he's the key to helping Beau. The scent of lavender filled the room, and its intended purpose relaxed Hattie, who fell fast asleep.

Hattie awoke to Queenie barking. Beau hollering.

"Hattie Brown, get this dog to shut up!"

Hattie raced downstairs, slightly annoyed he was making such a big deal of the dog, more annoyed he still used her maiden name. Then she remembered, the PTSD.

The commotion woke Ellie, who ran to the hallway.

"You know how the drill works, Beau," Hattie said calmly, not knowing Beau's current mental state. "First rule when meeting a new dog is to introduce yourself...so the dog knows you're not a threat. Let Queenie get familiar with you, your scent. Let her sniff your hand."

"Good Lord, I'd forgotten that, Aunt Bethie'd be disappointed," said Beau, staring at the quirky-looking dog. "What the heck is it, anyway?"

"I believe it's a jumbo-sized hotdog with legs," teased Ellie.

"Y'all know what they say," teased Beau as he looked up at Ellie. "Dogs and their owners resemble one another."

"Are you telling me I look like a plump hotdog?" Ellie asked smiling.

"Absolutely not," said Beau.

Hattie looked at Ellie's pretty pastel pink linen pajamas she was wearing. Beau was staring too.

"But my cousin does," teased Beau.

Hattie rolled her eyes.

Beau leaned over to stroke Queenie behind the ears. "If you's keep barking, old man Clifton, next door, gonna be over with his shotgun. He shoots at anything that keeps him from a good night's sleep. Then his gunshots will wake our other neighbors, Eduardo and Jeremy, and their yippy Chihuahua. After we kiss and make up, we'll be invited over to their house for creps and fraps at three in the morning."

"What are creps and fraps?" Ellie asked.

"He means crepes and frappés," Hattie interjected.

"I mean get the dang dog quiet."

"Hattie, I'll take the pain in the butt to bed with me," Ellie offered.

"We barely know each other," Beau smarted off.

Laughter followed. Queenie realized all was well. She finally stopped barking.

"Let's get to bed. Ellie, you're going on forty-eight hours with no sleep. Beau, you best get some sleep. Oh, before I forget, thank you for putting fresh lavender in the cottage. It's so welcoming and sweet of you, continuing one of Mema's traditions. That and leaving a light on in the window."

"Lavender? I didn't put lavender in the cottage."

"Somebody did, it's in my room, too," Ellie said as she walked down the hallway. "Perhaps the housekeeper did. Lovely, isn't it? Good night, you two."

Hattie and Beau looked at each other. They didn't have a cleaning person at the cottage. Never had one. Likely never would.

"Beau, if you didn't put the lavender in the cottage, was it a special lady friend of yours? Someone I should meet?"

"No. I don't get it, maybe it was Eduardo and Jeremy, the neighbors, they're master gardeners. I s'pose they saw I had guests and thought it a neighborly thing to do."

"Would they just walk in without asking?"

"Don't really know, they're really friendly types. Maybe."

Beau and Hattie made their way to their respective bedrooms.

"Beau, do you believe in ghosts?"

"That's sort of random."

"Do you?"

"I think of 'em more like guiding spirits. Now let's get some sleep. Oh, and Hattie, one more thing."

"Yes?"

"There's a ghost behind you," he joked, tossing a pillow at her.

Chapter 38:
Chasing Broken
Dreams

Hattie had deep, vivid dreams. She and Asher were on his sailboat. They were at his parents' having Christmas dinner, laughing, with his siblings. His sister sat next to her, happily conversing. The scene then switched, and Asher was smiling at her while she played with Queenie. They were living in a brownstone. The high-rise condo nowhere in sight.

She woke feeling happy, almost gleeful. It was Saturday. Asher's favorite day. She reached for him. The bed was empty, the sheets cold. Her heart raced; she looked around. She remembered. She was in Fairhope. She missed Asher, his warm athletic body sleeping beside her. His arm around her, resting on her tummy. Hattie missed his smell, the woodsy soap he lathered in. She sat up. She could hardly breathe, recalling the early days of their relationship, when Asher woke her early, at dawn, and they made love, and then they'd lounge late in bed half the morning, drinking coffee. She longed to have that back, knowing she'd never love anyone as much as she loved Asher. Her mind raced. What if he'd stopped by their condo, wanting to talk? Maybe he tried calling; cell phone service in Fairhope was hit or miss. What if he, somehow, had gotten hurt and needed her? She reached for her phone, texting him.

In Fairhope. Family emergency here. Text if u need me.

She climbed back in bed and laid her head back down. A strong scent of lavender blew in from the open window, making her sleepy. Just when her mind finally slowed down, her phone pinged. A text.

Asher is unavailable.

Hattie curled up in a ball, pulling the covers over her head, muffling the sobbing noises with a pillow. She knew in her heart, Asher was not alone.

* * *

"Good morning," said Hattie as she clunked her way down the stairs in her clogs. She was determined to put on a brave face. "I'm thinking of using the outdoor shower. Beau, did you by chance clean out the spiderwebs?"

"Nope, left the creepy-crawlies just for you."

"Of course you did. I'll shower inside."

"Actually, I replaced the wood floor in the outdoor shower last week and fixed the plumbing. The hot water is working, and it's never been cleaner."

"Well, I declare," Hattie claimed, exaggerating her Southern accent. "Mema be mighty proud. Ellie, is my cousin being a gracious host?"

"Southern hospitality at its finest. I'm enjoying the *New York Times* while drinking a cup of excellent coffee after an extraordinary breakfast. You didn't tell me Beau was such a good cook?"

"Did he tell you why he is good?"

"Beau, why are you a good cook while your cousin can't fry an egg?"

"Mema used to make me cook with her when I got in trouble. Her way of disciplining me, forcing me to stay inside. I cooked plenty in my childhood. Which is why goody two shoes over there can't cook and I can," teased Beau.

She stuck her tongue out at him.

"If you'll excuse me," said Ellie. "I'm going to use the indoor shower."

As Ellie left the kitchen and walked down the hall, Beau stood up from the table, watching her.

"She's pretty, isn't she?"

"She is and, man oh man, sassy as a toddler."

"I love her to pieces. So, be honest, how are you?"

"A few postwar ghosts to shake loose from this numbskull brain of mine. Overall, I'm fine. I'm home, ain't I?"

"I'm so glad of that."

"And, be honest," Beau mimicked her, "how are you?"

"I'm home, away from work?" She tried to look carefree. He tried smiling back. She knew they were both hurting.

After Hattie showered, she and Beau walked the perimeter of the cottage's lot, Beau explaining what needed to be fixed and updated.

"The property taxes are unbelievable. Fairhope's become a retirement haven. I'm hoping the brewery does well, and I'll make enough to cover the taxes. Then we can keep the cottage in the family. This place is a keeper, for our children and our children's children."

Hattie cringed. Here she was, a Harvard grad, investment banker, and didn't have a cent to help pay the property taxes. She'd made a half million last year. When Asher said his company needed money for real estate projects, she happily obliged. But now, for her own family, she had nothing to offer. She was too embarrassed to confide what she'd done with her savings to either Beau or Ellie. Beau would likely drive straight to Boston and kill Asher himself. Ellie would likely jump in the passenger seat and help him do it.

Hattie began scrolling through messages on her phone.

"Can't stay away from work?" Ellie inquired.

"Sorry, I've been waiting for my assistant to touch base," said Hattie, standing up. "I'm going to try giving Kayla a call. Then we can walk to town. I'll take you to the farmers market."

"Sounds good."

Beau came in from the mudroom with his toolbox. He was wearing a baseball hat, backward, and earbuds, listening to music. "Is it okay if I take Queenie? She can hang outside with me."

"Sure. Ellie and I are walking to the farmers market. She's cooking dinner tonight. I hope you can join us."

"Sweet! Love to. Hey, Queenie, let's go," Beau commanded. Queenie got up and followed him outside. Ellie shook her head in disbelief. "You Browns have the magic dog touch."

"Kinda do," said Beau as they went outside.

"Did you get ahold of your assistant?" Ellie asked Hattie.

"No, but it's Saturday morning and Kayla's likely sleeping off a hangover. She's young, into the club scene. Hey, let's clean up, head to town."

"What about your breakfast?"

"I'm not hungry," said Hattie.

"So? That's never stopped me."

Hattie had thrown on a white T-shirt, denim shorts, and her Converse tennis shoes. Ellie wore the blue-and-white sundress she purchased the previous day with a new straw hat. She looked every bit a Southern belle. Except, of course, when she opened her mouth, she was all Boston.

"Is the faaaarmers maaarkit faaar?

"Far enough to leave the stilletos at home and put some flats on," laughed Hattie.

Chapter 39:
An Insider's Guide to Training

"Hattie Brown, is that you?" a familiar voice hollered. It was Mrs. Perkins, her high school science teacher, wearing the same huge, round glasses she wore when Hattie was in school. She was walking a fiery little terrier, which was growling at the world.

"Hello, Mrs. Perkins. Good to see you."

"Yes, dear, wonderful to see you!" exclaimed Mrs. Perkins. "You were my favorite. I still brag about you to my students."

"I see you've got a new friend with you," noted Hattie.

"This is Scruffles. Frankly, he's as naughty as the kids I send to detention. Chewed the legs of my dining chairs and the corner of an oriental rug in my study. And the damage he's done to my shoes. If I recall correctly, you helped your mother with dog training. Care to give your former teacher advice?"

"Awww, yes, let me think. Since you're gone all day teaching, you'll likely need to crate Scruffles. Bored dogs get into trouble."

"I can't do that."

"Trust me, Mrs. Perkins. You can. The crate will become like a bedroom to Scruffles, a comforting place to rest."

"Well, dear, I am going to try your suggestion. After all, you were my smartest student."

"Good, if crating doesn't work, call me. I'm staying at Mema's cottage for a few more days. Goodness, Mrs. Perkins, I failed to introduce my dear friend, Eleanor Reade. We were roommates at Harvard. We're on our way to the farmers market—we've got to get there before vendors sell out of fresh produce! Good to see you!"

"Likewise. Thank you, Hattie. Oh, one more thing," said Mrs. Perkins.

"Yes?"

"I hear Beau's been getting into trouble. You best get a handle on it."

"Yes, ma'am."

"And I understand you are an investment banker."

"Yes, ma'am," Hattie said with pride.

"I never hold back from telling my students what I think about their choices. And you, dear, have so much talent. There's more to life than making money. Keep that in mind. People change careers all the time, to find what suits them best."

"Yes, well, thank you," said Hattie.

Ellie couldn't stop laughing when they were out of Mrs. Perkin's sight. "Does Mrs. Perkins have any other hobbies besides snooping on her former student's life?"

"Welcome to Fairhope. There's a reason I left."

Chapter 40:
Homegrown Folks

The Fairhope farmers market was bustling with activity—vendors selling organic fruits and vegetables, fresh-cut flowers, and baked goods. It was a sensory joyride.

As Ellie inspected a batch of cucumbers, Hattie scrolled through her emails. Kayla finally responded. *Nothing unusual at work. Enjoy the vacay!*

A yellow Labrador suddenly darted in and out of Hattie's legs carrying a French baguette in its jaw. The owner, a disheveled mom in a white sundress, hair pulled back in a ponytail, was dragging three young kids behind her, screaming, "Maggie, stop!"

"I should help her out," Hattie told Ellie. "That's Gay Sorenson. She goes to my church."

The Labrador stopped to chomp on the baguette. Hattie calmly walked closer, bending over to the Labrador's level.

"Come here, pretty girl," she said happily. "Come, girl." After Hattie offered up a friendly tone and a big smile, the retriever dropped the baguette and licked Hattie's face.

"Good girl!" Hattie said, petting the dog with one hand, reaching out to grasp the leash with the other.

The haggard-looking mom, with her youngest dragging behind her, raced to Hattie.

"Thank you!" she said gratefully. The mother, whose strands
of blond hair had escaped her ponytail, turned her attention to the
Lab, the she-devil voice returning. "Bad dog! You are a bad, bad
dog! I don't have time for this crap."

The Lab cowered its tail between its hind legs, wanting nothing to do with his mom.

"Gay Sorenson, right? I'm Hattie Sinclaire, Mema's granddaughter."

It was always an easy icebreaker for Hattie. Most folks at
church knew Mema. "I attend First Methodist, too," said Hattie.
"Rather, I used to. I live in Boston now."

"Why, yes, of course. I apologize. My children wanted to bring
the dog along. I accidentally dropped the leash to chase my three-
year-old. The dog took off. Makes me so crazy!"

"Dogs can do that to us," acknowledged Hattie. "Years ago, I
helped my mother train dogs. Some days I was so fed up I wanted
to quit. Mama taught me one particular trick of the trade that
made my life a whole lot easier."

"And what was that?"

"When you want a dog to come, skip the mad voice and use
a happy voice."

"What?" asked the confused young mother. "Why?"

"It's like this, a mad voice means she's in trouble. And she's not
interested in coming back only to lose her freedom and receive a
scolding."

Hattie realized her Southern accent was completely back. It
was nice, like reuniting with an old friend.

"Use a treat," continued Hattie. "Use praise. Even if y'all madder than a hornet, fake the happy voice. Believe me, it took a lot of convincing before I put it into practice."

"It's not how I raise my own children."

"And your children are wonderful, I can tell. I would never tell you how to raise kids. Dogs are different. They only know a few words, commands. Your tone really matters—the difference between a dog that runs and a dog that comes."

"I'll try," said Gay. "Thank you."

Hattie reached down to scratch behind the dog's ears. "And, Miss Maggie, I expect from now on when your Mama says 'come' in her sweet voice, you listen. Don't make a fool of me."

The Lab wagged its tail and licked Hattie.

"I think she understands."

The frazzled mother gave Hattie a half-hearted smile. "I hope so, again, thank you for the help."

"Of course."

"Shall we head back to Mema's?" Hattie asked Ellie.

"Who are you, Hattie Brown Sinclaire? Cesar Milan's second cousin? Fairhope's dog whisperer? You never told me how great you are with dogs."

"I trained dogs a lifetime ago. I've worked hard to get away from it. I assure you. Those days are behind me."

Chapter 41:
Afraid of the One
You're With

Queenie was not in her crate. She looked around. No chewing damage, no evidence of counter surfing. Hattie guessed she was with Beau.

She was right, finding Beau crashed out on a big oversize chair, his legs resting on a leather ottoman. Queenie sleeping on his lap.

"Suicide bomber on the left," Beau said, mumbling in his sleep. "Shoot 'im, now!" Beau's head was going forward and backward as if a boxer's punching bag. Queenie rose from her sleeping position, her thick front paws moving up until they settled on his chest. The dog stared at Beau like a doctor assessing a patient.

Hattie was afraid to move, fearing she'd be Beau's unintended target. Queenie, however, showed no fear and began frantically licking Beau's sweaty face. Slowly, the licks woke Beau from his nightmare. His arms stopped thrashing. Hattie marveled at what she'd just seen.

His eyes opened.

"What the heck? Stop licking me like I'm a popsicle."

His entire body felt soaked from sweat, his chin covered in dog slobber.

"You okay?" Hattie quietly asked.

"Yeah, just a bad dream."

"Do you have them often?"

"Wish I had them less."

"I'm sorry."

"Yeah, me too."

"Ellie is cooking us dinner. She wants fresh seafood. I'm going to take her to the pier."

"I'll take her. I know the guys there. Give me a minute to wake up, change shirts."

Hattie didn't know how to respond. Was anyone safe around Beau these days?

"I suppose," Hattie stuttered.

"Boy, you sound like a parent whose teenage daughter just got asked out for the first time. Listen, Ellie told me she's got a boyfriend in Paris. Give me some credit."

The boyfriend situation was hardly on Hattie's radar.

"Let me ask her? I'll be right back."

Hattie filled Ellie on what she'd witnessed.

"I got this, Hattie, it's me, remember, I survived childhood trauma. PTSD is one area where I actually know more than you."

In the end, Hattie reluctantly let Ellie go with Beau. Like an overprotective parent, she watched as they climbed in the truck. Ellie was still wearing her sundress and had put on her new pink strappy sandals. Beau put a baseball cap on over his sweaty hair.

"Okay, y'all be back, what in an hour, or so, right?"

"Depends," said Beau.

"Depends on what?" Hattie asked anxiously.

"Depends on whether your best friend is good at catching fish."

"Whaaat?" Ellie exclaimed. "When I said fresh seafood, I meant from a seafood market, the kind of place that fillets the fish, then beautifully displays the latest catch on ice for customers to admire."

"We can do one better," Beau interrupted.

Ellie groaned. "You're taking me fishing."

* * *

"How'd y'all do?" Hattie hollered to them from the garden as Beau and Ellie climbed out of Beau's new pickup. Hattie was dressed in Mema's wellies, torn-kneed blue jeans, and a T-shirt. She wore one of Beau's baseball caps to keep the sun at bay. She'd made great progress on weeding the garden beds.

"Your friend, here, caught some decent-sized grouper."

"I expected nothing less, Ellie salmon fishes with her grandfather every spring."

"Impressive."

"Charles didn't have a grandson, so I've pretty much done it all," shrugged Ellie. "I'm going to get cleaned up. I know you work tonight; dinner will be ready before you leave."

"Looking forward to it," he smiled.

Hattie sat on the porch swing with Beau.

"I love this swing, it's a gift to those of us who enjoy porch sitting."

"Thanks, just put it in last week."

"I love your touches. You've made it yours."

"This is your place, too. The door is always open."

"Thank you. I promise to be a regular visitor."

"I hope so."

"I'm going to head over to say hello to Pastor Luis soon. Call me if you need anything."

"Of course," said Beau. "Hey, you might as well hear it from me first."

"Yeah, what's up?"

"You know his girlfriend, Lauren, right?"

"Not well. She sang beautifully at Mema's service. She's lovely."

"That's not how I'd describe her but okay. Luis confided to me Lauren left Fairhope and is living in New York. Wants to jump-start her acting career. Guess she has higher aspirations than doing community theater in Fairhope."

"That's tough. It's not as if a pastor can commute on weekends to visit his girlfriend. You think Pastor Luis will leave our church and head to New York?"

"Not likely. Lauren fell in love with a 'suit' who works at Goldman Sachs. He's got big bucks. She asked Luis to ship her things."

"I don't even know what to say." Hattie was heartsick for Luis. "He didn't say anything."

"He doesn't talk about it much. Best not to say anything."

"I won't say a word, promise."

Hattie changed out of her gardening clothes, threw on a jean skirt, flip-flops, and a clean T-shirt, and headed to First Methodist.

"Hi Rebecca, is Pastor Luis around?" Hattie asked.

Rebecca was the church custodian. She filled in as receptionist when LeeAnne was at lunch.

"He's eating lunch in the church garden. I'm sure he'd love the company."

Peering through the pine trees, Hattie saw Pastor Luis sitting on a bench, eating. The same crazy cowlick that he so desperately tried to control the first time she saw him was still there, giving him a boyish charm.

"Care if I join you?" asked Hattie.

"Your timing is perfect. How about half a turkey sandwich and some Cheetos?"

"Aren't Cheetos for kids?"

"Absolutely not."

"I'll pass on the Cheetos, but half a turkey sandwich sounds good."

"Okay, but you're missing out on the beauty of eating Cheetos as an adult."

"And what's that?"

"As an adult, I know better than to wipe the orange stuff on my pants."

"Disgusting." Hattie laughed, wondering how Lauren could fall out of love with someone who was so kind and easy to be around.

"I've got an extra bottle of water, care for one?" Hattie asked, pulling two bottles out of her backpack.

"You're always prepared, practical. I like it."

"Practical is my middle name," Hattie said. "Which lately has not done me any favors."

"Why is that?"

"You don't want to know," she shook her head. "Besides, it's not about me. I came by to thank you for your help with Beau last night."

"Of course."

"The more I learn about trauma, the more I realize there are no easy answers."

"You're correct, it's far bigger than you and me. We need to offer it up to the Lord in prayer."

"I hope he's listening."

"He's always listening."

"You think so?"

"I know so."

"Lately, I'm not so sure."

"Let's give it a try, anyway. What do we have to lose?" Pastor Luis gently clasped her hand.

"Dear Lord and Jesus Christ, we ask you to guide your son Beau as he works through his emotional scars. As he fights an invisible enemy only he can see. We ask that you guide us in our words and actions as we do our best to help him. We accept that we can't fix him, and ask you to lead us to the people who can. In your name, we pray. Amen."

"Amen."

They ate in a comfortable silence.

"Beau should see a therapist," said Hattie.

"I agree."

"Anyone you recommend?"

"There are several excellent therapists in Fairhope who've helped several members of our church, but I have yet to found one who specializes in trauma."

"Does that mean he'll have to go somewhere outside of Fairhope for help?"

"It appears so."

"I researched trauma centers near me, in Boston."

Hattie described how they use nontraditional therapies such as yoga, meditation, music, even horseback riding to help people suffering from PTSD. She further explained how trauma affects the brain.

"I feel like I'm back at Harvard."

Hattie's face flushed in embarrassment. "I apologize. Asher says I have a tendency to be boringly academic."

"Not at all. You are blessed with a sharp mind. God calls us to share our gifts. In time, Asher will understand and appreciate it."

Hattie's eyes welled up, tears falling onto her cheeks like a dripping faucet.

"I don't think so. Asher isn't happy. With us. With me," she quietly confided.

Pastor Luis leaned in to look her in the eyes.

"He may be unhappy with himself, you know."

"No, it's me. I've tried so, so hard, to become the type of wife Asher wants me to be—pretending to be spontaneous, funny, even sophisticated. Top it off with a few pathetic attempts at being the life of the party—which by the way is difficult when you're more suited to being a wallflower."

Pastor Luis nodded knowingly.

"And as hard as I tried to live up to his expectations, the real me keeps popping out at the most inopportune times. I'm like the baby crying during your sermon, an annoying noise."

"Crying babies are part of life."

"The truth is, Pastor Luis, the real me is not enough."

Hattie's cheeks grew red and blotchy, her nose running. Pastor Luis handed her his handkerchief, like the ones Daddy used to carry in his hip pocket. It was soft and smelled like fabric softner.

"I've learned, the hard way, convincing others we are perfect for them is not our job," Pastor Luis said hoarsely, clearing his throat. "If we stay true to ourselves, be the person God intends us to be, we are always enough."

Chapter 42:
The Company
You Keep

Hattie walked in the kitchen and Ellie was hunched over her laptop.

"What y'all doing?"

"I keep my favorite recipes on my Mac so they are always at my fingertips. These are my babies."

"Gotcha."

Hattie watched as Ellie scrolled through the seafood folder.

"I'll make the pan-seared grouper and farro risotto with asparagus. The encore would be a strawberry shortcake served with the Guatemalan coffee I purchased at the farmers market."

"Boy am I glad you are my best friend."

"Back at you, girlfriend."

Hattie watched Ellie as she filleted the fish with the precision of a surgeon. She was dressed in her formal chef attire, blocking out everything but the meal prep, including Beau, who stepped in the kitchen to grab a couple glasses of sweet tea.

"Ellie, need any help?"

"You two go relax. I get very intense in the kitchen. You are better off outside."

Hattie laughed. "Hey, Beau, let's go on the porch."

Both sat down on the new porch swing.

"Why is Ellie here?"

"She's on break from school," said Hattie, her eye twitching, a Brown family quirk. "Her grandparents are celebrating their fiftieth anniversary next week, she's going to surprise them."

"And after traveling all the way from Paris, she drives here, isn't that a lot?"

Hattie inhaled air to calm herself. She knew where this was heading.

"Yes, it is. Ellie wanted to help me help you. Drive with me in the Jeep."

"Hattie, your eye is twitching like a June bug. You're not telling me the whole story."

Hattie pulled her phone out of her pocket, checking the screen. Asher still hadn't messaged her. If he wanted to reach her, he would have done so by now. It was time to tell Beau the truth, all of it. And for the most part, she did. The intimate details, though, she wasn't sharing. When she was done talking, Beau asked, "Do you want to be married to Asher?"

"I do."

"I hope he gets a clue then. Cuz he's ruining the best thing that's ever happened to him. I'd like to pummel some sense into the idiot."

"I'm a grown woman. I don't need you solving my problems, particularly with physical force."

"Oh, come on. Tell me it wouldn't feel good to see him get what he deserves."

"Beau, I'm warning you, stay out of it."

Ellie opened the kitchen window. "Dinner in a few minutes. I'm going to change into something cooler."

"Let's go in and help her dish up the food."

They heard someone sprinting down the hallway to the kitchen. Ellie ran straight into Hattie and Beau, who'd come in the kitchen to wash their hands.

"You look like you've seen a ghost," Hattie said.

Ellie was white as a sheet. "OMG, I just saw a shadowy figure standing in Mema's bedroom. It looked like the spitting image of your grandmother. When I took a second look, the figure was gone."

"You likely saw Mema. I've witnessed it myself lately," said Beau nonchalantly. "As I told Hattie, it's only a spirit that has a few loose ends to complete on earth. From what I sense, Mema won't be here long."

"Oh my gosh?" stammered Ellie. "You and Hattie and your ghosts."

"Calm down. No one ever died from seeing a ghost. Look, you're fine, right?"

"Uh, wow, well okay, I best get back to cooking. I don't want to overcook the grouper. And I'd take a shot of bourbon. Calm my nerves."

"I'll get you one. First, I'm going to run upstairs and change for work. Then I'm pouring you a glass of some of the finest Kentucky bourbon ever made."

"Be quick," warned Ellie. "Dinner is almost ready."

Beau returned wearing freshly laundered Levi jeans and a navy polo shirt with his brewery's logo on the breast pocket, joining

Hattie at the picnic table. Hattie wore white denim jeans and a chambray jean shirt.

Ellie planned the dinner outside on Mema's patio. A white linen tablecloth covered the picnic table set with Mema's china, a centerpiece of freshly cut flowers, and three lit candles. It reminded Hattie of Sunday supper at Mema's, which was always delicious with a lovely set table prepared for guests, a far cry from Mama's meals, which often were wolfing down a sandwich while standing so they could quickly get back to training dogs. Ellie came outside carrying a serving tray with dinner plates of seasoned fish, risotto with asparagus, and a slice of crusty baguette bread.

"This is like Sunday suppers when we were growing up; this reminds me of that. It's really nice. Thanks, Ellie."

"You Northerners aren't so bad," teased Beau.

During dinner Hattie and Beau shared childhood memories. Ellie laughed, enjoying their stories. Her blue eyes sparkled with laughter. Her blond hair glowed in the candlelight. Hattie thought Ellie had never looked more beautiful.

"It was an amazing meal," Beau said, placing his napkin on his plate. "I'm sorry to say, I have to head to work. I've enjoyed this. Please save me a piece of the shortcake."

"We'll leave the lights on," said Hattie. "Text if you need anything."

After dinner, Hattie cleared the table and washed dishes.

"The night's young. Do you want to watch a movie on Netflix?"

"In our jammies with a big bowl of popcorn?" Ellie asked.

"Yes! Like old times."

The movie lulled them to sleep on Mema's sofa with Queenie fast asleep between them.

* * *

"Morning, ladies. Y'all having a beach day?"

"We're hoping you join us," Hattie said.

"I've got lumber to pick up at nine to replace some wood rot. I could join up after. Which beach?"

"Dauphin Island, West End."

"Sweet. I'll bring a couple of paddleboards."

"Can we borrow the Jeep?"

"You can have it."

Hattie hated to admit she might have to take him up on his offer.

The beach parking lot was almost full.

"Must be spring breakers," said Hattie.

"Hey, there's a spot."

Hattie and Ellie unloaded beach chairs, a cooler, towels, and a huge umbrella. They headed up the sand dunes, finding a quiet spot hidden by seagrass.

"Want one of the books I brought?" Hattie asked. "I've got a couple of good mysteries."

"No, thanks. I'm going to close my eyes and soak up this gorgeous sun, get a much-needed dose of vitamin D."

Ellie nodded off in the beach chair, the warm sun making her sleepy and relaxed. She woke to two men shouting at each other.

"Sounds like trouble," Ellie said.

"Sounds like Beau," Hattie said, jumping out of her beach chair. "I better see what's going on."

"I'm right behind you," followed Ellie, not taking time to put on her swimsuit cover-up.

Hattie and Ellie took a shortcut down a steep sand dune to get to the parking lot. The volume and intensity of the argument was escalating.

"I think you meant to say to me, 'Welcome to the beach,'" Beau shouted at a skinny teenage boy wearing pants that hung low below his rear. He was shirtless with a half-inch gold chain around his neck.

"No, I said give me the F-ing parking spot, first come, first serve," the teenager hollered.

"You were too busy playing smooch face with your underage girlfriend to notice. The spot was free and clear when I pulled in," said Beau, untying the ropes holding the paddleboards on his truck.

"Get real. I was waiting for the Corolla to back out."

"No, you were making out. I gave you three full minutes and a couple of friendly honks before I took it."

"I don't have to take your crap," said the teenager, drawing a knife blade on Beau.

"We're calling the cops," Ellie bellowed like a ship's fog horn.

Beau was in fight mode. He had the teenager in a neck hold, grasping the gold chain as if he was going to choke the kid to death.

"Beau, let him go," pleaded Hattie. "He's a waste of time."

"Help me, God," she prayed. She tried redirecting, again.

"Beau," hollered Hattie, "bring the paddleboards over by where we're sitting, our usual spot, up over the sand dunes."

Beau stared at her blankly, his eyes glazed over.

"Ellie needs help putting the umbrella up."

Hattie glanced nervously at Ellie.

"Hey there, Beau," Ellie said in a seductive voice. "I really need you to fix our umbrella, the wind keeps blowing it away. And I've got this new green-and-pink bikini. My fair skin is burning up like bacon in the fryer."

Beau loosened his death grip. The young man dropped to the ground, gasping for air. Beau grabbed the kid's knife. The sweet young girlfriend was covering her eyes. Beau tapped her shoulder, handed her the knife. "This guy is a loser, dump him."

"Let's go, now!" shouted the teenage girl, who was crying uncontrollably.

The teenage boy jumped back in his car, flipped off Beau, and sped out of the parking lot.

Beau inhaled deeply, raking his fingers through his shoulder-length hair.

"Come on," Beau said tersely. "I came to teach you two how to paddleboard. Let's get to it."

Hattie and Ellie dutifully followed Beau like obedient soldiers to the shallow water.

"Let's start out on all fours, like you're giving a pony ride to a kid," Beau instructed.

Ellie and Hattie got the hang of it.

"Now, it gets harder, separates the girls from the women," said Beau. "Slowly, try standing."

Ellie stood immediately. Her strong, muscular legs from days spent as a chef in training made it look easy.

"Ace, you got it!" he hollered to Ellie. "Hattie, your turn."

Hattie, sitting all day at a desk job, had lost much of the leg strength she had as a trainer. She attempted to stand, each time the paddleboard escaping from her. After a half dozen falls into the water, she, too, finally experienced success.

"Hattie, you need to put some weight on, too darn skinny," Beau said.

"I'll gladly give her a few of my extra," Ellie said, her long hair clinging to her back and shoulders.

"Why? You look good."

"Please, I know you're being kind. Which isn't like you. Where's the Beau I first met?"

"You're right. I'm more like this," Beau said, tipping Ellie off the SUP board.

"You loser!" Ellie teased.

"Now that you've practiced falling and passed with an A," he laughed, "our next lesson is moving to a low stance, on your knees, paddling. Like this." Beau demonstrated.

Hattie and Ellie watched closely, then attempted it several times unsuccessfully.

"One more time, you almost got it. I swear."

Sure enough, Ellie was on her knees, paddling like a pro.

"Darn, girl, you're a quick learner. Position your feet where your knees are, slowly stand."

Ellie did as she was told, keeping her balance.

"Look straight ahead. Shoulders back. Try paddling!"

For a few solid strokes Ellie was amazing, holding her own. The wind picked up, the waves got bigger, and she was tossed upside down, looking like a kid doing a cartwheel. Beau dove toward her to help, grabbing Ellie's arm and the paddleboard.

"I say that's it for the day. You've done well, but enough is enough. The wind is picking up. And it's getting rough."

"Agreed. I'm feeling shaky, I need something to eat."

Beau raised his eyebrows.

"Don't say a word," Ellie warned.

"Ellie, you look beautiful," interjected Hattie.

"Totally agree. I was gonna say you fill out that bikini nicely. Thanks for asking me to check it out earlier."

"I only did that to distract you," Ellie scolded. "To stop you from beating up a stupid teenager."

"It worked. Really, thank you," he said squeezing her hand. "I mean it."

"I know you do."

"Have enough food to share?"

"A good chef always does."

Hattie watched as her best friend and cousin chatted so easily. She wished she'd been comfortable like that with Asher. She'd always been so nervous, afraid of making a mistake around him.

Ellie served up turkey sandwiches on whole grain bread with organic greens topped with slices of tomatoes and a chipotle sauce. The trio sat quietly eating, watching the tide. After lunch Beau began packing up the boards.

"Ladies, I better head back."

"Thanks for the lesson!" said Ellie smiling at Beau.

"We'll stop by the brewery later," said Hattie.

"Good, it's usually quiet on Wednesdays. Lots of folks like you."

"What's that mean?" asked Hattie.

Beau shrugged his big shoulders. "Book club folks. They've become my Wednesday regulars."

Hattie smiled. "Then we'll fit right in."

Chapter 43:
Party Crashers

Instead of a low-key night at the brewery, beer flowed like the Mississippi River. All the tables were filled. Hattie and Ellie sat at the bar. Beau made a point to stop and chat when he had a free moment.

The usual Wednesday night book club crowd was outnumbered by a large group of boisterous conventioneers staying at the Grand Resort. The group amiably called it a night.

"Ladies, looks like once I clean up, I can get out of here."

"Can we help you clean?" asked Hattie.

"I'll take all the help I can get."

Beau headed into the storage room to get cleaning solution and rags to wipe down the tables and bar. When he returned from the backroom, a local semiprofessional rugby team had arrived, fifteen minutes before closing time.

"Oh jeez," said Beau to Hattie and Ellie. "Look what the cat dragged in. I'm familiar with these guys. A local rugby team with the maturity of high school sophomores."

Hattie noticed the muscles in Beau's neck tighten as several rugby players strutted up to the bar.

"What can I do you for?" asked Beau.

"I'll have the cheapest beer you got," said one of the players with dark curly hair, wearing a shirt that said "Team Captain" on the back.

"We don't serve cheap, we're a craft brewery," said Beau.

"Then give me whatever the pretty blonde over there is drinking."

Hattie, Beau, and Ellie all turned to see who he was talking about. Sophie Bicksford. Sophie was as pretty as she was kind. She'd attended Ole Miss, where she met her husband. Her father was owner of First Bank Fairhope, her mother was a former debutante. A good family. Sophie, the Bickfords' only child, was an elementary school teacher, and her husband owned a small law firm in town that handled the brewery's legal work.

"I'll even leave a tip if ya introduce me to her."

The captain's teammates laughed and jeered.

"That fine woman is happily married," Beau said. "She won't be interested. She's here with her book club. Most of 'em are teachers. They all have kids."

"Sure is *perrty*," said the captain. "Does she mess around?"

"What did you say your name was?" asked Beau.

"Bud. Bud Hansen. Captain of the team."

"Bud, it'd be best to leave her alone," warned Beau. "Her husband is an attorney."

"My little woman is out of town," shared Bud. "And I'm looking for someone real cute to party with. She's real cute."

"Bud, I'll say it again. The group over there is a book club. They read books. Something I'm guessing you don't do much."

"I don't care what her IQ is."

"Listen, why don't y'all head on over to Lewy's, the pickin' is a whole lot easier over there. We're more of a family-friendly brewery."

"Are you kicking us out?" Bud sneered.

"Trying to help you find folks more to your liking."

"My liking is the blonde over there," slurred Bud. He downed his beer, belched, then staggered over to Sophie's table. He was drunk and loud.

"Looks like y'all might need some male company tonight," Bud said, placing his grimey hand on Sophie's shoulder. "Can me and my team buy y'all a beer?"

Sophie looked visibly uncomfortable. Caily Walight, the woman seated next to Sophie, pushed Bud's hand off Sophie's shoulder.

"No thank you," Sophie politely said. "Us moms are heading home shortly."

"Night's still young," argued Bud.

"Not interested," snapped Caily, a mother of five, four of which were teenage boys.

"I can make you interested," said one of the rugby players.

Hattie and Ellie watched as the tension in the room became palpable.

"This isn't going to end well," warned Ellie.

"Please leave," begged Sophie. "Before I tell the bartender you're harassing me and my friends." Sophie stood up, shoulders back, staring at the rugby team to show she was not easily intimidated.

"Loosen up," taunted Bud. "We're just lookin' for some fun. Not askin' y'all to get hitched."

Bud reached around, attempting to cup his hand around Sophie's breast. A rough hand grabbed Bud's forearm with brute force, preventing that from happening. "Not on my watch," said Beau, twisting Bud's arm so tight it could snap like a stick.

A set of knuckles hit the temple of Beau's head, sending him reeling.

Beau fought back. Two direct blows. The first was to the rugby captain's spleen area, forcing Bud to keel over; the second blow had Bud down on his knees, begging Beau to stop.

By the grace of God, Beau came out of his trance, stopped himself before delivering the third blow. "You ever try that crap on another woman, I'll kill you. I swear to God."

"This isn't the end of this," Bud sputtered out spit like oil on a hot pan.

Hattie heard one of the rugby players, an off-duty cop, on his cell phone to the sheriff. Sophie was on her phone, asking her lawyer husband to come down to the brewery.

Sophie's husband arrived on Pastor Luis's heels. The sheriff arrived shortly thereafter.

"That son of a bitch is way out of control," Bud shouted to the sheriff. "Arrest him. He tried to kill me."

Hattie watched as Pastor Luis was talking Beau down from a highly agitated state, asking him to take a few deep breaths.

"Sheriff, you have a minute?" Sophie's husband, Tom, asked.

"No Tom, I don't. I'm arresting Beau Brown."

"You are not," interjected Hattie. "He was not in the wrong."

"Sheriff, you should be aware that my wife is ready to file sexual assault charges against Bud."

"Excuse me?" the sheriff asked.

"Bud assaulted my wife. Sophie was here with her book club. She and her lady friends told Bud to leave them alone. He tried grabbing my wife's breast. Beau stopped him. It's all on video—her friend's cell phone."

"Are you telling me if Bud files charges against Beau, your wife is filing charges against Bud?"

"I am."

"We witnessed the whole thing," said Ellie. "Beau rescued Sophie tonight from that jerk over there who accosted her."

"Beau's a good guy," said Tom.

"Used to be. Trouble now. One more incident like that, I'm throwing Beau in jail."

The sheriff walked over to Bud.

"Hattie, got a minute?" asked Tom.

"Of course."

"I appreciate what Beau did for Sophie. I really do. But you gotta get Beau some help in controlling his temper. I can't keep bailing him out of jail. Sheriff is serious about locking him up."

"We're working on it together," said Pastor Luis, who was now standing next to Hattie. "I'll stay with Beau until close. Hattie, you head back home. Tom, I'll touch base with you later."

Hattie and Ellie were still up, in the kitchen playing cards, when Pastor Luis and Beau walked in.

"Smells delicious in here. Tex-Mex?" asked Beau.

"I've got enchiladas in the oven. Late-night margarita, anyone?" said Ellie.

"I'll take one," Pastor Luis said. "I'm starving. How about you, Beau?"

"Sure, but hold off on dinner for a minute or two. I have something I need to give Hattie," he said. "I'll be right back."

He went upstairs, taking the steps two by two.

"I've got to do something to help him," Hattie whispered to Ellie and Luis. "Sophie's husband warned me that the sheriff is watching Beau. If there's a next time, he'll throw Beau in jail."

The conversation halted when they heard Beau coming down the stairs. Ellie let out a gasp, almost dropping the pan of enchiladas when she saw Beau.

Beau was holding a gun.

"Y'all, don't panic," Beau said calmly. "This here gun was left to me by Mema."

"Mema would never have had a gun," Hattie said in disbelief.

"You're wrong. It's a family heirloom. Funny thing, still works like a charm."

"I'm so uncomfortable with this," said Hattie.

"Right now, so am I," Beau admitted. "For what it's worth, I've been having these dreams. Mema's in my room, talking to me, telling me what to do. She says Hattie needs Henry."

"Henry?" asked Pastor Luis.

"Henry is this here gun. It was owned by Judge Henry, who left it to Frank, Mema's husband. The Judge and Frank were best friends. After Frank passed, Mema inherited Henry."

"Mema's been talking to me too," admitted Hattie.

"It's another world down here," Ellie said, handing Pastor Luis a fork and knife. "First ghosts, now this."

An uncomfortable silence came over the room.

"Hattie, keep Henry," instructed Beau. "You may need it to protect yourself, maybe from me."

He coughed uncomfortably, trying to get words out.

"I don't much trust myself right now. If I'm out of control, use it if you need to. I won't blame you. Self-defense. Mema seems to know something we don't. I suspect we should follow her wishes."

Hattie silently accepted the gun from Beau, as if she were being handed a rattlesnake. Whether she needed Henry or not, she knew to keep the gun away from Beau.

"Okay, enough gun talk. I'm not even going to get started on what I think about people owning guns, so please eat," said Ellie.

"Terrific!" exclaimed Pastor Luis. "Everyone please join me in thanking Ellie, and of course, the good Lord, for this wonderful, much-needed meal."

They bowed their heads.

"Thank you for the food before us, thank you for family, living and deceased, thank you for bringing together old friends and new friends. Amen."

"This is my kind of Tex-Mex," said Pastor Luis, taking a huge bite.

"These are downright fantastic!" Beau exclaimed. "I could serve these enchiladas at the brewery and sell a ton of 'em."

"Not a chance," Hattie said. "Jean Paul has big plans for our Ellie."

"What kind of plans?" Pastor Luis inquired.

"Yeah, tell us, what kind of plans?" Beau chimed in. "Because your food and my beer could put us on the culinary map. I may steal you away."

Ellie smiled at the compliment.

"I've been offered a position as a sous chef to the executive chef of a five-star restaurant in Paris. Jean Paul is a food celebrity, of sorts, at least in France. I'll be working directly for him."

"When you get sick of snails and caviar, you know who to call," Beau teased.

Chapter 44:
Boston Calls

E arly the next morning, Hattie's phone rang. She headed out to the porch so not to disturb the others still sleeping.

"This is Hattie Sinclaire," she said, speaking softly into her cell phone as she looked out at the bay, hoping the calmness of the water would seep into her.

"Hattie, it's Richard. Do you have a few minutes to talk? Privately?"

"I do."

"I've got bad news. The Federal IPO is under government scrutiny. The SEC is looking into insider trading, perhaps someone at the firm."

"That's ridiculous. There's absolutely no way."

"I thought so too. Until I was informed someone purchased Federal stock two days before the IPO, then sold it the day of the public offering. Made close to a million dollars. The SEC is requesting a review of our protocol, emails, and correspondence, anything pertaining to Federal's IPO."

She didn't know how, or why, but she was certain Asher was involved. How had he gotten insider information? She hadn't told him a thing. He hadn't been in their apartment in weeks.

"I'll leave Fairhope immediately. And Richard, I promise you, I did nothing wrong."

"Good, then you can clear this up when you return Friday."

"Of course. See you then."

She hung up. It immediately rang again.

"Richard?" Hattie asked.

"No. It's Luis."

"Sorry, I thought it was my boss. Something urgent has come up at my office. I need to head back to Boston sooner than I planned."

"I'm deeply sorry. Beau and I have enjoyed you being here. When do you leave?"

"Today."

"Perhaps our prayers are being answered. I heard from a former Harvard classmate of mine who is friends with the chaplain at one of the Boston trauma centers. Apparently, he has some pull there. If you can get Beau to Boston by Monday, they'll see him for an evaluation."

"That's incredible timing, thank you."

"Not sure Beau will see it that way," cautioned Luis. "Why don't I head over and talk to him?"

"That would be wonderful."

"I'll be there shortly."

Hattie was shaky after Richard's call. She took a few deep breaths to compose herself, with her mind spinning, she proceeded inside to share the news.

"Hey, you two, looks like something's come up at work. I need to get back to Boston."

"Can't it wait a few more days, please," Ellie begged. "You deserve a week off, and I'm really enjoying your town."

"Unfortunately, no. My boss called, there's a mandatory meeting this Friday."

"Rats, I was really enjoying the company," Beau admitted.

"Why don't you come with us?" asked Hattie.

"No can do."

"Beau, please come. There's…"

"No," Beau interrupted. "I've got a brewery to run."

The doorbell rang. Ellie jumped at the chance to answer it.

"Aren't you a sight for tired eyes," Ellie said to Pastor Luis, who was standing at the front door with a drink carrier filled with four cups of coffee.

"Good morning, long time no see," he teased. "What's it been, six hours or so?"

"More like five," Ellie said, reaching for a cup. "Which is why I need this, badly. If you'll excuse me, I am going to shower. I understand we're leaving."

Hattie, Beau, and Pastor Luis gathered at the kitchen table. Beau's left leg was bouncing anxiously like a child waiting for the end of the school day bell to ring.

"The sheriff called me this morning. A courtesy call," Pastor Luis told them. "The rugby player you had a run-in with last night hired a lawyer out of Mobile."

"He's an idiot," scoffed Beau. "He assaulted a woman. I defended her. Plain and simple."

"The sheriff says he's giving you a pass since you're military. But he believes you have an anger-management problem. We need to show we've got a mental health plan in place, or we've got a problem."

"What about our deal—Sophie agreeing not to press charges against Bud if Bud didn't press charges against me?" asked Beau.

"The lawyer says the deal was struck under duress."

"Slimeball," Beau muttered.

"There are excellent therapists who specialize in what you're going through," Pastor Luis said. "Unfortunately, none in Fairhope."

"Looks like I best make the effort to go to Mobile, even Birmingham if I have to."

"The good news is Hattie and I found a great place for you, one of the best in the country."

"By the looks on your faces, it's not Mobile or Birmingham?"

"It's Boston," Hattie said enthusiastically.

Beau stood up from the kitchen table, throwing up his hands in frustration.

"Y'all planned this, didn't you?" he scoffed. "It ticks me off, Hattie, that you think everything's better in Boston. Get over yourself."

"Beau, don't be mad at Hattie. We did research, independently, and we arrived at the same conclusion."

"I hate the thought of leaving Fairhope. I've been gone so long. I love the people in this town. And darn it, they love me," Beau muttered. "I don't have a single friend in Boston."

"Apparently, I don't count," Ellie said, looking spectacular as she entered the kitchen. She'd washed her hair, put a touch of makeup on, and wore a pretty chambray sundress. "And if you have me for a friend, you've got my grandparents, Charles and Claire.

And then there's Queenie, likely the best friend anyone could ask for, and she'll be with us until a certain someone finds her a forever home. So that's already five. And you haven't even crossed the Mason Dixon line yet."

"This is a frickin' intervention," Beau snarled. "I need some air."

"Beau, wait," Ellie begged. "They're right. I know they are."

"You don't know a thing. I lost my best friend, my wingman. I was suppose to protect him. You've never been in combat, scared out of your mind that you're going to get blown away to pieces. And if you're lucky enough to get some sleep, it's mixed with nightmares so horrific you wish you'd never fallen asleep. On top of that, the nightmares become your thoughts. It's all you think about. Eventually it becomes your reality and you can barely tell the difference. You, my friend, don't know nothing."

"Actually, I do," Ellie said defensively. "I've lived the night terrors, the aggression, the agitation, the constant fear. Your mind and body gang up on you, making life a living hell. I understand what it's like to wonder how you'll survive one more day in an endless dark tunnel with no ray of light. Beau, I get it because I lived it."

"Yeah, what kind of trauma have you had with your billionaire grandfather, your Harvard degree, and your Paris cooking school? How can you possibly get it?"

"You may have lost your wingman, but I lost my parents. I was six years old. I came home one day after school. My grandparents were there, red eyes from crying. They tell me there's been a terrible accident. And that my parents didn't make it."

Beau leaned on the countertop, looked out the window. "Jeez, I'm sorry."

"I got kicked out of more schools than fingers on your right hand. I couldn't concentrate. I lived in fear, never knowing who or what would be taken from me next. And if that wasn't enough… never mind. Some things are too awful to share. I know about tragedy. And thank God, I got help. I won't hurt anybody and I won't hurt myself. My family wasted a lot of time with therapists who didn't know what they were doing. Go to Boston. Get the help you need. I promise you won't be alone."

"Yeah, right." Beau's broad chest caved like a captured soldier.

"It's worth a try. You can't keep living like this. It's not fair to you. It's not fair to those you might unknowingly hurt."

Beau quit pacing, sinking back down into a chair. He placed his hands over his face. After a few minutes of silence, he spoke. "Okay, let's get packed. The sooner we get going, the sooner I get back here. I'm driving. Queenie stays in the crate, the entire time. And I don't want to hear a peep from either of you about how fast I drive."

"Fine," Hattie and Ellie simultaneously agreed.

Pastor Luis prayed for a safe and healing journey. Hattie tried to concentrate on the prayer, she really did. But she was drifting, her eyes resting on Luis. Why hadn't she fallen in love with someone like Luis? A great man of faith, a good man with a tender heart.

The room filled with the scent of lavender, reminding Hattie to pack Henry. She'd almost forgotten the gun. It was the right thing to bring it with her. When Beau returned to Fairhope, the gun would be thousands of miles away. It was safer that way.

Beau loaded everything into the Jeep.

"Ellie, I'll sit in back," said Hattie, "I need space to work."

"Sure thing," said Ellie, giving Hattie a dirty look.

Ellie climbed in the front passenger seat, tying her hair into a messy ponytail. She immediately put her earbuds in.

Beau sped through Georgia, the Carolinas, and up the coast, taking breaks only to let Queenie out to do her business, and grab a Mountain Dew to keep him awake.

Hattie messaged her assistant, Kayla.

Please have all Federal's files and copies of all emails during the planning of the IPO on my desk before Friday.

Hattie was confident all the necessary paperwork would be there to prove her case with Richard. Kayla was well organized and tech savvy. Smart.

Kayla messaged her back. *I can drop files off at your condo Thursday night, if that helps.*

Hattie texted back. *Great idea. Leave the files with the doorman.*

Together they'd clear everything up.

Hattie received two text messages from Pastor Luis, one reminding her to have Beau fill out all the paperwork prior to arriving at his appointment. The second message read, *"When I'm afraid, I put my trust in you." Psalm 56.*

Chapter 45:
Unexpected Visitors

Hattie, followed by Beau carrying all the luggage, tailed by Ellie, with Queenie on her heels, entered the lobby of the Boston condominium building.

"Welcome back, Hattie, and entourage," said Cooper.

Queenie barked.

"Got yourself a new friend?" asked Cooper.

"This is Queenie. We're fostering until I find her a forever home."

"Awww, if you ask me, she's a keeper," reaching to scratch behind Queenie's ears. "You're back early."

"Something urgent came up at work," admitted Hattie. "Did my assistant drop off files?"

"She did. A couple of times, actually. She personally delivered them to your condo."

"Oh, okay," said Hattie, wondering how Kayla got in. "Cooper, meet my cousin Beau. He'll be staying with me for, well, I'm not sure how long, and you remember my friend, Ellie, right?"

"Of course. Beau, it's a pleasure. Your cousin is my favorite tenant in the building," said Cooper.

"Do you think you could get Beau a key to my condo?"

"I'll have it ready this afternoon. Stop by my office. I need to show you something."

"Sure. Let's head upstairs. Ellie, you're welcome to change before going to Charles and Claire's. Beau, you best rest after all the driving."

On the elevator, Hattie began searching her handbag for her condo key. Nothing. When they got off the elevator, outside the apartment, she began rifling through her duffel bag, recalling she'd put the key in one of the inside pockets. She saw something shiny at the botton of the bag. Dang. She'd forgotten she put Henry in there.

"Beau, here's the key," said Hattie, attempting to be inconspicuous as she covered a pair of pants over the gun.

As Beau inserted the key, the door flew open.

"What the hell?" Asher said to the Fairhope contingent.

"Why are you here?" Ellie snapped, glaring at Asher as if he was a cockroach in her kitchen.

"Hardly any of your business. But since you asked, I do own the entire building."

"Asher?" Hattie stood, stunned to see him there. She dropped the duffel and heard the gun fall out, hitting the tile.

"Which you bought with your wife's money," Ellie admonished.

"Title is in my name. Who is this guy?"

"I'm Hattie's cousin, Beau Brown," said Beau, extending his hand. "I'd normally say it's a pleasure. But hate to start the day lying like a politician."

Asher, in wool trousers, white dress shirt, and Italian loafers, rolled his eyes. "I always knew when I met your family they'd be white trash."

"You're a pig," snapped Ellie.

"Careful there, blondie," challenged Asher. "I'm not the one getting fat in Paris."

"Asher, stop!" begged Hattie.

"Ellie and I go way back, she knows me. Right, Ellie? We've got a history."

"I bet it's an ugly one," interceded Beau.

"Hardly," said Asher. "Hattie, since you're here, I've got the divorce papers drawn up, ready to be signed. I can go grab them. We can sign them right now, then you and your friends can be on your way."

"I live here," said Hattie. "You're the one who left. If you'll excuse me, I need to get ready for work."

"Sign the divorce papers, and you can spend every second at work. I'll keep all the furniture, which I picked out. But please get the stupid rocker out, the one your hillbilly family is so proud of. Your muscle man cousin can move it for you. I'll have someone pack your clothes. Send the boxes. I keep the condo. You never did appreciate my good taste, so you can leave."

Hattie felt a cool breeze, the smell of lavender surrounded them. Beau's face had gone scarlet. Like a lion he was ready to pounce.

"Lord God," Hattie silently prayed. "Please don't let Beau explode and do something he regrets."

"I agree, we need to wrap this up," she said, pretending to be matter of fact, as if she were about to sign a contract to buy a car. She didn't want Beau involved in her mess. He didn't deserve this.

"Let's all sit down so I can look this over," Beau said, taking control as he tried to walk in.

Asher blocked him. "I need a few minutes, to make a private call to my divorce lawyer."

"You got five, anything longer and I'm breaking down the door," Beau said as he met Asher's gaze.

They waited in the apartment foyer. Silently. Hattie protectively stood by her duffel, hoping the gun was well-hidden, out of Beau's sight. Five minutes felt like an hour. Finally, Asher returned.

"I'll take a copy of the paperwork," requested Beau, towering over Asher.

"I'm not sure a hillbilly like you can understand legalese. Do you want me to set up a conference call with my lawyer? She said she'd walk you through the divorce agreement."

"We won't need your lawyer," Ellie retorted, confidently putting her shoulders back, standing tall like a prosecutor ready to win a case. "I'll call our family attorney, Jim Dubois, who, by the way, is the best attorney in Boston."

Asher groaned, evidentally aware of Jim Dubois's reputation.

Beau pushed Asher aside. "Please, ladies, make yourselves at home. Because this is *your* home, Hattie. Until this chump buys you out, fair and square."

"Let's go to the dining room," said Asher. "No elbows on the table, please. It's glass and I hate smudges."

Hattie looked at Beau. His fists were clenched. She knew Asher was pushing Beau's hot buttons.

The four of them sat down. Ellie sat at the head of the table. Asher at the opposite end. Hattie sat next to Ellie. Beau sat across from her, flipping through the pages of the divorce agreement.

"You are doing the right thing, Asher," said Beau.

"What?" said Asher with a surprised look on his face.

"Just look at yourself in your high-priced Italian clothes, your gelled back hair, your alligator loafers. Heck, your cologne, alone, screams you need constant female attention."

"Shut up," exclaimed Asher.

"You're a pretty boy, not the kind who gets his hands dirty. I've been watching you. You want to kick that sweet dog for laying on your fancy white carpet. You can't imagine rescuing a dog, can you? Or for that matter, being a loyal husband."

"The dog is disgusting, like my wife, a disappointment."

"You're disgusting," chimed in Ellie.

Asher put his hands in the steeple position and sighed.

"You see, Hattie wants a predictable life," Asher said. "things like a boring banking job, a home in the 'burbs with a garden. She wants us to be a nice family with babies and dogs. It's not what I signed up for."

"Exactly what did you sign up for when you got married?" asked Beau.

"Someone fun, likes a good time. A party girl. Someone I enjoy." Asher pointed directly at Hattie. "Miss goody two shoes, right there, wants to be the corporate star. Always the teacher's pet. Wants everybody to know how smart she is. I want someone exciting. Someone hip. Hattie is dull, boring at work, boring in bed. The worst…"

"Excuse me!" Ellie snarled. "Hattie has supported you since the day you asked her to marry you. You should be grateful."

Hattie's emotions were all over the place, surging with feelings she'd never experienced, love crossing over into hate. It was time to end this charade of a marriage. Asher didn't love her. He was evil.

Closing her eyes, she silently recited Mema's favorite Bible verse from the book of Ephesians: *Therefore, put on the full armor of God, so that when the day of evil comes, you may be able to stand your ground...*

She prayed it a second time, her inner strength finally arriving.

"Asher, I'll sign the divorce papers—with one caveat." She grabbed a pen, writing an addendum to the agreement. "I remain in the condo until you buy me out at fair market value."

Asher looked from Beau to Ellie.

"Fine." He scribbled his name with a black Montblanc pen he pulled from his shirt pocket. "I want out."

Hattie breathed deep, scribbling her name with a ballpoint pen. "We're finished. You need to leave."

Asher turned to Ellie. "I'm a free man. Ellie, I'd love to reconnect. You're still hot. Had us some fun in college—that one night. But, let me guess, you don't remember."

"You drugged and raped me!" screamed Ellie.

"Yeah, right," scoffed Asher.

Horrified, Ellie lashed out, "I swear to God, I'll kill you if you don't tell them the truth. Hattie deserves to know the truth."

Asher laughed, sounding like a high pitched hyena.

"You're one sick dog," Beau said. Hattie noticed Beau was sitting on his hands. He was trying to hold back from punching Asher.

"No, that, there is a sick dog," screamed Asher, shoving his loafer in Queenie's face. The dog crouched further under the table, shaking in terror.

Still, Asher reached his leg further, kicking Queenie over and over like she was a punching bag. Queenie let out piercing yelps, so startling Hattie instantly covered her ears, begging Asher to stop. But he continued to strike. As Hattie dove underneath the table to protect Queenie, she watched Beau hurl himself across the glass table, reaching for Asher. Asher succeeded in kicking Hattie hard several times on the side of her head as she protected Queenie. Everything went black. Until the sound of two loud firecrackers. Wait, Hattie thought, those were gunshots.

Hattie glanced to her right. Beau was lying on the floor, Ellie crouched over him, screaming. Lying next to Beau was Henry, Mema's gun. Jeez. Hadn't she hidden it in the duffel bag? She remembered. It'd fallen out, slid on the tile towards the bedroom. But no one had noticed, or had someone? She reached for the gun. Glancing to her left, she saw Asher slumped over the table, the once smudge-free dining room splattered with blood.

It was the end of her world.

Chapter 46:
Man Down

"Who's in here?" the cop hollered, standing behind the marble column in Hattie's foyer.

"There's four of us," responded Hattie. The smell of lavender surrounded her, and she experienced a strange sense of calm as she stared at Mema's gun. "My husband, ex, actually, has been shot."

"Hold up your hands," shouted the second cop.

Hattie dropped Henry to the floor, then raised both hands in the air.

Ellie remained by Beau, tears of black mascara streaming down her cheeks.

"I shot him," Hattie said flatly, void of emotion.

One of the cops walked over to Beau, leaning over to check his pulse. Queenie growled, showing her canines.

"Easy, pup, checking to see if your owner is alive," the cop said to Queenie.

"That's my cousin, Beau Brown," Hattie pointed out. "You need to get him to the hospital. He's a Navy SEAL. Has PTSD. Please help him. He had nothing to do with this."

Asher's head hung low, like he'd fallen asleep. The younger officer checked his pulse. "This guy is dead."

"Two males, one shot dead, the other unresponsive, apparently has PTSD," the cop hollered into his police radio. "Send emergency vehicles."

A few minutes passed and in walked a man, wearing brown slacks, a white button down shirt with a brown tie. He began surveying the room. Four EMT attendants followed with two gurneys. After the EMTs put Asher and Beau on the stretchers, they pushed the gurneys toward the exit.

"Where are you taking him?" Hattie politely asked.

"What do you care?" asked the cop.

"I'm not asking about my husband," Hattie said coldly. "I want to know where you're taking my cousin," pointing to Beau.

"Likely Mass General," the second cop said as he handcuffed Hattie.

"Read her her rights," instructed the older officer.

Ellie was sobbing. "Hattie, I'll call Charles. He'll call our attorney. Expect to hear from James Dubois. Soon."

Hattie nodded. She trusted Ellie. Charles knew people. It mattered.

Cooper was standing behind the concierge desk as the police walked Hattie through the lobby in handcuffs, a cop on each side of her.

"Coop, take care of Queenie, please," begged Hattie. "Asher kicked her hard, over and over. She needs to be seen by a vet."

"I'm sorry I didn't call the cops sooner," Cooper muttered.

"You did your best," said Hattie.

"I hated him," muttered Cooper.

"You the owner of the dog?" asked the younger cop as they exited the building.

"No, sir, I'm the dog's trainer."

Chapter 47:
The Lowest Point

"Ain't you something special," remarked the uniformed guard, unlocking the cell door. "Police chief wants to see you."

Hattie nodded. She was shaking so bad the handcuffs would hardly go on.

"Hold still," the guard growled.

"I'm trying," quaked Hattie.

They walked through the jail, Hattie avoiding eye contact as they passed guards and people. They took a secured elevator up to the second floor, then down a long hallway.

"Chief, I got the perp," announced the guard.

"Thank you. We'll take it from here."

The police chief, a tall, dark-skinned, broad-shouldered man dressed in a finely pressed uniform, was watching her. Hattie blushed, guessing the chief was sizing her up. Was this her defining moment?

"Domestic situations, like yours, are the worst for us cops. Good people finding themselves backed into a corner." He shook his head sympathetically. "Follow me, young lady. Your lawyer will be here shortly. Jim Dubois. I know him. He doesn't represent just anybody. You're lucky."

Hattie wanted to scream this was Asher's fault. He was the bad guy, not her.

The chief brought her to a private room where a small group gathered, a man with the same dark hair and skin as Pastor Luis, only far more elegantly dressed. Next to him was a black Lab, wagging its tail. Sitting in a chair next to the man was a stunning woman, long black hair, deep brown eyes, dressed casually, leggings and a long tee, rocking a fussy baby with dark curly hair in footed jammies. Hatti longed to pet the dog and hold the baby. She thought of Mema's rocker. Why had she wanted a bigger life with someone like Asher?

"Mr. Dubois and Ms. Walters, welcome back," Chief Watson said as he watched Justice chasing her tail, the leash wrapping around Jim's loafers while the baby wailed.

"What in the world?" Chief Watson asked.

"I apologize," Jim said. Hattie noticed Jim was at least as tall as Beau and held a similar commanding presence even next to the police chief, who was built like an Alabama linebacker. "I'm training my dog to be a therapy dog. She goes where I go. We weren't expecting to be back here working."

"Jim, men like us shouldn't retire," said the chief. "Welcome back."

"I won't let Jim retire," Maxine stood with her baby. She was as tall as the chief and only a couple inches shorter than her law partner. "Not on my watch."

"On your watch, Maxine? From my office, I just watched you illegally park your SUV in a handicapped parking spot outside of my building," admonished the chief.

"Well, if anybody's handicapped, it's me with little Derrick."

The chief shook his head. "Some things never change. No one tells you what to do, Max. Especially your fine husband. Best detective on the force. Is he doing okay?"

"Loves being a dad."

"I bet he does. Got five of my own kiddos, all grown. Thank the Lord. Let me find you, and this petting zoo, a room to meet privately with your client."

"It's good to see you, Chief," said Jim.

"You too, Jim. Even you, Max," the chief teased. "I'll feel less so if your dog poops in my station or if one of you dumps a dirty diaper in my restrooms."

"Duly noted," promised Jim, attempting to get the leash unwrapped from his ankles.

"I got it under control," said Max as the baby started wailing.

"Sounds like it," laughed the chief.

Once in the conference room, Maxine set her baby down in the car seat. The black Labrador laid her head on Derrick's tiny feet. Soon the dog and baby were sound asleep.

"Would you look at that?" Jim marveled.

"I'm bringing your dog home with me," Maxine whispered.

"Ms. Sinclaire, you may sit here, next to me," Jim suggested. "And, Rusty, could you please remove her handcuffs? She may need to write some things down for us."

"Can't. She's charged with murder," said the husky guard, his cropped bleached hair and steel blue eyes glaring at Hattie under the fluorescent lights.

Maxine stood up, her six-foot-one frame looming over the officer. "Seriously, Rusty, there's as much chance of her running out of here as my baby. Take the cuffs off."

"Maxine, you're always pushing the limits around here, just cuz your husband is friends with the chief," Rusty retorted. "Let me do my job."

"Let us do ours," Maxine countered. "She'll need to write some thing down for us."

The guard unlocked the handcuffs and left, slamming the door behind him.

"I'm Jim Dubois. Charles Reade has retained me to be your lawyer. This is my assistant, Maxine Walters."

"I am so grateful Mr. Reade contacted you on my behalf," Hattie said, as tears welled up in her eyes. "He must be so disappointed in me."

"Disappointed in the situation, certainly, not you," corrected Jim. "Charles loves you like a daughter. He's determined that we help you, best we can."

"Thank him for me," Hattie said. Her body was shaking; she was having trouble focusing. Her hands were tightly gripped together as she silently prayed for strength to get through this.

Her lawyer was distinguished looking. Confident. Kind eyes. His assistant, Maxine, was tall and lean—the most beautiful woman Hattie had ever seen. Skin the color of a latte.

The dog got up from the corner, walked over to Hattie, nudged her thigh, then finally rested her head on Hattie's lap. Hattie petted her.

"Mama used to say dogs are heaven's angels working here on earth." She gently stroked her hand down the sides of the dog's long nose. "What's her name?"

"Justice."

"A good lawyerly name."

"My wife, Abby, named her."

"Nice. Down, girl," Hattie said, gently guiding the leash, encouraging Justice to lie down. "Stay."

Justice did as Hattie commanded.

"How'd you do that?" Jim asked. "I've been trying to accomplish it for months."

"I helped train dogs, years ago. Family business."

"Before Harvard?"

"Yes, sir."

Jim and Max spent all afternoon with Hattie. They covered Hattie's history, her marriage with Asher, the trip to Fairhope, and the call from her boss about the SEC investigation.

"What you tell us is attorney-client privilege. It doesn't leave this room. Let's walk through what happened this morning."

"Yes, of course. We, by that I mean me, my cousin Beau and my best friend Ellie, were all heading to my condo after being in Fairhope. Beau was going to stay with me, Ellie was going to shower, change clothes, and go see her grandparents. So, let me think, when we arrived, I had no idea Asher was there. He had moved out, we were separated."

"Did your doorman tell you Asher was there?"

"No." Hattie shook her head. "But now that I think about it, Cooper, that's the doorman's name, mentioned he needed to talk to me."

"Did you ever find out what he wanted?" asked Maxine, taking notes on her laptop.

"No, I didn't."

"Max, contact the doorman. See what he wanted to tell Hattie. Sorry, go on, Hattie."

"Beau, Ellie, and I rode the elevator to the twelfth floor. I was digging through my stuff to find the key. The door flew open, it was Asher. He said he had the divorce papers. We went inside the condo. Asher shouldn't have been there. I live there. He left me."

"Did you want to sign the divorce papers?"

"Well, no. I wanted my marriage to last, I believed in the whole 'until death do us part,' but Beau was there. I didn't want him getting upset. He has PTSD."

"And?"

"And so, I went along with it all, as calm as I could. I put my luggage outside my bedroom. I had originally planned to change and go to work. Then we all went to the dining room to sit down. Beau wanted to review the divorce agreement. Ellie offered to get me a lawyer to look it over. You, in fact. Beau took the divorce papers and was going through the document."

"Was there anything in the agreement that was unacceptable to you?" asked Jim, making notes on a yellow legal pad.

"Asher wanted me to leave the condo, right away. But I wouldn't, all my stuff was there. I had to go to work. Beau told Asher he'd have to buy me out. The thing is, I paid for the condo. I had nowhere else to go."

"Was Beau upset?"

"He seemed in control. Really." She was looking them both in the eyes, desperate for them to believe her.

"What was Ellie doing during this discussion?"

Hattie lowered her eyes, she paused.

"She was helping me."

"How?"

"Moral support. Then Asher started saying awful things about me, then her. Ellie began shouting at Asher. She was upset. Asher then went after the dog. Sweet Queenie. Asher doesn't like dogs. He kept kicking Queenie, over and over. She was yipping in pain. I crawled under the table to protect Queenie. He then was kicking me. The last I recall was Beau coming over the table to help. Then I blanked until the gunshots."

"Do you remember if Beau had a gun?"

"No, absolutely not. I took the gun from the cottage in Fairhope. I didn't want him to have it, in case. He didn't know I had it in my luggage. It was my Mema's, an heirloom."

"You inherited a gun?" asked Max, her eyebrows raised.

"Beau did. I took Henry, that's what Mema calls the gun, with me."

"Why?"

Hattie sat silently.

"Why did you take the gun with you?" asked Max. "Were you afraid of your husband?"

Hattie nodded no.

"Were you afraid of what your cousin might do?"

Hattie nodded no.

"Are you sure?"

Hattie rubbed her fingers across her forehead. "Only if he's triggered. It's not his fault. He's getting help." She started to cry.

"Okay, let's move on," said Jim. "What was Ellie doing while this was going on?"

"Screaming. Asher was saying such awful things about her."

"What kind of things?"

"Mean things."

"What kind of mean things?"

"I can't recall exactly. What I remember is there was a blast, like a firecracker. Another. Two gunshots. The blood. The police came. The ambulance. This whole thing is my fault." Justice remained by Hattie's feet.

"Were Asher and Ellie friendly? Prior to this?" asked Jim, tapping his pen.

"They went to the same prep school. Had mutual friends. But she was not friends with him."

Despite Max's best mom efforts, her baby's occasional fussing was turning into constant crying.

"I've fed, changed, burped this li'l guy. I got no more tricks in my diaper bag. I gotta head home," Max said shoving her laptop and yellow legal pad into the diaper bag. "I'll be working tonight. Call me, boss."

"I'll walk you out." Jim stood and stretched, pressing a button to come have a guard let them out.

"Hattie, will you keep an eye on Justice?" asked Jim.

"Of course," said Hattie gratefully. It seemed Justice was the only thing that kept her from completely falling apart.

* * *

"What did you think of Max?" Jim asked Hattie when he returned to the conference room. Justice was lying by Hattie's feet.

"Impressive. Street smart. Beautiful. Frankly, I'm a little intimidated," admitted Hattie.

Jim laughed. "Yeah, me too. Years ago, I hired Max away from the DA's office. Next to marrying my wife, it was the best decision

I've ever made. She knows her stuff. Part detective, part paralegal. Nothing gets by Max."

Justice woke, noticed Jim, and jumped up on his thighs. Hattie calmly reached for the leash and snapped it gently.

"Down, stay," Hattie said in a firm voice. Justice looked at Hattie. Hattie stared back. Justice blinked first and lay back down.

"Good girl," said Hattie, brushing the sides of Justice's nose.

Jim watched her, then stood.

"Hattie, your case is complex. There are so many unknowns. Max and I need to figure out more of these unknowns so we can build a defense. I have to ask, are you protecting someone?"

She didn't speak. She couldn't look him in the eye.

"I am sorry about all this," she admitted.

"Put aside my friendship with the Reade family. Did Ellie ever share with you that Asher drugged and raped her in college?"

"How do you know?"

"Max found it in an unfiled police report. A friend of a friend gave it to her when we walked in here. She's doing background checks on everyone that was in the condo when Asher was shot."

Hattie told him what she remembered from that night. She felt a nudge inside of her. She had to know.

"How does a date rape drug work?"

"Club drugs can come in the form of pills or powder, even liquid," explained Jim. "If mixed with a drink, it can taste salty; the scary thing is, many drugs don't change the flavor of the drink. They're easy to mix in. If I had a daughter, I'd tell her to order her own drinks, don't accept freebies. Leave a drink unattended, get a fresh drink. And don't *ever* drink anything served out of a punch bowl."

"Good advice," she said, recalling the evening she met Asher and Monte for dinner. Had Asher drugged her too? She'd only had one drink that night and couldn't remember a good portion of the evening.

"Hattie, I want you reconsider what you told police. I want you to plead not guilty tomorrow at the hearing. There's more here to this story."

A knock on the conference room door. It was the police chief's assistant and a new guard. "We need to get your client back to holding."

"I understand," said Jim. "Give me one minute."

The guard stepped back outside the door.

"Hattie, listen, the hearing is set for tomorrow at eleven. They'll bring you to the courtroom. I'll meet you there. If there's anything new that you remember, they'll let you call me. They know me."

As they put the handcuffs back on Hattie's wrists, Justice began whimpering. She looked back at Justice, knowing she'd give anything to be back training dogs.

Chapter 48:
Cellmate Confessions

Hattie returned to the holding cell, lying down on an empty bed, so lost in thought she ignored the coldness of the metal bed and the dirty, thin cushion masquerading as a mattress. She closed her eyes.

"You look familiar?" asked a woman's voice wrapped in a strong Southern accent. "Y'all from Birmingham?"

"No. I don't believe we've ever met," said Hattie in a defeated-sounding voice, keeping her eyes closed. All she wanted was sleep.

"That's cattywampus, I recognize y'all."

"You must have me confused with someone else. I'm from Fairhope. And I haven't lived there in years."

"Wait one darn minute. Sweet Jesus! You're all grown up! Y'all way more sophisticated and your Southern accent is almost nothing. But it's enough that I remember you. The smart girl on the bus. Going to Harvard. Remember me, Bess? I was heading to Boston to visit my cousin."

Hattie jolted up from the bed.

Hattie took in the woman's appearance, why yes. The woman looked slightly familiar. The stocky body like a bulldog. That was it! Hattie remembered. The blond pixie cut was gone; the woman's hair had grayed, now scraggly and unkept, as if she hadn't been to a salon in a long time.

"Bess?"

"The one and only!"

"How did you end up here?"

"More like, how did you? You were the one going to Harvard!"

"You were going on a vacation to visit your cousin."

"Never left," shrugged Bess. "My cousin's wife got sick, breast cancer. When she passed, I stayed on to help raise his little guy, Patrick. The boy was only six years old. Such a sweetie. Teenager now. And can't stand the sight of me."

"I was the same way with my mom when I was that age."

"Yeah? I never had children of my own, so it's a first."

"Bess, what happened? Why are you in here?"

"I discovered a priest who couldn't keep his devil hands to hisself," Bess sputtered. "Molested my nephew, an innocent altar boy. The priest was a pedophile, disguised as a man of God. My Patrick wasn't his only victim."

"I'm sorry. Shouldn't the priest be in here? Not you, right?"

"Hattie, darn it all. I'm a big old fool. I took justice in my own hands, slammed the priest against the church wall hard as I could. Then kicked 'em where the sun don't shine. Teach 'im a lesson. His secretary called the police. She makes me so mad. She's covered for him for years. She should be in here too."

"I'm so sorry," said Hattie, getting up to hug Bess.

"Yeah, thanks," mumbled Bess as she wiped her tears and runny nose with her sleeve. "But like I said, I shoulda let God be judge and jury, like the Bible says. I didn't listen, not that I always do.

And here I am. What happened to you, kiddo? You were a super-star genius kid."

"It's a long story."

"I got time," said Bess, releasing Hattie from the hug to look her in the eyes. "I know you's a good person."

"I stayed in Boston after I earned my degree, joined an investment banking firm after I graduated. Got married less than a year ago."

"Married? Why that's great."

"Didn't work out like I planned." Tears sprang from Hattie's eyes.

"Kiddo, what went wrong?"

"He was a bad man. I signed the divorce papers and we argued. My husband was shot and killed. I've confessed to murdering my husband. Rather, ex-husband."

"Must've been some kind of argument. Was he violent with y'all?"

Hattie shook her head.

"Hmmm, I'm bettin' another woman involved?"

"Probably scores of them. But that's not even the worst of it."

"What's worse than a cheating husband?"

"A husband who raped his wife's best friend. A husband who hacks his wife's computer and steals client information. Then makes a million dollars illegally, insider trading. Frames me for the crime."

"Dang, steal a woman's livelihood, steal her life."

"Amen to that," agreed Hattie, wiping her tears. "This is strange, isn't it?"

"What, us, in matching orange jumpsuits?"

Hattie gave her a half smile. She recalled Bess being good humored.

"Sorry, just trying to lighten the mood around here. Sounds like you work in stocks?"

"Investment banker. Trek Investments on State Street. I've been there since I graduated."

"I got me a neighbor who works there."

"Really?"

"She's young, perty as a peach, secretary to some bigwig. She's working on her degree at night. Or used to be, I think she dropped out. Got herself a new boyfriend who occupies her nights."

"What's her name?"

"Kayla Greene."

"Well, another coincidence. Kayla's my assistant."

"You kiddin' me?"

"I love Kayla to pieces."

"You's that important executive she works for! I knew you'd make it big!"

"Gosh, I don't think I'm big time anything. I didn't realize Kayla dropped out of night school."

"That's cuz you too good of a person to put your nose where it don't belong. Not me. I'm a snoop. It's the boyfriend. He arrives every night, late. From what I'm seeing, Kayla is hiding something."

"Why do you say that?"

"He never picks her up at her mama's house. Always at the corner, between my cousin's house and hers. It's real strange."

"That is strange," said Hattie wondering who Kayla was seeing. "I heard she's dating a broker at the firm. As you can guess, men in my office drool over her."

"Whoever he is, he's one good-looking guy. Sandy brown hair, gorgeous eyes. Knock your socks off if you saw 'im. Gets out of the jeep to open the door for Kayla. A real gentleman."

Bess continued, "The boyfriend must play sports. He's got a body to die for! Wears a BC cap. And you ain't gonna believe this, I believe he's got Southern roots."

"Why do you say that?"

"Drives a Jeep with Alabama plates."

It couldn't be, could it? wondered Hattie. Sandy brown hair, blue eyes, handsome. BC cap. "Bess, what color is the Jeep?"

"Dark gray."

Hattie gasped. The jail floor felt like it was spinning. Hattie reached for the bed. She needed to sit. The darkness was invading her vision like a monster entering a room. She felt like she was going to pass out. Then the scent of lavender flooded the cell, bringing Hattie back from the dark.

"Girl, you's as clammy as an oyster. Thought you was gonna drop like a swatted fly. Here, take a sip of water."

Hattie gulped the water, wiped her chin.

The guard returned. "Your lawyer is here."

"Me?" asked Hattie.

"No, her," said the guard pointing to Bess.

"May I make a call?" asked Hattie.

"Chief told me you got phone privileges. Both of you, follow me.

Hattie knew exactly who to call.

✳ ✳ ✳

"OMG, Hattie. I can't believe it's you," exclaimed Ellie. "I thought you could only make one call. Shouldn't that be to your lawyer?"

"I think it might be different than what we see on TV."

"Are you okay?"

"Would you believe me if I said I was?"

"No. I'm sorry. Do you remember what happened?"

"It's all a blur. How are you, how's Beau?"

"I'm as good as can be expected. Charles, Claire, and I went to visit Beau. He was transferred from Mass General to Saint Mary's, a psychiatric hospital. He's awake. Worried about you."

"Tell him I'm fine."

"I did."

"Tell him he needs to go to his Monday evaluation at the trauma center."

"I spoke with his doctor. If things continue to stabilize, it looks promising."

"Will you watch over him for me?"

"I will. But you'll be out on bail soon. Charles says the hearing is set for tomorrow."

"Can you check on Queenie?"

"I called Cooper. He says Queenie has no broken bones. Charles is picking her up now."

"Thank God."

"Hey, do you have any idea why Cooper wants to talk to Jim? He asked my grandfather for Jim's number."

"I have a hunch."

"What it is?"

"My guess is he saw Asher with another woman. Remember my assistant?"

"Who wouldn't?"

"I think she was having an affair with Asher."

"Jeez. How do you know?"

"Long story. But you need to call Jim. Tell him. I'm not sure how much longer they'll let me talk on the phone."

"I'll call as soon as we hang up. Anything else?"

"Call Luis. Tell him what happened. Ask him to help with Beau. I don't know if I'll ever get the chance."

Hattie began weeping. "Ellie, I don't think I can talk anymore."

"Wait, we're going to get you out of there. I promise."

"How do you know?"

"Because you look terrible in orange. And jumpsuits are out of style."

Hattie let out a combination giggle-sob. "You are so bad. This is not the right time to make me laugh."

"I think it's the perfect time."

"The guard is here, I've got to go. Love you, Ellie."

"Love you back, sister."

Chapter 49:
We Meet Again

"How'd it go?" asked Hattie when Bess returned to the holding cell.

"I don't know," said Bess. "My arms are pitted out, as stressed as a hydrangea with no water. I guess deodorant around here is a luxury we don't get. Sorry 'bout the smell. My lawyer thinks I should plead guilty; he'll see if they'll cut me a deal. My first offense and all."

"Do you trust your lawyer?"

Bess shrugged. "Court assigned. Ray's scrounging up cash to get me a different one, one his cop friends use."

"That's good. I'm not sure court-appointed lawyers are the most qualified."

"Yeah, I figured. He looks sixteen. Are you as exhausted as I am?" asked Bess, plopping down on one of the metal beds.

"I feel like I'm fighting in a war," commented Hattie.

"Let's say our prayers, get some rest. Tomorrow's a big day for you and me."

Hattie carefully lay down. The mattress was thin, lumpy—worse than the ones she slept in at college. This one was torn, foam seeping out. The sheet was itchy and looked unclean. Stains that hadn't come out in the wash. Her stomach ached, knowing this could be her life. She didn't want to think anymore. She closed her eyes, but sleep evaded her.

"Bess, you awake?"

"Yeah. Countin' sheep. What's up?"

"How is it, after all that's happened to you, you still have faith in God? I'm sort of struggling."

"Actually, I kinda gave up on the big guy."

"Yeah?"

"A miracle happened today, forced me to do a one-eighty, renewed my faith."

"What was it?"

"You. You and me, here, in this jail at the same time. Think about it. What are the chances two good people, who met years ago, end up in the same holding cell? When I saw you, recognized you, I knew God is as real as my cup of Dunkin' coffee I have each morning to get me jump-started."

"It is a strange coincidence."

"Ain't no coincidence. God's all over this. Look at us. We're safe. We're together. That, my child, is a God thing."

"Thanks, Bess. I really needed to hear something like that."

"Good night, kiddo."

"Good night." Hattie planned on calling Jim in the morning.

Chapter 50:
MIA

"This is Jim Duboise."

"Jim, it's Hattie. Say, did Ellie get ahold of you? Tell you about the information I learned from another woman, a sort of friend, in the same cell."

She heard Jim breathe and exhale. "Ellie shared the details. Max and I don't suggest putting a whole lot of faith in a cellmate. Usually they're just trying to sweeten their own deal with prosecutors."

"I know this woman. I trust her. She knew details that you couldn't make up. I swear."

"Let me get Max in here. Hold on."

"Maxine, can you come in my office?" Hattie heard Jim holler. "Hattie Sinclaire is on line one. Hattie, you're on speaker. Max is joining me."

It was so familiar. Like at the firm, when she stepped into Richard's office to talk to a client.

"Max is going to make friends with Trek's IT department. Max, see if you can find out if Hattie's assistant accessed her computer."

"I did give Kayla my password, in case she needed my customer information."

"Ouch! I'll get right on it. First, I got news," said Maxine. "Chief Watson called. Your cousin apparently broke out of the hospital. He's at the police station. Same one as you. Chief says Beau confessed to shooting Asher Sinclaire."

Hattie gasped. "He did not do it! I know he didn't."

"Calm down, girl," ordered Max. "We're getting to the bottom of this. Trust me. Your doorman is coming to our office soon. Cooper says he has a video that vindicates you."

"Really?"

"Yes, we'll know more when we see it," acknowledged Jim.

"Who is taking care of Beau?"

"Looks like for now it's the po-po," said Max. "Hope they do a better job than the hospital."

"This can't be happening," cried Hattie.

"Hattie, Cooper just arrived here. Plan on seeing us at your hearing, it's still set for eleven this morning."

"Thank you." Hattie hung up the phone. The guard was waiting for her, always watching her like she was a criminal.

* * *

Hattie paced nervously waiting for the officer to escort her to her hearing. Bess had fixed Hattie's hair, wiped the tears from Hattie's cheeks, helped her to look presentable for court. Now they waited. Hattie was too nervous for chitchat.

"Grab your stuff," a guard said, approaching the cell.

"Okay," said Hattie, taking the manila envelope the officer handed her. "Do I bring this with me to the hearing?"

"Ain't gonna be a hearing. Change of plans. You're free to go."

"Excuse me?"

"They found the perp who did it."

"Can you give me a minute?" Hattie said to the officer.

"Make it fast. Some of us got a job to do."

Hattie walked quickly back to the holding cell.

"Bess, I'm free to go. Not sure what's going on. But I promise I'll get you legal help. Good legal help. I'll ask my attorney. Hang in there. We'll get you out of here. I promise."

"Thanks, kiddo. I know y'all do all you can."

Hattie hugged the burly woman goodbye. "Bus friends?" teased Bess.

"Jail friends," said Hattie. "But not for long."

Bess smiled, a big tear rolling down her cheek.

Hattie exited the secured area of the police station. Jim Dubois was waiting for her. He was dressed in a suit and tie with Justice by his side. Maxine was on the phone, dressed professionally in a blazer with black wool pants and heels.

"Hattie, there's something you need to see. Let's step in here," said Jim, directing her to an empty room.

"Of course," said Hattie, reaching over to pet Justice. It felt so good to have a dog by her.

"The police are bringing your cousin Beau here. He should be here anytime."

"Okay."

Hattie cautiously sat down. She felt like the police were going to enter the room and arrest them. Beau walked in, wearing his camo jacket and jeans. He gave her a noogie on the head, like he did when they were kids. "It's going to be fine," whispered Beau.

"Cousins, let's step in here," ordered Max, pointing to another conference room.

"Evidentally, there were more people in the Sinclaire condo the morning of the shooting than we realized," said Jim, reaching for his phone.

"Who else was there?" questioned Beau.

"Hattie's assistant, Kayla."

Bess had been right. It was a God moment. He existed. Front and center in her life.

"We owe Hattie's doorman a big thank-you," said Maxine. "Cooper put up a camera outside your condo. The building apparently hadn't had security cameras installed yet, and he knew something odd was going on when you were in Fairhope."

Jim tapped his phone, started the video. Hattie took a deep breath, watching Asher show up with a couple of cardboard moving boxes. Kayla, dressed in a short green skirt, black low cut top, and ankle boots, arrived later with an armful of work files.

"Oh, she's a hot little number," observed Maxine.

Justice left Jim's side and trotted over to Hattie, gently nuzzling her head on Hattie's thigh. Mama always said dogs know when people need them. And she needed Justice.

Hattie stared at her feet, not sure she could watch. But she had to know. She must face the truth. Kayla was beautiful, confident, lively. Of course, Asher would be attracted to her. How could Hattie have been so clueless?

Jim stopped the video, interrupting Hattie's thoughts.

"Nothing happens for an hour. I'll forward the video."

"Oh, something happened, boss man," interjected Max. "Just glad we ain't watching it."

"The guy is scum," said Beau, who got up from the chair and began pacing the room.

Jim forwarded the video to the part showing Kayla leaving the condo approximately an hour later. Asher kisses her goodbye. A full-on intimate kiss. Hattie felt like a fool.

"Okay, now let's watch what happens the next day."

Kayla arrived with a small file. She uses Hattie's key to let herself into the condo.

"Keep watching, said Jim, forwarding through the video. "The video never shows Kayla left."

"She killed Asher!" Hattie gasped.

"Appears so. Ballistics is confirming the fingerprints now."

"How did the police miss her?" asked Beau.

"No idea. I think when Hattie admitted to shooting Asher, they figured it was a done deal; likely they didn't check things out like they should."

They continued watching.

Hattie breathed in a few more deep breaths, nauseated and humiliated.

"Hattie, I know this difficult," said Jim. "When I turn the volume way up, you'll hear the conversation on the inside of the apartment; the video, though, is only of the hallway. This is the part, you couldn't recall. Likely you were in shock. I won't make you listen to most of it, just one part, so you understand."

They all leaned in to hear.

"You are a liar," said a young woman's voice. "What about me? You said you loved me, only me! Why would you ask Hattie's friend out? WHY?"

The blast of a gunshot, then another.

Silence.

Why had Mema ever given her that stupid gun? And then she thought, what if Mema hadn't? Would she be dead now? Asher had drugged her once, he'd drugged Ellie, too. He was capable of evil. Maybe Mema had known. Maybe Mema was somehow protecting her and Beau.

The group continued watching video of the EMTs rushing in with two gurneys, then rushing out. Hattie walking out handcuffed. Ellie leaving with a detective by her side. Then nothing.

"Okay, I'll fast-forward," commented Jim. "This is, by the way hours later, around five at night. Long after police have left."

They watch a redheaded young woman in her early twenties leaving the apartment, managing to squeeze through the crime scene tape. She doesn't ride the elevator but exits through the emergency-only stairwell, not caring the alarm goes off.

"That's it. The original video was submitted to the DA. The judge is issuing a warrant for Kayla's arrest," explained Jim.

"I feel sorry for her," admitted Hattie.

"Why?" exclaimed Beau and Max at the same time.

"Asher was a con man. The best. He made you think you were the love of his life. He was easy to believe. I should have known better, but Kayla was so young, easy to con."

"In my fifty years of practicing law, I have found most people are good," said Jim. "Unfortunately, a few are truly evil. Some of them so smooth, they've fooled me a time or two. Hattie, you're going to get through this. Keep the faith."

Hattie nodded. Her husband was dead. Her loyal assistant a murderer. Where did she go from here?

"Girlfriend, I've seen far worse. You got to get back on the saddle of life. Maybe not today, or next week. But there'll be a time when you move on," advised Max.

"Listen to Max. She knows all. And she tells me it every single day," smiled Jim. "Now, you have people who are anxiously waiting to see you. Time for a quick hello, then we need to meet with the judge."

Chapter 51:
A New Plan

As they waited to go through security to get into the court-house, Hattie heard a bark. The happy kind. She looked through the glass. Ellie was with Queenie in the courthouse atrium. Hattie smiled. How in the world did Ellie talk the guards into letting her bring Queenie?

Queenie let out a howl at the sight of Beau and Hattie.

"We see you, Queenie." Hattie bent down to quiet Queenie and give the goofy dog a hug. Once Queenie was calmed down, Hattie stood and hugged Ellie, never wanting to let go. Ellie was family.

"Hey, there," said Beau to Ellie. "You, again."

"Yes, me, again." Ellie smiled. "You can run, Beau, but you can't hide. You were a bad boy yesterday," she teasingly admonished Beau. "I had some explaining to do to the hospital staff."

"Sorry."

"I forgive you."

"I forgive you too," Hattie chimed in.

"What are we, the three stooges?" Beau laughed. "Always getting into trouble without meaning to."

Charles and Claire approached the group, and Claire took charge. First hugging Hattie, then Beau.

"I'm never letting the two of you out of my sight," lectured Claire. "I've always thought about hiring a personal bodyguard for Ellie and Hattie, to look after them when I'm not there. When I met Beau, I decided it was unnecessary," joked Claire. "But apparently, Beau needs one too!"

They all laughed. Hattie couldn't recall laughing with family in a long time. And the Reades were family.

"Hattie and Beau, there's a coffee shop around the corner," interrupted Jim. "Let's meet there in five minutes. Then we'll head back to the courthouse together. I'll have my wife Abby pick up the dogs. Justice isn't well trained enough to sit quietly in the judge's office. And Queenie doesn't look ready for the task yet either."

Hattie looked around. Justice and Queenie were roughhousing, rolling over one another. She walked over, picked up both leashes. "Leave it!" she said sternly, snapping the leash. "Down. Stay."

"You just can't help yourself, can you?" Beau teased.

"I am my mother's daughter."

"The trainer," teased Ellie.

"Yes, the trainer," admitted Hattie.

Hattie grabbed her backpack and was following Jim when Maxine gently grabbed her elbow, whispering in her ear. "It looks to me there's a doggone sweet man over there, waiting for you."

Max pointed back to a quiet corner of the courthouse. "He's been getting your family coffee, praying with them and for them. He played with Queenie when she was getting wild in here. He's a bit sloppy, like my husband—I notice everything. Girl, he watched you come through security, looking like he'd waited a lifetime for you. Trust me, Hattie, he's the kind of man a woman doesn't let slip through her fingers. Go on, girl. Put him out of his misery and go over and give that man a hug."

There stood Pastor Luis with a quiet smile, his eyes welling up with tears. It was so Luis. Wrinkled clothes and the black Nikes back on his feet. His warm olive skin, dark eyes, and that darn cowlick. Seeing him gave Hattie the same feeling as sitting by a campfire on a cold autumn evening. He was all that a great man should be: faithful, good, kind. Hattie rushed over to him, spontaneously reached up to kiss him on the cheek. He turned too quickly, and Hattie's smiling lips landed on his soft smile. Her body jolted with electricity as she planted a warm, loving kiss on him. He kissed her back. She was breathless. After Asher, she never thought she'd feel this way about any other man, ever. She couldn't believe this. It was good and right and wonderful. And this time, she was enough.

Chapter 52:
Tough Love

"Judge Mulroney will speak first," instructed Jim. "She likes to make her point. Please be attentive and polite. Do not argue or disagree with her. She's got a stellar record and demands, and deserves, the utmost respect. I trust you both in that regard."

Jim exchanged pleasantries with the judge's receptionist, a young man dressed in a navy blazer, white dress shirt, tie, and navy slacks.

"You can follow me," the receptionist said, guiding them into the Judge's chamber.

Shelves of law books lined the back wall and a desk that looked like it belonged in the Oval Office. Portraits of famous Massachusetts judges and statesmen were neatly hung on the back wall. The judge, wearing a black-and-white herringbone blazer with black slacks, stood.

"Please be seated, all of you," Judge Mulroney directed, returning to her seat. Hattie thought the judge looked like a regular businesswoman; she had imagined she'd be in a judicial robe. Hattie noticed the judge's triple strand of pearls around her neck. Mema always told her strong, serious women wear pearls.

"I asked Mr. Dubois to bring you here to discuss the seriousness of what you, Hattie, and you, Beau, have done."

Hattie was sick inside. She didn't think she could take much more. Beau, however, looked as calm as Jesus halting a raging sea.

"Lies beget more lies. In my twenty-five years of legal work, the truth always surfaces."

Hattie felt shivers run down her spine, and the scent of lavender surrounded her. Surely as the sun rises and sets, Mema and the Holy Spirit were in this room.

"You've made a mistake trying to protect one another. In some ways, I understand it. We Mulroneys are a tight clan, too. However, in the eyes of the law, you lied to the police. The alleged criminal remained at large. More people could have been hurt. Despite your good intentions, it served no one well."

"Yes, ma'am." Beau acknowledged. "I apologize. I was wrong."

"Thank you. Beau, you served on SEAL team 6, with a distinguished military career. You have fought—and from what I understand—almost died for our country. You have been through enough. The only disciplinary action I have is for you to get the mental health help you need for PTSD. I understand you're headed to a trauma center. I wish you well."

"Thank you, your honor."

"Hattie," the judge said, looking at a sheet of paper on her desk, "you are a Harvard graduate, a successful investment banker, and I'm told by Mr. Dubois, an extraordinary dog trainer. You, obviously, are a highly motivated and successful individual."

"Thank you."

"However, I noticed in reviewing your credentials you have done little in the way of service and volunteer work since graduating from Harvard."

Hattie was shrouded in guilt. The judge was absolutely right.

"I'm assigning you 250 community service hours as restitution for lying to the police. With your background, I suggest you volunteer at a local animal shelter. Additionally, Mr. Dubois intends for Justice to become a professional therapy dog. I'm assigning you to be his trainer."

"Yes, ma'am. Thank you."

"And, I have a special request."

"Of course, your honor," Hattie said, desperately trying to please the Judge.

"I own the most brazen, untrained goldendoodle, who seems to enjoy terrorizing the streets of Boston. I am hoping you have time on your schedule to help train my dog, Atticus."

"Definitely," Hattie said, smiling at Jim.

"Good. You are free to leave. My assistant will be in touch. Don't disappoint me."

Chapter 53:
Closing Pandora's Box

Hattie desperately tried to open her eyes several times, but her lids felt like ten-pound weights. And the same dream kept replaying. She was reaching out her hands for Mema's. And as hard as she tried, she couldn't quite grasp them. Mema waved, turned, walked towards glowing rays of light. Mema turned one more time, blew Hattie a kiss, the rays of light surrounding her. And then she was gone.

Hattie woke when the midmorning sunlight streamed in on her. She remained in the Queen Anne bed, enjoying dual European comforters and pillows. The sheets were simple cotton, cream colored. Hattie appreciated the comfort. Asher had preferred dark satin sheets. It was hard to believe he was gone. She didn't hate him; she didn't love him. When it came to Asher, she was numb. She wondered about his family. Prayed for them. She knew she must also pray for Kayla. "May you, Lord, give them all the strength and your guidance to overcome this tragedy."

She thought of Ellie and the dark secret carried for so long. They'd need to talk. Was it too soon? Or was it too late? Had finding Henry been a curse, or a blessing? A family heirloom had done so much damage. It was all so complicated. She closed her eyes, continuing to pray.

She heard voices downstairs. She should get up. A green Boston Celtics T-shirt, leggings, and furry slippers were laid out on the bureau. Ellie, of course. Hattie dressed, made the bed, and sat down. She thought of Asher's family and what they must feel. Her head began to hurt.

There was a light knock on her door. "Hattie, are you awake? I've got breakfast ready. French toast and fresh fruit," announced Ellie.

"Just getting dressed. Come in."

Ellie walked in looking her usual Saturday casual—white oxford shirt, jeans, and suede loafers. Her hair was pulled up in a high ponytail.

"Breakfast for two."

"Where is everybody?" asked Hattie.

"Charles and Claire are giving Beau a tour of the brewing facility in Somerville. They just left. I don't think they'll be back for a while."

"How did Beau seem?"

"Fine."

Hattie smelled the cinnamon French toast and the coffee. "This looks divine."

"Speaking of divine, that was quite the kiss you planted on your preacher."

"I'm so embarrassed. I think it was a burst of some kind of crazy mix of emotions coming out of me. Did I embarrass him?"

"More like surprised him, but totally in a good way. From what I saw, he was grinning from here to Cape Cod."

Hattie smiled, liberally pouring the maple syrup on the French toast and took an elephant-size bite. "This is soooo good. You going to culinary school was definitely the right choice. Want to be roommates again?"

"Sure. Can you move to Paris?"

"No, haven't you heard? Here for a while. I'm assigned community service."

"Hattie, I'm just going to get this out on the table."

"Okay."

"I need to explain to you why I never said anything to you about the night with Asher when he…"

"Ellie, don't. I understand."

"No, please. This has to be said. I should have told you everything. It was all so confusing. A guy like Asher, who has women chasing him, does something like drugging and raping me. I didn't get it. I blamed myself at first. I'd been drinking. I couldn't really figure it out at the time, not knowing much about ecstasy and how it worked. I blamed the alcohol, thinking I'd somehow had a bad reaction and I'd lost control of my senses," she stumbled for words. "Then I began to learn more and realized it's criminal what he did."

"Ellie, I'm so, so sorry."

"I so regret not telling you. I thought I'd break your heart. And your heart ended up broken anyway. I hope you can forgive me."

"I hope you can forgive me. I thought only of myself this past year and a half. Asher was an awful person. To you, to me, to others. I'm only glad my parents weren't alive to see me marry the jerk. The way he kicked Queenie. Mama used to say if a man doesn't like dogs, run; if a dog doesn't like a man, run even faster."

"Maybe that's why Queenie can't leave Beau alone. He's a good man, Hattie."

"He told me what you did for him, at the hospital. Thank you."

"It was my pleasure."

"Does Jean Paul still have your heart? Cuz if he doesn't, I know a certain someone who has eyes for you."

"I honestly don't know," admitted Ellie. "And I think the only way I'll really find out is by going back to Paris. Plus, I need to finish school."

"I kinda figured that."

Chapter 54:
Life Marches On

Hattie and Ellie were on their phones sitting in the window seat overlooking Clarendon Street when the others returned from the brewery tour.

"We're back," Claire announced. "And we are starving. Ellie, care to whip us up something delicious?"

"I'd love to. Dinner at seven?"

"Perfect. Why don't you make a grocery list and I'll go to the market."

"I'll go with you," offered Ellie.

"Beau, you want to take Queenie for a walk with me?" Hattie asked.

"Sure, I could use some exercise."

"Let's take Queenie over to the Commons, good open space for you to toss her the ball."

Hattie attached the leash to Queenie's collar, grabbed a doggie bag, and threw a borrowed sweatshirt over her Celtics T-shirt.

"Let's go," Hattie instructed Queenie, whose tail wagged in excitement.

"You doing okay?" Beau gently asked as they walked down Beacon Street.

"Better than expected. You?"

"I woke up wanting to bail on this whole trauma center thing, but Charles offered me a personal tour of the Reade brewery. Made me excited. You know, Ellie's grandparents are good people."

"The best. They're like my second family."

"Yeah, not much left of ours, is there? Looks like it's you and me, kid."

"It's the quality, not the quantity."

"Then I hit the jackpot."

"Me too."

"We'll see. Got a lot to fix, up here," said Beau pointing to his head.

"Want to hear something strange?"

"Not really, but you're going to tell me anyway."

"Last night I dreamt I was reaching out for Mema's hands. She kept letting go. She was going somewhere, she was happy."

"Looks like Mema's job is done here. She needs to move on. The rest is up to us and the big guy. We're never ever really alone. Luis calls it faith."

"You think so?"

"I know so."

Hattie smelled lavender. She looked to heaven. And the scent got lighter and lighter. Until it was gone.

After dinner that night, Beau seemed tense and agitated.

Hattie was worried and mentioned it to Ellie.

"Let me go talk to him."

"You sure?"

"Positive."

Later Hattie and Ellie found Beau watching ESPN, Queenie by his side, his hand resting on Queenie's soft fur.

"Beau, I'd like to take you to the trauma center tomorrow morning," said Ellie.

"Don't. I'll be in a rotten mood. Therapy. Feelings. I hate discussing that stuff."

"You can't keep living like this," said Ellie, running her hand through her long blond hair. She leaned over the back of the sofa and rubbed his back until he finally relaxed.

"I don't know why not? That felt pretty nice," he teased.

Hattie watched the two of them. There was a spark. And they seemed so comfortable with each other.

Monday morning arrived. Claire served everyone coffee and pastries.

"Eight o'clock meeting," announced Hattie. "I've got to run." She hugged Beau goodbye. "They're going to help you, Beau. Listen to what they say."

"I just want to go home," said Beau. He picked up his small duffel bag, gently held on to Ellie's elbow, and with his other hand grabbed Queenie's leash.

"Let's go, dog included."

Chapter 55:
I Know the Plans I
Have for You

"Can I buy my best friend lunch this afternoon?" Ellie asked, walking into Hattie's office.

"I would love that. But first I need to clean out my desk. Pack up my stuff."

"Let me help," offered Ellie.

Hattie began tossing paperwork. She also tossed her wedding photo along with the expensive gold frame Richard had given her into the wastebasket. The rest she and Ellie put into a cardboard box.

"Okay, we're done," Hattie sighed. "Almost ten years here, and I'm packed up and gone in ten minutes."

She no longer belonged here. The staring eyes, the uncomfortable conversation with Richard. It was like she had leprosy and no one wanted to be around her. But Ellie, and Ellie's grandparents, loved her. Beau. Luis. And in the end, that was what mattered.

"Let me carry the box," Ellie suggested. "My car's outside."

Thank God, Hattie thought.

After Hattie and Ellie returned to the Reades' home, Hattie changed out of her charcoal gray business suit, threw on jeans and a crew neck sweater. She took a few minutes, calling the animal shelter in Jamaica Plain to see if they needed volunteers.

"Always," the shelter's manager told her. "Can you be here tomorrow?" the friendly voice on the other line asked.

Hattie left early the next day for the shelter, wearing old, but tougher than tough, jeans, a T-shirt, and Converse tennis shoes. Hardly comparable to the expensive Brooks Brothers suit she'd worn less than twenty-four hours ago. And like that, she was back cleaning kennels, just like she'd done for Mama.

✳ ✳ ✳ ✳

"How was work?" asked Ellie one evening when Hattie returned from the shelter.

"Lots of cleaning, just like I remember."

"Was it awful?"

"Actually, no. It was more like returning home, to my roots. Only I'm not angry doing the work like I was when I was a kid."

"Beau called. He thinks he'll get released Friday. I promised to pick him up. He's done a lot of healthy stuff. Meditation, music, therapy, even horseback riding. Said it feels so good to him. Like he's more in control."

"Thank you, God, for good help."

"Get this, the director thinks Beau's a great candidate for getting a service dog. He'd have to go to training. Beau says from what he learned from your mother, Queenie has the right temperament, very trainable. He's going to ask if he and Queenie can be a pair."

"Mama would love that."

"So would Queenie."

"Ellie, I'm going to miss you."

"You know I can fly here any time, if you need me."

"I know. And Charles and Claire are here, too. I'm so happy for you. Top of your class! You'll be receiving the James Beard award someday, I know it."

"And you'll be finding solid ground again. You're going to bounce back from all this."

"I hope so," said Hattie tentatively.

"I know so."

Hattie's schedule and responsibilities picked up quickly at the shelter. She'd also begun working with Jim and Justice, finding joy and satisfaction from training.

"You have three seconds after Justice does something good to praise, or three seconds after Justice misbehaves to give a correction," Hattie instructed Jim. "Otherwise, you've lost your teachable moment."

"A correction?" Jim asked.

"A verbal correction is a firm 'no,' or 'leave it.' It's not shouting at Justice. Too many people think the louder they scream the command at their dog, the more likely the dog will listen. Remember, it's the tone of your voice, not the volume. And if a firm no doesn't work, it's a snap of the leash. Just enough to get the dog's attention, not a hard pull of the collar by any means."

"Like this?" asked Jim.

"You got it!"

"Hattie, you definitely have a gift," said Jim. "I hear next week you're scheduled to begin working with Judge Mulroney's dog, Atticus."

Hattie prayed she'd be equally effective with Atticus as she was with Justice.

On Friday, the director at the shelter stopped to visit with Hattie.

"I hear you are quite remarkable with dogs. We're wondering if you can start training the dogs that have been here the longest. If they're better trained, the chances for adoption improve."

"Sure."

"Good. We'll have you start with Seamus, an Australian shepherd/lab. He's a runner. We've tried to place him with two families, but they tired of him running away. Seamus never responds to the 'come' command. We've had several trained volunteers work with him, none successfully. Perhaps Monday you can spend time with him?"

"Certainly. My mama was a master at teaching the 'come' command. I'll do it first thing, after feeding and letting the dogs out."

"Great."

"Oh, and will you," Hattie stuttered, her cheeks flushed, her hands sweaty, "sign my community service form for this week?"

"Of course. Do you have the form with you?"

Hattie pulled it out of her backpack. This was humiliating. Thankfully, the director signed the form without a need to ask more questions.

"We're grateful you're here, Hattie. Keep up the great work."

Chapter 56:
New Beginnings

When Hattie arrived at the shelter Monday morning, there were two new dogs people surrendered over the weekend. One was a Newfie, the size of a Mini Cooper, who was attempting to gnaw the leg off the lobby's imitation leather sofa. The receptionist at the front desk was having difficulty controlling the dog.

"Betsy, need a hand?" asked Hattie.

"This monstrosity of a dog won't stop chewing, or for that matter, drooling. His owner surrendered him a few minutes ago. Every time I turn around, the dog is back chewing something. He howls like a pack of wolves when he's in the crate so the director told me to make him comfortable."

"Let me see what I can do. What's his name?"

"Rufus."

"Hey there, Rufus, my name is Hattie," she said, slipping him a treat out of her fanny pack while stroking his soft black fur.

Hattie removed the dog's nylon leash, slipping on the preferred leather leash she used when training.

"I'm going to take Rufus for a walk. Get his energy level to a more manageable state before I try crating him," Hattie told

Betsy. "My mama used to say an exercised dog makes for a better behaved dog."

Hattie walked Rufus eight blocks. He attempted to pull, but Hattie had the time and patience to work her magic. Pull. She stopped. Start again. Pull. Stop. Start again. Repeat until the dog realizes he's no longer in charge. The two practiced this for a good forty-five minutes. When they returned to the shelter, she put Rufus in his new crate, and slipped him a treat.

After cleaning kennels, there was feeding and letting the other dogs out. Hattie was busier than usual because of the new additions to the shelter. The staff told her they loved watching when she trained dogs. They nicknamed her "the Trainer." She quickly became the go-to person when it came to questions about house training, jumping, sitting, down-stays. By the end of the week, no one used Hattie's given name. Phrases such as "get the Trainer," "we need help from the Trainer," "ask the Trainer" could be heard throughout the shelter.

The week flew by and Hattie felt stronger, lighter, less tense. She carried a deep sadness about the events that had transpired. Luis had advised her to seek counseling. And like Mama, work helped.

Friday night, fifteen minutes before the shelter closed, Hattie was the only worker still at the shelter. She was staying late to do an extra half hour of work with Rufus. His giant size made it even more important he learn commands and follow them, or he'd never find a forever family.

Rufus had a stubborn streak with a giant heart and childlike spirit. Somebody special was going to love this gentle giant.

Her last chore was to clean the lobby, so after she put Rufus in his crate, she began sweeping behind the front desk. The shelter's doorbell rang.

"Dang it," she thought, remembering she'd forgotten to lock the front door. Her heart pounded. She was jumpy and anxious since the murder of Asher. Her adrenaline kicked in, ready to dial 911. Instead, she turned around to greet the person who had entered the shelter.

"May I help you?" she said confidently, blowing her uncontrollable hair off her face. Her jaw dropped.

She could only see the man's back as he shut the front door. But she'd recognize the cowlick anywhere.

"Yes, I believe you can."

He was standing there in a jean jacket, a Harvard Divinity T-shirt, and brand-new white Converse tennis shoes. The black Nikes must have run their course.

"I'm relocating to Boston, a new job, leaving Fairhope, Alabama. And…I'm looking for a dog."

"Do you have a certain breed in mind?" she smiled, playing along.

"Not really. Must be friendly. A greeter, tail wagger. Especially on Sundays."

"Okay and what else?" Hattie laughed.

"Must like music, choirs, and a man who plays guitar. You get my drift?"

"Of course. Anything else?"

"Good with people of all ages, enjoys visiting hospitals and nursing homes."

"Hmmm, I know just what you need."

"What is that?"

"What you need is a church dog." Hattie smiled.

"Even more than that," the handsome pastor said, returning Hattie's smile, "I need a trainer."

Milton Keynes UK
Ingram Content Group UK Ltd.
UKHW041150170324
439554UK00013B/79/J